ASHES
OF THE
EARTH

ASHES
OF THE
EARTH

A
MYSTERY
OF
POST~
APOCALYPTIC
AMERICA

Eliot Pattison

COUNTERPOINT
CALIFORNIA

The author would like to acknowledge that the lyrics on page 240 are from Bobby Darin's song *Beyond the Sea*, first recorded by US Atco in 1960.

Library of Congress Cataloging-in-Publication Data is available.

ISBN: 978-1-58243-816-0

Cover design by Domini Dragoone
Interior design by Megan Jones Design

Printed in the United States of America

COUNTERPOINT
Los Angeles and San Francisco, CA
www.counterpointpress.com

CHAPTER *One*

*T*HE FACES OF the many child suicides Hadrian Boone had cut from nooses or retrieved below cliffs never left him, filled his restless sleep, and encroached in so many waking night mares that now, as the blond girl with the hanging rope skipped along the ridge above, he hesitated, uncertain whether she was another of the phantoms that haunted him. Then she paused and reached out for the hand of a smaller red-haired girl behind her. Hadrian threw down the shovel he was using to dig out the colony's old latrine pit, gathered up the chain clamped to his feet, and ran.

He scrambled up the steep slope of the ravine, ignoring the surprised, sleepy curse of his guard and the shrill, angry whistle that followed. Grabbing at roots and saplings to pull himself forward, he cleared the top and sprinted along the trail, his spine shuddering at the expectation of a baton on his back, his gut wrenching at the sound of a feeble shriek from the opposite side of the ridge. As he reached the open shelf of rock, he sprang, grabbed for the swinging rope that hung from a limb over the edge, heaving it up with a groan of despair. He froze as he hauled the child at the end of it back onto the ledge. What he found himself holding was an old coat fastened over a frame of sticks, and he was looking into the blank eyes of a pumpkin head with dried wheat for hair.

The shriek sounded again, and Hadrian suddenly realized it was one of laughter. The two girls behind him tittered with delight as he cradled the effigy in his arms. More children joined in the laughter, at least half a dozen in the shadows of the trees.

"No more, Sarah," he scolded the older girl as he rose, dumping the figure onto the ground. "Not this game. I taught you better." He saw now the photograph pinned to the effigy's chest, an advertisement torn from a long-forgotten magazine showing a woman driving a red convertible filled with joyful children eating bags of hamburgers. Such photos were considered by many children to be proof of the paradise on the other side and were the reason so many sought to reach the heaven they depicted. Carthage colony had long ago banned the private possession of salvaged books and magazines from the past century, which guaranteed their hoarding by the young. There were no more cars, no more drive-through fast food, and the only religion in most families was that invented by children as they tried to decipher the forbidden annals of a lost world.

"Why the stones?" he asked, bending to roll the pumpkin figure's head toward him. The eyes carved into the flesh, the most prominent feature of the effigy, had pupils of blue pebbles.

Sarah glanced back at a thin boy in the shadows, taller than the others. "Dax said his eyes would disappear. He's seen it, in the others who cross over. He says that's what you take with you to the other side, your eyes, because that's where your soul lives."

"To be or not to be, amen!" interjected the younger girl.

"To be or not to be, amen!" The children under the trees quickly echoed the words.

Hadrian shuddered at the strange, frantic homily, then braced himself on a tree trunk. His despair was like a physical weakness. He'd opposed the withholding of the truth from the younger generation, arguing, begging, and shouting until he'd been removed as the head of the colony's school. Left without the truth about their world, the young would always find their own version of it. Hadrian had begun to think of the children of Carthage as one more population of prisoners. He glanced at Dax, filled with foreboding over the boy's familiarity with suicides, then shook his head at the girls and began to dismantle the figure.

Sarah and her younger sister put on the wounded expressions so familiar to him at the school. "We found something special for you, professor," Sarah offered, handing him a little cylinder of rolled maple leaves tied with vine. "I was going to bring them to the jail window tonight after—"

The baton slammed into Hadrian's shoulder like a hammer, the first blow knocking him to his knees, the second causing him to collapse onto his hands.

"No!" the older girl cried. She lowered her head and charged the guard who'd materialized behind Hadrian, ramming him in the belly.

"Get back, you damned vermin!" Sergeant Kenton snarled, slapping the girl as he was pushed against a tree. "I told you last night your gangs are finished! I'll find your—" his fury melted into confusion, then fear, as he recognized Sarah. "I didn't mean . . ." he muttered to her. "We can't have prisoners escaping, Miss. You know the governor sentenced Mr. Boone to more hard labor for destroying government property again."

Sarah straightened, rubbing her cheek where he'd struck her. "And what, Sergeant," she asked in a stern, grown-up voice, "shall we tell our father when the prisoner he sentenced cannot work because of the beating you gave him?"

Kenton cast a baleful glance at Hadrian. They both knew he would be willing to haul dried dung himself just for a chance to use his baton on Boone. The burly sergeant swallowed hard, bobbing his head to the girl with ill grace. Governor Lucas Buchanan was the most powerful man in the colony of Carthage, on the entire planet for all anyone knew, but in his own household his daughters reigned supreme. "Lawbreakers owe a debt to all," Kenton murmured. It was the safest of responses, a slogan carved over the entry to the colony's courthouse.

Hadrian clutched his throbbing shoulder a moment, then rose, brushing dried leaves and dirt off his clothes.

"Did you know, Dora," Sarah declared to her sister in an exaggerated whisper, "that back in the days of the world Sergeant Kenton sold shoes?"

The younger girl laughed derisively and raised her necklace, shaking its amulet at Kenton, who reflexively jerked backward. It was a rattle from one of the local diamondback snakes, a favorite adornment of the adolescent gangs.

The policeman clenched his fists, then glared again at Hadrian, as though he must be the one broadcasting the sergeant's secret past. Kenton offered a servile nod to Sarah, then feigned a retreat for two steps before springing into the brush where he seized the lanky boy by his hair. Dax squirmed for a moment before Kenton brutally slapped him. "I'll have you begging with the half dead in another week!" he spat at the boy.

Blood streaming from his nose, Dax pushed back his shaggy blond hair and grinned as Kenton marched back down the trail. "Jackals run with ghosts!" Dax shouted at his back. "Keep hold of your eyes, Sergeant!"

Hadrian stared at the boy, as disturbed by his bizarre words as by the policeman's behavior, then turned to the girls with a disappointed gaze. "No more pretending about the other side," he said, the words strangely choking in his throat. The last time he'd found a child suicide, he'd not been able to stop weeping for an hour. He gestured toward the golden fields of grain and the sprawling town of log, stone, and scrap-metal houses beyond. "This is the paradise that belongs to you." He gathered up his chain and followed his jailer.

Five minutes later he was back in the pit of dried waste, shoveling the fertilizer into a tattered basket, then carrying the load to the wagon that would transport it to the fields. Glancing about to assure Kenton was nowhere in sight, he extracted the secret bundle from Sarah and with a surge of pleasure unwrapped it to find half a dozen pages torn from books. Quickly he stepped to the flat rock in the shadows where ten similar pages gleaned from the dried sludge lay after being washed in the bucket he was supposed to use for drinking water. He leaned against a boulder and studied the contraband Sarah and Dora had passed to him. Three pages from a history text, three of precious maps, colorful maps brimming with towns and provinces and countries that existed only in a few memories now. With a pang he gazed at other pages trapped in the dried sludge around him, ruined beyond salvage, sent for use in the latrine before the new bleaching mill began recycling old books into fresh paper. The last words of dead poets were there, histories of entire civilizations whose names would never be spoken aloud again, mixed with small useless objects like electric clocks, music players, and hair dryers, stripped of metal and discarded. The end of the world had no ending. Most of it had been annihilated in a few nightmarish days twenty-five years earlier. But the rest of it slipped away like this, one shard at a time.

He stared at one of the maps, of the eastern United States. He could still name people he had known in a dozen of the cities, though their faces had blurred in his memory. He put a finger on each city's name and mouthed it, as if to keep it alive. "Baltimore," he whispered. "Portland, Washington, Poughkeepsie, Philadelphia—"

The two movements from the brush came almost as one. First, a furious Sergeant Kenton emerged with a fresh hickory switch, pointing at Hadrian's illegal hoard, quickly followed by Sarah running with her sister on a course to block Kenton from reaching Hadrian. But the policeman's rage had burnt away the intimidation he'd felt earlier from the girls. He sidestepped them, reached Boone in two leaps, and slashed the switch across his face so violently it drew blood. Hadrian bent and took the beating, flinching with each blow, knowing resistance would make it worse, watching the girls through spasms of pain. Too late he realized they were prying up a weapon, a stout stick embedded in the dried sludge.

Dora, the eight-year-old, pulled so hard on the stick that she tumbled backward when it came free, causing Kenton to pause, as if considering whether to help the governor's daughter. Then the screams began, as the horror that had been pinned under the stick slowly rose from the surface. Dora shrieked and crawled, crablike, away. Sarah cried out in terror and darted behind Hadrian. An arm, a blackened, shriveled arm, reached from the sludge, extending its grisly fingers as if for help.

Lucas Buchanan, the governor of Carthage, always wore slate-grey suits gleaned from the warehouse stores during the frenzied scavenging of the colony's early years. Hadrian watched uneasily as the tall, lean man rose from his desk to put on his jacket before speaking, always a bad sign.

"There is only one reason we haven't permanently exiled you," Buchanan declared as he paced along the window of his second floor office. He seemed to be working hard to control his emotions. "If we voted today, the Council would toss you aside like the worthless salvage you are. Banish you to the camps or the forest to waste away with the other discards out there." He paused to straighten one of the many carefully selected photos on his wall. Abraham Lincoln sitting with his generals flanked Theodore Roosevelt posing with a dead buffalo. An image of a busy harbor with square-rigged clippers and steamboats hung over one of Thomas Edison beside his early phonograph. Buchanan was relentless in his efforts to wipe out the past few decades.

Hadrian clamped his jaw tightly, refusing to be baited by the governor's mention of the ghetto thirty miles away, the squalid camps where the survivors of radiation and other diseases from the apocalypse had been condemned to live. Slags, the exiles were commonly called, though many other epithets were used. *I'll have you begging with the half dead in another week*, Kenton had threatened Dax. Was he hinting at a coming purge of the gang leaders? The camps would be a living hell for the young teenager.

"But Jonah insists you are the only one he will work with, the only one who really understands what he's doing. I reminded him that many of us can read blueprints and follow designs. But the old man just gives me that damned monk's smile of his and says it's you or no one. As if he were our wizard and you the only apprentice able to read his runes." The governor's voice was heavy with resentment. "So when you complete your sentence you will be released into his custody," he added quickly.

Just the mention of the old man who had become like a father to Hadrian was a salve to his aching spirit. But after a moment he raised his brows. Ever since Hadrian had been pushed out of the Council and his schoolmaster's job, Buchanan had harassed him, ejecting him from his quarters at the school, arresting him on petty charges. "Why would you do that for me?"

"I told you. To help Jonah build our public works. He submitted a long list of proposed projects to the Council. He promises a brick factory soon, says he can even build a rail line to the mines in five years' time."

"I know you better." Hadrian shifted so he could keep an eye on the half-open door behind him. There should have been deputies frantically consulting, policemen conferring about the dead man. With a chill he saw several dirt-encrusted pistols hanging on belts from a peg on the back of the door, awaiting restoration.

The governor lifted a marble chess piece, an elephant with a castle on its back, one of the many random artifacts he collected. When he finally replied he addressed the rook in his hand. "I've discovered he keeps a secret journal. We've been unable to find it."

"Perhaps he's just putting your regime in historic perspective. I tend to think in terms of feudalism."

Buchanan's smile was as thin as a blade. "No one cares what you think anymore. But if the esteemed Jonah Beck were recording such careless thoughts and they wound up in our new newspaper . . ."

"You're asking me to spy on him?"

The governor toyed with the switch on an old gooseneck lamp. Government House was one of the colony's few electrified buildings, powered by bicycle generators designed by Jonah and manned by convicts in the darker, colder months. "We want only to protect him from himself. He trusts you. All I want are reports from time to time."

"I refuse." A drop of blood fell from Hadrian's cheek onto his tattered shoe.

Buchanan adjusted his jacket, which hung like a sack on his bony frame. Everyone had resembled scarecrows in the early years, but he was one of those who had never been able to regain their weight. "How many people in the known world, Hadrian? Nine thousand, maybe ten?"

"You always ignore the camps and the forest people. They probably make it closer to twelve."

The governor grinned, as if amused by the jibe. "And once you were with me at the very top, not just a founder, a leader."

"I don't recall worrying about what people called us. We were too busy keeping people alive."

"You played the survivor's game better than any of us. Now look at you. Can't even clean out dried shit without making trouble." Buchanan gestured toward a small stack of papers held together with a pin. "If I had enough paper to keep a thorough file on you, this would be a foot thick. You're a failure even at being a failure. There'd be little protest if I ejected you right now. Agree, or I'll have you declared an outlaw. No coming back. No more crying on the old man's shoulder. And no more interfering with my children," he added with extra vehemence.

Hadrian had been examining a photo of an old canal boat pulled by a team of mules. "Is that what this is about? Your daughters were toying with a hanging noose."

"A game."

"You and I have buried a lot of children through the years, Lucas. This is how the pattern begins, getting comfortable with the mechanics of it. I remember once when children joined Scouts and soccer teams. In your colony they join suicide cults. Surely you haven't forgotten how a little girl's neck looks when it's stretched? The bulging, surprised eyes, the laughter forever choked out of her? They don't move on to a more beautiful world, they just move into our nightmares. Each of their gravestones is a monument to our failure."

Buchanan gripped the rook so hard his knuckles whitened. "Since the day you were thrown off the Council and sacked as the head of our school you were no longer accountable for my children. Accept my generosity," he said coldly, "or I draw up papers today to exile you.

Push me and I'll banish Jonah too. I can't trust him if I have no leverage over him. Are you prepared to nurse him through the winter in some wattle hut in the camps? Frostbite will come first, then chilblains. After a couple of months he'll look like he had radiation sickness."

Hadrian stared at the little pool of blood on his shoe. He longed to be in the camps at that moment, sitting in a smoke-choked hut as some hairless, half-toothed bard sang the rock songs of their youth. But he couldn't bear to be forever parted from Jonah, and the old man wouldn't survive even a month of winter in the camps. He looked up into Buchanan's icy, expectant grin and slowly nodded.

Settling into his chair with a satisfied expression, the governor lifted a large silver ring from the desk. Hadrian realized he'd seen it an hour earlier. It had been on the finger of the shriveled hand in the sludge pit.

"We could have had this conversation next week when my sentence is up," Hadrian observed, his gut tightening. Buchanan had been making certain he had him under his thumb before demanding something more urgent.

"I want that body removed."

Hadrian closed his eyes a moment. Then he looked hard at Buchanan. "I'll need more than a shovel and basket. Tell Kenton to bring tools in the morning, a coffin if he can find one." Behind the desk was a plaque inscribed IN STRENGTH WE ENDURE. It had been Buchanan's political slogan when he was first elected so many years before. It had become his personal creed.

"You misunderstand. *Tonight.* Only you. I will order Kenton to release you after the evening meal, on parole until midnight. Take a lantern and whatever tools you need from the jail shed."

Once Hadrian had been welcomed there, in this office, once the two men had trusted each other. They had transformed through the years, trying to survive, each in his own way trying to build the colony out of the rubble of the world. Survival, he had learned, was not about merely adapting, but transforming. Those who had not transformed in the early years had died. You had to constantly slam the door on the thousand things that choked you with emotion, learn to be grateful for the scars that grew over your soft parts. Now whatever was left of either man from the old times was so disfigured as to be unrecogniz-able. Now they were in their final relationship. Buchanan had won, and Hadrian was becoming his secret slave.

"He was a big man. I can't do it alone."

"But dead for a long time," the governor observed. "There's prob-ably only . . . Surely the body's not intact."

"The sludge preserved him, like the old bog men."

Buchanan grimaced, then turned to gaze for a long moment over the harbor and the vast inland sea beyond before tilting his head toward a portrait of Sarah and Dora. "I lie awake sometimes," he confessed in a near whisper, "worrying that they think we are going to destroy the world again."

"Why wouldn't they?" Hadrian shot back. It was the endpoint of a thousand conversations they'd had over the past two decades, a reflec-tion of the strange, many-layered person Buchanan had become. He would gladly batter Hadrian in public, would shame him, would out-law him, but still, when they were alone, he could become the lonely widower, offering up the unguarded conversation they had shared in the early years.

"Sarah wrote something on the wall by her bed. *We know what we are but know not what we may be.* I asked where she got the words and she wouldn't say. Which means they came from you."

"You flatter me. I only recommended she read more Shakespeare." Free from the contamination of the modern world and being so widely available to the early salvage crews, the Bard's works filled several stacks of the colony's collection of approved books. "Fascinating, don't you think, that *Hamlet* would resonate with her? The destruction of a royal family."

Buchanan glared at him. "I am going to make you repaint the slogan you destroyed on the wall of the town square," he growled. "Say it. I want you well practiced when you recite it to the assembled children."

Hadrian returned the smoldering gaze. "Four weeks of hard labor was my sentence. Nothing was said about becoming part of your propaganda machine."

"Did I mention another week for escaping today?"

"I refuse."

"I can picture old Jonah now, frost in his hair, his teeth chattering."

Hadrian hung his head. "We have not lost our history. We are free of history."

A victorious grin split the governor's flinty features. He turned again, this time to watch a plume of smoke on the northern horizon, a steam-powered boat working one of the sea's endless schools of fish. "Be at the sludge pit at dusk. You'll have help," he said, and pointed to the door.

The corridor outside was empty. Hadrian stepped to the front window to survey the street below. Kenton, obviously assuming the audience would take much longer, was rolling a cigarette by a row of bicycles, sullenly observing a group of teenagers beside one of the horse-drawn machines used for scraping roads. Hadrian watched the sergeant, the skin on his back crawling from the beating to come, then shot down the stairs, stole a hat from a hook to conceal his face, and climbed out a back window.

Ten minutes later he stood in the entrance to the two-story log building, designed like a great barn, that housed the colony's library. Wiping the blood off his face, he watched the dusty street for the brown uniforms of Buchanan's policemen, then pulled the hat low and stepped inside. He slipped into a side chamber, pausing for a satisfied look at the shelves of books that had cleared the censors, then studied the stairway and the landing above for signs of a sentry before ascending, a volume of Dickens in his hand for cover.

He paused when he reached the threshold of the large chamber, gazing through the gaping door upon the slender figure, once the head of a great university, at the worktable. The sight of the grey-bearded man working with his nib pen on a sheet of heavy handmade paper always soothed Hadrian's tormented spirit. The page was from Jonah's secret chronicle of life in the new world, and every time Hadrian discovered him bent over the project—often by candle at night—he saw him as a monk from a thousand years earlier illuminating a manuscript for the ages. As he laid his hat on a chair and silently stepped closer, he saw that his friend was completing the details of a small sailing boat in the lower margin. Green vines brimming with pumpkins edged the top corners, autumn flowers the bottom, with elaborate flourishes connecting them.

Jonah looked up with a gentle smile. "They're giving tea breaks to the labor crews now?" he asked in a chagrined but good-natured voice, then gestured Hadrian toward a nearby stool before returning to his work. Hadrian glanced back at the door, aware that he had no more than a quarter hour before Kenton and his men began looking for him. He sat uneasily for a moment, then wandered around the chamber, a place dearer to him than any in the colony. He studied the mounted specimens of small forest mammals on one shelf, the volume of the ancient Chinese poet Sutungpo beside dried flowers on another. As he examined the working wooden model of an astronomical observatory with a telescope mounted on a pivoting frame, he thought of how the governor pined for public works to jump-start his new civilization, while the wizard of Carthage colony yearned to look at the stars.

At last Hadrian became aware of Jonah patiently watching him. His page was completed.

"You need to start a second journal, my friend," Hadrian declared. "Something simple, with designs for possible buildings, observations on the weather and stars, notes on crops, with some measured criticism of the government to keep it authentic."

Jonah cocked his head to one side like a curious bird. "The governor has been chatting with you."

Hadrian glanced back at the freshly illuminated page. Did Jonah keep only one page of his journal out at a time as a hedge against Buchanan's suspicions? "The governor," he replied, "is going to find a way to exile me." Hadrian clenched his jaw against the heartache that rose at the thought of being separated from the gentle old man, whose serenity and intellect had nourished him for so many years.

"The governor," Jonah observed with a wry smile, "is above all a practical man. You were there when we opened the public baths last month. The people were ready to kiss his hand for putting running water on every block. I have shown him designs for a new flour mill, a steam timber mill, even a rail line. As long as we keep building new projects, he will stay in office. And I've explained to him it is impossible for me to proceed without you. If he insists on constantly arresting you on petty charges, I told him I'll need a cell too, for we must be together." He paused, wincing, to knead his shoulder with long bony fingers. "I'm aging fast, my arthritis worsens every day. I need your hands and legs. You and I will do the detailed designs here. Then I'll watch in my glass"—Jonah gestured to the telescope on the veranda outside his workshop—"as you manage the construction. You will be restored, rehabilitated, you'll see. We'll build you a room on my cabin and train the warblers to eat from our hands. Rehabilitated," he repeated. "Back the way we were."

The words brought a strange sadness to Hadrian. He watched the flickering waters of the inland sea. "I wouldn't recognize myself," he whispered to himself.

But Jonah had heard. "Inside, we haven't changed," he said. Then he cocked his head again. "What happened today?"

"We found a body in the old latrine pit."

Jonah shrugged. "Surely you're no longer frightened of the dead."

"No," Hadrian admitted. "What frightened me was the children playing with a hanging rope again."

Jonah replied with a sad, knowing silence.

"All I've done, for all these years, doesn't mean a thing." The confession leapt from Hadrian's tongue unbidden, as if something deep inside had pushed it out. His despair was like a living thing gnawing at his heart. "I always told myself I survived for a reason. It was a lie. Thinking I could make a difference was the biggest lie of all."

After a moment Jonah lifted Hadrian's hand and dropped a familiar agate disc onto his palm, a meditation stone worn smooth from years of rubbing. "Borrow this," Jonah said. "Go back to your cell and use it. Reach inside. Stop trusting your emotions. The colony needs you more than ever. And stop escaping. Your bones will start breaking if you keep giving Sergeant Kenton so many reasons to beat you."

"I agreed to spy on you, Jonah," Hadrian confessed, unable to look the old man he loved in the eye. "Buchanan is going to start a new campaign to weed out those who don't support him."

"Which is why I made sure you were coming to live with me."

"He doesn't trust you."

"Nor I him." Jonah pushed Hadrian's fingers closed over the stone. "But he desperately needs me. And together we will devise the tales for you to carry back. Making a second journal that you can share with him is an inspired suggestion. If he insists on turning life into a chess game, then surely we can outplay him. He has no mind for subtlety."

"You refuse to accept how dangerous he is."

Jonah offered another serene smile. "I have ways to deal with our governor." He jabbed a bony finger at Hadrian's heart. "We haven't changed," he insisted, "not in the important places."

"Those places are lost to me," Hadrian replied, his throat tightening. "And I don't want to be what I have become." He ran his hand over his shaggy hair. "The only thing that gives me hope, old man, is that you still have the capacity to hope."

Jonah's reply was to gesture Hadrian to follow him onto the veranda. The view was spectacular, overlooking the town below, the vast, glistening inland sea to the north, to the south the stables and fields framed by hills streaked with crimson.

"It's the best crop ever," the old man said, waving at the fields beyond. "A surplus," he added in a pointed tone.

Hadrian studied him, knowing how carefully Jonah always chose his words. "You mean there's enough to ship outside the colony."

"I told the governor that if you and I agreed to start building his new brick factory, there must be one more project started at the same time. Our bridge."

As the words sank in, Hadrian's heart raced. They had dreamt of this for years, a bridge across the steep ravine that cut off all direct passage to the camps of the untouchables, otherwise requiring a day's journey.

"Our bridge!" Jonah repeated in a joyful tone. "The beginnings of the new world you and I have longed for." He stepped back to his table and, after a moment's fumbling through stacked papers, produced a sketch of a cantilevered bridge built of logs. "Buchanan's agreed that the first vehicles to cross it will be wagons of grain for the camps! It will mean a difference between life and death for some of the oldest!"

Hadrian saw the sparkle in Jonah's eyes. Most of all, it would mean the contact between young and old needed to heal long-festering wounds and a release of the flood of knowledge dammed up in the camps for so many years.

"So, you see, things are already getting better, my son," Jonah said, and paused to pluck a fading bloom from one of the potted roses he kept on the veranda. "We *will* make a difference, you and I. This is the way to change things. There are engineers in the camps, and teachers and poets. Everything will be transformed when we set them free. We will build a new school, a college even, and you will be its head. The Dark Ages had to come before there could be a Renaissance."

Hadrian had seldom seen him so animated, so happy. Jonah had not been able to make the arduous journey to the camps for nearly two years, had no idea how desperate conditions there were or how many of their aging friends had died. And he had no inkling of the many ways Buchanan might be lying to him. But looking into his radiant eyes, Hadrian had no heart to tell him. "A Renaissance," he echoed, forcing a smile. Then he accepted Jonah's embrace.

THE HUT WAS covered with flowering vines, surrounded by patches of herbs once neatly tended but now overgrown. As Hadrian dropped his armful of firewood by the stone threshold, a woman appeared in the doorway, acknowledging him with a sad yet grateful smile. She was hairless and careworn, aged far beyond her years, though her high cheekbones and intense green eyes reminded him that once, back in the days of the world, she had been a fashion model. He handed her a dozen sheets of newly bleached paper, stolen from a desk in Government House. "For your poems, Nelly," he said.

Inside, on a pallet beneath the solitary window, lay an old man of Asian features. His breath came in long, wrenching rattles and his eyes were unfocused. Propped on a stool next to him was an exquisite, nearly finished painting of a thrush on a willow branch. "He hasn't lifted a brush for days," the woman said over his shoulder. "I try to feed him but he says it tastes like mud. It's all I have."

On the floor Hadrian saw the wooden bowl half-filled with a yellow glutinous substance, gruel made of cattail roots. The winter before, she had killed their beloved dog to feed her husband, calling it squirrel. All summer, whenever he had seen movement in the shadows, the nearsighted old artist, a television reporter in the former world, had called out the dog's name and laughed.

"If I can get away this afternoon," the woman said, "I think I can find some tadpoles to boil."

As she spoke, Hadrian's belly exploded in pain.

"Get up, you son of a bitch!" spat Kenton.

Hadrian sat up, gasping, clutching his stomach. The sergeant hovered over him in the dusk, twisting the end of his truncheon in his palm. Behind him Lucas Buchanan leaned a bicycle against a tree.

"Quit your dreaming!" the governor snapped.

But Hadrian had not been dreaming as he lay waiting by the ravine. He had been simply reliving his last visit to the camps.

The governor lifted a pick and lantern from a pile of tools lying in the shadows, then pointed Kenton toward a large boulder near the road before gesturing for Hadrian to follow him into the ravine. Not daring to ask why Buchanan himself had decided to help with the grisly chore, Hadrian retrieved a shovel and hurried down the path, not missing

Kenton's ravenous glance as he took up his sentinel position. Escaping twice in one day guaranteed a double beating that night.

The two men worked feverishly at the body in the pit, clearing an arm, a hip, a leg, a foot as darkness overtook the ravine. The dead man was clad in sturdy traveling clothes, wore the leather beltpack commonly used by trappers and others who ventured into the wilds. His countenance, shriveled and stained nearly black, was that of a strong man in his twenties, ready to challenge the world. Or what was left of it.

Hadrian studied the stricken way the governor stared at the face. "You knew him," Hadrian declared as Buchanan lit the lantern. "You knew who it was when you saw that ring."

Pulling the ring from his pocket, Buchanan held it in the pool of light. "We had them made last spring so they could be sent back as a token with a message, to authenticate the source."

Hadrian bent to examine the ring. Engraved on it were a seagull and a pine tree, the symbols of the colony's flag. "He was working for you."

"There were two of them," Buchanan explained. "We had a private dinner where I gave them a send-off speech. Long recon." It meant a distant scouting expedition, in search of new sources of salvage.

Hadrian searched his memories of the spring before. There were always public announcements, public banquets before the long recon teams set off. "You kept this mission secret."

"They were one-man expeditions. They were supposed to leave before dawn, this one on foot, the other in a sailing canoe bound for the seaway. The other was brought back three weeks later in a trading boat from the northern settlement," he explained, referring to the tiny band of survivors who eked out their sustenance on the far shore, 150 miles away. "They found him floating facedown halfway across."

He looked at the dead man. "This one's Hastings, one of our most experienced woodsmen. Micah Hastings. He volunteered instantly the moment I mentioned I might send out new scouts. His mother comes every week to ask if we've heard from him."

"He never left," Hadrian observed as he scooped away more of the dried sludge from the man's side. "But why keep a salvage mission secret?"

Buchanan ignored the question. "All these months I've been imagining that he'd found a road that had not been made impassable by overgrowth, that he had gone far to the south and was mapping new salvage yards." Salvage yards. It was one of the colony's euphemisms for the ruined towns that were prized for the pieces of metal they contained. Humanity's technical progress was held hostage to the discovery of new junkyards. Buchanan paused, his voice growing more distant. "I had a dream a few nights ago, that Hastings found a family of elephants escaped from some zoo and was bringing them here." He contemplated the rising moon. "Do you suppose there are any elephants left on the planet?"

Hadrian was beginning deeply to resent the moments like this, moments when Buchanan pretended they were still old friends. "I don't know. Probably not."

The answer brought an odd quiet. The governor paced around the corpse. "That thing burrowing into his hand," he murmured in a tone of disgust. "Get rid of it."

Hadrian hesitated, then raised the lantern over the blackened hand. Something long and thin extended from its closed fingers. He realized that what Buchanan had mistaken for a worm was an encrusted strand of leather. As he pulled it, a flat oval slid out of the dead man's grip, an amulet of some kind. Hadrian spat on it and wiped it clean, revealing a piece of copper crudely etched with a doglike figure standing on two legs. It could have been a wolf. It could have been one of the voracious martens the new generation had taken to calling tree jackals. As he extended it to Buchanan, he recalled the strange words spoken by the leader of the gang that morning.

"What does it mean?" he asked.

Buchanan stared at the amulet with a worried expression before tossing it into the shadows. "Nothing. A coincidence, a piece of trash that tangled with the body."

"Jackals run with ghosts," Hadrian ventured, echoing the boy's words to Kenton.

Buchanan's eyes flared and he looked over his shoulder as if suddenly frightened. After a moment he muttered a low curse and leaned on his shovel. "He drank too much at the banquet, the fool. It was before we opened the public bathhouse." As Hadrian continued digging, Buchanan spoke in a slow, deliberate voice, as if rehearsing his official explanation. "Afterward he came here to use the public privy near his mother's cottage, tumbled over the side, and sank in. He was drunk and that railing on the back was never high enough."

Hadrian stopped his work, staring with new foreboding at the now fully exposed torso. "He did collect a little salvaged steel."

"What are you talking—" The words died in the governor's throat as he lifted the lantern and spied the blade of reworked metal between the man's ribs. "Noooo!" he moaned. "No," he repeated after a moment, in a steadier, contemplative tone, as if rejecting what he saw. He stared at the makeshift blade so long Hadrian went back to work, freeing the man's legs.

At last Buchanan straightened, stripped off his jacket, and laid it over the body. "I'll get a canvas to roll him in," he announced. "And a cart to carry him to the harbor. Find some stones for his shroud."

"He was murdered."

"You will row him out half a mile and drop him in."

"Jonah and I will need to study his body, to understand what happened."

"He was martyred in the service of the colony. There are all kinds of dangers lurking in the ruined lands. Everyone knows how many of our scouts never return. The world resists being rediscovered."

"He was murdered," Hadrian repeated.

"We don't have murders. We have never had murders in Carthage."

"No history. No murders. What's your next decree, no more disease?"

"You, Hadrian," the governor growled, "are in no position to—"

The sound of the bells rose slowly through their words. First one, then another as the alarm was taken up across the town. Hadrian and the governor darted up the trail to the top of the ravine.

"God, no!" Hadrian cried as he spied the flames on the hillside half a mile away. Spotting the governor's bicycle leaning against a nearby tree, he spun about and shoved Buchanan against Sergeant Kenton. "Find Jonah!" he shouted as he mounted the bike, ducking as the policeman recovered enough to swing his truncheon at him. "He'll know which books are the most important to save! He has places there where he stores colony treasures!"

Weaving through the crowd of frightened onlookers, he cycled past the fire brigade frantically trying to lay hoses from the nearest cistern. As he threw the bike down and darted into the burning library, men and women were beginning to empty buckets of water on the flames, while others were carrying out books and furnishings from the lower floor. Holes licked by flame were already appearing in the cedar shake roof as Hadrian bounded up the stairs toward the workshop. As he reached the chamber, he froze, a desolate groan escaping his lips as he collapsed onto his knees. Hadrian had found the colony's most important treasure.

Above his burning worktable, Jonah's body swung from a rafter.

CHAPTER *Two*

H ADRIAN WAS NOT aware of moving, only of realizing suddenly that he had grabbed the bucket from the stunned policeman who appeared at his side. He tossed the water on the table, dousing its flames, grabbed the knife that lay there, leapt onto the table, and cut the rope on the rafter.

He was on the floor beside Jonah an instant later, cradling him, pulling off the noose. The old man seemed to gasp and, with frantic hope, Hadrian laid him flat and pushed his abdomen before realizing it was just the dead air escaping his lungs. Through the tears that filled his eyes he saw men and women streaming into the room, emptying more buckets of water.

"Hadrian," a woman in a long white apron called in an anguished voice, "let me help you take him outside."

But Boone lashed out, shoving her away, raising his fist to warn off others. He lifted Jonah in his arms, cradling the grey-whiskered head to his shoulder as he carried him out. Collapsing onto the grass, he took one of the ink-stained hands in both of his as a long sob wracked his body. The end of the world had come again.

Through his fog of pain he became gradually aware of a company of prisoners being marched double time onto the grounds, of a fire hose sputtering then filling with water to spray the building, of Lucas Buchanan shouting orders then gasping as he saw Jonah. He watched, numbed, as prisoners hauled armfuls of books out of the building, then he struggled to his feet and joined the effort.

An hour later, his arms and face blackened with soot, he stood and watched the smoke rise from the smoldering library. Half the roof was gone but the rest of the building had been saved. Police whistles trilled as more onlookers arrived, clogging the street. Sergeant Kenton shoved Hadrian toward the rank of prisoners being formed for the march back to the prison. He resisted for a moment as Kenton put manacles on his wrists, then saw that Jonah's body was gone and, as if in a terrible dream, let himself be led away.

HALF THE INDIVIDUAL cells in the long two-story stone building housing Carthage's prisoners were usually empty. Most of the inmates, convicted of mere misdemeanors, were kept in shared barrack cells where they could easily be checked by guards between card games. A few of the youngest now hooted as Hadrian was shoved into their midst. He was something of a hero to them, not just for being the oldest of the repeat offenders, but also for his well-known feud with Kenton. The remaining prisoners stared coolly at him. They were old enough to remember he'd held office in the government of Lucas Buchanan.

A young prisoner tossed a tattered, soot-stained towel to Hadrian and stepped back from a basin of grey water. Hadrian was the last to wash up. Over a dozen men had already used the water to clean themselves after the fire.

"They'll get the roof back up in a week, Mr. Boone." Nash was a habitual burglar from one of the outlying farms, who had been a pupil at the school when Hadrian still ran it.

Hadrian covered his face in the filthy towel for a moment. Jonah's dead countenance seemed to be everywhere, even when he closed his eyes. He clenched his jaw, struggling not to weep. Most of the prisoners were grinning at him, mocking him, when he looked up.

Collapsing into the deep shadows of his bunk, he felt his grief gnawing away at his heart, and for a long time he lay as if paralyzed. Then, with great effort, he pushed the pain back. There would be only one way to deal with this agony, only one way to carry on his life. He had to understand what happened, had to find those responsible. Replaying the terrible scene at the library workshop in his mind's eye, he went over it again and again, finally considering the flames and the pattern of destruction. The papers on the top of the desk had just begun to ignite when he arrived, but two stacks of shelves had already burnt so intensely they'd set off the roof above. Under the desk had been shreds of colored paper, which he had furtively collected, and below the burning shelves had been the remains of the two oil lamps Jonah used for writing at night, a dozen feet from the desk. They could not simply have been knocked down by Jonah's flailing feet. Rather, they'd been lifted from his desk and thrown against the shelves. The papers on the desk had been lit by a stray ember.

Left on the desk had been the unfamiliar heavy knife Hadrian had used to cut the hanging rope. His palm and fingers were slightly burnt where he had held the knife. He studied the pattern of reddened skin. The hilt had been brass and disproportionately thick, the blade also was very thick, with a cupped guard around the hilt. It had not belonged to Jonah.

He sat up, looking for Nash. The other prisoners were in their bunks, but the young thief had washed his socks and was trying to dry them over the solitary candle lantern on the table.

"Swords," Hadrian said as he approached him. "Who has swords? Why would one be cut down into a heavy knife?"

Nash shrugged. "Everyone loves a sword when one turns up in salvage or the black market. But then they get it home and realize it isn't so useful. Practical men, they'll grind them down to a useful size."

"What kind of practical men?"

"Farmers," the youth offered, then considered the point a moment. "Fishermen, millers, maybe butchers and carpenters, even—"

A low singsong whistle cut Nash off. He scowled at the brutish man sitting on a bunk near the door. "Fuck you, Wade," the youth spat, then turned so as to put his back to the bearded prisoner.

"If you wanted to get into the library at night," Hadrian continued, "how would you do it?" The whistle continued, and Hadrian looked back at Wade. It was a prisoner's taunt, a warning about those who sang out secrets.

"But, Mr. Boone," Nash said, "I would never . . . not the library. My momma goes there. She'll come into town, all those miles, just to borrow a book."

"But just suppose."

Nash bit his lower lip. "I would bet old Mr. Jonah never locked those doors on the upstairs balcony he used for experiments. Wouldn't be hard to put a ladder up there. But probably no need. The librarian works late a lot. She leaves the front door open for people to return books."

Hadrian gave the boy a grateful nod and returned to his bunk. He was so deep in thought he failed to notice the shreds of paper until he sat on them. He shot back up, straining to see in the dim light. There were dozens of paper strips. As he scooped up several and took them to the lantern, Nash retreated uneasily.

With a shudder he saw they were fine vellum, some covered with a classical typeface, others with the bright inks of a map. Low, gravelly laughter rose from near the door.

He threw the shreds in Wade's face as he reached the big man.

"You stole a book tonight!" he spat.

The cell's bully held up an elegantly bound volume entitled *World Geography 1900*. "I liberated a month's worth of ass wipes. Stuff they put in the latrines is like sandpaper."

"It's irreplaceable!" Hadrian clenched his fists.

"So's my arse!" Several men in the adjacent bunks joined in Wade's jeering.

"It belongs to the colony."

Wade, a fisherman imprisoned for slashing his opponent in a bar fight, opened the book to a page captioned *Lands of Asia* featuring a color plate of the Great Wall. With glee he tore the page out, jerking a thumb toward Hadrian.

"Our distinguished visitor is still full of hisself," the burly prisoner declared as the other prisoners surrounded Hadrian. "I think he suffers from a misunderstanding of what is important in this world."

Hadrian felt hands close around his arms. "*Himself*," he said. "Of *himself*. You should have stayed in school, Wade."

Wade guffawed again. "Maybe his highness is just hungry," he quipped with a nod. It was a signal. Hadrian was flung to the floor. Three prisoners knelt on his arms and legs, another clamped his nostrils shut.

Hadrian held his breath as long as he could. When, at last, he opened his mouth, gasping for air, the wadded page was shoved inside. One of the men seized his chin and worked his jaw, opening and shutting it so that he chewed the paper, leaving him gagging and choking. He crawled to the piss bucket and vomited up the ruined page.

When he finally collapsed onto his bunk, Hadrian faced the wall and clamped his hand against his chest. They did not know he still had a dozen salvaged pages inside his shirt.

IN THE MORNING Hadrian was left in the cell as the other prisoners were marched out on work detail. Wade had sneered, making a slashing motion across his throat when the guard announced Hadrian was not to join the detail. They all knew he was the governor's favorite dog for kicking, and Buchanan would be in a kicking mood. He paced the cell, pausing at Nash's bunk as he saw its bloody blanket. The young thief had been beaten in the night.

He gazed out the window at the smoldering library on the ridge above, expecting the lock on the door to rattle open at any moment. Then he realized Buchanan would have been up most of the night and not be seeing anyone until the afternoon. He lay on his pallet, trying to sleep but seeing Jonah's body hanging from the rafter every time he closed his eyes. He paced the cell, tested and rejected the old porridge left for breakfast, now cold and thick as paste, then paused by Wade's bunk. It took him only a moment to find the old book, hidden in the horsehair stuffing of the pallet. He considered whether to hide it elsewhere, or even to throw it through the hatch on the door for a guard to find, then leafed through it and studied the beautiful hand-painted maps, nearly twenty in all. If Wade couldn't find it, he would beat Hadrian. If a policeman found it, he would probably take it for his own latrine. Hadrian began tearing out the maps and stuffing them into his shirt.

He stood at the door for several minutes, pressing his cheek against the barred hatch to watch down the empty corridor, then used wood splinters to pin the filthy towel over the hatch. Jammed in his sock were the pieces of parchment he had scooped up from under Jonah's table when he had gone back to fight the fire. He extracted them and arranged them, inked side up, on the table. He started with the outside edges first. As he connected the brown and purple vine that wound its way around an inch-wide border, framing a little sailing ship at the bottom, he realized the page was familiar. It was from Jonah's secret journal, the page he had seen him working on the day before.

It was a work of art, painstakingly detailed. Only the right-hand border was incomplete. Two semicircular pieces had been torn away, leaving two gaps on that side.

The elegantly inked text in the center of the page read like a poem:

Over the golden water this dawn could be seen the ten steamers of the fleet, the wanderers all returned home. The harvest fair continues, with wagons in from distant farms and children wide-eyed over giant pumpkins. Pipe and fiddle music rose with the moon last night. The dance stage was a joyful drum echoing down the valley.

Up from the meadows rich with corn, clear in the cool September morn. Round about them orchards sweep, apple and peach trees fruited deep. Fair as the garden of the Lord.

It *was* a poem, or at least the last paragraph was. Hadrian puzzled over the words. They sounded vaguely familiar, but incomplete. The last couplet was not finished. He pushed the edges closer together, as though new words would appear, not knowing what he had missed but with a rising suspicion that there was something else, a hidden message. Jonah Beck had delighted in the mysteries of language, in word plays. The passage on its face was a lyrical description of the major event of the past week. It could have been published in the daily paper. Yet it had been part of Jonah's secret journal, had been quite deliberately destroyed. He paused, looking out the window. But when? During his murder, or just before?

Hadrian separated the pieces and slowly reassembled them, taking several to the window to hold them in the sunlight, marveling again over their artistry. He knew from experience that Jonah might spend as long as a week on a single page, working on it in the late afternoon and evening as one of his many pastimes after long days bent over blueprints and designs. While he had not exactly hidden his journal from Hadrian, he had never spoken of it in detail. Hadrian had always assumed it was simply the old man's account of daily life in the colony.

Fatigue swept over him as he stared at the page in frustration. Gathering up the pieces, he stretched out on his pallet.

IT WAS NEARLY noon when a square-set figure roughly tapped Hadrian's stomach with his truncheon. "You need to clean yourself up if you're going to see the governor," Sergeant Kenton growled, pushing Hadrian down the corridor to the horse trough outside. When he finished, Kenton tossed him a yellow armband, the mark habitual criminals were required to wear in public. The sergeant wore an expectant expression as Hadrian slid the band over his sleeve. He had not yet punished Hadrian for the day before. Kenton was biding his time, waiting for the governor to draw first blood.

When Kenton left Hadrian in Buchanan's office, the governor acknowledged him only by shoving a thin newspaper across his desk. The colony did not have enough paper to circulate the news to all its citizens. Only senior officials received personal copies, with the remaining ones posted on boards scattered about the colony.

With an angry heart Hadrian quickly read the first article, its headline announcing the suicide of legendary scientist and Council member Jonah Beck. Police arrived moments too late to resuscitate him but then discovered a fire that had tragically broken out elsewhere in the building. Courageous efforts saved the structure and most of the book collection. Governor Buchanan had declared the next day an official day of mourning, with a state funeral at noon.

When Buchanan finally looked up, Hadrian spoke first. "You don't need me. You've already settled everything. Jonah succumbed to a suicidal compulsion. You decreed that the fire was unrelated. Hastings's body by now is no doubt under a thousand feet of water. You've done what you do best when reality overtakes you. Manipulate the truth in the name of public order."

Buchanan was silent a long time. Low voices rose from out in the hall. Hadrian's eyes widened as he turned and saw the policeman at the reception desk being relieved, handing over his pistol to a tall blond bull of a man.

"My god!" he said. "You think you're next."

Buchanan rose. "No one comes in, Bjorn," he instructed his new sentry, then shut the door.

"You tell the colony Jonah was a suicide," Hadrian spoke slowly, studying the governor, seeing now the lines of worry around his eyes. "But behind closed doors you fear the killer."

The governor stood at the window, gazing out over the inland sea, grey and choppy under a brisk autumn wind. "These are unsettled times. I haven't endured all these years just to have a blade shoved in my ribs."

Hadrian's mind raced. "Something in Jonah's death frightens you." It was a statement, not a question.

"The killer must be stopped."

"You've told the world there is no killer. So there is no one to stop. We have no murders in our paradise on earth."

"You can stop him." Buchanan's face was tight. "You must stop him."

"Tell me, Lucas, why would I want to do that?" Hadrian asked.

The governor spun about. Hadrian half expected him to leap at him across the desk. Buchanan paused, taking a deep breath. "I'm giving you your freedom," he replied in a simmering voice. "No banishment."

"My sentence is up in four days anyway. We both know with the stroke of a pen you could make me an exile five minutes after I walk out the door."

"It shall be recorded in the Council's ledger. No exile. Official freedom to come and go. An expression of our gratitude for the way you helped at the fire."

"I'm not sure I want to live in your colony anymore."

Buchanan's eyes burnt into Hadrian's. "Damn you! What do you want?"

"My armband comes off. Stop putting your slogans on the walls. And the bridge. You promised Jonah to build one over the west ravine."

"You go too far! You will not dictate the use of public resources."

"After the bridge, there will have to be a road. Then wagons of grain. The colony silos will be overflowing soon."

"Ridiculous! That grain is our lifeblood! Without it we'd never survive the winter. I keep telling the Council we must expand the plantings."

"More has been harvested than ever before."

"And we have more mouths to feed."

Hadrian stared at him. "You never intended to construct the bridge," he finally said. "You lied to Jonah, to appease him. My grandfather once told me that a lie to a dead man always comes back to haunt the living."

"It's impossible. The people won't allow it. You know how they hate the slags."

"Only because you taught them to." Hadrian rose as if to leave. "I can wait until my sentence is up, then disappear into the forest, let you spend the next year jumping at every shadow. I wonder what people will think when suddenly they see you surrounded by bodyguards after you've already assured them Jonah's death was just another suicide."

Buchanan grimaced. He was clearly struggling to keep his voice level. "We must get the new roof on the library."

"Split the crews. But I won't do your dirty work for you until I see work begun on the bridge. Jonah already gave you a set of drawings. First come the anchor piers on this side of the ravine . . ."

"Extortion of the governor is treason."

"There's no such law. It will be fascinating to hear how you explain to the Council why you need one now."

Buchanan seemed to flinch at the mention of the Council. His hold over the supreme political body of the colony was tenuous. He had firm control over only three of its seven votes, and the vacancy caused by Jonah's death meant even more uncertainty.

"Go back to the hole you crawled out of," Buchanan said through clenched teeth.

Hadrian shrugged. "The killers left a knife on Jonah's table. Did you see it? An old sword, cut down, heavy and sharp as a razor. A blade like that will slice your heart in half before you even feel it."

A CITY WORKER was lighting the fish oil lanterns hanging at each street corner. Hooves clattered on cobblestones. A bawdy song rose from a tavern near the waterfront. A horse nickered in a stable. Hadrian, enjoying his newfound freedom, paused to watch the moon rise over the endless water, then slipped through the rear door of an L-shaped log and stone building, the largest in the colony except for Government House.

The woman who sat at the kitchen table by the huge woodburning stove didn't see him at first. Her brunette hair, streaked with grey, hung over her face. She stared wearily into the steaming mug in her hands. The white apron she wore was frayed and stained with blood.

"I'm sorry about shoving you away at the library, Emily," he said softly.

Her head came up slowly as she straightened her hair and scrubbed at her cheeks. The sturdy, unshakable head of the colony's hospital had been crying.

"Did you, Hadrian?" she said. "I didn't notice."

"You're lying, but thank you."

It had been four months after the founding of the colony when Hadrian had found Emily ten miles inland, caring for three dying children in a cave. He had stayed with her until their struggle ended, then dug the graves before bringing Carthage its first doctor. During the past year they'd sat up many nights nursing Jonah through his bouts of illness. She rose now and poured him tea from the pot on the stove.

"I just came to beg a little soap and water."

Emily lifted an oil lamp toward Hadrian and winced. "A little? Weeks in jail, hauling old manure?" She jabbed a finger into his chest, pushing him onto the back veranda, then pointed to a metal bathtub sitting in a corner. She cut off his protest with an upraised hand. "You are not going to bury Jonah smelling like a latrine."

A quarter hour later Hadrian was luxuriating in hot water from the tank attached to the stove. A match flared as Emily settled into a rocking chair ten feet away and lit a small tobacco pipe.

"He was murdered, Em," Boone said.

"I am the known world's foremost authority on the damage done by hanging nooses. Asphyxiation by rope was the official cause of death."

"He would never commit suicide. Not Jonah. Life was too precious to him. He had too many unfinished projects."

"Above all here in Carthage we know the pathology of the human spirit. I could give you twenty reasons why he might suddenly give up. His arthritis was getting worse by the day. Do you have any idea what constant pain can do to you?"

"Give up and also try to burn his life's work?"

"Half a dozen reasons."

"Of all the scenarios you could postulate, surely murder is at least one of them."

The head of the Carthage hospital was quiet a long time, gazing at the tobacco smoke that drifted through the moonlight. "Two of his fingers were broken. There were marks on his upper arm where someone with a hand like a vise had gripped him."

Hadrian lowered his voice. "Does Buchanan know?"

"He was there when I cleaned the body. I showed him. He immediately reminded me that murder was a legal construct, not a medical concept, then insisted the injuries were made when Jonah dropped to the floor from the rafter. When I disagreed, he said we had a duty not to panic the population, that Jonah would want his death to be used for the betterment of the colony."

Hadrian leaned back in his cocoon of warm water and moonlight. Near the horizon a trail of sparks marked the late return of one of the steam fishing vessels. Above it the aurora shimmered. Jonah had kept his astrophysics alive by studying the northern lights and had been writing a scholarly pamphlet on why their display had increased over the past generation.

It was Emily who broke their silence. "An old man died out here last week," she said in a melancholy tone. "He had no family left, made his way as a carpenter, but in his spare time he tried to start little churches. Baptist first, then Episcopal. The final attempt was Buddhist. They always failed. He came out here on his last night. I found him dead at dawn, leaning against a post, looking upward. In his lap he had left a slip of paper. I thought it was going to be a prayer or a last bequest. *After the earth was in ashes*, it said, *I could see the stars more clearly*."

"Jonah was the best of us, Em," Hadrian said after a long silence. He wasn't sure she had heard him.

When she spoke at last it was in a whisper. "He was always about getting on with life. The world may have ended for the rest of us, but he treated it like a bad accident we had to just walk away from."

"At first I thought it was because he was callused," Hadrian replied. "But I quickly learned that wasn't true. It was just courage. More than I ever had."

"I read old books on psychiatry. Sometimes I think we are as disabled on the inside as the exiles are on the outside. But not Jonah. I never knew how he did it. As if he were the last real human on earth."

"On his body, was there anything else? A knife wound?"

"More like a line where blood vessels had been crushed, high on his neck, but just a shallow cut. A knife could have done it, held close to the neck. Nothing else remarkable. Just some blotches of color on his lips. Little brown and purple spots. An allergy, perhaps."

As Hadrian puzzled over her words, Emily stood. "There are clean clothes on the chair by the door, and you can use the bed in the exam room off the kitchen, provided you give me ten minutes first. Second floor, north corner."

She was taking the pulse of a young man when Hadrian arrived upstairs. Her patient was barely out of his teens, a handsome youth whose face strangely sagged along the left side. Emily lifted his left arm and dropped it. The limb was lifeless.

"Not a mutation, not a birth defect?" Hadrian asked.

The doctor shook her head. "His name is Jamie Reese. He's worked in the fishing fleet for years, the son of the captain of the *Zeus*, one of the old sailing trawlers. His crew found him like this on his bunk one morning. If he were fifty years older, I'd say it was a stroke. There's paralysis, probably nerve damage. He can't talk, can't write. Drifts in and out of this coma."

"He could have been hit on the head, but the concussion had a delayed effect."

"That's how it was first reported. But there's no sign of a blow. None of his crew would talk when I went to the docks to ask about a possible accident."

"Reese . . . Why do I know that name?"

"The hero from the sinking of the *Anna*. He was one of the two survivors. Saved the captain."

Hadrian looked at the patient with new interest. The *Anna* had been the first of the colony's steamboats, lost in a storm more than a year earlier. Reese and the captain had survived in a dinghy for several days before being picked up by another fishing boat. He paced around the bed, lifting the youth's arms, pushing back the sleeves.

"What are you looking for?"

"I don't know. A tattoo. Or a mark of some kind."

"His mother came every day at first, but she's stopped. She was quite emotional. I thought it was grief, but on her last visit it was more like fear. Two men came yesterday, smelling of fish. They wouldn't step into the room, just looked at him from the door. I asked what was wrong. They asked if he would live. When I said he probably would they didn't seem relieved, they just backed away."

Hadrian now noticed a leather strap around the fisherman's neck and pulled it out. It held a piece of tin stamped with an image, a wolf on two legs. But unlike the medallion gripped by the dead scout, this wolf stood in a tree. Not a wolf, he suspected now, but one of the vicious pine martens that had multiplied in recent years. A tree jackal. *Jackals run with ghosts.*

"Do you know this?"

"Just a cheap piece of jewelry."

"No. It's more. The mark I was looking for." He studied the youth again. Reese had been feted for his heroism after the shipwreck, would have had his choice of jobs in the fishery. "The two visitors. Did you know them?"

Emily shrugged. "They smelled of fish. And something else—spices. Cloves and cinnamon. I assumed they were friends of his. They asked how he fared and I said he should survive."

"What sort of friends stand in the hall and point?"

The doctor gave another weary shrug. "Fishermen and hunters get more superstitious every year. Haven't you heard? We're retreating backward in time, reversing history. We'll have witch trials and exorcisms before long."

Hadrian stepped to the end of the bed and laid the shreds of paper from his pocket on the blanket. "These were under Jonah's desk."

"Hadrian, I don't have time."

He held up a restraining hand and assembled the scraps quickly, then pointed to the missing arcs along the right margin. "Brown and purple spots, you said."

The doctor cocked her head, then lifted a piece from the margin to study under the oil lamp.

"Brown and purple ink. He bit off these pieces before he died."

Emily's brow creased with worry as she nodded her agreement. "But it's nothing," she said as she quickly scanned the pieces on the bed. "A diary."

"Jonah spent hours on this. A different page each week," he explained. "All I know for sure is that there's more to it than you and I can see." He gazed at the comatose sailor, then tore a slip of paper from the chart hanging from a peg by the bed and quickly wrote a note. "Give this to the governor in the morning."

As Emily read the note her mouth twisted as if she had bit into something sour. "A police guard? He'll never agree."

"You're on the Council."

"Why would I want some brute in uniform hovering over this poor boy?"

Hadrian stepped toward the door, fighting an overwhelming fatigue. "To protect the truth," he said, and slipped away.

AN HOUR AFTER dawn he found Emily back in the kitchen, instructing her nurses at the big table by the stove. She offered him a haggard smile as he poured himself tea. The only other medical personnel to have found their way to Carthage had been a chiropractor, a dentist, and two medical students. She was not only the head physician and hospital administrator but also chief instructor of its fledgling medical school.

Outside, he drank the strong brew and braced himself for the painful day ahead. The scent of fresh loaves wafted up from a bakery near the port. Trawlers were leaving the wharves half a mile up the shore. From the edge of town, cows mooed. The mechanical breath of a steam thresher starting its day's work rose in the distance. He drained his mug, set it inside, and began climbing the hill.

At the library crews were clearing out the debris from the fire. They said nothing, only stepped aside as he mounted the stairs. Jonah's workshop lay in ruin, apparently untouched, cordoned off by a rope at the entry. Charred roof shingles cracked underfoot. The old man's precious collections lay scattered about. Books lay in pools of water. The marks of heavy boots stained the shelves where firefighters had climbed to aim their hose.

He circled the big table, despairing of finding any evidence in the chaos, struggling once more to visualize the chamber as it had been when he discovered his old friend's body, before the fire and fire crews had destroyed it. Hadrian could see the fresh chips on the rafter where he'd hacked away the hanging rope. He found the knife where he had tossed it against the back wall. Lifting it now, he admired the finely worked hilt, noted the mark of a Philadelphia maker and a date. 1861. As Nash had explained, such a blade was too useful to have been preserved simply because of its Civil War vintage. It had been ground down to a size that made it useful for assaulting old men.

He stuck the blade into his belt, his heavy wool shirt concealing it, then studied the chamber again. The desk had been moved nearly two feet to position it under the rafter. There were footprints on it, those of the flat-soled shoes worn by Jonah but also boot prints. It would have taken two men to move the heavy desk. There had been at least two killers. With the knife at his throat, the scientist had been forced to step onto the chair, then the desk, had stood as the noose was tightened, and then been shoved off the makeshift scaffold. But if they had had such a knife, why go to the trouble of the hanging?

He touched the scraps of Jonah's journal in his pocket. There must have been a moment when he had seen them coming, had recognized their intention. He could have run to the balcony to call for help. But instead he had grabbed his illuminated page and taken two bites out of it, then ripped up the remainder.

Hadrian paced slowly along the shelves. Most of Jonah's prize exhibits had been damaged or destroyed. He ran his finger along the edge of several shelves, wiping away the soot on the inscriptions his friend had carved into the edges of the thick boards. KNOWLEDGE IS THE CONTAGION THAT ALL TYRANTS FEAR, he read, then WONDER IS THE BEGINNING OF ALL LEARNING. He picked up the stuffed grouse, broken beyond repair in the chaos of that night. One leg had been broken off, the other barely attached. Its head was gone. He paused. The head had been severed. He pulled out the knife, examining the blade, finding a tiny feather pressed against the hilt. He picked up another animal, and another. Each had been mutilated. For Jonah, it would have been like witnessing torture. On the floor were the remains of the intricate model observatory. It had been sliced into splinters.

A low moan escaped Hadrian's throat as he recalled Emily's report of broken fingers. They had not come to kill Jonah. They'd come to torture him, to obtain something from him. Knowing how treasured his exhibits and models were, they had begun by mutilating them. Jonah may have been weak in body but his was the strongest spirit Hadrian had ever known. Even after breaking his fingers, even after slicing into the skin of his neck with the knife, his torturers had failed. They had attacked his collections, held the knife to his throat, put the noose around his neck. But the old scholar would have shown no fear, would not have given them the satisfaction of begging for his life or bargaining with what it was they sought. Jonah had taken two bites of his page and let them hang him. But why burn the library, he asked himself as he lifted a book from the floor and returned it to a shelf.

Because they had failed, he realized. If they couldn't obtain what they sought from Jonah, they had tried to make certain no one else could.

He stared absently at the book he had shelved, then paused over its title. *Favorite American Poets*. He carried it back to the desk and again assembled the torn page. *Up from the meadows rich with corn*, the verse began. Over two dozen pages had been marked with folded corners. He began scanning the marked pages. Longfellow, Frost, Riley, Holmes, Emerson. Then the words of Whittier were in front of him, leaping off the page, completing the verse. *Fair as the garden of the Lord*, the poet had written. "To the eyes of the famished rebel horde," he read aloud to himself.

The missing words sent a chill down his spine. They seemed to cast the entire page in a different light. To anyone solving its riddle it was not so much a celebration of the harvest festival as a reminder of the misery of the exiles. Hadrian had never before heard Jonah refer to the exiles as rebels. There had been talk of open insurrection from the camps years earlier, only to die away as the leaders of the movement had succumbed to disease. Hadrian stared at the words with new foreboding, trying to convince himself they were just the musings of an aging scholar.

He stepped out onto the balcony that adjoined the workshop, where he and Jonah had stood only two days earlier, when Jonah had been so full of hope, had spoken of the renaissance to come. He lifted his face into the cool breeze and gazed out over the water. Once it had been called a Great Lake but the term had been lost. Survivors strangely avoided the old place names, as if they too had been extinguished in the destruction. Everything was the same but everything was different. Jonah had died and everything was different.

Hadrian fought a new wave of emotion, a despair so intense he had to grip the railing for support. As he did so his hand touched a groove in the wood, a slender eighth-inch channel cut at an angle, spanning the entire width of the plank that capped the railing. It might have seemed innocuous, a random defect, a carpenter's error, but he knew it had not been there when they'd constructed the building. It had been deliberately cut afterward, and Jonah never engaged in random acts. Hadrian searched the entire railing, finding two more grooves, each at different angles.

Retrieving three pencils from the desk, he laid them on the grooves. They all pointed to the tripod telescope in the center of the balcony, its position fixed by marks on the floor near each leg. He swiveled the instrument to the bearing indicated by the first cut. The end of the long ridge to the west of Carthage leapt into view, on the other side of the deep ravine that separated the colony from the reviled camps. He increased the magnification and a dead oak at the end of the ridge filled the lens. Hawks sometimes perched there, and a bird roosted there now. The tree had become part of the colony's folklore. Vultures were said to rest there after dining on the dead of the camps.

He reduced the magnification and turned the scope to the second mark. Town buildings leapt into view. A corner of Government House. A tavern. The colony's two theaters. Then, increasing the magnification again, the most distant of the structures leapt into view. It was the fish processing plant—more specifically, its roof.

The third mark aimed directly at the steep slope of the ridge that formed the settlement's eastern boundary. Nothing was there except large trees, misshapen from the prevailing northwest wind, and a clearing at the top where townspeople liked to take picnics. He paused for a moment, remembering that Jonah kept another, stronger lens tube somewhere, one they sometimes used to study the moon. He turned to survey the wreckage inside, spied a wooden box that had been knocked from a shelf, half its contents spilled onto the floor. Pen nibs, several old chandelier crystals, a paper knife. Remaining inside was the little tattered cardboard carton that held the lens.

A moment later he had inserted the lens and turned the scope back to the first site. The dead tree could be seen in great detail now, the bird at its top resolving itself into an eagle. Below it, on the lowest limb, was a flash of color he'd not seen before. Three long strips of bright cloth fluttered in the wind, a blue one flanked by two red ones. It was a signal.

A rustle caused him to spin around. A young woman was collecting charred papers from the desk.

"No cleaning in here!" Hadrian snapped.

"I was told to help," the woman stammered, glancing nervously at Hadrian before gazing at the floor.

"Not in here, not until I say so."

"You misunderstand, sir. I mean the governor ordered me to help you."

Hadrian set the papers back on the desk and studied her as she brushed aside a strand of long russet hair. She was a first-generation colonist, in her midtwenties, and would have been pretty had her face not been so heavily mottled. One in five children born in Carthage had pigmentation problems. She lifted the book of poems from the desk.

As Hadrian reached out to pull the book away from her, he noticed the brown tunic under her quilted jacket. "What exactly is your job, officer?"

She stepped back from the desk. "Sergeant. Sergeant Jori Waller," she said nervously. "I usually compile evidence for the tribunals hearing cases, show it to the judges."

Hadrian frowned. "You mean you're an investigator?" Carthage was still a small community in many ways but—probably because it was so small—many of its citizens kept aspects of their lives secret. So many participated in the black market that its shadow touched every street. So many had two faces that old timers joked the population wasn't nine thousand, it was eighteen. The job of the police, Jonah once had quipped, wasn't to penetrate the secrets but to make sure people kept their faces straight. Hadrian had never heard of a real investigator in the colony.

Sergeant Waller shrugged. "Mostly I just compile the facts in police reports. Our crimes are always straightforward, usually settled by the testimony of the arresting officer. A clerical job, really."

"But you're a sergeant."

She seemed embarrassed by the comment. "I'm in charge of the office." Then she added. "There are two others. Paper pushers."

"And what exactly did Governor Buchanan say I was doing?"

"Trying to learn who caused the fire."

Hadrian inwardly cursed Buchanan. Though he'd promised Hadrian freedom to conduct his investigation, he still had to have his watcher. Hadrian pointed to the door. "Go back to Government House. In a few days I'll come tell you what I found."

The young woman looked at the floor as she stepped back over the rope and shut the heavy door behind her. He frowned, then glanced at the book still in his hands and thought of the exiles. He would have to get word of Jonah's death to them, even if it meant making the arduous trip himself. Mail to the camps was forbidden, the trail there often patrolled to discourage travelers.

He worked feverishly, mindful of the midday funeral, looking at every loose paper, leafing through every book for the slips Jonah often set between pages. There were notes for manufacturing water pipes and household plumbing systems, designs for building a steam laundry, even a steam-powered printing press. Yet there was no sign of the rest of Jonah's secret journal, no pile of layered ashes where it might have been burnt.

He paced around the chamber, absently restoring more fallen objects to their shelves, then paused and turned back to gaze at the desk with new realization. Jonah had known the governor wanted his secret chronicle. He would not have kept it in the library.

His old friend had loved games. Once on Hadrian's birthday he'd designed a map with the location of little gifts indicated solely by Latin riddles. Stumbling through the mess underfoot, he absently kicked a shard of pottery under the desk.

Kneeling to retrieve it, he glanced up under the tabletop, saw words, and turned on his back to read them. He recalled helping build the oversized worktable years earlier out of wood salvaged from shipping crates. The container ship they'd discovered wrecked on the coast had provided most of the colony's early salvage. Several sets of words were scattered across the underside of the table. THIS END UP. LIFT HERE. KOREAN SHIPPING COMPANY. And a long set, in black like the others, but in smaller letters of what appeared to be an Eastern European alphabet. No. They were backward. A casual observer would have dismissed them as vestiges of some foreign tongue gone dead. But this tongue wasn't dead in Carthage, not so long as Hadrian lived. The words were in Latin. He found a piece of broken mirror and laid it on the floor to read the words reflected. QUAERE VERUM IMPRIMIS. Seek truth among the first things. The thrill of the discovery died, giving way to despair again. Jonah's strange humor was going to doom Hadrian's search before he got truly started.

In the distance a bell began to peal, calling citizens to the funeral. Hadrian darted out the door so quickly he almost missed the shadow that followed him down the stairs.

"You!" he exclaimed to Sergeant Waller. "I told you there was a mistake. Go back to your office."

The policewoman straightened. "I don't know why I am being punished," she said. "But I do know I am not permitted to abandon my assignment."

"Punished?"

Waller looked toward her feet as she replied. "You are a known criminal. Not just a criminal. A saboteur, a dissident," she added, as if that was his greatest crime of all. "Everyone in the corps knows the governor has a file on you."

"Why would you be punished for leaving when I ordered you to?"

"I failed my last assignment. If I fail another, Lieutenant Kenton will have me mucking out the government stables for the next six months."

"Lieutenant? Since when?"

"Since yesterday."

Hadrian winced at the news. "I'm supposed to feel sorry for you because you were sent to spy on me?"

"If I help you in any real way, the governor will pronounce me a conspirator too. If I don't help you, he'll say I disobeyed him."

"So what will you do?"

"Pretend to help you?" the sergeant suggested.

Hadrian gave a bitter grin. "Fine. Here's what you do. Find out if anyone was working in the library when the fire started. If so, pretend to ask them questions about who was here, what Jonah was doing, whether anything strange seemed to be going on."

She offered a hesitant nod.

"Walk along the street. Ask passersby if they saw anything. Then write up your report. Write what the governor wants to hear. Use bold words. Spice it with rumors gleaned from the street. *The citizens grow concerned over public safety. The people are thankful that running water had been installed in time to fight the fire. They wonder if damaged books will be auctioned off for personal latrine use.* Twenty pages at least. The governor favors quantity over quality."

The sergeant brightened, tore out the frontispiece of the first book within reach, and began writing.

Outside, a bass drum began to beat.

The governing council of Carthage declared a state funeral once every two or three years. Children would be released from school. The colony's antique hearse would lead a procession of somber leading citizens, followed by one of the town's two bands playing a dirge. But for the burial of Jonah Beck, the governor had called out both bands and erected a speaker's platform at the edge of the cemetery.

Hadrian stood in the shadow of a maple tree, listening as the leaders of Carthage extolled the old man. The Savior was invoked, and St. Peter too. The town had long ago forgotten that their resident wizard was a Jew. A woman waved a stick of incense over the coffin. An elderly matron famed for starting the colony's first bank took the podium and described seeing Jonah flying toward the moon in the shape of a great white bird. It wasn't so much a funeral as a somber circus. Jonah would have loved it.

Hadrian found a patch of grass on a knoll above those gathered and sat. It was a crisp day, the changing weather pushing vast flocks of geese and ducks southward, the colony's green and blue flag fluttering at half mast on the white-washed pole in the graveyard's center. Police in brown tunics paced along the fringe of the crowd. An enterprising vendor sold hot cider, fresh apples, and black armbands. Four men with shovels waited by the open grave. A square-shouldered man in a suit, smoking as he leaned against a tree, turned away as he met Hadrian's gaze. Hadrian had enough of a glimpse of his face to realize

he'd seen the man half an hour earlier, outside the library. Was he following Hadrian?

Hadrian tucked his knees against his chest and tried to focus on the
speakers. But his gaze kept returning to the gaping grave, and his grief
returned. *Seek truth among the first things.* Jonah's voice spoke the
words inside his head, stirring him from his numbness. It could have
been a simple reminder to make truth his priority. It could also mean
to seek it among those at the highest level of authority. He watched
absently as Kenton, wearing his new lieutenant bars, approached
Buchanan. The two men urgently conferred, Kenton pointing vaguely
toward the back of the crowd before retreating with a scowl, clearly
unsatisfied.

A moment later his stout figure broke through the edge of the
crowd, his hand on his truncheon as he marched toward Hadrian.

"If I see a slag within five hundred feet of the governor," the lieutenant snapped, "you'll be spending the night in the hospital."

"I'm sorry?" Hadrian muttered. He became aware of movement
behind him but did not break away from Kenton's angry stare.

"I don't play your goddamned games, Boone. I will gladly—"
Kenton's words choked away as he looked over Hadrian's shoulder.

Hadrian turned. He was surrounded on three sides by children. The
boy Dax was on one side, Sarah and her sister on the other, with at least
a dozen others behind them.

The lieutenant glared at the children. "You have no idea!" he spat
out before hurrying back to the graveside. For once Hadrian agreed
with him.

When he turned again to ask for an explanation, the children were
gone, slipping over the crest of the knoll. Only little Dora was visible.
She hesitated, giving Hadrian a quick, self-conscious wave. Then someone yanked her arm and she too disappeared from sight. He turned

back to the mourners. Kenton was nowhere to be seen. The man by the tree had lit another cigarette. He wasn't watching the crowd. He was watching the knoll. He was watching Hadrian.

There were few lives in the colony that had not been touched by Jonah, and the eulogies were many. Last came Lucas Buchanan. Standing close to him was the blond bodyguard Bjorn.

"Friends," the governor began. "I owe more tears to this dead man than you shall see me pay." Hadrian stared in surprise, heard the murmurs in the crowd. Buchanan wasn't quoting the words, he was appropriating them for his own. Did he truly not understand that one of the many strange consequences of his censorship policies had been to turn his populace into experts on Shakespearean dialogue?

The eulogy quickly moved into a litany of Jonah's many extraordinary contributions. Designer of the dams and gear works for the water-powered mills that ground their grains, cut their planks, powered their carpenter shops. Designer and chief engineer for the fleet of steamboats. Original organizer of the children's orchestra. Longtime director of the annual George Bernard Shaw festival. The sounds of weeping grew ever more audible.

It was peculiar, thought Hadrian, how funerals for the older generation were devoid of references to their lives or accomplishments from the prior world. *Author of books on astrophysics*, Hadrian was tempted to shout out. *Chancellor of the region's university. Holder of patents used in outer space. Father of three children. Husband to a renowned medical researcher.* But Jonah had already died that death, on endless nights long ago. His wife, his children, his university, and the city that hosted it had been wiped out in one blinding flash. Even the discipline of astrophysics had died, at least for another century.

He closed his eyes, steadying himself, then gazed toward the sky. Once Jonah and he might have gone birding on a day like this, Hadrian helping take notes on the strange plumage variations starting to appear. He glanced toward the haunted tree on the western ridge, then paused. There was a large bird in the tree again. He squinted, shielding his eyes. Not a bird, but a person in a cloak, watching the funeral.

Hadrian looked in alarm at Buchanan, now reviewing the civic awards bestowed on Jonah. The governor's back was to the dead tree. He droned on. "Chairman of the Science Advisory Committee, Citizen of the Year—" Buchanan's words choked in his throat. His mouth hung open as he stared at the stone cottage nearest the cemetery. A man in a black coat holding a long musical instrument resembling a recorder sat on the chimney. The wind stopped. Not a word was spoken. Only one bitter syllable broke the silence.

"Slags!" Kenton shouted.

Then from behind the chimney a hairless woman in a grey cloak emerged. The recorder began to play a slow, graceful tune that Hadrian did not recognize until the woman began singing in a powerful, lilting voice.

"*Amazing Grace, how sweet the sound,*" she intoned, "*that saved a wretch like me.*" Other voices slowly joined in, from below, until, despite Buchanan's furious attempts to quiet them, nearly the entire assembly was singing. "*I once was lost but now I'm found, was blind but now I see . . .*"

Hadrian was grinning until he saw Kenton race off with several officers. He leapt up himself. "Nelly!" he shouted in warning to the woman as Kenton disappeared into the cottage. But his cry was drowned out. The citizens of Carthage kept singing even after the policemen appeared on the roof. They stopped only as the police began to club the intruders.

Then in the uneasy silence came a strange echo. Buchanan spun about and cursed, bellowing for his police. But they took only a few steps and stopped as the wind renewed, carrying other voices toward them. Lined up on the ridge at the far side of the ravine, far from their reach, were at least fifty more of the bone-thin exiles, many with hoods covering their ravaged features, singing the eulogy for beloved Jonah, the last real human on earth.

CHAPTER *Three*

THE CABIN TUCKED between two steep ridges sat as it had for over a century, flowering vines creeping up its stone walls, touched by nature but not by the ruin of man. A sense of melancholy overtook Hadrian as he approached it along the well-worn path. In his fatigue he saw Jonah waiting for him, inviting him to sniff the fresh herbs in the kitchen garden before gesturing him inside. In recent years Jonah had spent most of his days, and many nights, in his library workshop, but this had been his home, and the birthplace of the colony.

Hadrian paused, wiped at the moisture in his eyes, then looked back up the path. The plainclothes policeman had reappeared when he had walked into town from the cemetery, lingering half a block away whenever Hadrian stopped, once conferring with another man in casual clothes. He had ducked down several alleys and doubled back before slipping into the trees on the far side of the ridge. The path behind him now was empty. With a sigh of relief he opened the door and froze.

The ruin of man had reached the cabin after all. The floors were covered with debris thrown from shelves and drawers, much of the furniture in splinters. The kitchen, the sitting room, the bedrooms had all been ravaged. He righted a ladder-back chair and collapsed onto it, his head in his hands. Here had been his one possible sanctuary, here he had expected to feel the restorative presence of his friend again. Instead it felt as if he had stumbled upon a continuation of Jonah's murder. It was as if the killers hadn't only wanted the old scientist dead and buried, they wished his very existence pounded into dust and cast into the wind.

For a moment he was back at the grave, to which he had returned an hour after the burial, sinking in grief to his knees. He had wanted to apologize somehow. For the colony's parting message to Jonah had been the senseless beating and arrest of the two exiles, one of them an old friend of theirs. Hadrian had found himself thrusting his fingers into the freshly turned earth as if reaching for his lost friend when his fingers unexpectedly touched something that didn't belong, something dull grey and plastic. The object was so alien he simply stared at it in confusion after bringing it to the surface. He was holding a small phone, a model that would have been old even at the time the world shifted. Someone had secretly buried a cell phone with Jonah. Yet he had watched the grave from a distance as the crowd thinned and had not seen anyone bury anything.

Hadrian did not know how long he sat in Jonah's house, the memory of the phone only adding to his despair. Eventually he became aware of the lengthening shadows and the chill in the sitting room. He lit a candle, then a fire in the stone fireplace, and began to clean the cabin.

He lost himself in the task, carrying what he swept up outside to a pile at the edge of the garden. Not stopping at righting the work of the killers, he filled a bucket from the hand pump in the kitchen sink, collected rags and soap, and scrubbed, feverishly cleaning windows. As tears welled again in his eyes, he worked even harder, losing himself in memories of earlier days there.

Emptying his bucket near the little herb garden, he paused, seeing again in his mind's eye the reverse writing on the desk in the library. *Quaere verum imprimis.* Seek the truth among the first things, in the first things. His interpretation may have been wrong. Perhaps it referred to a location. He dropped the bucket and ran to the fireplace, running his fingers over the stones along the side of the chimney until he found the loose one he sought, pried it away, and extracted a key wrapped in a scrap of leather.

He walked with a lantern along the cliff face behind the cottage, probing the vegetation hanging on the rock with his hands for nearly a quarter hour before finding the one place where the surface underneath was not natural ledge stone but mortared rocks. He and Jonah had erected the wall years earlier to obscure the opening, leaving only room for a man to slip sideways into the narrow passage. Hadrian raised the lantern over the small but heavy-timbered door with the iron lock plate, which Jonah had helped his father erect fifty years earlier. Jonah's father, owner of an engineering firm, had insisted the cavern chamber was necessary to preserve his wine collection. When the wine had been depleted at the first Carthage Thanksgiving, Jonah had decided to use the chamber for something else. A brittle, dusty paper with a carefully rendered skull and crossbones was tacked to the door, over a hand-lettered sign that warned TOXIC CONTAGION: ENTRY WILL RESULT IN FATAL EXPOSURE.

Only the older among the colony's inhabitants would remember the great debate about the bodies of the wretched souls who'd stumbled into the fledgling settlement dying of typhus. Sure of his own immunity, Jonah had insisted on singlehandedly sealing the tightly wrapped bodies inside the little crypt, taking the corpses away over the ridge in a handcart at night.

Now Hadrian nervously held his lantern close to the door. The dust of the years coated the wood, but the lock plate was clean. Clenching his jaw, he inserted and twisted the key. The door swung open with a groan. With a hesitant step he entered the vault, lifting the lantern to survey the chamber, then stepped inside and shut the door behind him.

Knowledge is the contagion that all tyrants fear. At least one of the old man's jokes had outlived him. Here was no crypt, but rather a secret vault of knowledge protected by the myth of contagion. As he began lighting the candles scattered around the room, Hadrian remembered once encountering Jonah bringing a dinghy to shore late one night. No one would have questioned Jonah about the bodies at the time, but Hadrian realized now they had been given a watery grave.

Above a table made of planks and crates and lining the adjacent wall were shelves of books, scores of books, many of them banned by the government. On the table, beside a magnifying glass, were more volumes, of medicine, pharmacology, and chemistry. Jonah must have collected them in the early years, secreting them when the censorship campaigns had resulted in thousands of books being sent for recycling. With an unexpected rush of emotion he sat on the stool at the table and found himself facing a plank hanging on the wall inscribed in Jonah's careful hand. DO NOT GO GENTLE INTO THAT GOOD NIGHT, it said. OLD AGE SHOULD BURN AND RAVE AT CLOSE OF DAY. RAGE, RAGE AGAINST THE DYING OF THE LIGHT. The plank was at eye level for a reason. Jonah wanted to see those words of Dylan Thomas's every time he sat at the table.

Hadrian pulled his own meager hoard of words from his shirt, laying the precious book pages he carried before him, then extracted the sword-knife from his belt. As he set it to the side, he noticed a small stand beside the table covered with a tattered square of linen. Holding his breath he lifted the cloth.

His heart leapt as he lifted the book from the stand. Jonah had tooled the thick leather cover of his secret journal with images of oak and maple leaves. The title, inscribed in elegant calligraphy on the first page, was simply *Chronicle of the New World*. Nearly three inches thick, the book was bound with strands of leather tied at the back so that adding a page simply required untying it and removing the back cover. He turned to the one most recently added. Like the others, it had a date penciled on the back, in the bottom corner. It was from the week before. He read the first paragraph and smiled. It was not about secrets of state, it was about secrets of the spirit.

> *Ten thousand geese we have counted this past week, more than double the migration rate of five years ago. Nature is well pleased with her scoured planet. Once I dreamt of fixing a camera to the leg of one of these feathered vagabonds. Now I dream of becoming one.*

The earliest of the pages read like an almanac, giving a statistician's review of life in the colony, listing number of inhabitants, babies born during the past year, cows, horses, and pigs in the colony farms, the size of the grain harvest, milk production, tons of flour produced, even the gallons of syrup gathered in the maple groves. Every page had the same format, elegant text framed in a box, the shaded borders containing artwork and sometimes brief aphorisms or quotes, several in Latin.

An unexpected contentment settled over Hadrian as he ranged through the journal. His old friend was still alive in the pages, his presence so real he could smell one of the sassafras twigs Jonah often chewed when coming in from the forest. He couldn't help taking pleasure in the accounts of the little events that made up life in Carthage.

A pet goat followed a girl into the school building. Two hundred pies were consumed in the last night of the midsummer fair. A new schooner had been launched to haul lumber and salt from up the coast.

Surely this had been Jonah's real goal, simply to document the normalcy, show the colony as a living organism, demonstrate how, despite all their trials and the self-destruction of advanced societies, individual humans would find a way not only to survive but also to celebrate life.

Every few weeks came a different type of page, ones filled with drawings and instructions, like little manuals for civilization. These recorded the designs for the equipment and buildings that had advanced the colony. The pile driver used for building the docks, the water-powered saw mill, the first steam boiler.

He found himself gazing at the darkest corner of the vault, where Jonah had leaned wide planks, pinned to which were detailed drawings of his future projects. Hadrian stacked these planks against the bookshelves, exposing an obsolete highway map that he pulled away from the wall. Then he choked with emotion as he brushed away the dust accumulated over years. Waist high on the wall were six rows of identical marks cut into the wood. Hadrian did not need to count them. He himself had carved ten in each row, twenty-five years earlier.

This was the place of first things.

It was a storm, Hadrian had told himself when he glimpsed the first flashes on the horizon. Hiking in the mountains by the lake, he had been in a low ravine when he'd seen the brilliant flashes of light reflected off the clouds and felt the first gale-force winds. He had gone in two days ahead of the rest of the family to do repairs on their little cabin deep in the mountains and felt it prudent now to descend closer to the lake to find phone coverage, to tell his wife to wait at home with the children until the weather improved.

The storm was like none he'd ever seen, with intense bursts of light on the horizon yet no rain, only long angry strokes of lightning arcing across the sky and violent blasts of wind that began leveling trees along the ridgetops. He was not surprised to find no phone service by the time he reached the water and had been about to return to the cabin when he first heard the frantically ringing bell. Running down the coastal trail toward the sound, uneasily watching the strange white-capped roiling in the water, he nearly stumbled over the bearded man hammering the old bell mounted at the edge of a high cliff, a vestige of an old fog warning system. Neither man spoke, for they had both caught sight of the large sailing yacht struggling to reach shore, her mast broken, a makeshift sail shredded in the wind. Suddenly a huge wave appeared and just as suddenly swallowed the boat. Tears streaming down his cheeks, the stranger had turned and pointed toward a little cabin tucked into the bottom of the ridge.

In the house two other men waited, a pair of hunters who'd also fled toward the bell. The four of them had watched in disbelief the horrific, confused television reports of rogue nations engaging the rest of the world with nuclear and biological agent strikes. First one station, then another had abruptly left the air, until the only one they could receive was Canadian, from across the vast lake. Those final broadcasts had lasted a few more hours, then with one more blinding flash on the horizon they too were silenced. There was no more television, no more radio, but they had heard enough to know that those who had survived the initial blasts would likely die of radiation or biological poisoning.

Their host, a retired professor of astrophysics, they learned, had brought them to his wine vault, insulated under two hundred feet of stone. He had quickly explained that it had a filtered ventilation system that had been overdesigned by his father, and they had frantically stuffed the vault with food, bedding, and every candle and oil lamp they could find. Their host did not know how long they would need to hide underground but gave his scientific opinion that sixty days should be sufficient for the air to clear. Winding an old alarm clock, he set it to ring every twelve hours. After every two rings, Hadrian had sliced a mark into the wall.

For the first few days they had spoken of their families, pretending they would see them again, and how they hoped the roads would not be too clogged when they finally drove home. After the first week Jonah had sat for hours at his table making calculations. It was then that he'd begun to speak in colder technical terms, about the reach of warheads and the half-life of radiation, the depletion rates of biological agents. He had worked in weapons research, developing models for the government demonstrating how once the low-quality, wide-ranging biological warheads favored by lesser nations had been deployed they would contaminate the entire planet, would wipe out nearly all human life as well as other higher life forms.

In the long silent hours, Jonah had developed a new model, using weather data from the last newspapers, showing how their location— one of the most remote in the eastern part of the continent and protected by the high ridges—had been spared the worst contamination by an unusual shift in wind patterns.

His three guests—but almost never Jonah—had sunk into dark, silent depressions lasting days at a time. In the night, in the blackness when the last candle was extinguished, they wept.

HADRIAN STAYED IN the vault for hours, reading many of the pages but also exploring the shelves. They held not only rare volumes—everything from common cookbooks to popular bestsellers to foreign dictionaries—but also glass tubes and columns containing the remnants of experiments, stacks of old magazines, even, in an old shoebox, a hand calculator and half a dozen corroded batteries. Hadrian had been the old man's closest friend in Carthage, but still Jonah Beck had kept many secrets from him. Much of what was in the vault was illegal. But that did not explain why Jonah's journal was so secret, or why Lucas Buchanan so urgently wanted to find it.

At last he returned to the stool and studied the little plaque again. *Rage, rage against the dying of the light.* It wasn't just a reminder. It was a manifesto. Jonah had been nearing the end of his tragic life. But there had always been one tragedy he thought he could reverse. On the very day he died he had spoken to Hadrian as if he were on the verge of doing so. With a new, rising pain, the realization came to Hadrian. Jonah had accepted death not simply because he thought he had saved the exiles, but because giving in to his killers' demands would have jeopardized those plans.

He sifted through the pages again, pausing over an entry made eighteen months earlier, mourning the loss of the colony's first steamboat, the *Anna*, in a storm, listing the names of the two men who drowned and mourning the loss of the sturdy little fishing vessel, named after Jonah's long-dead daughter.

Hadrian arranged on the desk the shreds of Jonah's last ornamented page, more frustrated than ever by his inability to understand the real reason Jonah had tried to destroy it.

He lifted the magnifying glass, then examined one piece of the colored margin after another. He studied the vines, looking for a pattern. Their twists and turns suddenly seemed to him not entirely random. He spotted a numeral two formed by the vine over one pumpkin, then saw a three in the one at its side. He found another number, then a letter. Stopping for a moment to reconsider the image as a whole, he began a more systematic search, starting at the bottom of the page.

As his eyes adjusted to the puzzle, the words leapt out to him. *Auribus tener lupum.* I am holding a wolf by the ears. He stared uneasily at the declaration, then worked his way up the unbroken left side and along the top. But there were no more words, only letters and numbers. H2GMAN4MGSS3GBC2CC, the series began. The remainder had been in the pieces his friend had bitten off.

"Jonah!" he cried out in frustration, pounding the table with his fist. Why had it been so necessary to hide the words and letters? From whom was he hiding them? Surely his friend had not died over a jumble of letters and numbers. He did not know how long he stared at the paper fragments but at last he returned the journal to its stand, blew out the candles, and left.

Back in the cabin, he replaced the key behind the chimney stone and made himself some tea in the kettle hanging in the fireplace. It was two hours before dawn, but he could not sleep. He carried a rocking chair out onto the porch where he and Jonah had spent so many evenings. His gaze drifted up toward the moonlit clearing on the cliff where the old bell had stood. It had hurt to find the secrets in the hidden chamber, but he slowly realized that Jonah had kept the secrets from him to protect Hadrian. Something in the vault, Hadrian was certain, was the reason Jonah had been murdered. He had held the wolf by the ears, but the wolf had turned on him.

As he watched the stars setting, he felt more alone than ever in his life. His discoveries had brought back pains he believed he'd banished years earlier. Distant memories flickered in his consciousness, and suddenly he smelled licorice and was with his long-dead son, teaching him the constellations, hearing the boy whisper his questions, as if he feared to upset the beauty. His son reached to hold his hand as a shooting star streaked overhead. He felt the touch, as real as the stab of a blade. Tears welled in his eyes. In the early years Jonah had often assured him that in time all wounds would heal, but it had never been so for Hadrian. His soul had been cauterized twenty-five years before, but the scar kept cracking open, letting the pain ooze out again and again, numbing him to the life around him. It had been the reason for his recklessness, why he had lost everything in the colony.

He blinked through his tears, struggling desperately to keep his son with him, whispering to him the names of more constellations and planets, now pausing as a new, brighter star appeared on the horizon. Suddenly he froze, scrubbing at his eyes.

It was not a star but a lantern, a bright lamp blinking on and off in the clearing above the lake. It was, he recalled, where Jonah's telescope on the opposite side of the ridge would be aimed if it was aligned with the easternmost mark on the railing.

Ten minutes later he stood behind a tree at the edge of the clearing, watching two men with a large box lantern into which baffles had been inserted. They were using it to send signals toward the lake as they spoke in low, urgent tones. Hadrian dared a step closer, desperate for a glimpse of their faces, then was suddenly wrenched off his feet by the violent blow of a stick. He grabbed at his assailant's legs as he went down, and they landed together in a tangle of limbs.

"Punic prick!" the man spat. He stank of fish and spices.

Hadrian twisted, avoiding a punch, taking hold of the man's ankle so that he was thrown off balance as he tried to rise. Hadrian rolled as the man fell again, hearing now laughter from those at the lantern. A fist hammered into his ribs. His opponent, heavier than him, groped for something in his belt. But before he could extract his knife, Hadrian grabbed a rock and hammered it into his knee.

"Bastard!" the man moaned, clutching at his leg.

Hadrian sprang to his feet and ran, staying on the trail for only fifty feet before veering off into the treacherously rocky field along the slope. He knew the terrain better than his pursuers. He crawled into the deep shadow under a ledge, then listened as they searched, until a man shouted from above and they retreated. Daylight was coming, and these were creatures of the night.

Lafayette Avenue at dawn had an atmosphere of old Europe. The founders had had grandiose visions for their town once they had realized the colony was going to succeed. Hadrian had been in the meetings where municipal names had been chosen. Washington Boulevard. Edison Park. Hannibal Square, in a gesture to the name givers of the original Carthage. Among them, Lafayette Avenue was the one street that carried a sense of a civilized past. The cobblestones wet with a predawn shower, the stalwart stone buildings, the slow clip-clop of a milk-wagon horse, the scent of baking bread in the cool autumn breeze refreshed Hadrian as much as an hour's nap. He settled onto a bench near the library, watching the little shop across the street as he considered his encounter on the hill.

Punic prick, his attacker had muttered. It was not an epithet used by those of Carthage. Rather it had been born in the camps, where some former scholar had recalled the adjective used for those from ancient Carthage. Futilely he tried to piece together the bits of conversation he had heard from those operating the signal lantern. He had not heard enough to make sense of the words, but there had been something in their patterns, an uplifting in tone at the end of sentences. He realized now he had heard it as a youth when visiting the maritime provinces of what had been Canada. Yet discovering someone from such a distant, scoured place would be as likely as encountering a little green man in a spaceship.

He watched as a policeman progressed along the street, snuffing out the night lanterns, then stepped to the shop door and tried the latch.

"Closed!" came the voice of a harried woman in the kitchen as he stepped inside. "Thirty minutes!"

Hadrian pulled out a stool and sat at the counter.

The compact figure who appeared at the kitchen doorway wore a spattered apron.

"If you ever got all the flour out of your hair, Mette, I know we'd find a thirty-year-old beauty underneath."

The woman's peeved expression evaporated. "Hadrian!" she cried, stepping around the counter with arms outstretched. With a grin he accepted her hug.

"You look like a man who needs breakfast," she suggested.

"And yesterday's lunch and supper," he replied, suddenly famished.

She disappeared into the kitchen, calling out orders to her assistants, before returning with a steaming mug of chicory coffee and one of her famous maple sugar pastries. Mette Jorgensen had been one of fifteen vacationing Norwegian birdwatchers who had staggered out of the wilderness into the original Carthage settlement. The Norgers, as they had come to be called, had created a vibrant subculture in the colony, and provided the best of its shipwrights. "Scrambled eggs and bacon in ten minutes," she said, then sobered. "I'm so sorry about Jonah."

"I want to ask you about that night," Hadrian said between bites.

"Whatever I can do, you know that."

Hadrian always felt guilty over the gratitude Mette had shown him for so many years. He had intervened as a Council member when the tribunal selected by Buchanan was marking citizens for exile. Mette's husband had suffered wasting nerve damage from radiation that left him with a useless arm. Hadrian had insisted it was from an accident, had given a sworn statement to the tribunal. Though her husband had died only a year later, Mette's gratitude continued unabated.

"I've lain in bed awake, thinking about it," she told him. Her expression was suddenly grave.

"Jonah wasn't suicidal."

"Hadrian, he came in here every day for coffee and a roll, always with a smile and full of plans. Last week he stood at the window and gestured for me to see a butterfly that had alighted on his finger. The smallest joy was a great one for Jonah."

"Did you see anything at all that night?"

"It wasn't like I was standing watch. In the evening I might sit out front for a pipe. At bedtime I usually glance outside as I adjust the upstairs curtains."

"And?"

"When I was out on the bench there were two people in cloaks on the other side of the street. They walked past the library, as if they were studying it. I waved. They didn't wave back. Five minutes later they walked by from the other direction."

"Two men?"

"I don't know. They had cowls over their heads. It was getting chilly. After they passed the second time, they disappeared into an alley in the shadows between the lanterns. I had the impression they were waiting for me to leave. When I looked out from upstairs there was no sign of them."

"How long before the fire was that?"

Mette shrugged. "Half an hour."

"No one else?"

"The police patrol, an hour ahead of their usual schedule. Usually they stop for a smoke on the bench, but that night they kept moving."

"Had you seen Jonah earlier that day?"

She nodded. "More than usual. He came for coffee in the morning, then stopped to have tea late in the afternoon. Most days he holes up in his workshop until after dark, even sleeps there quite a bit. He had his tea, then left. Down the street. But he came back later. I saw the light from his workshop reflected onto his balcony."

That would have been after Hadrian had visited him. "Tell me something else, Mette. Do you recall ever seeing him with Micah Hastings, one of the young market hunters? It would have been maybe six months ago."

The baker shrugged, then paused to gaze out the window. "There was a boy, in green and brown clothes. He stopped Jonah one day as he left with his tea and they sat on the bench outside. They spoke for a long time. I had the impression Jonah was trying to talk him out of something, and failed. He looked upset. He drank all his tea there, watching where that boy had gone as if thinking of following him. I remember because he always takes his tea right back to his workshop. *Took*," Mette added in an anguished whisper before disappearing into the kitchen.

"You ask better questions than the police," she offered as she returned with a plate heaped with eggs, buttered bread, and bacon.

Hadrian shot her an inquiring glance as he chewed.

"There was a young woman, one of those with the spider-web faces," she said matter-of-factly. "She asked if I'd seen anyone running from the fire, that's all. Like she was going through the motions. She was very quiet, ordered a cup of tea and nursed it for a long time. Then suddenly she up and asks if you were the same Mr. Boone who used to organize poetry readings for the school classes."

Hadrian stopped chewing. He could not have heard correctly. "I'm sorry?"

"I swear, Hadrian. I had to ask her to repeat herself. She said did I ever hear Mr. Boone recite poetry. I just said you were the head of the school, then she got quiet again and left. Except she insisted on paying for her tea. Police never pay. Kenton didn't pay when he showed up a few hours later, and he had a whole meal."

"Asking about the fire?"

"Not at all. Asked if a Sergeant Waller had been here. I said there'd been no introductions but I'd been visited by an officer with mottled skin. He asked what she'd said, then asked about you, if I'd seen you, if I knew things about you."

"Things?"

Mette busied herself in wiping off the counter. "Where you were sleeping," she replied, a new awkwardness in her tone, "where you were getting meals, questions like that." The kind baker had always acted as if Hadrian's plummet through society had never happened. She paused. "Then I asked if I could send some bread to those two in prison. He laughed again and warned me not to let the governor hear of such talk."

"Were you there, Mette?"

"At the funeral? Of course I was there. I started the singing down below, after poor Nelly led the way."

"That," Hadrian said, "is what you don't want the governor to hear."

He felt like a soldier in hostile territory as he approached the decrepit mill, the first built by the colony but abandoned years earlier after construction of the terraced ponds that powered newer, bigger mills. A lookout in a tree called a warning to those inside. A youth stepped from behind another tree, aiming an arrow at Hadrian.

"I came to see Dax," Hadrian declared in a level voice. He glanced over his shoulder to make sure no one had followed.

"Hickory dickory dock, mice run up the clocks," the boy intoned. He had a disquieting, feral air about him.

As Hadrian studied the young guard, who kept his arrow aimed at his chest, he became aware of other shapes in the shadows. "Hey diddle, cat and a fiddle, the cow jumped over the moon," he offered.

The bowman cocked his head, confused, but did not lower his weapon until a sharp whistle came from overhead. Dax looked down from the top of the large waterwheel where he was moving his legs at a relaxed pace, keeping up with its movement so that he remained stationary. Two other boys emerged from the brush, holding bows at their sides, as Dax stepped into one of the catch chambers of the wheel, riding it down and jumping off as it approached the bank. He landed lightly in front of Hadrian.

"I want to know about the jackals," Hadrian declared.

Dax frowned.

Hadrian reached into the pouch on his shoulder, extracted a fresh loaf, still warm from Mette's ovens, and tossed it toward the gathering boys. Dropping all interest in playing the stern sentinels, they gleefully ran to a log bench to share it.

Dax looked at them with disapproval. "We ain't going back to any classroom. They treat orphans like pet dogs there."

"You forget I was thrown out of the school." Hadrian glanced uneasily at the coils of rope by the log bench, several with familiar knots at the ends. The children had been practicing tying nooses. "I'd be happy just to have you stop playing with death."

"The jackals don't force anyone to take the ride." The boy pulled a copper medallion out from under his shirt.

With a speed that obviously surprised the boy, Hadrian grabbed it, turning it over in his hand. It was the same shape as the other medallions, but it bore no markings. Which made Dax what? A would-be jackal? A probationary jackal?

"Better keep it covered," Hadrian advised as he stuffed the necklace back in the boy's shirt. It was illegal to own copper in Carthage, and any known bits of the metal were government property, for coins.

"Kenton will arrest you for that copper alone. He'd be happy to send you to the heavy salvage crews."

"Been assigned before," Dax said defiantly. "A month hauling iron rails over the mountains to the foundry."

As he followed the gangly youth into the mill, Hadrian gazed at the worn wooden mechanism, remembering how Jonah had labored to find the right proportions for the gears in this, the first of the colony's mills. The rest of the chamber was filled with the gang's particular artifacts. A television without its tube, puppets on strings hanging in the open space. A hair dryer into which a battered toy rocket had been stuffed as if it were a launcher. One wall was nearly covered with photos torn from yellowing magazines.

"Train rails?"

"That's what the crew chief called 'em. *Train rails*. All in a line, though you had to dig away the brush and weeds to see 'em. Heavy as hell. Nailed right into the earth."

Hadrian paced along the wall of photos. "Do you know why those rails were laid on the ground, why they were always so straight and the same distance apart?"

Dax shrugged. "You take the salvage where you find it." The phrase had become part of the vernacular, a way to dismiss any need to explain the original function of the mysterious objects found in ruins.

Hadrian gestured at the images of obsolete objects, pointing to the first one. "This is a toaster, for warming bread slices. We had one in our kitchen, and my mother would get mad because I tried to put cookies in it." He indicated another. "This is a record player. You put black discs on it, and you would hear music. This is a man playing golf," he said of the next. "It's a game. You hit a little white ball around mown fields, trying to sink it in a hole." He looked into the boy's uncomprehending eyes and gestured to one more. "A toy spaceship like I got for Christmas once."

Some hay trickled down from the loft overhead, and Hadrian looked up to see three pairs of eyes looking out of the shadows. One of the children leaned forward. It was Dora, Buchanan's younger daughter. "What's Christmas?" she asked.

Hadrian sighed. "We call it the Year-End Festival now."

He pulled a photo of a locomotive from the wall and pointed to the rails underneath. "What did you think those rails were for? There is no one waiting on the other side to take you for a ride on one of these. I used to travel on those trains when I was your age. They're not on the other side, Dax, they're in the past. Gone."

"That's what you say, to keep us from taking the ride." A chill ran down Hadrian's spine. "We've heard them tell us in their own words," Dax declared stubbornly.

"Tell you what?"

"About the dead land. The ghosts go into the dead land and come back. Then they tell us about it. They eat hamburgers and have bicycles that ride without pedaling."

"Toy trucks and baby dolls!" Dora exclaimed from above.

Hadrian lowered himself onto a bench by the wall. His voice cracked as he spoke. "People don't die and come back."

Dax grew very solemn. He suddenly seemed years older. "The first time I seen it I was so scared I ran into the forest. He was dead, dead for hours. Then he sat up and opened his eyes. Bloody hell, those eyes."

"His eyes?"

"The pupils were pale blue, like the sky all washed out after a storm. Almost like he had no eyes at all, 'cause he left the real ones on the other side to keep watch. We all ran, because we knew old books about monsters coming from the other side. Zombies, they call them.

But he just laughed when we ran. Later he found us and told us about the beautiful things he had seen, said the ones up on Suicide Ridge had been right, that he seen them playing on the other side."

Hadrian shuddered, as much from Dax's earnest tone as his words. The boy truly believed in what he was saying.

"We weren't sure either until he began bringing things back for us."

Hadrian stared at him, filled with new foreboding. "What things?"

Overhead, Dora disappeared, then came down a ladder stair clutching something wrapped in old sacking. When she reached Hadrian she uncovered the object. It was a large, exquisitely worked blond doll in a white dress that could have been fresh from a store shelf thirty years before. When Dora reached the wall she pointed. Following her small finger, Hadrian saw that it was not simply another photo, but a color plate torn from a Bible. It portrayed a blond angel with rays of brilliant light emanating behind it. The girl held the doll up to a crack in the boards, causing it, too, to be illuminated from the back by shafts of sunlight.

From behind Dora a boy approached, extending a shiny new toy truck exactly like one in another ad. As Hadrian stared in disbelief, Dax disappeared into the shadows at the back of the mill and returned carrying an object wrapped in deerskin. It was a brilliantly painted six-inch-high figure of a bearded wizard with a small dragon resting on his shoulder.

"It's salvage," Hadrian said, well aware of the pleading in his voice.

"No one's ever brought anything like these back from salvage," Dax countered. "Salvage is old. Salvage is rusty and dirty."

Hadrian sighed heavily. "How many of these ghosts are there?"

"Three that I've seen," Dax reported.

"People you knew before?"

"People from away I think. They had the smell."

Hadrian tensed. "Exiles?"

"From away."

Away. It could mean the outlying farmers, or exiles, or the hunters who stayed distant except to bring in hides. Perhaps even those impoverished survivors who eked out their sustenance on the far side of the sea. Hadrian then remembered the odor of those who had assaulted him in the clearing. Emily too had spoken of visitors who smelled of spice. "Please," Hadrian said. "Please don't try for more, don't take a ride looking for such things."

Dax began rewrapping his wizard. "The jackals ain't going away. The jackals have big work to do."

"And what's the price, Dax? What are they forcing you to do to become a full member?"

The boy just smirked.

Hadrian wearily rose, searching for something on the young faces, on the magazine pages, that might explain the mystery these children guarded. He should have been angry, yet all he could feel was a deep sorrow. His eyes settled on a solitary advertisement on the back of a door. REACH OUT AND TOUCH SOMEONE, it said. With a shaking hand he pulled the ad from the wall. DON'T FORGET THOSE YOU LEFT BEHIND, read another that touted a cellular phone.

"It was you at his grave!" *Why would you bury an old phone with Jonah?* he was about to blurt out. Then he saw the pain in the boy's eyes. "How did you know Jonah?" he asked instead.

"He would visit our fields sometimes," Dax explained, gesturing toward the fallow patch of ground outside. "Looking for insects, birds, even flowers. We would help him. He brought books to us, sometimes he read to us. About a great white fish. About Indians. Last month he brought that book about pirates and we sat around a fire as he read. 'Fifteen Men on a Dead Man's Chest.'" For the first time

Hadrian noticed a shelf of books by the aisle that led to the rear of the mill. He saw *Treasure Island. Kidnapped. Ivanhoe. Robinson Crusoe. Huckleberry Finn. Swiss Family Robinson.*

Hadrian felt a flush of shame. If he had not been drunk or in jail so often over the past few months, he would have known, probably would have joined Jonah on such trips. "What would you want him to talk about if he called?"

Dax shrugged. "Say I'm sorry about the saw pit."

"Saw pit?"

"He was going to meet us there in two days. To read the end of the pirate book. And explain the pictures."

"What else, Dax? You didn't bury a phone to apologize about missing a reading. What else would you ask about?"

The boy shifted uncomfortably. "About who's got the words now. About the running."

Hadrian gazed at him, struggling to understand. "Are you saying you were doing work for Jonah?"

Dax gazed at him in silence for a long moment then spun about to the crew of his strange little ship. "Man the boats!" he called out.

Like mice in the night Dax and the children disappeared into the shadows.

A THIN, BLACK-HAIRED doctor was bent over Jamie Reese writing on a medical chart as Hadrian arrived at the second-floor room. The comatose man still lay on the bed where Hadrian had last seen him.

"Any change?"

The doctor started, caught off guard, then straightened. "None for the better," he muttered, then passed Emily as he slipped out of the room.

"You can't just walk in like some kind of intruder, ignoring the woman at the front desk," Emily groused. She was out of breath from running up the stairs. "She wanted to send for the police."

"I thought the police were protecting him."

"The governor declined your request."

Hadrian lifted Reese's hands, the scarred, callused hands of a fisherman. "What else have you learned about him?" he asked.

"He shouts out sometimes, like he's having nightmares."

"Shouts what?"

"More like cries of terror. Nothing coherent. Once he sat up shaking with fear and said a flock of snakes with wings was chasing him."

He reached over to open the man's eyelids.

"Hadrian, no, let him be. He—" Emily's protest choked off with a gasp.

The patient's irises were pale blue, almost so light in color as to be invisible against the whites of the eyes. Hadrian was looking at a ghost.

As Hadrian stared in disbelief he became aware of movement behind him, followed by another cry of alarm. Sergeant Waller stood at his shoulder.

"Does it mean he is dead?" she asked in a frightened whisper.

"No, Jori," Emily replied. "He still has a strong pulse."

Hadrian stepped between Reese and the police officer. "I told you I would find you in a couple of days."

The sergeant seemed to struggle to turn her gaze from the figure on the bed to Hadrian. "I didn't know you were here."

Emily put a hand on his arm. "Jori's from a good family, Hadrian," she said, as if apologizing on her behalf.

Hadrian looked in confusion from one woman to the other. "Where the sergeant comes from," he said slowly, "is the governor and Kenton.

She's been assigned to report on me. She is a brilliant actress. Wanted me to believe she was just a middling clerk."

Before Waller could reply, Emily pulled on Hadrian's arm as if to distract him. "What do you expect? Buchanan would never give you a free hand without keeping watch."

Hadrian stared at the doctor, struggling to understand why she seemed to be defending the sergeant. "Perhaps you forget I used to award badges at our police graduations," he said, an edge of bitterness in his voice. "That's when they take a vow to maintain justice and protect the people."

His words seemed to disturb Waller. She slowly looked up. "My father was a policeman in the . . . he was a policeman before," she said in a tight voice. "All he had were daughters. I was the oldest."

Emily seemed unaware that her hand was still on Hadrian's arm, or how tightly it was squeezing him. "You need to go, Jori," she said. There was an odd entreaty in the doctor's voice.

Hadrian looked down at Reese. "You mean you came to see him?"

Sergeant Waller pursed her lips together and nodded. "When I used to investigate on my own, my cases never came together. Then the governor began to take a personal interest in my work, as if he were training me for something. My last big case was in the fishery. There was reason to suspect smuggling by the head of the fishery guild, Captain Fletcher. Fletcher the One Eye, the working man's representative on the Council. The governor gave me papers that said I was a health inspector. Then Fletcher offered me a bribe to leave him alone. I said no. I think that's what caused him to suspect me. He tried to scare me away. I finally found a crew member willing to talk about trips in the north, about fish being offloaded illegally outside Carthage and other cargoes being loaded. About strangers from outside Carthage meeting on fishing boats."

Hadrian considered her words a moment, wondering whether she was acting now. He regarded the figure in the bed. "You mean the hero from the sinking of the *Anna* was your source," he said.

"I think the governor had a plan to arrest one of the biggest criminals in Carthage, then put his own man in charge of the fishery. But then Jamie disappeared. Never showed up at a scheduled meet, never came back aboard his ship when it docked."

"Not," Hadrian suggested, "until he had had his accident."

"The governor was furious. He called me incompetent. He said I didn't have a clue about how life worked in Carthage."

Hadrian weighed her words. "You mean you were supposed to accept the bribe," he said after a moment. "It's the world Buchanan lives in. He was certain Fletcher would offer a bribe, certain you would accept it. Then he would confront Fletcher."

"But Fletcher was on the Council by then," Emily inserted. "Buchanan wouldn't want the scandal."

"There would be no scandal. Buchanan wouldn't want to arrest Fletcher, he would want to control him. The sergeant and Fletcher would become new pawns because Buchanan could throw them in prison at any time. Except," he added, "the sergeant upset his plans with her unexpected honesty."

"He put me on suicide patrols for a month," Waller said, "watching tall trees on the ridges, and threatened to fire me if I failed him again."

"You came here to resurrect your old case?" Hadrian asked.

Waller looked down at Reese. "What if what happened to him was because of me?"

Hadrian gazed at the sergeant as if seeing her for the first time. "Dangerous sentiments for someone working for the governor."

"Working for the governor," Waller replied, "is an honor few members of the corps ever get."

"That's better," Hadrian said as she cast him a smoldering glance. "Now tell me. The two men who follow me. Do they report to you or Kenton?"

She grimaced. "Officially they are assigned to me. But Kenton gets whatever information he wants from them, whenever he wants, without bothering to ask me."

"Let them keep up their playacting," he instructed her. "And resurrect your old case by all means. I don't need to see you again. Write up your report on me and give it to the governor in a couple of days. Mark it secret, so Kenton will be sure to read it. Show them at last you have grasped the essence of good police work. Say your subject exhibits dangerous antisocial behavior, that he harbors delusional suspicions of criminal conspiracies taking root in Carthage. If left unchecked, he threatens to be the seed for a whole new hooligan class. Don't forget his psychotic tendency to believe only he knows how to discover the truth."

Emily fixed him with a withering gaze. "I have medicine that will shut him up, Jori." She moved closer to Waller as if to protect her.

Hadrian smiled grimly. "I took my last medicine twenty-five years ago, Em, and never woke up."

CHAPTER *Four*

ADRIAN WATCHED FROM a window in an empty hospital room as Sergeant Waller conferred with her two men on the rain-slick street below, pointing to the second-floor corner room where she'd last seen him. Then he darted into the corridor, down to the kitchen, and out the back door. Minutes later he stood at a large building whose four chimneys churned out clouds of wood smoke. The textile works in its early years had been constructed to turn salvaged fabric into fibers for papermaking. It had eventually expanded and now took in raw wool to be processed into cloth for the colony's apparel makers.

"I'm looking for the owner," Hadrian said to the woman who sat at the front desk. She appraised him coolly as he self-consciously pushed back his ragged hair, then she disappeared behind a closed door. He waited several minutes before she reappeared, gesturing him inside with a frown.

He followed her past great steaming vats, through a room stinking of wet wool, into a huge chamber filled with carders and spinners, then up a staircase to a quiet room where half a dozen large looms were being worked. Hadrian stood uncertainly after the woman turned and abandoned him. Looking about, he saw a stocky, bearded man by a rear window, who gestured to him with his pipe.

Hadrian knew Hastings from years earlier, when the burly man had supervised the construction of the school, but had had little contact with him since he had gone into private enterprise. He stood silently as Hastings filled and lit his pipe, puffing out richly scented clouds.

"I'm not sure how this is supposed to go," the mill owner stated. "Am I supposed to cooperate with you because the governor finally took the yellow band off your arm or throw you out for being the feckless antisocial ass he has always told us you are?"

Hadrian breathed in the fragrant tobacco smoke. There was something almost church-like about the quiet industrious air of the loom chamber. "I think I'd rather you cooperate because I *am* the feckless antisocial ass he warned you of."

Hastings grinned, then spoke in a near whisper. "At bedtime when the youngsters climb under their comforters my wife and I tell them of the way it was when we were young. But we make them promise never to speak of it at school."

It was an extraordinary confession, a gesture of trust, a renewal of old friendship.

Hadrian offered a grateful nod. "Including your son Micah?"

"When he was younger, yes."

"Is that why he was so eager to go on a salvage scout?"

Hastings round face seemed to grow thinner. "I told him more than half never make it back. Hell, we don't even know if it's disease or radiation or wild beasts that take them. But at that age they feel immortal. He had become a market hunter. He knew the woods, thought he'd be the one to blaze new trails, like those early pioneers in the lessons. Every day his mother keeps hoping for a message from one of the other hunters. I keep reminding her that his was a long scout, beyond the usual hunting lands."

"Did he tell you where?"

"Southwest somewhere, he said. "Then Buchanan wanted him to follow the old canal there toward the old factory towns along what was the Hudson River. Christ knows I told him those towns got hit hard," Hastings muttered, "that they still could be hot with radiation. He could hike a month in a hot zone and never know until he dropped. I wanted him to learn this business since he was the eldest but he said I had other sons for that."

Hadrian hesitated over the distant way the father spoke of Micah. "Before he left, was he in some kind of trouble?"

"Trouble?"

Hadrian shrugged. "With the law. With the gangs. With paying debts. There are a lot of reasons someone might want to leave for a few weeks or months."

Hastings gazed at him as he worked the pipe stem in his mouth. "Of course not," he said, then hesitated. "Not that I know of," he amended with an edge of worry in his voice. "He was making new friends, frequenting taverns along the waterfront. He'd moved into rooms with a friend from the fishery. We hardly ever saw him."

The low murmurs of the looms filled the silence that followed. Hastings turned to face the window. "There's folks who say that Buchanan thought Jonah Beck was getting too powerful," he said abruptly.

Hadrian grew very still. This was dangerous ground. "I was just wondering about the fire."

"There was a fireman who saw Jonah hanging," Hastings said. "He got drunk, starting saying the fire didn't start elsewhere in the building, but right there in the workshop. And not where Jonah could have started it by kicking a lantern. People are saying we can't trust the newspaper anymore." He fixed Hadrian with a somber gaze. "If you're so interested in the fire, then why ask about a scout patrol five months ago?"

Hadrian didn't reply. The starting place wasn't the scouting mission, it was the link between Jonah, Buchanan, and the scout.

Hastings waved his pipe toward the courtyard below, where a thin, careworn woman was watching two small children play in the puddles. "Don't burden her with all these questions, Boone. She's troubled enough not hearing from Micah."

Then the woman looked up, telling the children to wave to their father, and suddenly Hadrian had the answer he had come for.

THE OLD MILL appeared empty as Hadrian approached. There were no boys with lethal bows nor any acrobat on the waterwheel. He stepped cautiously inside, studying the old works, running his hand along the tops of beams, testing for a loose floor board that might conceal a hiding place. He froze as overhead the ceiling creaked. Footsteps rose, then faded, moving toward the ladder at the far end of the building. He waited, listening. When no one appeared from the corridor of small chambers below the ladder, he stole into the shadows, remembering now how Dax had momentarily disappeared when retrieving his precious figurine.

The boy was in what had been the mill foreman's office, lying under a hanging lantern on a bench that extended the length of one wall, gazing intently at the little wizard in his hand. From just beyond the entry Hadrian studied the chamber, trying to discern where the boy kept his treasure hidden. There was a wooden bucket with a sack in it. A work station was built into the opposite wall, consisting of a narrow desk with a single small drawer. Above it were planks with rows of nails where once had been pinned orders and invoices. One plank was slightly ajar.

"That day up on the ridge," Hadrian said abruptly, standing in the doorway to block any attempted retreat, "Kenton said he'd seen you the night before, spoke about looking for something you had. What was it?"

Dax, holding the wizard to his chin as if for protection, watched him warily, not offering a reply.

"I am trying to help, Dax. What do you do for the jackals?"

"We do fine without help."

Hadrian realized how little he knew about the boy. He was not quite a child, nor yet an adult. Now he recalled the boy speaking of orphans. "What happened to your parents?"

"Crossed over, years ago," Dax answered in a flat voice. "My uncle says he don't have time for delinquents whenever he sees me."

"What did Kenton do the night before?"

"Cornered us in one of the stables. Took two of the older ones for a salvage crew, hauling rails over the mountains for a couple months."

"Older?"

"Eleven, maybe twelve. Says he will keep taking one of us every week."

"But surely their parents—"

"Orphans too. Live at the school, like I do when it gets too cold to sleep here. Kenton fixes things with the teachers when he wants us."

Hadrian could barely contain his emotion. The police corps seemed to be spreading its tentacles further every week. "He threatened you but doesn't take you. Which means he took the others as salvage slaves to put pressure on you. What do you have that he wants?" As he spoke Hadrian stepped away from the door, to give the boy a chance to escape. Dax did not move, except for the tiniest flicker of his eyes toward the desk.

Hadrian was an instant faster than the boy and already had his hand on the loosened board when Dax grabbed his arm to stop him. Hadrian pulled the board out, reached inside, and extracted a rolled-up piece of paper.

Dax seemed to coil, as if to leap at him. But Hadrian shoved him forcibly onto the bench and unrolled the paper on the desk.

It was a hand-drawn map. Its central feature was a long, arcing curve facing east below a meandering line with little waves above it. There were no other features except the image of a snarled, dead tree to the west of the curve and small circles placed equidistant along the arc, all with dates below them. Ten circles, seven of which had X's inscribed in them.

Hadrian looked to Dax for an explanation but the boy just stared woodenly at his wizard. He pointed to the waves. "The lake," he observed, then put his finger on the withered tree. "The haunted oak above the ravine." He pointed to the space above the arc, just below the lake. "The fishery plant would be here. Is this what you do for the jackals, keep secrets for them?"

Dax said nothing.

The first dates under the circles were from three years earlier. The realization began as a pinching in his throat, then fell upon him like an anvil. He dropped unsteadily onto the bench beside the boy.

"Suicides," he said slowly. "The children." He recognized several of the dates, had helped recover more than one body after responding to the screams of parents out searching for a tardy son or daughter. In recent years the ridge had turned into a favorite location for child suicides. A groan escaped his throat. "Why would you record the suicides? Why would Kenton care?"

He moved his finger along the dates and circles, then suddenly found his finger touching the next empty circle, with a date a month into the future. He grew very still. When he finally spoke his voice seemed frail. "How long have you had this map?"

"A year, maybe more."

Hadrian closed his eyes for a moment. It wasn't a record of suicides. It was a master plan for them. He indicated the empty circle. "A suicide has been ordered for there next month."

The boy did not argue. "People decide for themselves when to go."

"People? These are children."

Dax spoke in a whisper, not to Hadrian but to his little wizard. "Some were parents who crossed over looking for a child that went ahead." He glanced up. "There are no more suicides now than before."

It took a moment for Hadrian to digest the words. The boy had thought about them before, or else was well rehearsed. They were correct as far as he knew. The rate of suicide, though horrifically high, had not really changed in recent years. "So what does that make you, a travel agent for the dead?"

The boy looked up slowly, as if fearful of making eye contact. "Travel agent?"

"You show them how to use the rope, where to hang it, how to start their journey. The road to take."

"Not all of them. The young ones, mostly. They think about it, talk with the group. Once they decide, we just help them. Sometimes they like to hear about the ghosts. Sometimes Sarah comes and reads from Shakespeare. That Shakespeare knew all about ghosts. 'I am thy father's spirit,' that old ghost tells Mr. Hamlet."

It wasn't so much the boy's familiarity with suicide that Hadrian found so unsettling, it was the matter-of-fact way he spoke about it. "That day on the ridge by the sludge pit. It wasn't a game, it was a practice." There had been half a dozen children there, Hadrian recalled, including the governor's own daughters. Was one of them to be the next?

Dax did not reply.

Hadrian had a hard time speaking through the tightness in his throat. "Do you ever see them, Dax, afterward? Have you ever cut one down?"

"I leave them alone. It's a time for quiet. Sometimes you do. I've seen them hide, waiting for someone to pass. Usually it's police, but sometimes it's you. You're the cheater, the cheater of death, I heard them say once when you went by, who wants to keep them from their treasure."

Hadrian clenched his fists. "So this map is what Kenton wants?"

"He heard rumors. I don't think he knows for sure it exists. The police stop the suicides when they can. They take us to the station every few months, interrogate us about a suicide cult. Ain't no cult I tell them, just an after-school club."

Dax stood and eased the paper out of Hadrian's hand. Hadrian did not resist.

"If you're so sure about the treasures on the other side, Dax, why haven't you gone for them?" It was a brutal question, and Hadrian felt a flush of shame as it left his tongue.

The boy rolled up the grisly map without speaking. Only when he had returned it to its hiding place did he face Hadrian. "What about you, Mr. Boone, where do you think they go?" The boy asked in an earnest voice. "I've seen the ghosts, but Sarah showed us a Jesus book once that has angels. They're nothing like the ghosts I know. Angels stay in heaven. Is that what you think?"

Hadrian felt like he had been kicked. There had been a crippled priest who had found his way to the colony in the early years. He used to hold court in a tavern over a whiskey bottle and preach that after the apocalypse heaven was full, that St. Peter had put out a no vacancy sign. For his part, whenever Hadrian tried to imagine an afterlife all he ever saw was his family in the last moment of their lives, looking at him accusingly while the flesh burnt from their bones.

"What I think, Dax," he finally said, his voice strangely hoarse now, "is that your life doesn't belong entirely to you. We need you here, we need all the children here. There is still a good life to be built in the world that you know."

"Mr. Jonah didn't think so."

The words fired an unexpected anger in Hadrian. He stood and grabbed the boy by the shoulders. "Jonah did not kill himself!"

Dax ignored his words. Pulling himself free, he faced Hadrian. "Maybe it don't matter who put the rope around his neck. Maybe what matters is why the secrets in his head were worth taking to the other side."

Lucas Buchanan was whistling as he entered the dimly lit cellar of the governor's mansion. So intent was he on finding a bottle he failed to notice Hadrian shutting the door behind him until the deadbolt clicked into place.

"Micah Hastings took the name of his stepfather," Hadrian abruptly declared. "You were hiding that from me. But I saw his mother today. It was Jenny Standish. I forgot she remarried."

Buchanan cursed under his breath. "How the hell could you know I'd be down here?"

"Because I poured out the bottle of brandy you kept upstairs."

For a moment Hadrian thought Buchanan was going to strike him. "You fool! No one's making brandy anymore!"

"And you may have the last six bottles in the world right here." Hadrian stepped to the wine rack and removed one of the precious bottles, absently looking at the label. Buchanan froze as Hadrian extended it by the neck over the stone flags of the floor. "You weren't scared just because Jonah was killed. You were frightened because of the pattern no one else could see. Hastings was not Micah's father, his father was Henry Standish. Which makes the connection you wouldn't speak of. Standish and Jonah. You and me. The four original colonists, the founders."

"Micah wasn't alive at the time," Buchanan said with a frown.

"His father was lost on a salvage run in the third year, when Micah was an infant. Fell in a biological sink," Hadrian recalled, referring to the low swales where lethal gases had lingered. "It's why Micah wanted to go on that scout, isn't it?" Hadrian tossed the precious bottle from one hand to the other, then extended it at arm's length. "To finish something. What was he looking for?"

Buchanan stared at the bottle, his expression troubled.

"I remember that year," he continued·when Buchanan did not reply. "Jonah found some regional maps and newspapers from just before the end. He spent days making calculations, pushing pins into the maps to mark sites of likely blasts. Then he used weather reports to identify communities that may have been sheltered, the ones in deep valleys below ridges that were perpendicular to the blast sites. Half a dozen candidates within a hundred miles. Standish volunteered to lead those scouting parties. I remember when he came in after a month, more dead than alive, shaking from the horrors he had seen. But when he recovered he was excited about one of the valleys, the last one he'd visited, far to the southwest, near the old canal. He had studied it from the ridge above, made a crude map of what survived. A long, narrow valley with commercial and industrial structures still standing, then blocks of well-built houses at the far end, above a river.

"We sent six men and a dozen horses, more than we could afford to lose. Two months later one man came staggering back, half-blind, his lungs corroded beyond repair. They had reached the valley and in their excitement had galloped into a biological sink along the river bottom. He was the only survivor because his horse had gone lame and Standish and the others got out ahead of him."

Buchanan grew somber as he listened but continued to stare at the bottle.

"Jonah then burnt his maps and refused to help plan any more expeditions except those to the train lines in the mountains."

"You're talking ancient history. Pyramids and black plague. Who can remember such things?"

"What was Micah looking for on his secret scout?"

"What every scout looks for. Glory and gold."

"He knew about that valley."

"Ridiculous. He was a baby when his father died."

"His father liked to write notes about his travels. And there was that survivor."

"He was worthless. A raving lunatic when he returned. He never really recovered."

"You mean you exiled him."

"Of course. You were either an asset or a liability. Liabilities were pushed out. That's how we survived. How we still survive."

"Jonah knew, didn't he? He knew about Micah's mission."

"Not from me."

"Micah knew Jonah would remember. A good scout would try to find out as much as possible about his destination."

The governor did not argue. "Either an asset or a liability," he repeated with a pointed gaze.

Hadrian did not resist as Buchanan wrapped his fingers around the neck of the bottle and pulled it away. Suddenly he felt very weary.

He settled onto a high stool by the wine rack. "Why would you need such secrecy around your scouts?" he asked. "The government has been sending out salvage patrols for years."

Buchanan frowned, then sighed. "Salvage on the rail lines isn't affected. They just follow the old train routes in the mountains."

"You're saying something happened to the others? When was the last time one got through?"

His companion loosened the cap of the bottle and lifted it for a long swallow. "Nearly a year."

Hadrian stared in disbelief. "But your guns. You have new guns."

"No. What has expanded is the rehabilitation we do on the old guns we recovered through the years. Such as we have. Some have gone missing," Buchanan confessed.

"Guns have been stolen?"

"I don't know. Stolen. Mislaid. We had a couple dozen shotguns. No one can find them."

Hadrian weighed Buchanan's words. The police had never really needed guns before, but the shotguns would have been the heaviest weapons in their makeshift arsenal. "Were there other scouts killed?"

"One missing. Then that one who drowned out on the lake. Another was going south on horseback last year and woke up one morning to find his horse's throat cut. He walked back and took up farming." He glanced up at the half window that opened out onto the street.

"But salvage continues. The government still collects duties."

Buchanan stiffened. "It was all restructured last year. The master of the merchant's guild came in with a business plan. They would be granted exclusivity for salvage so long as they could guarantee an increase in customs duties."

"You gave them exclusivity? There was no announcement." Hadrian was incredulous.

"Privatization it used to be called. Much more efficient for everyone. No need for public hoopla. The Council agreed."

"So you agreed to stop sending salvage patrols and kept doing so anyway. And what about your suspicions about smugglers working out of the fishery?"

"The agreement with the guild was that they would use only designated overland routes. We have the right to verify, to audit books."

"Sergeant Waller wasn't sent into the fishery for an audit."

Buchanan's eyes flickered with anger. "There were unsubstantiated reports of ships unloading salvage. Sending Sergeant Waller was a mistake. She has no appreciation for the subtleties of affairs of state." Meaning, Hadrian knew, that he was furious with her for revealing to him her mission into the fishery. "She's too inexperienced to rely on. Her first surveillance report was rife with speculation and extraneous, worthless details. She said she saw a wagon of grain driven into the fishery at night. Ridiculous. She even reported seeing ten steamboats in the harbor one morning. I had to remind her only nine are left in the fleet. She'd forgotten one sank last year."

Hadrian stood and paced along the racks of wine bottles, digesting Buchanan's words. "So you let the government be intimidated out of the salvage business."

"Ridiculous. It was not our priority. A bargain was struck that reallocated resources for the good of the colony."

"A bargain with whom exactly?"

"I told you. Head of the merchant's guild. The Dutchman."

"Van Wyck," Hadrian said. "He was on the Council when I still served."

Buchanan seemed amused. "He pointed out that salvage was too dangerous for small parties, and government resources stretched too thin. Later we agreed the guild would take over administration of the inspections and duty collection. He guaranteed that revenues would rise ten percent a year for the next five years."

"Very generous of him."

"He demonstrated how his guarantees assured the ongoing construction of public works, allow us to plan projects for the next five years."

"So the government really doesn't know what is coming in from the outside."

"Nonsense. The guild files reports. We have the right to audit. Van Wyck is a great supporter of my initiatives, a positive influence on the Council."

"Sounds more like he sold his vote to you in exchange for a monopoly."

Buchanan gave an impatient sigh. "You know nothing anymore about the workings of the Council. He is an active member, regularly makes suggestions for improvements."

"Suggestions?"

"Streamlining the government oversight of the guilds, so they can be more autonomous. More self-policing in the fishery."

Hadrian weighed what he was hearing. Fletcher, the head of the fishery guild, had joined the Council as well. The fishery and merchant guilds were responsible for well over half the commerce of Carthage's economy. "You mean giving the guilds more ability to operate in secrecy."

"I thought you opposed keeping all the power in the governor's office," Buchanan shot back.

"Maybe you're not really controlling Van Wyck's vote. Maybe he and Fletcher are controlling yours. Your house looks more and more like a palace. You have the most exquisite collection of salvaged furniture in the colony."

"It's the governor's mansion," Buchanan said bluntly. "The guild wants to show its appreciation to the people, and the government is their representative."

"Meaning Van Wyck offers gifts suitable to your status. I saw a grandfather clock upstairs that would have been worth a fortune even in the old world."

"Van Wyck is a patriot. He has an instinct for what we need. An ally for progress. Just last week he sent in a suggestion to privatize the police launch."

"Sent in?"

"He's been ill. He stays on his horse farm in the far south now. He sends correspondence sealed with his signet ring."

"A medieval touch. For how long?"

Buchanan hesitated a moment, lowering his voice. "A few months. Perhaps six or seven."

Hadrian did not miss the nervous glance the governor cast toward the little window high on the cellar wall. "Who would have thought after all this time you would start being afraid of tree jackals."

The words shook Buchanan. He took a long swig of his precious brandy.

"On the street there're rumblings that a killer may be roaming the colony," Hadrian ventured.

The alcohol quickly restored the familiar Buchanan, releasing the anger simmering just below the surface. He had not intended to confide so much in Hadrian. "But you have not found a killer," he parried. "As usual you just complicate my problems. I have persuaded the Council that there will be need for a public execution when I present the killer. We will have to suspend construction of your precious bridge. Instead a gallows will be built."

Hadrian's mouth went dry. "We aren't even close to understanding the killings."

"Killing," Buchanan corrected. "At the appropriate time we will have a memorial service for the scout Hastings who like his father died a distant, lonely death while performing his patriotic duties." He paused. "I anticipate a double hanging."

Hadrian's mind raced. "No!" he protested. "They came only to honor Jonah."

"Two slags infiltrated the colony. I am beginning to think they were on the roof to celebrate the success of their assassination."

"You told the world Jonah was a suicide!"

Buchanan ignored him, taking another sip from his bottle.

"You may as well declare open warfare on the exiles."

Buchanan shrugged. Upstairs his new grandfather clock chimed the hour. "I have a working firearm for almost every officer in the corps now. I've been thinking about this the wrong way. Jonah's death isn't a crisis. It is a window of opportunity."

"Killing exiles brings you no closer to the truth, no closer to finding the real murderer."

"Look for tomorrow's paper. There will be an editorial bemoaning the gradual breakdown in public order, suggesting that the Council give me more power to deal with bad elements. On the front will be a headline about how I have discovered our beloved Jonah Beck did not die at his own hand after all. Our fellow citizens will read of the murder charges I am filing against two illegals who sought to undermine our government by killing a member of the Council. It's time people saw an execution. Puts things in perspective. Our citizens take too much for granted. They become lazy, losing the vision of our greatness. They need a common cause to unite them, to restore their backbone." The governor raised his bottle in salute. "In strength we endure."

"I remember sitting at campfires with you and Jonah in the early years. We were going to plant fields of flowers and never talk of war. We were all so scared of the guns from the early salvage that we threw them into the lake." He slowly raised his head to meet the governor's gaze. "Don't do this, Lucas, I beg you."

Buchanan gave a humorless laugh. "It's been decided. For the good of the colony those slags will have a fair trial. Then they will hang."

WHEN HADRIAN APPEARED at her table in the coffee shop near Government House the next morning, Sergeant Waller leapt up to flee. He grabbed her shoulder and forced her down, then sat beside her.

"Those two exiles took a great risk coming to town to mourn Jonah. They are as innocent as you and me."

She shrugged. "A few days in jail and then they will be escorted to the border."

Hadrian unfolded the paper he'd just ripped from a public board down the street and shoved it across the table. Waller paled as she read the headline.

"I keep wondering why Emily wanted to tell me you came from a good family. Perhaps she wanted me to forget that you've been lying to me, Sergeant, that you are charged with special missions for the governor, that he gave you at least two operatives to follow me. But then you did warn me that you would only pretend to help me."

"I can't just—"

Hadrian raised a hand to interrupt her. "So I am going to pretend to save you."

He watched as her school-girl expression faded, replaced by a scowl. "Good," he said. "First, I will pretend you know Lieutenant Kenton can't be trusted. Next, that the truth meant something to your father if not to you. And that you don't want to live in a town that hangs innocent people. Finally I am going to pretend you understand the only two people in the colony who can do something about that are sitting at this table."

Waller stared into her mug of brewed chicory. When she looked up she began slowly shaking her head. "I was in class one of those times you got removed by members of the Council. I could hear you arguing in the hallway, pleading, almost weeping. It was embarrassing. You were supposed to be this great wise founder and you turned out to be this bitter ne'er-do-well who couldn't control his emotions. We could see you in the window sometimes crying as you watched us play. We had chants we used when we played jump rope. *Boone, Boone, Boone,* we sang, *he's a loon, loon, loon.* You want me to stop pretending? Fine. Buchanan means to be rid of you once and for all. That's the evidence I am assembling, the file to convince the Council to expel you permanently. I meant to ask you about *hooligan.* Is that with a *u* or two *o*'s?"

"Listen to me. There isn't a soul who survived from the old world who isn't a lunatic in some way. It's the ones who don't show it you have to worry about."

"He's given me a whole sheaf of fresh paper to write up my report."

"Kenton, Buchanan, and I pulled a body out of the sludge pit. It was the scout Hastings, stabbed in the gut months ago. Jonah was tortured and hung that night. The killings are connected somehow."

"You're lying to save yourself."

"You're becoming part of the lie, Sergeant. Which means you are helping to protect murderers. Do yourself a favor. Try to find out where Kenton was the night of the fire. Everyone else was pitching in to save the library. He was off disposing of Hastings's body in the lake. He got promoted the next day."

"*A loon, loon, loon,*" the sergeant sang under her breath as she rose. She tossed several coins on the table and headed for the street.

HADRIAN HAD NOT set out for the long-closed saw pit, had only been in desperate need to clear his head in the chill morning air, but when he suddenly realized he had walked past the fields at the edge of town he paused, recognizing the overgrown path beside him. The little canyon had been one of the most active venues of the early colony, chosen for the way its low ledges eased the skidding of logs into place for sawing with the long two-man blades. He and Jonah had spend many hours in the pit dug between two of the ledges, pulling the long blades on the downstroke, steadying them on the upstroke as they cut planks for the first houses, then resting in shifts in the little log hut near the pit. They had been long and happy days, spent in the special camaraderie of those who share arduous labor.

He followed the path for several minutes, then with a melancholy pang he saw the faded chalk drawings on the long slate wall that lined one side of the canyon. The children who had watched had entertained themselves by sketching the workers and other scenes of colony life. Jonah was going to explain the pictures, Dax had said. Hadrian had thought it strange that Jonah had chosen the pit to meet the children. He had misunderstood. He had assumed Jonah was going to explain the plates in *Treasure Island*. But he knew now that Jonah was going to explain the chalk drawings, the forgotten pictographs of the early colony.

He walked along the wall, lost in a flood of memories. The drawings, sheltered by an overhanging ledge, had aged surprisingly well. The first crude rendering showed a team of horses pulling a log toward stick men waiting with a jagged object that must have been a saw. Next came a group of women who held up a net stuffed with fish. He remembered the happy day when the first net, fashioned with thread unraveled from sweaters, had harvested dozens of fish and provided the biggest meal they had had in months. More drawings showed the house built from the first planks with a proud family holding hands in front of it, then soapmaking at a kettle, a moose chasing a woman, a small structure with a bell tower that had been the first school, run by Hadrian.

In another, figures with uplifted heads watched the moonlit sky with a dozen arcing lights. Jonah had referred to those months as the summer of the satellites. Without their ground support, satellites had begun falling from the sky, the biggest a space station that had become the tomb for a dozen astronauts who had watched their world flicker out below. Children had exclaimed with glee and made wishes on the falling stars.

He found himself at the sawman's shack, opening the flimsy door on its rotting leather hinges. Jonah would have brought a surprise snack for the children, would probably have invited them into the little structure where so many original colonists had rested, making bold plans for the future. The rough table used for meals was still there, with a heavy chair beside it, as were all the initials and messages carved into the wood of the posts and beams. He ran his fingers over the names of old friends, many lost in the expulsions, then looked back at the chair. It was a sturdy wooden armchair, not part of the original furnishings. Near the chair the flotsam that littered the table had been cleared away to make room for an assortment of tools. Neither the chair nor the tools had any dust on them. They had been placed there recently. Had Jonah made an advance trip, preparing for the visit of the children? With new curiosity he stepped closer, studying the objects by the chair. Four short lengths of rope. An old soldering iron, the kind left to glow in coals before use. A rusty pair of pliers. A sewing needle, the heavy kind used for sail making. A carpenter's clamp.

Suddenly he recoiled in horror. Someone was meant to be tied to the chair. Jonah was expected but had died before his visit. Someone had been preparing to torture Jonah in the little isolated canyon.

He found himself outside, his heart hammering in his chest, suddenly fearful now that he was being watched. He picked up a piece of wood to use as a club and pressed himself against the outside wall for several minutes, studying the rocks and stumps along the trail, finally reassuring himself that no one waited in ambush. As he hurried away he paused only at the pit. Several of the covering logs had been rolled away. As if someone had planned to dispose of a body in the hole.

Suddenly he was running, stopping only when he reached an outcropping that gave a semblance of protection. His fear was irrational, he knew, but it was real. Cold-blooded killers had been there, preparing to torture and kill Jonah. But someone had beaten them to it. No, he told himself, as he collected his thoughts. There was only one team of killers. They had planned Jonah's killing, apparently planned it far in advance, using a secret from their young jackal recruit. His old friend had already been marked for death when Hadrian had last met him in the library. But the killers had changed their plans. For some reason they had to kill Jonah two days early. But why, what had happened? Hadrian fought the answer, tried futilely to escape its torment, tried to convince himself there was no proof, but it would not be denied. The killers had suddenly attacked Jonah in the library because Hadrian had uncovered the murdered scout.

UNDERCOVER POLICE WERE a recent innovation in the colony, and Hadrian almost felt sorry for the two who inexpertly tailed him as he left the coffee shop.

He led the two men on a stroll along the waterfront, weaving around horse-drawn wagons and bicycles, then pausing at a shop to watch their reflections in the glass. He paused again to study the little stall where a tinker bent over a brazier, heating an iron to solder a metal pot. Hadrian had watched the man trade with his customers before and spotted a familiar leather pouch between his feet. He breathed a silent apology and stepped into the shadow of an alleyway.

"Officer Jansen, isn't it?" Hadrian asked as the older officer passed by, nervously scanning the street. Jansen blushed, then awkwardly accepted one of the two cheap cheroots Hadrian extracted from his pocket. "If I'm not mistaken, I was there with the Council when you received your badge." Hadrian struck a match on the wall.

Jansen, a sturdy, unpretentious man, hesitantly accepted the light. "That was years ago," he said uneasily, a hint of Norwegian in his voice.

"Point taken," Hadrian admitted as he lit his own cheroot. "Times have changed. You're a leading officer of the law and I'm an ex-prisoner."

The Norger glanced at Hadrian's sleeve as if looking for an armband. "Habitual offender," he added.

"Ever hopeful of reform," Hadrian offered. "And still offended by other lawbreakers."

Jansen looked at him uncertainly.

"There's still a bounty on undeclared copper if I'm not mistaken."

"Fifteen percent."

"You could buy your wife a nice trinket. If you're quick." He nodded at the stall across the street. "That tinker will take payment in kind. He's been collecting little seashells with treasure inside that should have been declared long ago."

Jansen cast a confused glance at the tinker.

"Watch him carefully. When you approach he is going to drop something to cover the little pouch between his feet."

Jansen studied Hadrian suspiciously. "It will take me a while to finish this cheroot," Hadrian told him, then watched as the stalwart policeman puffed up his chest and stepped to the stall. The tinker pushed a rag from his knee onto the pouch. Jansen pushed him aside and grabbed the pouch, dumping its contents onto the tinker's counter. At least two dozen little electric motors tumbled out. Jansen picked up the tinker's hammer and tapped one. The motor popped apart at its pressed metal seam, revealing the bright copper wire densely wrapped around the apertures. Jansen's eyes went round. The motors would yield enough for at least a fifty-dollar coin, a month's wages for many in the colony. The tinker turned pale, then darted away through a line of wagons filled with firewood. Close in pursuit was Jansen's partner. The Norger hesitated, glancing at Hadrian, then grabbed the pouch and joined the race, no doubt worried about his claim to the bounty.

Hadrian slowly stepped into the street, laid his cheroot on the tinker's counter, helped himself to the hammer, and trotted away in the opposite direction.

THE ADDRESS LISTED for the comatose patient was in the warehouse district, a rundown loft in one of the old buildings thrown up in the early years. It was a brute of a structure with a first floor consisting of heavy logs lined with large metal sheets cut from shipping containers. At the top of the stairs that ran up the rear of the building, the door was fastened with a padlock. With a single stroke of the hammer he knocked away the flimsy lock and stepped inside.

The salvage stacked along the walls of the apartment was no real surprise. Half of the young males in the colony dreamt of making a black market fortune. Most of the stock cluttering the rooms was familiar. A box of razors. A carton of plastic toys. Piles of corroded pots and pans. Toothbrushes. More cartons contained small vases, glass paperweights, and other baubles being hoarded for the holiday markets. Several smaller boxes were lined up on a table by a cold pot of vermilion wax, waiting for a forged tax seal. Hadrian paused and looked out the kitchen window. The apartment was at the edge of the woods, half a mile from the clearing on the ridge where he'd been attacked. Someone familiar with those paths would have no trouble bringing the contraband to the apartment in the predawn hours.

He began a closer search of the apartment, pausing more than once as an item stirred some distant, blurred memory. A metal lunchbox with a large brown cartoon dog. Crayons still in their golden box. A little bronze rendering of the Statue of Liberty. There were tattered suitcases filled with girls' party dresses and three flattened soccer balls awaiting discovery of the pump needed to inflate them.

In the kitchen he opened every drawer and cabinet, then the icebox. Inside were two wooden containers with sliding lids that he lifted out and set on the table. The first was full of cinnamon, laced no doubt with the powder smugglers used to cut the spice. The second was filled with salvaged tins of spices, the containers rusty and corroded but their contents still fragrant. Marjoram. Nutmeg. Cloves. Cardamom. White pepper. All exotics, probably worth as much as all the other salvage in the apartment combined.

Hadrian pushed back furniture from the walls, revealing several lewd renderings scratched into the plaster but nothing more. The drawers of the chests in the two bedrooms yielded nothing but men's clothing. But lying on top of one of the chests was a hand-carved fish on a lanyard. On its belly was inscribed the word *Zeus*. Hanging from a bedpost in the second room was a carved deer on a leather strap. Hadrian stared at it, then reexamined the clothing in the nearby chest. On two shirts he found a faded name inked along the tails. Hastings. The dead scout and the fisherman in the hospital had lived together.

Suddenly the floorboards by the entry squeaked. He grabbed the hammer from his belt and flattened himself along the wall, inching toward the door to glimpse the intruder.

The figure there stood very still before lifting the broken lock from the floor, then stepped inside and closed the door.

"I couldn't have you think all of us are as incompetent as Jansen and his fool," came a tentative voice.

Hadrian lowered the hammer and revealed himself. "Jansen was doing his patriotic duty, Sergeant," he observed. "Probably his biggest arrest in months."

Jori Waller nodded slowly. She seemed to have aged since he had seen her last.

"Jamie Reese is dead," she said abruptly. "I went back to see if he'd regained consciousness. The nurses were wrapping him in a sheet. That doctor of his, Dr. Salens, was already reporting it as an industrial accident. But I told them I needed to examine his body, alone. I looked at his eyes. They weren't white anymore, they were pink. Blooming with broken capillaries. I looked in his mouth."

"His mouth?"

She reached into her pocket for a folded square of cloth. From its creases she lifted a tiny feather. "From the back of his tongue. I found another in his nostril. The hospital uses goose-feather pillows."

Neither said anything for a long time. Hadrian became aware of the hammer in his hand and dropped it onto a crate. Jamie Reese had been smothered with his own pillow. "You should report it," he said.

The sergeant looked at the floor as she spoke. "I asked the doctor for paper. I sat by the bed for an hour writing it up, linking it back to my smuggling case. I tracked Kenton down to submit it, but he only laughed at me and tore it up."

Now she noticed the disarray of the furniture in the bedroom behind him. She stepped past him and began to move the chest of drawers away from the wall, revealing a carton on the floor that had been concealed underneath. It was filled with cheap metal spoons.

Hadrian watched her, realizing he was more confused about Jori Waller than ever. "Exactly how close are you to the governor?" he asked abruptly.

His words took a moment to sink in. Her lips twisted in anger. "To hell with you!"

He stared at her.

"The governor was against me being admitted to the corps," she explained in a brittle voice. "When a few Council members supported me he decided I was political, a player in his world. He has that small team that does special assignments for him. His flying squad, he calls it. Bjorn and two or three others. I went to him with a theory about the smuggling, made a proposal to him. He decided to audition me."

"What theory?"

"Smuggling has always been for entrepreneurs. If someone was out of work and had the spine for it they could make one trip into the ruined lands and earn enough to support them for a year. After the governor reached his accord with the merchant guild, more goods were coming in through the licensed gates but more forged tax seals were appearing as well. Smuggling was happening on a much bigger scale."

"You mean it became more organized. The deal with the guild became a cover for more sophisticated smugglers."

"No one really cared. Revenues were up, enough to pay for the new colony projects."

"Meaning Buchanan had no cause to tamper with the status quo." He cocked his head at her. "Until you came in with evidence. And he knew you had the ear of at least one member of the Council. If he didn't listen, he knew Emily would."

"The corps had been told to stop worrying about the salvage trade. What was good for the guilds was good for the colony."

"What exactly was your evidence?"

"I got identified as the expert on official records because of my job for the court. The clerk in charge of the fishery records came to me. The ownership files of three of the boats were missing. But I found the retired clerk who originally recorded them, and she had a great memory. Companies controlled by the Dutchman own them, charter them out to Captain Fletcher. If you want to bring in very large objects, you need to use boats. I joined night patrols for a few weeks. On four different occasions boats came in before dawn, met those heavy ice wagons. I told the governor they unloaded no ice, took no fish to the plant. I suggested that Fletcher needed to know we were watching, just to discourage him. Maybe tell him we had grounds to perform an audit." She halted, frowned, and cast a sidelong glance at him. She had not intended to confide so much.

Hadrian considered her words. He knelt at the box of spoons, lifting several. "This is the best your mastermind can do?" he asked as he dropped them back inside. "A few pounds of spoons and spices? I could find a dozen caches of contraband better than this one."

The sergeant studied him a moment, trying to understand. "Not worth being killed over, you mean?" She gazed around the room. "What's left?"

He pointed to the bed, custom-made of heavy timber, with a bulky headboard. It covered much of the wall at that end of the room. They struggled to move it, sliding it inches at a time until they glimpsed a new structure behind the headboard. With one last shove they pushed the bed clear, revealing a small hatch built into the wall, its plank door locked with another padlock. Hadrian gazed at the sergeant, expecting her to stop and summon help.

But she kept staring at the padlock. "The streets were nearly empty during the fire, so someone whipping a cart horse toward the water-front got noticed. The harbormaster said Kenton just demanded one of his dinghies, then ordered him to go help with the fire." She did not wait for Hadrian to respond but simply retrieved the hammer and smashed the lock away.

The low, long space was lined with birch planks, keeping it dry and strangely luminescent. When he brought back the lantern from the kitchen the sergeant was already inside, kneeling by a crate of whiskey bottles.

"Worth their weight in copper," he observed.

There was only one other container in the hidden chamber, a wooden crate made as carefully as a cabinet, with handles on each side and a lid that slid back in carefully shaped grooves like a giant candle box.

Inside were more than two hundred little cylinders inserted into racks that had been drilled to accommodate two dozen apiece. Jori lifted one of the stubby cylinders by its brass base and cast him a quiz-zical glance.

"Shotgun shells," he explained as he lifted out the top rack and pulled a cylinder from the rack below it. "I haven't seen so much ammunition since . . . in all these years. One of these can kill a man. Two or three, if they're standing close together."

The shell in Jori's hand was old, its plastic casing familiar to Hadrian from long-ago hunting trips. But the one in his hand was new, the old brass cap fitted with a waxed, brown-speckled pasteboard casing. Someone wasn't just hoarding ammunition. They were illegally making it.

"The governor claims he has enough guns for almost all his police now," Hadrian observed. "But they must be random. Different calibers, different types, with the only ammunition probably what was found in the magazines."

"There's barely enough ammunition to load each gun," Waller admitted. Fear was entering her eyes. She seemed to understand. Their motley store of weapons offered little protection against shotguns with unlimited ammunition.

Hadrian sat back against the wall and pulled out one of the irreplaceable bottles of whiskey, broke its seal and took a swallow. He had been ready for a surprise in the apartment of the dead scout, but nothing like this. Buchanan had said the government's small inventory of shotguns had disappeared. His foreboding was like a cold, living thing worming up his spine.

"With these," he said, "someone could start a war."

CHAPTER *Five*

*T*HE JAILERS WERE so accustomed to seeing Hadrian marched
through the prison doors they barely looked up as Sergeant
Waller shoved him into the entry, arms manacled behind
him.

"I need a quiet cell," she declared as she lifted a long truncheon
from a rack by the door. "A special project for the governor. And I do
not want to be disturbed in my work."

The senior guard, a white-haired survivor, looked up from his
gin rummy. "Boone." He uttered Hadrian's name like a curse. "The
best for interrogation is the far corner on the second floor, but that's
reserved for our slag guests. Next door to it should do though I can't
guarantee the quiet. That bitch likes to sing. Sounds like an old cat in
heat." He gestured toward a ring of keys on a peg and waved them
through. The sergeant shoved Hadrian again, drawing a laugh from a
passing guard. They climbed the central stairway and went straight to
the corner cell.

The man and woman inside were not asleep rather only half-
conscious. The interrogation of the exiles had not been gentle. The

sergeant unlocked Hadrian's manacles, and he gently lifted the bald woman into a sitting position against the wall. Her face was bruised, her lips cracked and swollen.

"Nelly," Hadrian whispered, reaching inside his shirt. "I brought apples. And bread."

The woman's eyes fluttered open, and she made an effort at a grin as she recognized Hadrian. "You damned fool," she said. "You know that even on a good day I can't do much chewing." The radiation Nelly had fled from had destroyed not only her hair follicles but also nearly all her teeth.

She accepted the mug of water he pressed to her lips, drank thirstily, and passed out.

"She knows you?" Waller asked in a perplexed tone.

Hadrian looked up and saw the revulsion on the sergeant's face. "She arrived in Carthage during the first months. We'd been building the colony together for nearly three years before the vote was taken to expel them."

"Slags lived here?"

If there had been a mirror nearby Hadrian would have told the woman to look at herself. She seemed to have forgotten the disfigurement of her own skin. "A lot of them worked in the hospital. Nelly was there, served as a delivery-room nurse. She was probably in charge of the nursery when you were an infant. She would sing, like no one else could. People said what the wars took away from the rest of her they put back into her voice. There was never a baby who didn't stop crying when Nelly sang. She was our angel."

Waller's awkward laugh brought heat to Hadrian's face. "Or the closest to an angel we're allowed in this particular world. Now break up some of that bread so she can soften it in the water when she wakes." The sergeant quieted and did as she was told.

Hadrian turned to the other inmate, a compact, muscular man with a bony, scarred face. He wore a red wool cap that Hadrian knew covered curly black hair, kept long to cover the bare patches where follicles had died. Hadrian could not place his name but recalled that he'd been a small child when the worlds shifted, a boy whose parents had died in the first winter after their exile. Hadrian had seen him before in the camps, one of the few men strong enough to chop and carry timber from the forest. There was hatred in his eyes as he stared at the newcomers.

"My name is Hadrian."

"Hadrian Boone," the man growled. His face was sullen. "One of the founding dictators." Hadrian just stared at him expectantly.

"Shenker." The prisoner grudgingly offered his name.

"You upstaged the governor at the funeral, Shenker. A rotten idea."

"Once Nelly declared she was going to sing for Jonah no one was about to stop her."

"And you came along for the fun?"

Shenker slowly shook his head. "I came along to protect her."

Hadrian was familiar with his type among the new generation at the camps. Iron hard and filled with self-loathing but with one or two soft spots that defined their lives. "The governor means to hang you."

"So we have been led to believe," Shenker said. He turned his head to let Hadrian see the deep bruising on the left side of his face. Beside him on a cloth lay a bloody molar. Eyeing the sergeant, he pulled in his legs as if armoring himself against another attack.

"The police are going to claim you were in town the night Jonah died. They will produce witnesses who will say they saw you at the library. Help me find evidence that says otherwise."

Hadrian did not understand the perverse grin that rose on Shenker's face.

"But we were," the exile declared.

"Were what?"

"In town, by the library."

Hadrian stared in disbelief. "You were in Carthage that night?"

"It's a free world."

"No it's not. Not in Carthage, not for a member of the camps."

Shenker sneered. "Member of the camps? Don't bullshit us. Say it. *Sla—aagg.*" He drew the word out. "Though I hear some of you older Punic pricks prefer the term *tent niggers*. Is that what you call us behind our backs?"

"Did you kill Jonah?" Hadrian demanded.

"Nelly loved him like an older brother."

"Then help me help you, Shenker. Otherwise you both will hang."

"Buchanan's bluffing."

"The governor has already ordered the gallows built, at the edge of the cemetery," the sergeant put in. She was leaning against the door, studying the prisoners with an unsettled eye. "He wants it conspicuous, for the watchers on the ridge. He'll hang you just to spite them." She studied the two men a moment. "He met with all the senior officers yesterday," she explained hesitantly. "He told us he was done being patient, that now we have proof that the colony cannot survive without more order, without removing its enemies."

From behind them Nelly stirred. "Our crops failed this summer, Hadrian," she said softly. "Blight in the potatoes, rust in the wheat. Do you have any idea what that means this winter? Slow death for a quarter of us at least."

"There's food here," Hadrian said. "Our silos will soon be full." He paused, remembering his last conversation with Jonah, when the old man had spoken of taking wagons of wheat to the camps. He'd known about the crop failures.

"We don't need your damned help," Shenker snapped. "Or that of your dappled girlfriend."

Waller abruptly shifted from Nelly's side, took a single long stride, and kicked Shenker in the ribs. Despite his obvious pain, Shenker grinned. "Lose a couple clumps of hair, beautiful, and you're just another slag."

Hadrian stepped between the two. "How did you get to town?" he demanded. "Where did you hide? Two exiles don't stay in town for three days without help."

Shenker only kept grinning.

Waller bent over Nelly as the woman shifted, offering the water again. "Our interrogators have been asking that ever since they were arrested," the sergeant said. "The owner of that house whose roof they were on was detained today. The governor decided to brush off an old law. Anyone found to have aided exiles may be exiled himself."

"We're not your enemy, Shenker," Hadrian said.

"You've had us pinned under the heel of your boot so long you don't even notice us in the mud anymore," the exile spat.

"For an oppressor, Shenker," Nelly broke in, "Hadrian knows a lot about swimming in mud."

She offered a contrite smile as Hadrian turned to her. "I'm sorry, Hadrian," Nelly said. "My protector recently salvaged a collection of essays by Marx and Mao. It almost makes me believe in censorship." She offered a grateful nod as she dipped a piece of bread in the water and chewed it.

Hadrian cast a quick, pointed glance at the sergeant. Nelly hesitated, then nodded her acknowledgement. The exile camps had their own governing council, called the Tribunal, of which Nelly was the longest-serving member. Nelly understood he wished Jori Waller to remain unaware of the fact.

"Nelly, if you don't think Buchanan will hang you, you don't understand how much he has changed."

The exile woman lifted another morsel of bread and stared at it. "Did you know Jonah kept a tattered map of the moon pinned to one of the walls in his cabin? Once he told me the names of its largest craters and lunar seas. Early in his career, you know, he helped with some of the explorations there."

A ragged laugh escaped the sergeant's lips. "On the moon?" she asked sardonically.

"A hundred years ago men were walking on the moon, you stupid bitch," Shenker snapped.

Waller looked at Hadrian, her old schoolmaster, as if he should correct Shenker. When he did not she looked strangely hurt.

Nelly seemed not to notice the exchange. "There were craters that only had numbers," she continued. "Jonah said Carthage and the camps should form a joint commission, to christen them with real names."

Hadrian fought a sudden melancholy that was so intense it seemed to paralyze him. He felt a pressure on his hand. Nelly pulled him down to sit beside her. As she broke off some of the bread for him she began to hum a low song without words, using her throat as her instrument. It was a sound all her own, one she had developed after the breaking of the world. He closed his eyes, letting the song work its calming magic. After nearly a minute he pulled out his pocketknife and sliced the apple. Waller nervously lingered at the door, as if to encourage Hadrian to leave. She had taken a big risk in agreeing to Hadrian's request to secretly take him to the exile prisoners. Now she stared at Nelly with a confusion that bordered on fear. The police sergeant was glimpsing a world she had never seen before.

"Nelly, I just want to get you home," Hadrian said, handing her an apple slice.

"You haven't seen our home lately," she said wryly.

He stepped to the window, clenching the bars for a moment. "Why did he have to die?" he questioned the shadowed trees.

"Jonah knew more than anyone in all the world," came her cryptic answer.

"Why were you going to see him?" he asked.

"I don't know."

Hadrian gazed with despair into his hands. "So now you don't even trust me with the truth."

"It is the truth," Shenker growled. He inched closer to Nelly, as if he would have to protect her. "She got an urgent message from Jonah saying he had to see her. We don't know why."

"What were the exact words?"

Shenker's fists clenched. "I told you. Interrogation is over. Get out or I'll—" his protest was choked away by a hand on his knee. Nelly had leaned forward to calm her fiery companion. With her other hand she reached inside her tunic and offered up a tattered slip of paper.

Hadrian's mouth went dry as he read it. *Come at once*, it said in Jonah's familiar hand. *If the world is going to shift let us be the reason.*

He allowed himself be pulled by the sergeant out of the cell, Shenker lifting the note from his hand as he left. "If they come again," Hadrian instructed the exiles, "pretend to be unconscious." He extracted his arm from Waller. "Put me in the next cell," he said to her.

"You're not a prisoner." Conflicting emotions swirled over her face.

"I need sleep. And you need to assert your authority." He stopped halfway into the open door of the next cell.

"I'm sorry?" She did not see the group of men approaching behind her.

"Hit me."

"I'm not another—"

"You really are just another slag bitch at heart, aren't you?"

Hadrian had seen the fast, powerful reaction following Shenker's gibe. Her hand came up in a blur, swinging back and hammering his jaw.

He stared at her and smiled as the blood welled up in his mouth and dripped down his chin.

"Excellent, Sergeant!" boomed the deep voice behind her. "The long quick arm of the law at work!" said Lucas Buchanan.

Hadrian retreated into the cell as the governor stepped beside Waller, with Kenton, Bjorn, and a prison guard a step behind him.

"Did you know Sergeant Waller was once a young star in the lacrosse league, lieutenant?" the governor asked Kenton. The sport was one of the few old world traditions of the region he had allowed to continue. "Don't get inside her elbows. They're deadly." All the police laughed, except Waller. She stared with cool resentment at Hadrian.

"The others?" Buchanan asked.

"Nursing their injuries," the sergeant reported in a wooden voice. "Not much good for talking right now."

Buchanan frowned. "And citizen Boone's project? The evidence on the events at the library will need to be—" he searched for a word, "refocused."

"We are making progress," Waller replied.

Hadrian hung his head, scrubbing at the blood on his chin.

Kenton muttered something to one of the guards, who stepped to the next cell. Hadrian heard the heavy door creak open, watched the shadow of the guard as Buchanan stepped past him into the cell. Bjorn lit a cigarette, one of the Booksticks brand—tobacco rolled in an old book page—that had become so popular in the colony. The governor emerged a moment later, wearing an air of satisfaction.

"The owner of the house has changed his mind," Kenton reported. "The slags forced their way into his dwelling before the murder, leaving him gagged and bound to a chair. He agrees now that their clothes may have been singed upon their return the night of the fire."

Buchanan fixed Hadrian with a venomous stare, as if defying Hadrian to challenge him. "Write it up," he ordered Kenton.

Kenton wore a gloating smile as he pushed Hadrian into the empty cell and locked the door.

Retreating to the small window at the rear, Hadrian studied the landscape, revisiting in his mind the many escape scenarios imagined during other long nights in the prison, and how he might free the two exiles. There was no outside wire, not even guards patrolling the grounds, nothing but the window bars, recast from railroad iron. He twisted his hands around the bars, futilely pounding them with his fists.

He was no closer to understanding the murder of Jonah. His old friend was as much an enigma in death as he had been in life. Every path led only to more questions and greater danger, and the truth seemed less and less important to all the other players in the strange, treacherous game.

He dropped onto his cell cot, surrendering at first not to sleep but to a storm mingling memories and nightmarish images. Jonah and Nelly performing a violin duet before an audience of exiles fifteen years before. The boy Dax lying dead, his body strangely punctured with shotgun shells that had not been fired but driven into his body like stakes. Buchanan and Hadrian covered with sawdust as they labored years earlier, making up songs to the rhythm of the saw blade. The exile camps in the coming winter, bodies stacked like cords of firewood because the survivors were too weak to dig in the frozen ground.

Jonah had fought bitterly against the expulsion orders, but when Buchanan had prevailed by holding a public referendum, he'd felt it his duty to escort the first caravan of exiles leaving the colony. The fate of the burnt ones had been sealed when one of the silos of precious grain had been found empty, its precious contents secretly consumed by those unable to earn their sustenance. Buchanan had prophesized the colony's doom if a third of its population could not support themselves. By the time the final vote was taken, thefts of food and blankets were becoming rampant. Worst still, deformed, mutated babies had begun to be born.

Jonah and Hadrian had sat most of the night before the exodus making plans with Nelly for the new community of exiles. As the caravan left the city Jonah fiddled a jaunty tune and Hadrian carried a crippled boy on his shoulder, encouraging the other children to skip along with the music. After the first five miles the police escort had decided the two Council members were slowing the column and forced them to return to Carthage. Jonah and Hadrian had tried to travel every few weeks to the new camps, helping to build tent platforms, carrying in potbellied stoves on packhorses. After the first month a cemetery had been started. After the second, twenty graves had already been dug and they had been treated like unwelcome intruders. On their next visit they had awakened to find all their horses butchered for meat. They had focused then on helping two old friends secretly flee from Carthage into the mountains before they were swept up in the second wave of expulsions, and vowed to organize new relief for the camps by the next spring. But by then the censorship debates had overtaken Carthage.

JONAH HAD FOUND Hadrian in his office, hurriedly packing books before the newly formed book audit committee had arrived to examine his shelves.

"I won't last as head of the school, will I?" Hadrian had asked as his old friend dropped into a chair and picked up a volume of twentieth-century history. The committee would send it for recycling if they found it.

Jonah shrugged. "You still have many supporters," he said wearily.

"I'm not sure anymore if we are the spark of civilization. Maybe we are just the dying ember."

His friend did not seem to have the energy to protest. They had spent most of the day arguing with the rest of the Council over the censorship measures. The proponents had been passionate, and unwavering. A woman had testified that she had found her teenage daughter crying after reading an account of the last century, telling her mother no matter how hard she tried, how hard her own children tried, they would never have a world as good as that she read about. The testimony had become repetitive, reduced to a few poignant sound bites. You can't teach a little modern history without teaching all of it. Teaching about modern civilization was like describing a doomed airline flight— perfectly wonderful until the landing when the plane crashed and all on board died. Revealing modern history to your children was like telling them they had a genetic disease.

A woman had asked those present when was the last time they had volunteered something about the end of the old world to their children. It was true. Even without a law no one had such conversations. The ending was indeed like a disease no one wanted to spread.

Jonah had hidden the book inside his shirt before replying. "We have to move forward, Hadrian. Maybe it isn't so important. Just imagine we landed from a different planet and our young don't even understand astronomy. It doesn't make them less precious, or our survival less important."

"You should have been governor all these years, Jonah," Hadrian said.

"No. It was better for the colony that I work on my projects. You were the one." Even as he spoke the words the scientist grimaced, as if wishing he could take them back. They both knew the reason Hadrian wasn't governor was his paralyzing bouts of depression. There had been long spans during the early years when his grip on reality had been frail indeed. More than once Jonah had discovered him in conversation with his dead children. "We'll find a way, Hadrian," Jonah said, "a way that lets us show our faces again."

He hadn't thought much of it then, but those words had eventually echoed in Hadrian's mind and stayed with him all the years since. Jonah hadn't been talking about the censorship, he had been talking about the exiles, about his festering guilt, about how he and Hadrian couldn't pretend to be saving civilization if they couldn't save the exiles first.

IT WAS TWO or three hours after midnight when a key rattled in the lock and the door swung open. Sergeant Waller threw him a policeman's tunic and a wool cap as he groggily sat up. "Put them on," she ordered. "And not a word, damn you, or I will leave you here to rot."

Outside it was a raw, windy night. One of the cold northern storms, early for the season, was moving in across the inland sea, the air filling with wind-whipped leaves and occasional snowflakes. Waller led him to a rack of bicycles reserved for government business. Hadrian selected one and followed her, the tires hissing on wet cobblestones, leaves churning up into his face. The only sign of human activity was a dimly lit bakery where loaves were filling the ovens.

After a mile the sergeant halted. She dismounted and let her bike drop to the ground. They had arrived at the old warehouse at the edge of the woods. As Hadrian followed her up the same stairs he had mounted the day before, she paused as if to collect herself, then pushed the door open.

"It seemed too important to be left alone," she declared in a taut voice. "The home of two men who have died."

"Who have been murdered," Hadrian corrected.

"I came back," she said slowly. "I thought there must be something we missed."

Hadrian saw the legs first, extending from the bottom of the makeshift sofa. "Mother of God!" he gasped as he saw the blood-soaked chest, the face rigid with a questioning expression. It was the place of three dead men.

"Jansen was always pestering me for more interesting assignments. I brought him here, swore him to secrecy, said to keep watch until I returned, and to detain anyone who arrived. He was excited, said it felt like real police work for a change."

Hadrian recognized the corpse now as the officer he had tricked the day before. He bent over the body. It had two gaping wounds in his chest, centered over the heart. "You need to get Emily," he said. "Quietly. Now."

"First you and I move that bed again," the sergeant said.

"The chamber will be empty," Hadrian said, pointing to the low table beside the sofa. The whiskey bottle he'd opened earlier was there, now half-empty.

When they pushed the bed away even the padlock, a precious commodity, was gone. The only thing remaining inside the low chamber was the cap of the whiskey bottle. Waller, looking as though she were about to weep, turned and silently left.

Hadrian wandered through the apartment again. The only changes since his first visit were subtle. The carved deer that had belonged to the dead scout was gone, as were the boxes of spices. Traces of powder were on the kitchen table, beside a knife. The remains of three cigarettes were in an ashtray, the cheap, farm-made variety favored by laborers. He sat across from the murdered policeman, holding the whiskey bottle in his hand and gazing apologetically at him. The unspoken question on Jansen's face seemed directed at Hadrian.

He remembered Jansen now. There had been a terrified teenage boy with the Norwegian birdwatchers who had descended out of the mountains. This was not the life, or the death, the blond boy had expected when he had packed his binoculars in Oslo all those years ago.

Hadrian lifted the bottle to his mouth, but stopped, gazing at the amber liquor, then lowered it. "I'm sorry about yesterday," Hadrian whispered to the dead man. "Nothing personal." He rose, drained the bottle into the sink, then unbuttoned his borrowed tunic. As he bent over Jansen he paused, noticing now the white patches on the dead man's fingertips. He leaned closer. Powder, like that on the kitchen table. Looking into the questioning face one last time, he draped the tunic over the policeman's head, then opened the window. A stench of death was rising in the room.

A cool anger had settled over Emily's face by the time she reached the apartment with Sergeant Waller. She did not take well to an unexplained summons, doubly so if, as Hadrian expected, she was on one of her rare off-duty nights. She seemed about to erupt with anger at him.

"My God, Hadrian!" She began, then dropped to her knees by the body. "What have you done?"

"Hadrian," Waller interjected, "was in a cell when this happened. Officer Jansen was here on assignment."

Emily cast a worried glance at the sergeant, then pulled off the covering tunic.

"I don't believe," Hadrian said to her back, "that Carthage has ever before lost an officer in the line of duty."

Emily bent low over Jansen's eyes, studied his hands, then opened his shirt. She muttered a low curse as she saw the wounds. "What exactly were those duties?"

Jori Waller stared at the dead man's face. "Confidential."

"This is the apartment where Reese lived," Hadrian stated.

Emily looked up with a worried glance, then lifted the hand with the traces of powder. "He'll have to be brought to the hospital. The governor will have to be told first. There will need to be some sort of announcement." She rubbed a little of the powder on her own finger and touched it to her tongue, wincing as if it were bitter.

"He was stabbed by smugglers," Sergeant Waller hastened to say. "Who no doubt are deep in hiding by now."

"I don't think you understand, Sergeant," Hadrian corrected her. "Those aren't stab wounds. Officer Jansen was shot."

Waller went very still. "Ridiculous. People don't have guns."

Emily extracted a pair of long forceps from her leather medical bag and probed the topmost wound, pushing into the red, still-oozing tissue. A moment later she pulled out a small, bloody bullet, extending it toward them. The sergeant leapt to the open window and vomited over the sill.

PEOPLE DON'T HAVE *guns*. The words echoed in his mind as he watched the thin silver fingers reach out over the water, the first hint of dawn. There had been a strange anguish in the sergeant's voice, but when she had turned back from the window, looking at Hadrian and Emily, condemnation was in her eyes. Not only guns and bullets had crossed over from their old world, now also there was murder.

The words Hadrian had spoken to Jonah days earlier came back, like bile on his tongue. Nothing he had done in all the years of the colony mattered. The time between ends of the world just kept getting shorter.

He was not sure why he'd come to the clearing where he had been attacked, had known only he needed to leave the apartment before more police arrived. For long painful moments he considered ways to provoke Buchanan into exiling him immediately so he could leave the colony and its woes behind. But he could not turn his back on Nelly. He had taken slim comfort in the fact that the two had been locked in their cell at the time of the murder. But then just as she was leaving the apartment Emily had turned to reassure the sergeant.

"There are patrols out already, Jori. Word came to the hospital to watch for them, in case they sought medical attention. They won't get far."

"I'm sorry?" Waller had replied.

"The exiles you were holding. Their cell was found empty. Lieutenant Kenton has ordered all police on duty to be armed, and all paths leading toward the camps to be blocked."

Hadrian had stared at her in confusion. He had been in the adjacent cell and had heard no forcing of the door. Had they escaped while he slept? "They didn't kill Jansen, Emily," he had insisted.

She was silent a long time. "I went to see them yesterday," she finally replied. Hadrian reminded himself that once Nelly and Emily had been good friends. "She's changed. She has a new fierceness, a deep anger. Her husband died of malnutrition as much as anything else. The exiles have been backed into a corner and have nowhere to go," the doctor warned. "I'm sorry, Hadrian. But don't be misled by who they were twenty years ago. She is capable of anything now. The time for the camps is running out and she knows it."

Nelly had indeed changed. But perhaps, Hadrian told himself as he watched the dawn's rays touch the water, it was only the ones who hadn't changed who couldn't be trusted. *What is the truth you wish to find?* Jonah had asked him more than once when he had found Hadrian in one of his despairing moods. Now the better question was, why did he want the truth? For Buchanan? For Nelly? For the colony that had turned its back on him?

He settled onto a log worn smooth from use as a seat and watched the world come to life as the sun edged its way over the rim of the planet. A huge raft of geese rose from the cove below to continue its migration. A solitary trawler left the fishery and steamed toward deep water. In the distance a chorus of cows lowed as they waited to be milked.

Sitting there, Hadrian considered again how the smugglers had signaled from the clearing in front of him, and glanced back at the path that ran from the hill to the apartment. A signal from the ridge could be seen by a boat far out on the water, far enough to be invisible to those in town. A lantern might call in a waiting ship to unload in the cove below, out of sight of town, then the cargo could be carried over the ridge down the path. But why go to the trouble? Waller had confirmed that the smugglers were not shy about taking their goods to the fishery docks. It was as if there was another layer of smuggling within the smuggling ring, a crime within a crime.

He closed his eyes as fatigue overtook him. When he stirred a few minutes later, a small figure in a red shirt sat cross-legged in the grass ten feet away, at the very edge of the cliff, facing the water. At first he could not understand why the boy would seek him out, then realized he wasn't there because of Hadrian. The cliff provided a unique unobstructed view of town and sea, a sweeping perspective of many miles.

"I didn't mean to take your seat, Dax," he said.

The boy shrugged without turning. Hadrian realized the boy must have seen him already and had chosen to stay. He rose and sat beside him on the grass.

"The old professor and I," Dax said after a moment, "we would come up here. He told me the names of birds and trees and stars, said you could never unlock the mystery of anything unless you knew its name. He told me the names of some of the mountains on the moon. Sometimes when it was full we would howl at it like wolves. Once I asked him why and he said because we were alive and needed the world to know it." He pointed to another, smaller group of white birds beginning to move in the water for takeoff. "Snow geese, getting fat for their migration. When they finally move they will fly thousands of miles, Professor Beck said. He said they see things that no man in Carthage ever will," Dax added in an awed whisper.

After a moment Hadrian gestured over the water. "They used to be called the Great Lakes. There were five of them. This was one of the smaller ones."

The boy cast him an uncertain look. "I don't see how," he said in an earnest tone. "If that were true there wouldn't be any room left for the land."

Neither spoke for several minutes.

"Men come here at night sometimes, Dax. Just before dawn. With a signal lantern. Did Jonah know about them?"

The boy slowly nodded. "He knew most everything."

"You told him?"

"He saw them in his telescope."

Dax pointed to an osprey diving for a fish. They watched it carry the breakfast back to its nest.

Jonah knew about the smugglers. Did it mean he knew about the arsenal secretly being assembled in Carthage? Hadrian reminded himself that Jonah had started referring to the exiles as rebels. "There was a killing in town, Dax," he finally said. "A policeman. They will be furious. Stay away from Kenton."

"Kenton don't know as much as he thinks," the boy shot back, then grew more contemplative. "A policeman?"

"At a smugglers' roost."

"There'll be a price to pay for that," he rejoined. Not for the first time Dax sounded wise beyond his years.

"What is it, Dax, what is the name of that thing that hangs over us?"

When his companion hesitated, Hadrian saw the worry on his face. "I think it's an old world name," the boy said heavily.

His words tore at Hadrian's heart.

"Then tell me this, what was it you were doing for Jonah?"

"Some days his legs were bad."

Hadrian looked over the water, watching a small, fast flight of terns. "You mean you were his runner. Carrying messages in town, like you do for the jackals." The boy, he realized, was the perfect secret messenger. He certainly knew every alley and shortcut in town, as well as many hiding places, and townspeople were accustomed to seeing the orphan boy turning up unexpectedly, alighting nowhere for long.

"With him it was different. He wanted to pay me but I said there was no need. Learning from him was different than learning in school."

"Running to where?"

"Wherever. The hospital. People with books. The tin smith and glass maker, that one made him things by blowing in a tube," he added, as if to impress Hadrian. "Sometimes he would have me meet him with the reply at the Norger bakery, because he knew how much I like the maple sugar pastries."

Hadrian recalled quizzing the boy about the telephone in the grave, what he would ask if Jonah called on the phone. *About who's got the words now*, he had said. As if Dax sensed something vital, something urgent in the messages. As if he sensed something undone.

"Once he had me leave a message at a birch tree a couple miles up the coast."

Hadrian considered the words carefully. "You mean a tree beside a steep trail into the mountains?"

The boy nodded. "A week later he sent me there again. There was a flour sack, all sewn up, for me to take back. But not as heavy as flour."

That, Hadrian told himself, had been a reckless thing for Jonah to do, something he never would have done lightly. It had been many years since they helped their friends Morgan and Helen escape the second expulsion and secretly taken supplies to the couple as they built their remote, hidden home. Morgan knew the forest, and those who traversed it, better than any man Hadrian knew.

"On a day like this, without wind, it's like they're running in wet sand," Dax said abruptly. "Can't hide. Anyone could see," he added pointedly, as if to say he was betraying no confidence.

"I'm sorry?" Hadrian followed the boy's gaze toward the water, not understanding.

"The fishing shoals are there," Dax said, gesturing to the north.

Hadrian scanned the horizon in confusion, then froze. Although the boat was nearly out of sight, with no wind the smoke of its steam engine etched a long track in the dawn sky. The vessel wasn't heading to the fishing grounds, it was going west. Following a prohibited course toward the exile camps.

CHAPTER *Six*

HADRIAN ARRIVED OUT of breath on the balcony outside of Jonah's library workshop, panting from the run down the hill. He quickly swung the telescope toward the shoreline. The boat now was a speck on the horizon but its trail of smoke still plainly visible. He straightened, studying the harbor, watching as the morning breeze filled the sails of two of the old sailing skipjacks and pushed them northward. He bent back to the scope, lining it up with each of Jonah's railing marks in turn. In the clearing above, Dax's red shirt was visible as the boy stood staring out over the rafts of waterfowl.

Hadrian swung the lens back to the middle mark, bringing into view two men on the roof of the main fishery building with smaller telescopes in their hands. They could have been watching the skipjacks, could have been watching for signs of fish. As he watched they swung their lenses toward the smaller wharf closer to the center of town. Jonah's third mark took him back to the ragged spar at the border of the exile lands. The three cloths still hung like flags from the tree. Yellow, red, yellow. He straightened, puzzled, trying to recall the colors he had seen before. Red, blue, red. They'd changed.

He watched the plume of smoke until it finally dissipated, then focused on the fishery again. The two men were climbing down through a roof hatch. They hadn't been watching the sailboats or fish. They had been waiting for the steamer, and its smoke, to disappear. He studied the waterfront again. They had been watching the steamer but had also been keeping an eye on the boatshed where the police launch was kept. As he watched them disappear into the building, he recalled Buchanan's criticism of Jori Waller for overcounting the steamboats in the harbor. The governor's words had been gnawing at him. Then, as he looked out over the water, he recalled other, similar words appearing in Jonah's journal from the week before. Striving to capture the splendor of the day Jonah had described ten steamboats in the harbor. But Hadrian knew, and Jonah knew, that one had sunk. Only nine existed. Five were in the harbor now but that meant nothing since they often stayed out overnight, especially this late in the season when they were trying to fill their holds before the ice set in.

He stared absently at Jonah's marks on the railing. How the old scientist had delighted in riddles! His fingers wrapped around the cool stone in his pocket and he pulled it out, gazing at the intricate patterns in the agate. He would never understand the killings until he understood the mysterious patterns of Jonah's life. He looked back at the signal flags on the exiles' tree. There had been one signal when Jonah was killed. There had been a new signal now, when someone had stolen Nelly and Shenker out of prison.

As the sun's early rays reached the balcony, he basked for a moment in their warmth to the sounds of the town coming to life. And a sudden smell of onions. He spun about to see a tall blond man leaning against the doorframe, a half-eaten onion in his hand. He nodded at Hadrian as he took another bite. It was Bjorn, the stone-faced bodyguard.

The Norger policeman spoke while still chewing. "He says you are to come with me. Now." When he straightened he filled the entire doorway. With a helmet on his head and a battle ax in his hand he would have made a perfect Viking.

They drove in a covered buggy that waited behind the library, the big Norger cracking a whip over the heads of the team as they sped out of town onto the southern road. His escort ignored Hadrian's questions, speaking only to the horses, expertly weaving the team around farm wagons, the wheels clattering loudly as they raced over a covered bridge. They were nearly five miles from town when he pulled the team to a stop beside another, empty buggy, tethered at the base of a steep wooded hill.

Before he stepped onto the path Bjorn turned to face Hadrian. "Was it over quickly? Did he suffer?" Even after all the years, there was a hint of an accent in his voice.

For a moment Hadrian gazed in confusion. "Jansen? No. It was probably over before he realized what had happened. I'm sorry. Was he—?"

"My cousin," Bjorn replied without emotion.

When they reached the top, Hadrian saw Jori Waller first, seated on a rock, her face drained of color. She offered no greeting, only a look of apology. Lucas Buchanan stood twenty feet away beside a large log. A terrified boy with a bow and quiver of arrows sat against a nearby tree.

"He and his older brother were hunting when they found this," Buchanan explained in a tight voice. "The brother galloped to town, straight to my office. Sergeant Waller was there speaking to me about Officer Jansen's unfortunate demise."

Hadrian saw now the skeletal legs draped across the log behind Buchanan, a femur exposed through rotting trousers. He forced himself to step forward and examine the corpse. Part of the skull gleamed white through the rotting flesh of the man's face. Clumps of brown hair flecked with grey had fallen from the scalp. His eyes were gone and mildew clung to his clothes. A vine curled around one leg.

"His hands were tied around the log," Buchanan continued. The corpse's arms were stretched along either side, disappearing underneath. "As if he were left here to die."

"As if he were tortured," Hadrian corrected. "Who is he?"

"God knows. A hunter. A farmer with a feud with a neighbor."

A dead man without a face. A scout stabbed and left to drown in sewage. His closest friend tortured and hanged. Hadrian's fear was slowly replaced with a cold anger. "That day we found Hastings, who did you and Kenton speak with about it?"

Buchanan looked up from the grisly scene. "No one, you fool," he muttered.

"Someone knew about it. It was why Jonah died that night."

The governor glanced pointedly at Waller and Bjorn, his eyes filling with warning. "It was a state secret," he snapped, then gestured Bjorn toward the body. "Release the hands."

The Norger opened a pocketknife and reached under the log, then backed away as the arm stretched out. The fingers had been chewed on by small animals, but one finger was entirely gone, neatly severed above the knuckle.

Hadrian studied the hair and the structure of what was left of the face, then knelt to examine the remaining clothing. It was all fine wool and linen, with a trace of embroidery on the pocket of the shirt. He looked up at the governor. "Like you said, he was having health problems."

"What are you talking about?"

"It wasn't any finger that was severed. It was the ring finger, because it bore a signet ring, the seal of the guild. What did you call him? Your most important political ally? The most powerful businessman in the colony? I'd say the Dutchman has been exercising his power from the grave for the past six months."

What little color was left in the governor's face drained away. "You can't know it's Van Wyck."

"Look at the shape of the face, the hair, the fine clothes. What's left of his expensive shoes." Hadrian bent and reached into the pocket of the dead man's shirt, pulling out and unfolding a slip of paper. He read it, then extended it to Buchanan. "A bill of sale for a new horse, made out to Van Wyck. This is the road he would have taken to his farm in the south."

A twig broke behind him. Sergeant Waller was approaching. She was forcing herself to look at the evidence.

"Who would dare torture him?" The governor's voice had gone hoarse. He had been invoking the Dutchman as a political ally on the Council, using his vote, reading his statements into the record, for months. "There's no sign of a death blow. It must have been an accident. He was being pressed for something and he had a heart attack."

Hadrian leaned over the body, studying the ruined torso, noting now the long striations in the remaining flesh. "They cut deep into his belly before he died."

"To what end?" Buchanan glanced with worry into the shadows of the forest.

Hadrian paced around the log, studying the surrounding ground, seeing now that Bjorn was staring at a large hole fifteen feet up an old maple. The shape was familiar, as were the scratch marks below the hole. "It would have been in early spring," he said. "The marten that used that hole had young. The slices were to ensure there was an irresistible scent of blood."

"I don't understand," Waller said behind him.

"They have four, even six babies. After the first few weeks the pups are ravenous for fresh meat." He turned to face her. "Van Wyck was tied here to be finished by a frenzy of tree jackals feeding on his belly."

Something like a sob escaped the sergeant's throat. Buchanan retreated behind Bjorn.

Hadrian touched the sergeant's shoulder and pushed her away from the grisly sight. "Why not just kill him?" she asked.

"He was being punished, I wager," Hadrian said. "Made an example of. There were probably others here, brought to watch."

"But who?" Buchanan asked. "Who would engage in such butchery?"

Hadrian fixed him with a cold gaze. "The ones who have been working with you to control the Council."

THE ENDING OF the world had been hard on the devout. For most their faith had not only been broken, it had been shattered, not simply forgotten but rather the butt of bitter jokes and jibes. In the early years survivors had turned their backs on their religious upbringings, losing themselves in the ordeal of staying alive and the abject pain of their losses.

As Hadrian watched the compact figure in brown homespun working in the garden of his little white chapel, he realized the man might well be the only one left in all the world able to perform a religious ceremony that would have been recognized in the century before. Yet Father William had not even tried to replicate or invoke the old institutions. He had sought to honor spirituality, not the traditions of earlier centuries, adapting to the new realities of the colony and the cultural markers of its citizens. There was no liturgy as such in his services, there was debate on "the slings and arrows of outrageous fortune." There were no sermons, there were soliloquies involving skulls. In a colony where it was more likely in most households to find a volume of the old poet bard than a Bible, it was no surprise that William's flock called themselves Shakespeare Christians. They were as likely to solemnly quote a verse of MacBeth as a passage from Ecclesiastes.

While on Sundays William played the priest to his congregation, on other days he was the solitary monk, roaming the forested ridge above the chapel, meditating, and tending the little shrine overlooking the lake. When Hadrian arrived he was dividing flower bulbs dug up from his chapel garden. The monk nodded silently as Hadrian dropped to his knees and began helping with the chore. Hadrian knew better than to raise the first word with William, who had been known to take a vow of silence that would span the entire week between worship services. It was far from the first time Hadrian had joined him in his chores. Months earlier William had dragged him, in a drunken stupor, out of a gutter and put him to work plaiting beehives, had encouraged Hadrian's frequent return to divert him from another alcoholic binge.

When they finished with the bulbs, William produced two stiff brushes and handed one to his visitor, who began cleaning a marble cherub mounted on a whitewashed fence post. Such little stone figures adorned nearly every post, and the window sills inside the chapel, all donated by salvagers. Hadrian and William knew the weathered figures had been gleaned from ruined cemeteries but never spoke of it.

"The Lord is my shepherd," the monk murmured as he began cleaning a limestone lamb. Part of William's ritual was a quick invocation over each before he worked on it. "He that sheds his blood with me, be he ever so vile this day shall gentle his condition," he recited when he reached a small statue of a Christian warrior.

After several minutes he finally looked up. "One of the Buchanan girls came to me yesterday—the older one, Sarah, clutching one of those magazine ads. Came to me here," he added.

Hadrian glanced at the ridge above them. The little clapboard chapel wasn't William's main church. It was a shrine of solace built below Suicide Ridge. "Please tell me it was not about a trip to collect toys on the other side."

His companion's face tightened. "I'm sorry?"

Hadrian gestured to a bench. "Have a seat, Father," he said, then gazed out over the water as William settled onto the bench. With a sigh he began to explain how ghosts had been giving gifts to the young.

The monk stared unseeing at his garden as he considered Hadrian's words. "Who would do such a thing, who would treat eternal souls as playthings?"

"Sarah is stronger than that."

William slowly nodded his agreement. "She asked for you, Hadrian, said she'd been trying to find you. When I said I didn't know where you were she sat on the bench as though going to wait for you. She sat there and sang under her breath, just staring out over the water. After an hour she finally decided that I would do, and started speaking." The monk absently plucked a dried flower stem and twisted it between his hands. "But I still don't know exactly why she came. She has a restless spirit, that one, but there is something more going on, more than the emotional squalls of an adolescent girl. She said her father is wrong to hoard the past as if it was just another of his antiques. When I asked her what she meant she said he pretended that life always had been easy and cheerful for them. He tells the girls about the splendid festival meals their mother loved to prepare for them before she died. But Sarah remembers long winters of being always hungry. Once she found her mother chewing on acorns in order to save bread for her daughters. Buchanan got furious, told her not to tell such lies in front of her little sister.

"Then she pulled out more magazine ads—more than a dozen, all with photos of homes and families playing. She had drawn circles around things."

"What things?"

"Random objects. Porcelain. A glass fish. A brass table lamp. A grandfather clock."

"Salvage. All things she has seen before in this world."

"A grandfather clock?" William asked in surprise.

"There's one in their house. The governor's mansion." Hadrian paced along the perimeter of the garden, touching each of the statutes on the posts as he passed. Their heads were shiny from being stroked by mourners. "I remember before, when you had just a garden and some log benches, up higher on the ridge."

The monk nodded. "We could see the lake better from there."

"And more of the land on the other side of the ridge."

"What do you mean?"

"I don't know." Hadrian began working on a pair of marble doves. "I remember an article in the paper when this chapel was dedicated. The building itself was paid for by the Dutchman."

"Van Wyck is a supporter of our flock. With his help the merchants' guild funded the construction. There's a plaque by the door."

Hadrian stepped to the door, reading the wooden plaque with the carved expression of gratitude to the guild, looking inside at the half-dozen benches and simple altar adorned with candlesticks and more gravestone carvings. More than once he had calmed himself in the little sanctuary. Over the altar hung a simple wooden cross and a long slab of wood that William had inscribed with elegant letters. WHAT A PIECE OF WORK IS MAN, it said, HOW NOBLE IN REASON, IN ACTION HOW LIKE AN ANGEL, IN APPREHENSION HOW LIKE A GOD.

He sensed William at his shoulder. "Did they tell you to build down here?"

"The old site wasn't suitable for building. Van Wyck sent a contractor who selected this one, even purchased the land from the Council."

Hadrian turned to face the monk. "Van Wyck is dead," he said abruptly.

William closed his eyes, pressing a hand over the little wooden cross that hung on his chest. "May he find eternal peace. I had heard he'd been ill recently."

"He died months ago. He was tortured, then murdered."

The monk squeezed his cross tightly. "Surely you are mistaken. He sends money for our support. He still sends the little statues."

"But they actually come from the guild."

Worry creased William's round countenance. "Yes," he confirmed, "they come from the guild."

Hadrian ran his fingers over a lamb. "Salvage," he said. "It's all about smuggling." He explained what he knew about Van Wyck's death and the use of his signet ring to manipulate the governor.

William lowered himself onto a bench again. When he finally spoke it was in a whisper, as if he did not want the lamb to hear. "You mean his murderers paid for my chapel. But why?"

"They must have an interest in the ridge above. An interest in steering attention away from it, an interest in keeping the suicides coming. No one goes any higher but those suicides. Their families come to mourn but they don't go beyond your chapel, not as high as your old shrine." Hadrian kept his eyes on the ground as he explained the map secreted in the mill. "The same people are responsible. They want the ridge to be haunted, a no-man's land."

It was a long time before the monk spoke. "I have a theory about the ending of civilization," he said quietly. "First you hit a few buttons and millions of strangers die. Then you start cheating at cards and forgetting your mother's birthday. Before you know it you're teaching children to commit suicide."

Something new rose in William's eyes when he looked up, a glint of anger. "Christ's bones! They've been using me as another puppet, using the children!" He rose and gestured up the ridge, then set off at a determined pace. Hadrian watched him for a moment, then followed.

Half an hour later they stood at the little clearing, now overgrown with weeds, that had held the former shrine. Hadrian paced along its perimeter, glancing uncomfortably at the forested slope behind him that had been the site of so many suicides. He mentally cataloged the landscape below. The edge of the town, with its shops and residences. The cemetery, where Jonah's fresh grave was a brown slash in the scythed grass. The fishery. The ravine, over which towered the gnarled old signal tree.

"What am I missing?" Hadrian asked. "What else did you see from here?" Then he corrected himself. "Whom did you see?" Perhaps it was not so much a place he sought as the unexplained movement of people. "If I were a smuggler," he added, "why would I worry about this view?"

"A smuggler can secretly cross the border in any number of places," William replied. "But here it makes no sense." He gestured to the deep chasm that defined the border of the colony below the ridge. "There is no crossing possible over the ravine. I have heard of a bridge being started, but it's at the south end of the ridge."

"But if you were moving goods in and out of boats, this place gives you a bird's-eye view. It has to be movement from the docks they worry about."

"But the new chapel overlooks the road from the docks to town," William pointed out.

"Not the road from the docks to the shipyard," Hadrian said. "Not the road to the icehouse." He walked to the western edge of the clearing, where the ledge dropped away in a nearly vertical cliff. Far below them, out of sight, was the entrance to the cavern used for storage of the ice blocks cut from the lake in the winter. A well-worn dirt track ran into it. He gestured to a faint line of shadow that ran from the trace and disappeared into a grove of trees.

"There was another cavern tested first for storage of the ice," William explained. "They abandoned it because the access to it was too dangerous, a track along the ravine's edge where wagons could easily slip and fall. They found the one below and just widened its entrance instead."

"Show me what they abandoned."

William, who often patrolled the ridge for suicides, was more familiar with it than anyone Hadrian knew. The monk silently led him through a labyrinth of winding deer trails, over the crest, and then down a steep slope thick with stunted laurels and evergreens.

Hadrian's companion offered not a gasp of surprise when they reached a well-groomed roadbed, but rather the growl of an angry animal. The passage to the cavern may have been abandoned once but it had later been completed, creating a roadbed wide enough for a wagon. Hadrian took a few steps toward the lake and saw how the secret road rose out of the trees near a sharp hairpin curve around a tall outcropping that concealed the remainder of the path. The entire pathway was hidden, both by the outcropping and the steep, nearly vertical slope above. Anyone at the top would assume there was nothing but the ravine below. The only ones who could see it would be exiles looking from across the ravine. He turned and followed the road until it terminated a quarter mile later at a set of heavy timbered doors.

The double doors were closed with a wooden bar and a lock set in iron staples. He picked up a rock with a sharp edge and began pounding one of the staples. After a minute William raised another, heavier rock, slamming the staple with alternate blows. When the soft metal finally gave way they pushed away the lock, lifted the timber bar, and swung the doors open.

The chamber inside was packed with goods for as far as they could see. A battered armchair stood at one side of the entry, opposite the stuffed head of a moose suspended from one of the beams that supported the door frame. Tables were stacked with clothing, candlesticks, paintings, lamps, kitchen utensils, and hundreds of other items. Along the wall under the moose was a long workbench. At its near end was one of the crude stamping machines used to forge customs seals. At the other was a hand-powered grinding stone. Beside it were three swords, one of which had been cut down to the size of a knife. Hadrian's hand trembled as he lifted the blade. "One of these," he declared, "was used by Jonah's killers."

He wasn't sure Father William heard him. The monk stared numbly at the smugglers' trove, then slowly backed out of the cavern. As he retreated down the road Hadrian wandered along the tables, pausing over a table of mint-condition toys, most still in their original packages. The ghosts were subverting the children with such treasures. The next table was stacked high with small wooden boxes such as he'd seen in the kitchen of the smugglers' apartment. They were filled with the mélange of spices that had been the black market's premier product for years, a composite of whatever a salvage party might find and the powder used to dilute them. The men signaling at the cliff above town had smelled of spice. Emily had said the fishermen who had watched Jamie before his murder had smelled of cloves and cinnamon. Jansen had had powder on his fingers when he had been killed.

Hadrian searched in vain for weapons or more ammunition, then moved back to the table of new toys and began stacking them in his arms. Carrying them to the ravine, he tossed them over the side. It took him five trips to clear the table.

When he was done he collapsed into the overstuffed chair by the door, feeling weak. He had been so blind, they had all been so blind, obsessing over politics while organized crime was extending its tentacles into the colony. He extracted Jonah's worry stone and began rubbing it, staring into the mocking eyes of the moose.

Finally he rose, shut the doors, and secured them with the bar, then slowly made his way over the ridge. When he first glimpsed the little chapel from above, William was moving frantically in and out of the doorway, carrying armloads of objects outside. As he reached the ledge just above it, the building exploded into flame. William stood with one of the stone cherubs cradled in his arms as if comforting it, watching his precious chapel burn. What a piece of work was man.

HADRIAN PAUSED AT the top of the hill that adjoined the fishery compound. The sprawling complex of stone, wood, and salvaged metal sheets had quickly become the colony's industrial anchor after Jonah had perfected the steam engines that enabled the fleet to reach farther, with larger loads, than the older sailing vessels. Production of fish for food had been the priority, but soon processes were developed for fish oil to fuel lamps, fish meal to fertilize crops, and half a dozen other products like sturgeon-skin purses and Angel Polish, the shimmering cosmetic cream that was all the rage among the growing number of women with uneven skin pigments.

The night trawlers had emptied their holds and were cruising back toward the fishing grounds, a line of four steamers with two sail skip-jacks staggered behind. Four tall brick chimneys coughed up smoke from the factory boilers. He could hear the low, heavy wheeze as the steam pipes leading to the meal plant began to build pressure for the next processing run. A wagon appeared below him, bearing a delivery from the icehouse. Another dropped lumber near the ship works, where the wrights were crafting a long, narrow hull for one of the iceboat freighters that brought salt from up the coast in the winter.

The big wooden pier was alive with activity. Mates yelled orders as a net was arranged on the deck of one trawler, firewood unloaded onto another. Hadrian picked up one of the empty baskets used to haul fish and walked with a deliberate air, reading the nameplates on the berths. He balanced the basket on his shoulder and kept his head down.

The slip where he finally stopped was at the end of the wharf reserved for the skipjacks, the sailing trawlers. The name he stared at was the one he'd seen inscribed on the wooden fish at the dead sailor's apartment. *Zeus.* He glanced back toward the other berths he had passed. *Perseus. Prometheus. Jupiter. Poseidon.* Carthage's first generation had a classical education second to none.

"They're gone," came a voice behind him. "Out with the first run this morning. Poor swabs are working almost round the clock these days, trying to beat the cold. Double shifts."

Hadrian turned to face a man with an unkempt beard, a leather bag of shipwright's tools slung over his shoulder, clutching a large hand auger. He'd been replacing one of the wharf boards.

Another man with tools paused behind the first, eyeing Hadrian suspiciously.

"I thought they might be having some sort of service for the boy who died."

The bystander spat tobacco juice toward Hadrian's foot and moved on.

"Too late, friend. Young Jamie was put to his rest the very eve they brought his body up from that damned abattoir of a hospital."

"The only fresh grave at the cemetery is the one for the old professor," Hadrian observed.

The carpenter rubbed his hand over his brow. "Wrapped in an old sail and taken a mile offshore. His mother said he always enjoyed the view of the ruined lighthouse out there."

"Is she here then, his mother?"

The wright seemed not to hear. "The boy used to come into the shops, when he was no more than knee-high, just to sit and watch. He was there the day we laid the keel for the *Zeus*. After a few weeks he'd memorized the sequence of the tools I needed, would just hand them to me without my asking. I told his ma he should apprentice to me, that he had an instinct for working with wood. But she said she had to have him on the boat. And there's no denying Captain Reese." A steam whistle sounded. The man paused. "She's the skipper of the *Zeus*," he explained, "took over when her husband died years ago. Steer clear of her," he added before moving away. "She chews fish heads for breakfast."

Hadrian lingered at the vacant slip, feeling adrift, not even certain why he felt the need to speak with Reese's mother. He returned the empty gaze of a seagull on a piling, then wandered to the main wharf and sat on a piling himself to watch the workers passing by. A middle-aged man carrying a basket of fish offal walked past, followed by a youth wearing the heavy gloves of the ice handlers. Then a young woman in sunglasses caught his eye. A familiar medallion hung around her neck. He eased off the piling and followed her into a large stone and timber building at the center of the complex.

Stacks of empty wooden barrels lined the passage, waiting to be filled. One of the youths heaving a barrel onto a hand truck wore sunglasses too. The woman made for the central hall where workers relaxed between shifts. Hadrian watched as she spoke with two rough-looking bearded men wearing the canvas tunics of fishermen, then she stepped into another passage marked with a sign, WAREHOUSES.

He followed her down a narrow corridor connecting the structure to a building filled to the walls with barrels, then, as she slowed down, slipped behind a stack of barrels and waited. The air was pungent with the scent of hickory and oak, salt brine, and the onions mixed with pickled fish. Suddenly there were other scents, close by. Beer and unwashed bodies.

Hadrian spun around to face the pair of bearded men he'd seen chatting with the woman.

"You were asking about the Reese boy as if you had unfinished business with him," said the taller of the two, a thin, sour-looking man.

Hadrian backed along the barrels as the two men closed in. Each wore a brass medallion with a jackal etched on it.

"It was personal." Hadrian kept an eye on the woman, who watched with amusement as the second man picked up an iron crowbar.

"What business do you have with a dead fisherman?"

"We were friends."

A new voice rose from the shadows. "There's a lie." The man who stepped into the light had a face that seemed all scar and bone. "The boy wouldn't have gone anywhere near you, Hadrian Boone. You expelled him from school when he was fourteen."

Hadrian's heart sank as he recognized the man. Fletcher was the head of the fishery guild, and a member of the Council, but the eye patch he wore made him look like a pirate. "If that's true, it would have been for good reason." In truth, he'd only expelled students who committed repeated assaults on other students. "And it would have been a long time ago."

"Not to him. When his friends were still in school he was out on the water because of you, his hands raw and bleeding from pulling in nets in freezing rain. He was a good lad. A hero. Saved me when the *Anna* went down." Fletcher turned toward the woman a moment, then pointed down the passage. Hadrian inched closer to her as she whispered a protest, apparently disappointed at missing the coming entertainment. As Fletcher gestured again, more insistently, Hadrian ducked and darted toward her, brushing her head with his hand so that her glasses fell off. She did not move, only sneered at him.

Her eyes were nearly entirely white, the irises washed out. Fletcher spat a curse and with remarkable speed slapped the woman. Biting her lip, she retrieved her glasses and retreated. As she left, a teenage boy ran up to Fletcher, whispering close to his ear before speeding back down the passage.

Fletcher's smile was cold as ice as he turned back to Hadrian. "You've been up on Suicide Ridge. The chapel is burning."

"I have a thing about organized religion."

Fletcher's laugh echoed off the stone floor. "You're a homeless drunk who stays alive by spying for the governor. How the mighty have fallen, eh?" As he stepped closer, Hadrian saw that Fletcher had a tattoo of a snake on his neck, arranged like a necklace.

"I've heard the best tattoo artists are in the camps on the north coast," Hadrian observed, ignoring the taunt.

Fletcher aimed the back of his hand at Hadrian's cheek. He ducked too slowly, so that it connected with his forehead, the captain's heavy ring opening the skin. Blood trickled down his temple. "Hold him down, Scanlon!" Fletcher ordered the tall, thin man.

Scanlon grabbed Hadrian's arm and gestured for his companion to seize the other. The pair pinned him against a stack of barrels as Fletcher produced a long filet knife. "You will stay out my fishery, Boone." He sliced open Hadrian's shirt at the shoulder, then ripped off the sleeve. "You never heard of Jamie Reese or the *Zeus*. Come back and we'll drop you in the fish chopper. You'll end your days as fertilizer for next year's crops."

The tip of the blade pierced the skin over his bicep. Fletcher expertly slid the knife over his skin, making a slit around his entire arm. "Stay the fuck out of other people's business, schoolteacher! Buchanan may have let you take your armband off but you need a reminder that no one wants you, no one trusts you. Let's make it permanent." A second, parallel cut was made three inches below the first.

Hadrian struggled not to scream. "Their eyes!" he shouted above the searing pain. "What are you doing to their eyes!" The blood was flowing freely now, down his arm as another incision was made connecting the two cuts.

Fletcher paused, flattening the blade over the skin between the two cuts. With sudden horror Hadrian realized he was going to slice away the skin, make an armband of scar. As Hadrian squirmed the captain gave another raspy laugh.

"What the—" Scanlon growled as his companion buckled at the knees and fell to the floor. With a blur of movement a crowbar pounded into Scanlon's ribs. When he did not drop an elbow cracked into his chin, throwing him back against the barrels.

Fletcher spun about with the knife still raised and froze. Jori Waller stood four feet away, holding the bar at arm's length, ready to swing again.

"You bitch!" he spat. "You're another who has a hard time learning her lessons."

She raised her other hand, holding something small and dark.

"It's a goddamned pistol!" Scanlon gasped as he struggled to his feet.

"The governor is getting desperate," Fletcher said with a lightless smile. "But he has more guns than ammunition. He's not going to trust you with any of his precious bullets."

"This man is my prisoner," Waller declared, gesturing Hadrian behind her.

Fletcher glanced at the knife in his hand, dripping with Hadrian's blood. "Boone has no idea of the dangerous ground he treads on. I will gladly save the colony the cost of his prison upkeep."

Suddenly another knife appeared, in Scanlon's hand. There was a click as the hammer of the gun hit an empty chamber. Fletcher grinned and advanced, then the gun gave a short, sharp crack. The knife in Scanlon's hand flew through the air.

"Fuck me!" he groaned, and held up his hand. Waller had shot off his little finger.

The fishermen stood in stunned silence as the sergeant shoved Hadrian toward the passage and began backing away. By the time they were outside her hand was shaking so violently Hadrian had to take the gun from her to get it back in its holster.

THEY FOUND EMILY rocking on the back veranda of the hospital smoking her pipe, a tall bottle beside her. She raised a hand in warning before Hadrian even put a foot on the steps. "You can't come in, Hadrian. If I help you again he says he will assign half a dozen policemen to the hospital, hovering over everything we do. In last night's Council meeting he had us ratify his choice for Jonah's replacement on the Council.

The head of the shipwrights' guild, who's probably wrapped around his little finger. Then he announced the Dutchman has died at his farm, so he named another replacement, the new head of the millers' guild. But he needs us to ratify if the man is to sit for more than an interim period. I said things are moving too fast, that most of the guild heads are now men we don't know well. When I even hinted at resistance he proposed a new licensing body. Every doctor and nurse to be reviewed by a politically appointed panel to adjudge their fitness for the colony payroll. Then Kenton came by this morning looking for you."

Jori Waller spoke over his shoulder. "The Dutchman didn't die at his farm. He was murdered. At least six months ago."

Emily looked up with a shocked expression. "No. Impossible!" She thought a moment. "He's been on the Council, casting his vote."

"And he hasn't attended meetings for all these months," Waller said. "Buchanan saw his body. There's no mistaking what happened. But he somehow forgot to inform the rest of the Council about that detail."

Emily opened her mouth as if to speak again but said nothing and finally just lifted the bottle to her lips. Hadrian caught its sweet scent.

"It's not even noon, Emily," he observed, "a little early for corn whiskey."

She turned the bottle toward Hadrian, displaying its medical label. "We put in some tincture of hellebore and call it anesthetic. And it's not early for me. I haven't been to bed. In surgery all night. Some fool announced he could fly and jumped off a barn." She took another drink. "You need to get out, Hadrian. The paper has begun to criticize the governor, blaming him for Nelly's escape. Now he has to deal with a dead policeman. And Buchanan has the notion that all his troubles are somehow your fault. Find one of your holes and disappear for a month or two, let things cool off. Go to those friends of yours in the mountains."

Instead he stumbled up the stairs as the sergeant shoved him forward.

"Dammit!" But Emily's protest died away as Waller pulled away the policeman's tunic that covered him, revealing his blood-soaked shirt. Fletcher had sliced deeply. "You sorry bastard," the doctor muttered, then motioned him inside. Hadrian picked up the bottle as he passed the rocking chair.

When Emily left them in the little exam room off the kitchen, he drank deeply, then turned to the sergeant. "This is where I thank you and say goodbye."

"I didn't do it for your thanks," the sergeant said stiffly. "You saved me last night in front of the governor."

"I save you, you save me. The trouble is, Sergeant, both times it was me who took the beating." He forced a small grin.

Her expression did not change. "Tell me why Fletcher was so worried about you or we go straight back to the prison."

"You're probably the first Carthage policeman to ever fire a gun in the line of duty."

The sergeant shrugged. "The pistols were just issued."

"I was impressed with your marksmanship."

She blushed, looking at the floor. "I was aiming at the barrel beside him."

"Reducing the criminal population one finger at a time." Hadrian closed his eyes for a moment against the rising tide of pain. "Fletcher was scared of me for the same reason he was scared of you," he said. "He's worried that we might start following the trail you found last summer." His arm felt as if it were on fire. "Kenton or Buchanan told someone about discovering Hastings's body. The killers found out and for some reason had to attack Jonah that very night. We need to find out whom they told. Kenton probably went back to the prison when I went missing that afternoon. Someone there helped Nelly escape."

Waller seemed not to hear. "What did you expect to find at Jamie's boat?" she asked. "Why trail that woman?"

"Why follow me?"

"I wasn't. I was looking for the *Zeus*, thought Jamie's mother might be more interested in talking now that he's dead. But some carpenter said I should get coordinated with the old schoolmaster and pointed inside. Why did you follow that woman? Why let Fletcher trap you like that?"

"You don't understand, Jori," came Emily's voice over the sergeant's shoulder. "Hadrian's life is all about doing penance. He decided long ago that the end of the world was his fault. If on a given day someone doesn't kick him, cut him, or beat him, he'll find a stick and flog his own back raw."

Jori backed away as the doctor pushed Hadrian onto the table. He helped peel away the blood-soaked shirt for Emily, grimacing as the fabric stuck to his skin. "A permanent armband," he said, and tried to grin through his pain.

"We should have thought of it years ago," Emily muttered, then pushed him flat.

He clenched his jaw as she poured alcohol over the incisions.

"Fishing crews are working double shifts," he explained as she began stitching his skin together. "Everyone's on edge. I saw people wearing sunglasses for no good reason."

"It's a fad, that's all," Emily replied as she worked. "The old man who grinds lenses down the street says suddenly there's a demand for them. And the sunny season is over."

Hadrian bent his head up. "Why would you ask him?"

Emily pushed him down. "The day after Jamie was admitted some-one left a pair of sunglasses by his bed. I didn't really think about it but after he died I realized they must have known what was going to happen to his eyes."

Hadrian studied his friend, recognized the lingering anger on her face. "That's enough to make one a little curious. But what made you mad enough to do something about it?" he asked.

"Yesterday Buchanan came with his Norger brute while I was in surgery. He got one of the junior doctors to sign a statement saying that Jansen was stabbed. The bullets I extracted have disappeared from my office."

Hadrian glanced into the shadows. Waller sat in a chair by the door. She was very still. He flinched as the suture needle entered his skin again. "One of the people wearing sunglasses had washed-out irises. No one is born with eyes that color."

"No one is born that way," the doctor agreed.

"No one in their right mind jumps off barns to fly." His words quieted Emily. Her face began to cloud with worry. "In college I knew people who would stay awake for days straight, people who would lay as if in a coma then wake up with a smile. Some might try to fly off a barn."

Emily frowned. "Lost world. Lost technologies." She paused and tilted his head, holding the bottle to his mouth.

Hadrian watched the doctor in silence, seeing not just exhaustion and anger there now, but an edge of something that could be fear. "There were a lot of types, lots of names—speed, ecstasy, acid, meth, fly powder."

"This is Carthage, Hadrian. This is the other twenty-first century."

"Different world, different technologies. You make your own anes-thetic. Who else would know how to manufacture drugs today?" It wasn't just the alcohol that was setting his head in a spin. He was finding no answers, only more questions. Smugglers. Drugs. Murder by jackal. Munitions. Jonah had started calling the exiles rebels.

"Jonah. Me, when I have time to think about it. Our pharmacy, for making the extracts and tinctures out of the plants the herb collectors bring us. I don't know of anyone else. We don't teach much chemistry beyond what they need in the foundry and processing plants."

Jonah. Suddenly Hadrian remembered the books spread out over the desk in his secret vault. Biochemistry. Physiology. "Did Jonah use your lab?"

"Of course. Has all these years, at night or when others didn't need it. But when it comes to producing synthetic chemicals like those that people used as hallucinogens, it would take special materials and equipment. We have the most advanced lab in the colony and we couldn't do it."

There had been another book on Jonah's desk. Botanical chemistry. "What if they were using plants like you do?"

She dripped more alcohol over his wound as she closed it. "Of course there are native plants, dangerous as hell. Nightshade, foxglove, mayapple—not to mention twenty kinds of mushrooms." Emily slowly shook her head. "No. They're unpredictable, more likely to kill you if you don't know how to handle them."

"I don't understand what you're calling *dangerous drugs*," Waller inserted. "You use drugs in the hospital."

Emily frowned. Hadrian realized she'd forgotten the sergeant was still in the room.

"In the old world there were pills that would take over your mind. Make you do things you'd never think of without them. Make you forget even who you are. Make you crave still another pill, and another, until eventually you'd do anything for just one more."

The sergeant was clearly struggling to understand. "You make it sound as if they enslave people somehow."

The doctor slowly nodded.

"But there are other people who know about them," Waller continued, "who remember them."

"We regularly work in the lab with many plants. Nightshade can make belladonna, a good sedative. Foxglove makes a heart medication if processed carefully." Emily turned back to Hadrian. "These are not recreational drugs. You're talking about complex compounds that couldn't be made in the simple lab we have. My staff wouldn't even *know* about the kind of drugs you're talking about. No one in Carthage."

"No one in Carthage," he repeated, fixing the doctor with a pointed stare.

Emily said nothing, just finished his sutures, jerking the last knot closed so hard Hadrian flinched in pain. As he tried to sit up he swayed, feeling light-headed.

"You have to stay still, dammit. You lost a lot of blood. Two, three days at least," Emily declared as she begin wrapping a strip of linen around his arm. "The shed out back has a couple of old mattresses. Technically that won't be in the hospital."

Hadrian looked up at Waller. "Two mattresses. You can lie down and watch me suffer." The sergeant made a wincing expression. "Or you can go back to that loft. The killers weren't there only when they killed Jansen. They'd been using the place, probably came and went for months. They must have left signs. Witnesses along the street perhaps. And there's a boy named Dax who carried messages for Jonah but he also does favors for the jackals." He gave her an assessing look. "Or maybe you're better off going back to being Buchanan's goon." His head began to spin and he lay back onto the table, throwing his arm over his eyes.

He heard the two women take steps toward the door. There was a oddly forlorn tone in the sergeant's voice as she spoke to Emily. "I remember him, from school," she said in a near whisper. "He would say funny things, but sometimes they were inspiring. He would bring in baby animals and read poems. Now he wears borrowed clothes and sleeps in sheds. He plays games with me like I'm still a little schoolgirl. He lies even. Does he always lie, Doctor?"

A blanket was thrown over Hadrian. "He never lies about the important things, Sergeant. Remember that."

Five minutes later Emily returned and pulled away the blanket. "You're not asleep, Hadrian." As he rolled over she extended a clean shirt.

The stitches pinched his flesh as he sat up. "You've never told me why you help her, why you defend Sergeant Waller."

"I've known her family a long time. She deserves my help."

"Why, Doctor, does she need your help?"

Emily helped him into the shirt. "Her father was ill from the start, one of those who kept his condition hidden to avoid being expelled. Her mother started a business to support them. He died when Jori was only ten or twelve. When she applied to the corps after school and the question of her acceptance came before the Council, Buchanan laughed, said we needed our young breeding stock focused on making babies. I said he was a damned fool, that he was going to accept her and promote her, to give encouragement to other young women. He reminded me I was demanding the Council pay for a new wing on the hospital."

"What new wing?"

She cast a peevish glance at him.

"Christ, Em," he said as realization sank in. "You gave up your new wing to get her into the police corps?"

She shrugged. "He would have found some other way to block it." She tightened the bandage covering the wound on his forehead. "I've been to their house for dinner many times. The last time, Jori was on duty. Her mother showed me her room. She has an old photo of her father in his uniform, with his badge, on a little table like a shrine. Her mother hates it, says the only way Jori will ever succeed with the police is to become like Kenton."

"Kenton," Hadrian replied, "will wise up and give her a new assignment any day now. In another week she'll be calling on farmers to collect the cattle tax."

Emily said nothing, just pulled out her pipe and lit it. "Buchanan," she confided with a glance at the door, "has ordered the recruitment of a dozen new police, with bonuses to be paid for signing on. He's building an army."

"Buchanan hasn't a clue about what's going on. He's been played like a puppet for months. Now he reacts the only way he knows how."

"There're rumors about more exiles hiding in town," Emily said. "Kenton's talking about doing a sweep of every block. God help Nelly if she's caught."

"Do you still keep that old nag at the flax farm south of town?" he asked as she turned to leave.

"I keep my well-seasoned mare there, yes," came Emily's taut reply. She paused as she considered Hadrian's words. "You're in no shape."

"No shape to walk thirty miles over the mountains, no," he agreed. "And I'd rather not have to steal the horse I ride." He returned her cool stare. "Buchanan has told the colony that Nelly was Jonah's killer. Now he has to blame Jansen's death on her. He will never allow her to elude him for long. He will hang her, the truth be damned. I owe Jonah the truth, whatever the cost."

Emily stared at him silently, pleading in her eyes.

"I can't sleep without seeing his dead face. He had grand plans, Em, plans to fix all our past sins, and someone has perverted them into death and greed. I have to stop them."

The doctor sighed. "When's the last time you were there, Hadrian?"

"A few months ago. In early spring I hauled in a packful of grain and cut firewood for a few days."

"You mean you stole a packful of grain from the government silos," Emily said with a shake of her head, then worry creased her face. "Things have changed a lot. The softness is gone in the survivors. They're—" she searched for a word, "antagonistic. They will know what Buchanan plans for Nelly, and they won't hesitate to commit violence against one of us."

Hadrian lowered his legs to the floor, fighting the pain and dizziness as he stood. He pulled away the now bloody bandage from his head. "You misunderstand, Em," he said. "I'm not one of us anymore."

CHAPTER *Seven*

*H*ADRIAN COULDN'T SHAKE the sense that he was in some bizarre dream of the old American West, limping into the ragged, dusty town, leading his exhausted horse as fearful children ran to announce the stranger's arrival. Every step brought new pain, not only to his arm, where the wounds kept opening, but also in his legs and back. The aging horse had been steady and forgiving in her gait but he had passed out twice on the trip over the mountains and fallen, the mare nuzzling him awake on the ground.

His mount now saw the watering trough in front of a crude log building. Dropping the reins, he let her trot past him, then stumbled the last few feet to the trough. With his last ounce of strength he loosened the saddle and knelt, gulping down the fresh water, then sluicing it over his head. Ignoring the rivulets of blood flowing down his arm, he sat propped against the trough and studied the main thoroughfare of the exile community. Heads poked out of tattered platform tents, erected during the original expulsion, that some exiles still called home. Here and there could be seen a new log building with roofs thatched with marsh grass and reeds, though most of the homes were the decrepit clay-and-wattle structures put up in the early years.

Men and women moved by, some observing him with suspicion, others with idle curiosity. More than a few hobbled on crutches or leaned on canes. Several wore strips of cloth around their faces to hide disfigurements. He watched for familiar faces but received only hesitant, nervous nods from a few older men and women he and Jonah had helped years earlier.

His head began to throb. The mare gazed at him, her nostrils flaring. She smelled fresh blood. Hadrian looked down to see another, new red patch swell across his sleeve. He grabbed the side of the trough and heaved himself up.

The world spun as he took a step. His head swam and he collapsed, his eyes fluttering open and shut as he sank into unconsciousness. True to his dream, the last thing he saw was a tattooed Indian hovering over him.

He awoke on a straw pallet in a pool of light from the afternoon sun. A familiar figure wearing a brightly embroidered skullcap sat beside him, washing his still-seeping wound.

"The fugitive finds her stalker," he said to Nelly. "Ever the contrarian."

"It wasn't you I was escaping from, old friend," the bald woman said with a sad smile.

As he sat up the pain from his arm made him wince. "I dreamt an Indian was attacking me."

"An Indian," Nelly said slowly, gesturing out the open rear door of the little cottage, "who wisely carried you here before an angry crowd gathered around the trespasser from Carthage." A large, swarthy man could be seen chopping firewood.

"We used to be welcome here."

"Amazing what being treated like diseased animals for a generation can do for diplomatic relations."

Hadrian looked back outside. As the man chopping wood bent to pick up a piece, Hadrian saw that half his face was obscured in patterns of ink. "Really an Indian?" he asked in disbelief.

"They call themselves First Bloods. I found Nathaniel washed up on the beach last spring after a storm, more dead than alive."

"From the far shore?"

"From one of the original tribes. I'd almost forgotten there had been a large reserve to the north. Nathaniel says many of his people who survived have gone back to their old ways. A lot of them are trading, picking up such work as they can find. There's half a dozen in the camps now. As you well know, we've been in need of strong backs for a couple decades."

A few strong backs were making a difference, Hadrian saw as he sat alone by the entry to Nelly's home an hour later. She had gone to forage for food in the forest and insisted he stay behind to recuperate. Now he saw the little improvements. Yet, too, there were the new setbacks that inevitably afflicted the exiles. The gardens at first seemed in better shape than he had ever seen, tilled and cleaned of rocks, many with new rail fences. But most also had smoldering stacks where blighted potatoes and pumpkins were being destroyed. A small windmill had been erected to power a water pump, but its wind-catching blades were torn and tattered. Several passersby seemed better dressed than usual, wearing salvaged clothes, yet others were wearing little more than scraps of canvas. One woman limped by wearing a vest of woven reeds.

He dozed off, leaning against the door frame, and awoke to find a mug of hot tea on a three-legged stool beside him. He did not recognize its mix of herbs, at once sweet and acrid, but drank deeply and found himself remarkably invigorated. Finding no one inside when he set the mug on the kitchen counter, he wandered along the dusty street to the crest of the hill that overlooked the camps' modest harbor. When he'd last seen it, it had held only the rundown pier for the exiles' fishing dinghies. He froze now, confused. The old pier was still there, dilapidated as ever, but another more substantial one was there as well. Beside it was a sturdy boathouse.

Hadrian slipped off the road, to the shadows at the edge of the woods, where he perched on a boulder to study the harbor. The muscular workers at the piers did not appear to be from the camps, though there were ones with fair hair as well as several First Bloods. A pile of firewood lay by the boathouse. Only Carthage's steamboats needed such fuel. Any calling here would have incurred Buchanan's wrath if he knew of it. But the new pier and stack of firewood said that at least one of the large fishing boats was calling there regularly. Yet there was no sign of a fish works, no sign even of fish being sold.

He studied the main street of the settlement again, gazing at the hobbling, deformed inhabitants, the gaunt faces, the decrepit homes. He caught sight of a woman wearing an ancient but well-preserved football jersey with a large number on its back. Nelly had told him there was trading going on with those in the north but had failed to say how the starving colony found resources to pay to salvage traders. The exiles had nothing of value.

Working his way farther down the slope, he now spied a small, sleek sailboat anchored beyond the boatshed. Two tall men, one of them a First Blood, judging from his size and long black hair, walked up a shore path past the boat, toward a point of land where smoke curled up from some hidden source. Keeping in the shadows, Hadrian descended the hill until he could see its source. A cluster of log buildings had been erected on a little peninsula that was connected to the shore by a narrow, ten-foot-wide isthmus. The complex was protected not only by its location but by a recently built palisade of logs. As the two men walked through a gate in the wall, a third appeared, a sentry holding a shotgun, waving them through.

Hadrian felt as if he had stepped into a dark, chilling shadow. He could make no sense of the scene before him, but the sight left a cold, metallic taste in his mouth.

Retreating farther into the forest, he emerged half a mile beyond Nelly's cottage, giving the appearance he'd wandered to the south, then lingered to play with a boy and his dog. The boy's deformed foot made it difficult for him to keep up with his pet. Ignoring his aches, Hadrian lifted him onto a boulder and coaxed the dog into retrieving a stick as the boy threw it. A quarter hour later, as he bent to pick up the stick for the boy, a boot slammed down on it, snapping it in half.

"She's worried about you," came a sharp voice. "You disobeyed her."

Hadrian looked up into the hard countenance of the man he'd last seen with Nelly in the Carthage prison. "So have you come to help me, Shenker," Hadrian asked, "or to punish me?"

"I am here to bring you to dinner," the exile gruffly replied.

Hadrian followed a step behind his escort, pausing to uneasily glance at the boy, now limping away. There had been fear on his face when he saw Shenker.

"Hadrian, you remember Dr. Kinzler," Nelly suggested as she gestured him to her dinner table half an hour later. Before them was a loaf of bread, a bowl of steamed carrots and mushrooms, and a whole roasted salmon on a plank, an extravagant banquet by exile standards.

Hadrian nodded to the diminutive, pockmarked man in gold-rimmed spectacles, probably the best-groomed figure he'd ever seen at the camps. Kinzler was dapper in a blue suit jacket and white shirt. Even the patches on his khaki pants had been meticulously sewn.

Shenker took the last chair at the table.

"Dr. Kinzler is now the chairman of our Tribunal," Nelly continued. "He is building a whole new sense of community. We even have a name after all these years. New Jerusalem."

Hadrian raised his brows in surprise. There had been other names applied to the camps through the years. West Carthage, at first, but when it had been abandoned others had been tried, depending on the namer's perspective. Purgatory. Slagtown. Cemetery Creek. "A name full of promise," he offered. "The improvements are already noticeable." Hadrian looked back at Kinzler. "I can't help but wonder what your field of study was, Doctor," he added after a moment. "Urban renewal?"

Kinzler's smile offered no warmth. "Early in life I was a civil engineer, building shopping malls and highways mostly," he said with a shrug, as if acknowledging the lack of demand for those talents in the new world. "Later I took a doctorate in chemical engineering. Even as boy I was happy only when I was playing with wrenches and screwdrivers or the contents of my mother's spice cabinet."

"Which is what brought about the changes in our affairs," Nelly interjected as she served the fish.

"I'm not sure I follow."

"Dr. Kinzler is a tinkerer by nature. I told you I found Nathaniel nearly dead on the beach. The next day the crippled boat he'd been thrown from limped in seeking repairs. They fish with handlines for those big sturgeon. On board was a hunter who'd been returning in a canoe from a long-range expedition."

"You mean a long-range salvage hunter."

Nelly nodded. "They call themselves prospectors. He had half a dozen mechanical devices, none of which worked. Windup clocks, pocket watches, old rotary peelers, and the like. Dr. Kinzler offered to look at them. The next day he had two of the clocks working and offered to fix everything else. The First Bloods were so grateful they gave us a huge sturgeon. We had a feast together, like a Thanksgiving. People brought in roots to boil, made johnnycakes of cattail and acorn flour. The First Bloods asked if they could bring more machines to be fixed, with payment by them in fish and goods. Real trade started. It was a turning point for us. We haven't been able to spare people for salvage for years. Now they even ask what we want them to look for."

"All in exchange for repairs?"

Kinzler shrugged. "They have the muscle, we have other ways to add value. I believe it is called specialization of labor."

Hadrian studied his hosts. "The First Bloods don't have steamboats," he observed.

"But they cut wood for them," Nelly explained. "The fishermen are happy to buy it since it goes for well below the price in Carthage."

"Not something the authorities in Carthage would permit if they knew."

"Governor Buchanan is against anything at odds with his particular sense of world order," Kinzler observed with another of his narrow smiles.

"Which means what, that you are working on a new world order?"

Kinzler, still smiling, pushed the bowl of vegetables toward Hadrian.

"You wouldn't tell, Hadrian," Nelly said, an edge of worry in her voice. "About the wood."

"Of course not. Jonah and I both always wished the best for the camps, you know that. It's only curious that a fisherman would take the risk of helping you escape simply because he likes cheap firewood. If Buchanan knew, he would seize the boat."

Shenker squeezed his mug of water so tight his knuckles grew white. Nelly picked at her plate. "The cell door was opened before dawn by someone we couldn't see," Shenker told him. "And the rear one at the bottom of the stairs was ajar. We made our own way as best we could across the border. Fishermen would never take the risk to help us."

He was lying, Hadrian was certain. But why? Of course he'd want to protect the fishermen who had helped them back to the camps. But it hadn't been a fisherman who arranged the escape from the prison.

Hadrian silently studied each of the three in turn, nodding slowly. "I have always wished the best for the camps," he repeated.

"And what is it exactly you are helping us with on this visit?" Kinzler asked after a moment. A memory of the man's wife suddenly came to Hadrian. She had developed a wasting condition like leprosy and had taken years to die, in one of the group hovels with nothing but a mud-and-stick fireplace at either end for heat. Scars from such an ordeal would run deep in a man like Kinzler. It wasn't his lightless smiles that caused Hadrian to distrust him. He distrusted him because he didn't show his scars.

"Jonah's murder still needs to be resolved."

"A crime of Carthage," Kinzler reminded him. "I still am at a loss to understand what help you bring now to New Jerusalem."

"Governor Buchanan has already named his prime suspect. To back down now would be a political defeat. He will send a small army of police to seize Nelly."

"He can try!" Shenker spat.

"Every man he sends will have a firearm."

Hadrian did not miss the alarmed glance Kinzler threw at Nelly. "We can hide her," the chairman suggested. "The forest is deep."

"The truth would be better," Hadrian countered. "Help me find the real killer."

"We know nothing." Kinzler seemed to sense he had spoken a little too quickly. He shrugged. "The citizens of New Jerusalem hardly have incentive to assist Carthage."

"I believe Jonah died trying to help the camps. That very day he spoke with me about building a new bridge, about sharing our grain."

Kinzler removed his wire-rimmed spectacles. Rubbing the bridge of his nose, he said, "Perhaps we should take you on a tour of our cemeteries. Two out of every three graves are there because of your colony's refusal to help. They may have been sick but it was malnutrition and the cold that ultimately took them."

Hadrian broke away from the chairman's disapproving gaze and turned to Nelly. "You were in Carthage when Jonah died. Surely you must have some notion as to why he had summoned you."

"Healing," Nelly replied, drawing a chastising frown from Kinzler. She continued. "He was confident there would be a thaw in relations soon. He asked what were our priorities, which should come first, food or clothing."

"Asked how?"

"Letters. I told him neither. It was medicine we wanted. We had survivors with new children, healthy, normal children who were dying of pneumonia and fevers. He asked if we could find willow bark, and when I said yes he told us he'd found an old recipe for making aspirin out of it. It worked! Soon he was sending suggestions for other medicines."

Hadrian nodded. Nelly never lied, simply managed not to tell the whole truth. He remembered the books hidden in Jonah's secret vault, remembered Emily's description of her lab's experiments with more potent herbs. "You thought he had more urgent news about a medicine?"

"He had asked for a list of our common maladies. I had consulted with all our midwives and sent it to him the month before. I thought he had made a new batch, something he wanted us to have right away."

Hadrian was about to remind her he had seen the note about the shifting of the world. But a new emotion swept over him. "He never told me about it," Hadrian said instead, flushing at the bitterness that had crept into his voice.

"Hadrian . . ." Nelly began. She looked down at her food. "He spoke often of you in his letters. Being picked up for public drunkenness and vandalism, spending frequent nights in jail. How could you be trusted with such secrets?"

It was Hadrian's turn to stare silently at his plate. He gestured to the throbbing wound on his arm. "I think I need to lie down."

Shenker grinned.

Nelly helped him to his feet.

THE POET BARD was working at the table when he woke. It was probably two hours before dawn. In a pool of moonlight at the far end of the table was a stack of books. He watched from his pallet in silence as Nelly read from a thick volume and took notes with a quill pen, remembering the warmth, even hope, with which he had once watched Jonah bent over his own manuscript.

When at last he stirred she rose and poured him a mug of tea from a battered pot on a brazier, then gestured him to the table as she returned to her work. Once he had known her only to write poems and reconstructions of old songs. But that wasn't what she was doing now. "Herbal infusions," he read from the heading at the top of her sheet.

"These books turned up in salvage a month ago. Nineteenth-century pharmacology. Much more useful than anything later, since it doesn't require equipment we don't have." Nelly offered a quick smile, then returned to her work, pushing a candle closer to her notes.

"What do the salvage teams have to report when they return?" Hadrian asked after a long silence.

"Not much."

He regretted the words at once, for the chill they cast. Even after so many years, salvaging for many felt like raiding tombs. Speaking about the objects collected was inevitable, but talking about the ruined lands was taboo.

But clearly Nelly herself had already asked. "The skeletons are mostly gone now. Nature has reclaimed everything less than a square mile of pavement. The few high-rises left are completely entangled in vegetation. Lots of predator animals. Some say animals that escaped from zoos are cross breeding. Lions and cougars. Grizzlies and black bears. So many rumors, crazy rumors. A colony of meat-eating monkeys. Pythons hanging in trees." She shrugged. "Who knows?"

He lifted a piece of empty paper waiting beside Nelly's books, admiring the weight and texture. It was handmade. "So much better than anything I've seen in Carthage." The sheet beside it was transcribed with music. An old folk song, "Fifteen Miles on the Erie Canal."

"An artisan in the northern settlements sends it. It holds the color of our berry inks perfectly."

Hadrian laid the paper in front of him. There was nothing quite so hopeful as a sheet of fresh, blank paper. "I thought the north only had some struggling fishing camps."

Nelly chose not to reply. She got up to lift the kettle to refill their mugs. "I need to know you believe, Hadrian," she said suddenly.

"Believe?"

"In our work. In the future."

The words were simple, almost silly, but they brought a strange tightness to Hadrian's throat.

Nelly covered his hand with her own a moment. Then she rose with a glint of excitement before gesturing him to wait as she stepped into the drafty little room that served as her sleeping quarters. She returned moments later carrying a bulky, squarish object covered with a cloth, setting it in front of him with a conspiratorial gleam.

"They brought this in and Kinzler's shop fixed it." With a ceremonial air she lifted the cloth, then opened the tattered case underneath.

His fingers trembled as he reached out and touched the old typewriter, one of the black boxy portables from the 1940s. He thought he should say something but his voice cracked. She put a hand over his again. "When I first saw it I broke down and cried like a baby," Nelly confessed. She produced a pocketknife, sliced away the bottom of the paper she had been writing on, and fed it into the platen, gesturing to him expectantly. "I dab pokeweed ink onto the ribbon," she explained. "I think I'll be able to saturate some strips of linen to use."

Hadrian lifted his fingers to the keyboard and after a moment typed eight words. *Do not go gentle into that good night.*

She leaned over his words, a thoughtful expression on her countenance. "It's going to be different, Hadrian, I can feel it. Jonah felt it." She ran her own fingers over the keys and typed another line. *Rage, rage, against the dying of the light.*

He stared at the exhortation, remembering the last time he had seen it. "Why do you mention Jonah?"

"He used these words with us," she said. "His way of reminding us, of keeping our heads up."

"He was feeling his age."

Nelly paused, fixed him with a look of uncertainty. "Hadrian, surely you understand. He wasn't referring to himself. There wasn't an ounce of self-pity in Jonah Beck."

"But that's what the poet meant. Rage against old age, against death," he explained, looking back at the typed letters. For the first time he realized they could have a different meaning.

"Jonah wasn't speaking about the light of his existence. He was speaking about the light of humanity. He meant it was time to take action."

Hadrian stared at the words again. The pain of Jonah's loss never seemed to dissipate, only took on new dimensions. "Carthage still runs this world of ours, Nelly."

She unrolled the paper from the machine and handed it to Hadrian. "Nobody rules us here," she said defiantly.

"Because the camps remain unimportant to Lucas," Hadrian replied. "He's always assumed they would eventually die away."

"If Carthage lets us die, then the best parts of Carthage die too. Don't you understand?" There was a new torment in Nelly's voice. "It's what Jonah was talking about. It was why he died."

"Buchanan also senses things are changing. Even in the colony people are becoming too independent-minded for his liking. He gives speeches in Council about how vulnerable Carthage still is, how it constantly totters at the edge of destruction."

"Uttering such phrases is just part of who he is. We are the shadow that gives meaning to his light. If he didn't have a real threat, he would have to invent one."

Hadrian studied his friend with fresh worry. "Meaning he has a real threat now?"

Nelly returned his steady gaze without speaking.

"Things *are* going to be different," he said. "He's been looking for a reason to clamp down, to secure more power." He looked away, apology now in his tone. "One of his policeman was murdered, Nelly. The night you escaped."

Her breath choked. She dropped into her chair.

"Who helped you at the prison?" he asked. "You were on that steamboat that sailed out at dawn, you must have been." He sighed in frustration when she didn't answer. "Buchanan wants to be able to call it a budding insurrection. It's the opportunity he has been waiting for. He will use the exiles as his scapegoats and take more power as a result. If he can't destroy you, he'll simply annex you and throw all your leaders into prison."

Nelly looked out the window into the darkness. "Every night since I heard of Jonah's death I've had the same nightmare. I'm in a chair on a porch, rocking in the dark. Jonah appears and puts his hand on my shoulder. Not Jonah. His ghost. He says he forgives me for his death. It makes no sense. It tears my heart out."

Once more Hadrian had the sense that it was Jonah who'd set in motion the machinery that seemed to be grinding them all up. He recalled the ominous message Jonah had sent to her. "What did he mean, Nelly, about the shifting of the world being upon us?"

"I told you I didn't know. But it wasn't a message I could ignore. Shenker had just come back into camp from one of his travels. He said we had to go, right away, he promised to go with me. We signaled immediately that we were coming."

"You mean with the tree on the ridge." She did not respond. "But I think you had some idea of what he wanted."

"Something about the medicines, that's what I assumed."

"You said you made a list of illnesses."

"Carthage needs medicines too. I think he thought that working jointly to heal the sick would bring us together."

"What illnesses? What were the ones you told him about?"

"Influenza. Dysentery. Typhus. Snow blindness. Dropsy."

"Snow blindness?"

"It's what they're calling a new disease among our young. They go into intermittent comas. Their eyes go all white. Three or four have died."

Hadrian stared at her in silence. "In Carthage," he said, "we call it an industrial accident." He began to explain what he knew about the death of Jamie Reese. "It had something to do with the murder of that policeman, I am sure of it," he concluded. "What was it, Nelly," he pressed, "why did Jonah have to see you so urgently?"

"Don't you think I've been trying to understand ever since I saw you with his body that night?

"You saw me?"

"I was in the crowd, with my cloak over my head. I was about to run inside to look for him when you came out carrying him. Shenker pulled me away, said police would be swarming over the building soon."

"But you had been watching the building, waiting for a safe time to go in to Jonah. Surely you saw something."

"We were waiting in the shadows for more than hour. Two families came out carrying books. A delivery boy took in what looked like a tin of food, ran out a few minutes later. A police patrol went by. I've replayed it in my head again and again. There was nothing suspicious."

"You watched the rear door too?"

"Shenker did. Whichever entry cleared first we would use to go to Jonah. A janitor left, he said. A garbage wagon was emptying bins."

"His funeral was two days later. Where were you? Not at his house. I was there."

"I was there too, long enough to see through the window that it had been ransacked."

"Where were you?" he asked. "Maybe I can find witnesses who will help, at least make it clear you didn't kidnap the owner of that house."

"Sanctuary is where you take it," came her cryptic reply.

It was daybreak by the time Hadrian gathered his backpack and had checked on Emily's mare, praying that Nelly's influence would keep the horse from exile stewpots. He moved up the rutted road away from the harbor, toward the plateau where most of the camps' population lived. Kinzler's improvements faded quickly as he walked away from the waterfront. A scarecrow in a field resolved itself into a woman who pried with a stick at frost heaves, looking for potatoes that had escaped the blight. At the other end of the field a pig, less discriminating, rooted among a pile of the diseased tubers. A goose waddled by, extending a broken wing.

A tall man, thin as a stick, struggled with a shovel in the rocky soil at the edge of the cemetery. With a sagging heart Hadrian saw the row of fresh graves, most marked only with makeshift pine crosses or upended flat rocks. Beyond lay a row of shabby cottages whose roofs at least signaled the benefit of the new salvage trade. Two were covered with large sheets of plastic cloth, another with a mosaic of automobile license plates wired together like shingles.

He thought he recognized the face of a man walking with a cane and lifted his chin in tentative greeting. The man glared at him, then hobbled on. The haggard face would inhabit his nightmares now.

Hadrian had been the most persistent of all the founders to seek out other survivors, ignoring the warnings of Jonah and Buchanan when he had pressed farther and farther toward the ruined cities. There had been ten in the last group he had found, wandering along a stream in search of roots and amphibians to eat. Every one of them had been sick, damaged by radiation or the diseases of the malnourished. They had not welcomed him, they had thrown stones at him. He had to call out from behind a tree trunk to explain who he was and where he wished to take them. He'd emptied the food from his pack and watched them devour it like animals, then retch most of it back up as the fresh grain and meat hit their ravaged stomachs. They had encircled him, staring with wild, hateful eyes, as if he were responsible for their plight, then they had jumped him, ripping his clothes, kicking him until an older woman with a crutch had beat away his attackers. Once in Carthage, half had died within weeks. The other half were exiled months later. He had stopped searching for survivors.

He sat on a stump, watching the morning chores and remembering. Jars of night soil were being emptied into communal sewage pits. A child ran past him. A bird trilled from the forest. A goat bleated from a shed by the trees, waiting to be milked. Another child ran past him. Hadrian paused as a third child emerged from a house at a trot. The children were all running to the goat shed. No. He stood, watching more closely. They were being summoned by the bird in the woods.

Two minutes later he was crouching by the shed, watching as they gathered around a lanky, fair-haired boy sitting by a rolled-up blanket. Dax looked worn from his travels but seemed to take strength from the children, who were anxious to share the tattered magazine he produced from his bedroll. Only when he pushed the roll to the side did Hadrian see the canvas pouch hanging from his shoulder, the size of a courier bag. He crept back into the shadows. The boy had beseeched the dead Jonah for words to carry and now he had some.

There was a patient, almost gentle air about the boy as he entertained the little ones, a kindness Hadrian hadn't seen before. Dax had the manner of an older brother. Hadrian rose, about to descend toward the group, when the wind died and he caught a snippet of the conversation. The boy was explaining a glossy photo of an airliner with children waving to it. "On the other side each of us gets a big silver bird," Dax said, "and we flies inside it beyond the sky, all around the world, just 'cause we can."

He sank back into the shadows. Minutes later he returned to the woods and began to parallel the boy's path as Dax rose, leaving the magazine with the bewildered children. Toward the harbor, a man cleaning a stable waved at the boy and Dax handed him a folded piece of paper before trotting to a woman at a laundry tub. She joyfully accepted an envelope, then gave him a grateful hug.

Hadrian strode ahead to a point where he could see the waterfront. Two men at the boathouse watched the dusty road as if expecting the boy. Two others were splitting firewood and stacking it by the dock. Dax paused as he crested the hill, looking first at the waiting men and then beyond them before breaking into a desperate run. Hadrian strained to see what so worried the boy, cupping his hand over his eyes to look toward the rising sun. Then the morning wind pushed the cloud cover stretching toward the north. It seemed but a thread in the sky at first but as he watched it grew steadily bigger. One of the steamboats was coming.

When he looked back, Dax and the men who had awaited him were disappearing into the mysterious compound on the little peninsula. Hadrian abandoned his caution and began running toward the water's edge.

Gasping for breath, squeezing his throbbing arm, he watched from the shadows as the guard at the gate was called inside the palisade. The man returned wheeling a wooden barrow bearing a single wooden keg. As the man headed with his cargo toward the boathouse, Hadrian moved along the shore until he was directly across from the rear of the palisade. Spotting a gate open in the rear wall, he lowered his pack and entered the water at a run.

Moments later he leaned against the log wall, dripping wet. He hadn't been spotted but soon would be in plain sight of the approaching boat. He slipped through the gate into the nearest shadow, nearly gagging from the acrid odor that filled the confined space. It was a small lean-to piled with kegs, several of which were leaking their contents. He dipped a finger in the pool at his feet and sniffed. Turpentine. The year before a farmer living between the camps and Carthage had opened a mill to process the pungent solvent from the pine trees on his land.

He stole along the rear of the nearest building. Through its window he saw stacks of supplies inside, most in kegs and rough crates, with pieces of salvage hanging from pegs. Voices rose, and he heard the crackle of the wheelbarrow on the gravel. He ventured a look around the corner and watched as another keg was carefully loaded, as if it might explode.

Through a window of the largest building Hadrian glimpsed Dax, a frightened, guilty expression on his face as he gazed at the men gathered around a chair in the center of the room. Only when Shenker raised his hand to slap the figure in the chair did the others step back enough for Hadrian to see.

Jori Waller's face was already swelling from her beating. Blood trickled down her chin.

"When are the others coming?" Shenker was shouting loud enough to be heard outside. "Buchanan didn't send his slag bitch for nothing!"

Hadrian retreated along the wall, desperately scanning the grounds for a means of distraction. Rags were piled against the wall of the storage shed. A smoldering brazier sat near the gate where it had warmed the night guards. He snatched up several rags and darted back to the lean-to, dipping them into the puddle of turpentine. Watching as the next keg was wheeled from the compound, he ran toward the gate, tossed the soaked rags on the brazier, and disappeared into the shadows along the far wall.

The explosion of flame brought frantic cries from inside the main building. As the blaze licked around the gateposts, three men ran out, shouting, clearly frightened the flames would soon reach something else.

Shenker, standing just inside the door, gave a surprised gasp as Hadrian slammed his shoulder against him, knocking him to the floor.

He had his knife open and had cut half of the ropes on the sergeant's chair before the men from outside returned, with fury in their eyes and clubs in their hands.

He was on a train, holding his grandfather's hand as he nodded off to the regular hissing, chugging sounds of the wonderful antique locomotive. He could smell the hot dog the boy in the next seat was eating. His grandfather had promised him ice cream when they reached the station.

Gradually other sounds and smells began to stir Hadrian from his slumber. He groggily nestled into his grandfather's shoulder. Suddenly something cold and slimy pressed into his cheek. He sniffed and nearly gagged from the stench of putrid water and long dead fish, regaining consciousness in a fit of coughing and retching.

Someone pulled his shoulder up, lifting him out of the foul air along the bottom of the dark chamber. He shook his head violently from side to side, trying to regain his senses, feeling now the throbbing aches on his shoulders and back where he had been beaten.

"If that's how you rescue me," came a hoarse voice, "remind me to apply for a new hero."

"Sergeant?" He struggled with his words. "You weren't supposed to be in the camps."

"I didn't know where the boy was bound when I started following him. You said he was carrying secret messages. I certainly didn't know he had discovered me tracking him."

"Dax turned you in?"

"I am such a fool." Her tone was bitter. "I watched him hail someone working at a field by the woods, watched the two of them speak, even saw the stranger run toward the waterfront. I never imagined it was about me. They gave him a fresh loaf of bread and some dried herring after four of them cornered me at the edge of the village. That's what I'm worth. A fish sandwich."

A sudden violent lurch that sent Hadrian reeling against the wall left no doubt where they were. On a boat that was out in the swells, straining its engine. "What direction?" he asked as he looked at the partially open hatch overhead. Without a ladder they had no way out.

"North."

"You should have turned back when you saw the camps, Sergeant. You have no idea what you stepped into."

"And you do?"

"They are conspiring to take over Carthage. Buchanan and his police have become their sworn enemies."

"That's the trouble with you old survivors. You overdramatize everything. Feast or famine. Utopia or apocalypse. If this was a war, I'd be dead."

"The most convenient killing ground is the middle of the lake. Did they take your gun?"

She gave a resentful nod.

"In the old days a policeman losing a gun had to get it back to restore his honor." Hadrian regretted the words even before he felt her baleful stare.

Waller muttered a curse and stepped to the far side of the hold, making sure with a stomp of her boot to splash bilge water on Hadrian. He leaned against the bulkhead, knees bent, burying his head in his folded arms. He could not understand why he always felt compelled to taunt the woman.

The sturdy vessel was steadily picking up speed as she moved out of the shoreside currents, settling into a rhythmic heaving motion as she crested low swells. After several minutes he rose and began studying the beams and planks, running his fingers along joints that seemed familiar.

He suddenly froze and surveyed the hold and what he could see of the wheelhouse through the hatch. The *Anna*. It was impossible. Yet he was certain he recognized the boat, recalling how he had joined in her construction years earlier when Jonah had become impatient to install his first steam engine.

He felt the sergeant's stare and turned for a moment. "The tenth boat," he said. "You were right. It turned into a phantom. The *Anna* never sank, she was stolen."

Jori replied with a grim nod.

Jonah and Hadrian had both felt a personal loss when the *Anna* had been reported lost, though by then the shipyard had grown more sophisticated, had moved on to larger and more functional workboats. The *Anna* was small and fast. A smuggler's dream.

His mind raced as he tried to understand how her loss could have been fabricated. He'd attended the hearing, had heard how a sudden gale had overtaken her as the crew had shut down the engine to repair a leaking pipe. He closed his eyes, recalling the witnesses, the two heroic survivors who'd clung to an overturned dinghy for two days. They were Fletcher and Jamie Reese who, with unfortunate timing, had agreed to leave the *Zeus* to fill in for an ailing crew member. They had testified that the two other men on board had drowned, and so a wreath had been laid for them in the cemetery. Flynn and Wheeler. He remembered the governor calling out their names in the roll of the colony's heroes. Jonah had given a speech.

Suddenly he went still. On his last journal page Jonah had written how he had seen all ten boats of the fleet. *Wanderers all returned home.* Jonah had known, had deliberately recorded the truth, as if it would have been meaningful for someone who understood his secret journal. Hadrian had not fully appreciated the journal. It held secrets within secrets.

Hadrian studied the bulkhead that divided the hold, a new wall erected to create a separate compartment in front of the engine room. He touched his pocket and to his surprise found his knife still there. Settling on a large knot in the wooden planks, he began chipping away at its edges.

Ten minutes later he had his eye pressed to the open knothole, gazing into a small chamber with an elevated floor. The hatch cover overhead was ajar, allowing enough light for him to plainly see six of the small kegs that had been wheeled out of the compound, carefully secured with rope to cleats on the wall. He felt a touch on his shoulder and straightened to let Waller look.

"What could the camps make that would be so valuable to some impoverished fishermen in the north?" she asked.

"Gunpowder."

"No," the sergeant shot back. "I went to the library two days ago, looked in the old science textbooks. Nitrate, charcoal, and sulfur is what is used. The sulfur is yellow and stinks like sour eggs."

"All of which they could find if they look in the mountains. You forget that many of the original exiles were scientists. Jonah had no trouble setting up a gunpowder workshop when they needed it to blast channels for the water works."

"I remember going to that workshop. It had that terrible smell. There was nothing like that at the compound. They ignored me at first when they took me, just kept me tied and gagged while they readied this shipment. The kegs have smaller kegs inside, wrapped tight in deerskin and sealed with wax. There were other smells, like spices. And that strong stuff they use in paint."

"Turpentine."

Hadrian bent and stared at the kegs at long time. Whatever was inside was Kinzler's brainchild. Kinzler, the camps' answer to Jonah.

He stood and braced himself against the bulkhead, filled with new foreboding. If they didn't contain gunpowder, they contained something just as dangerous. Somehow Jonah had understood and would have known how to deal with whatever alchemy Kinzler was wielding. Jonah would have been a threat to Kinzler.

Waller settled below the hatch, where she watched the sky. "Have you been there?" she asked. "In the north."

"No, Sergeant, I haven't."

She cast an annoyed glance at him. "My name is Jori. Not Sergeant. Not Waller."

"No," he offered again, feeling an unfamiliar awkwardness. "No, Jori. I haven't been there." As far as Carthage was concerned, there was no *there* in the north, no real settlement, no community, no one, and no place that mattered to the colony.

"The reports all say it's just a few hardscrabble farms and fishermen living hand to mouth."

"The reports," Hadrian reminded her, "all come from the fishery."

Jori looked as if she had bitten something sour. "What happened?" she asked toward the sky. "All these years life goes slow and steady in Carthage. Then suddenly I don't recognize the world I live in. Every day it gets . . ." She searched for a word.

"Bigger," Hadrian suggested after a moment.

She sighed. "Bigger," she agreed. "I asked about that afternoon before Jonah died," she added after a moment. "No one saw Kenton. He wasn't at the prison. He probably just went to the races at the fair like half the other officers on duty."

Hadrian replied with an absent nod. He had realized others could have seen Hastings's body. Two young girls had definitely seen it. He bent and retrieved a small brown husk from the floor of the hold, then saw another, and another.

"Grain?" Jori asked as he dropped the husk into her palm. "The farmers don't use boats."

The little husks sent a chill up Hadrian's spine. "They're moving grain," he said. "You saw grain moving into the port at night. The millers were smuggling."

"No," the sergeant protested, "the governor explained I was wrong." But she could not argue against the proof in front of her. "God no, not our grain." It was the lifeblood of the colony and, as such, strictly controlled, stored only in five huge government silos at the edge of town. "They couldn't. The millers' guild watches over the harvesting and processing. The police guard the silos."

"This boat smuggles goods to Carthage, then brings grain back," he observed, though he had no idea of where it could be going. Those exiles he'd seen in the camps surely were not benefiting from it.

"Near that harbor," Jori ventured in a worried voice. "I was studying the settlement from the hill above before I was captured. I saw an island with tall windowless cabins, by a small dock. Like square silos." She picked up another of the husks. "I don't understand. The smuggled ammunition. These secret kegs. Now the grain. What does it mean?"

Hadrian had no answer.

Half an hour later the hatch was pulled back and a bucket was lowered containing a jug of water and four apples. Hadrian ate in a brooding silence, trying to make sense of his discoveries. As they were finishing their meager meal a familiar figure dropped through the opening. Hadrian sprang up to catch the boy, then saw that Dax was hanging by his hands from the hatch frame.

"Ain't it prime!" exclaimed the boy, swinging himself back and forth. "The wind and the water and millions of fish all around! I saw the back of a sturgeon at the surface, as long as a hay wagon!"

Hadrian grabbed the boy and pulled him down. "You turned her over to them, Dax. She's a police sergeant."

Dax eyed Jori a moment then shook his head. "Not outside Carthage, that's what they said. Outside Carthage she's just some nosey hag."

"It's Carthage you have to worry about, if you ever mean to go back. She didn't tell anyone there about your connection to the jackals."

"You can't know that," Dax shot back. "You were in the camps before she came." He eyed the sergeant suspiciously.

"I know she wouldn't do that," Hadrian insisted. "Not yet. And she was with me at the apartment where that policeman was killed." Then he added, "If Kenton finds out you're connected with the jackals, he'll probably pull your old mill down."

Dax's face darkened but he said nothing.

"How many?" Hadrian asked. "How many messages for Jonah did you carry to Nelly?"

"Once a month," came the hesitant reply. "Four letters, once a month, for Miss Nelly. She would give me things. Little carved animals. One of those knives with a turtle shell handle they make in the camps."

Four letters. Jonah had composed one journal page a week, Hadrian reminded himself. Four a month. As if he had been reporting to Nelly what he recorded in his chronicle. "Did you ever read any?"

"Never in life! The professor trusted me to keep them secret. Miss Nelly kept them secret too, locked in a box."

"Did anyone else see them?"

The boy frowned. "That Shenker. Lieutenant Shenker, he makes the others call him in that compound of theirs. Once he blocked my path. When I tried to get out of the way he hit me. I told him I was a jackal when he took my letter, but he only laughed. He read it over again and again, as if he had trouble understanding. When he gave it back, he said there was no need to tell Nelly he had seen it."

Hadrian hesitated as Dax reached for the water jug. "Who did you tell about Jonah meeting you at the saw pit, Dax?"

"No one," the boy said insistently.

"I was there. Someone had brought in a chair and tools. They were expecting Jonah. They were going to torture him and kill him there. Jonah was going there because of you, because of the book he was reading to you. They were going to be waiting."

"That's a lie!"

"No. Something happened that made them act sooner. But if Jonah hadn't died at the library, he would have died two days later. They would have tied him to that chair. They were going to burn him, to break his bones, to cut into him. Who did you tell, Dax?"

The boy's face darkened but he spoke no more, just took the apple cores and empty jug, dropping them into the bucket before grabbing the rope and whistling for it to be hauled up. As Hadrian watched Dax rise through the hatch, he wondered at the many boys who lived inside him. He was the orphan, struggling for years to stay alive on his own. He was the smuggler, the messenger for criminals. He was also the boy who listened, enthralled, to Jonah reading *Treasure Island* and wanted to learn about the stars. He was the jackal who ran with ghosts. And, Hadrian reminded himself, on arriving at the camps the boy had not gone straight to Kinzler but rather sat with the children like an older brother, then distributed secret letters to exile families.

IT WAS LATE afternoon when the *Anna* began to slow, buffeted by a chill autumn wind that quickly subsided as they entered a small bay. Hadrian and Jori had been released from the hold an hour earlier, arriving on deck as a man in soot-stained coveralls berated two teenage boys who had collapsed, clearly exhausted, by a pile of wood at the stern.

"Goddamned lubbers!" the man roared. "You'll be fish bait when I'm through with you!" As the youths spun about, Hadrian saw the fear on their faces. They were wan, thin boys, sons of New Jerusalem being sent north. Being sent to serve those of the north, he realized as the man—clearly the engineer, in charge of the engine below—violently threw a log at the nearest boy. It hit the boy in the chest, knocking him backward. As tears welled in the boy's eyes the engineer laughed, then turned to Hadrian and Jori. "Wood," he commanded, gesturing to the pile of fuel. "Down to the engine. Now."

They worked in silence, grateful at least for the fresh air. After his third trip Hadrian stole a quick glance at the boiler, confirming that it bore the numeral one on a brass nameplate that read CARTHAGE WORLD INDUSTRIES, one of Jonah's little jokes. The old scientist had fussed over the construction of the engine, finally deciding it was overdesigned and using a simpler version on subsequent boats. But Jonah had always been fond of the *Anna*, named for his long-lost daughter, and the vessel, a prisoner herself in a way, somehow felt like an old friend to Hadrian. Building her ten years earlier had been a labor of love, an important benchmark in the development of the colony's economy. The day of her launching had been declared a festival day, and Hadrian had arranged for wide-eyed schoolchildren to take rides on her across the bay.

As he climbed onto the deck for another load of wood, a boathook flashed out and grabbed his ankle. He stumbled painfully against the rail, then a boot on his back slammed him facedown onto the deck. Rolling over, he froze.

"Wade!" Hadrian cried. It was impossible. He was in prison.

The bearded man glanced at the wheelhouse, where Hadrian saw the wheel tied to a peg, then tossed the hook from hand to hand. He leaned so close Hadrian could smell his sour breath. "Ate any good books lately?" he asked with a guffaw. As Hadrian desperately looked about for a club, a length of rope, anything to use as a weapon, the boat lurched against a wave. Wade spat a curse, then tossed the hook into the wheelhouse and leapt to the helm.

The rest of the crew seemed to warm to Hadrian as he worked beside them and made no effort to return he and Waller to the hold when the engineer declared their work done. By the time they entered the harbor, one of the men, a giant with long black hair plaited in a tail at the back, joined Hadrian at the rail to explain the strange little community they approached. The big man, a First Blood who introduced himself as Sebastian, pointed to the long two-story stone structure that dominated the village.

"Long before the ending," he said, "this was a convent. St. Gabriel. Famous for making lace. When it shut down it was bought by a farmer. There were four such buildings, the nuns' cells on the top and working rooms underneath. It was already a century old even then, and he converted one to his home and the others to chicken barns. When the big blasts came, they were all from the north, from the cities along the shore. The buildings were parallel, identical stone structures. The other three shielded the last, so that when it was over just this one stood. When my family came out of the cave we hid in, there was nothing left, so we went to the lake and worked the fish along the shore to survive. Weeks later we came upon this, the only intact building anywhere, with three huge piles of cut stone ready to be used. A couple of weeks later others showed up, a band of men in grey clothes. We agreed to share the place."

"We always thought people up here were living in tents and crude lean-tos." Hadrian said with an uneasy glance back at the wheelhouse. Wade was distracted with the docking of the boat. When asked, Jori had confirmed there had been no other report of escapes from the prison. Wade was meant to be serving a month for stabbing a man.

"Some of my people still do, by choice. Some, like my brother Nathaniel, are making their way in the exile camps. Most of the salvage teams are from my tribe. My youngest brother left on one months ago and we haven't seen him since."

An ache grew in Hadrian's heart as he gazed at the old convent building. The two-hundred-foot-long structure was the most elegant building he had seen in twenty-five years. Nearly fifty people lived in apartments in the old chicken house, Sebastian explained, with another three hundred in the sturdy stone houses constructed about the land-scape on either side of the large structure. Their roofs used the same jumble of materials as in Carthage's early dwellings, split logs, pine bark, metal sheets, even thatch—but the walls were of the same precisely cut grey stone. Yet something was jarring about their lines, something incongruous.

Sebastian saw the way he cocked his head toward them. "We didn't know how to make good mortar or even how to lay stone until a few years ago," he explained. "We call them the crooked houses." The thick walls, though made of perfectly squared stones, bulged and twisted.

Hadrian looked back at Wade, speaking with the engineer now, then scanned the handful of rough-looking men and women at the waterfront, busying themselves with ropes for the berthing. There seemed to be no armed escort waiting for them. Jori looked almost wistfully at the hold where they'd been kept, as if ready to make the return trip. Suddenly a young girl ran out of a nearby shed and up the gangplank. Sebastian bent over as she whispered in his ear.

"You're with me," the tall First Blood said. As he pressed his hand tightly around Hadrian's wrist, two men moved up the gangway. Hadrian heard Jori's cry of alarm and turned to see the engineer grab her as she tried to flee. One of the approaching men laughed. It was Scanlon, whose finger Jori had shot off. Without speaking, and with no warning, he raised his good hand and slapped her so hard she dropped to the deck. She was unconscious as they dragged her off the ship.

CHAPTER *Eight*

*H*ADRIAN, TOO, WAS a prisoner, he realized as Sebastian
guided him beyond the waterfront. He was being allowed
to wander among the crooked houses of St. Gabriel but it
soon became clear he would not be allowed to stray beyond the reach
of Sebastian's long, powerful arms. The First Blood, however, was an
affable enough watchdog, letting Hadrian choose their course along
the perimeter of the settlement, not hesitating to answer his questions,
though shoving him forward whenever he hesitated to look back at the
building where they had taken Jori.

As they walked Hadrian contrasted the image of the northern community he was seeing with that conjured up by the Carthage fishermen.
The sparse population of the myth lived in primitive conditions and
their home did not even have a name. They were just *the northerners*,
and the term was always spoken in a tone of pity.

The real settlement was far more interesting, and far more unsettling, than its fabled counterpart. The town of crooked houses was
flourishing, many of its inhabitants attired better than the average citizen of Carthage. As they rounded a corner and came into the central

square, Hadrian's heart leapt. A market was underway, with vendors selling from tables arrayed along the edge of the square. Their wares comprised a rich assortment of salvage.

"The destruction here must not have been as severe as in the south," Hadrian ventured, noting now nervous glances being cast toward Sebastian. He had almost forgotten that where he stood once had been a different country from his own. Canada had always tried to remain on the sidelines of international disputes.

"Not much difference," Sebastian replied. "All the government efforts at peace for all those years just meant forty-eight hours' delay before the destruction came. But last year we found a corridor of warehouses four days' ride to the west, where half the buildings still stood. I was in the hunting party that discovered them. At first they looked like just more hills but when we got closer we saw they were structures covered with vines and brush rooted in their roof cracks. Our pack trains have been slowly emptying them."

Hadrian's eyes widened as he took in the breadth of goods. Soaps and cosmetics in original wrappers. Stacks of apparel, including T-shirts and ball caps emblazoned with the emblems of extinct teams. Board games. Toy trucks. Dolls in their original boxes. Comic books, their colors still vibrant. As he watched, a woman purchased a table lamp refitted to take candles, tendering three copper coins. Carthage dollars. She gestured for another woman, much more shabbily dressed, to carry her purchase. He realized more men and women in the crowd were carrying heavy loads, all wearing drab grey or brown clothes, all with their eyes lowered.

"Servants?" he asked.

"Indentured. Those who can't make it, those with no one to provide for them can sign on for five years to serve a household in exchange for room and board. It's how they survive."

Hadrian studied the averted eyes, the empty gazes on several of those who wore the drab clothes. "They don't look too happy about it."

Sebastian shrugged. "Sometimes troublemakers get assigned to indenture. Cheaper than a jail."

They roamed now past small shops and then beyond another row of crooked houses, eventually arriving at a knoll overlooking the settlement. Hadrian surveyed the landscape, realizing that each new piece of the puzzle made the whole harder to grasp. "Where are your farms, your food?"

"Some grains are grown on farms near here," the First Blood explained. "The rest we hunt or buy."

"Fish from Carthage."

"More than fish," Sebastian said, then he frowned. Hadrian sensed he was worried about revealing too much. "Most of the land beyond here was agricultural, for two hundred miles. Half our people had starved to death by the time we found them." He grinned at Hadrian's confusion, then relented. "Cattle and sheep gone feral, meat on the hoof. Huge herds now, in the thousands. Keeping long stretches of the old pastures grazed down."

"I thought hunter-gatherers were supposed to have a more hand-to-mouth existence," Hadrian said, looking back at the town. By many measures it was a prospering community but as he watched more of the servants he noted their looks of melancholy, if not outright suffering. They weren't servants, they were slaves.

"With all those who died of starvation in the early years no one begrudges a full belly now."

Changing the subject, Hadrian asked offhandedly, "Who teaches the children?"

Sebastian shrugged. "Why?"

"In my experience only two things are of real importance in life—who teaches the children and what they teach them."

"The mothers have a group, do the best they can. My own mother runs a school for the tribal children but she insists it be away, in the deep woods. We have artisans," the First Blood added, "wood carvers, pot makers, a couple of painters."

"And a paper maker," Hadrian surmised.

Sebastian nodded. "Just off the square. The old woman makes heaps of the stuff."

Ten minutes later they were stepping into the shop. In a side room a young woman in a grey tunic was ripping salvaged clothing apart at the seams, tossing it into a boiling vat for recovery of its fibers. Hadrian touched a stack of paper sheets on the counter. They were too thin to be used for the smuggled shotgun shells, but they were of the same speckled pattern, the same texture. It would not be difficult to make a heavier version. He watched as a silver-haired woman directed another indentured worker to carry what seemed to be heavier sheets through a doorway at the rear of the room. As Hadrian made a move to follow, Sebastian pulled him away.

They wandered along the waterfront in the fading light, pausing to watch a line of silent, fatigued riders with packhorses arrive at a building that had the look of a warehouse. Sebastian put a restraining hand on Hadrian's shoulder as he stepped toward the salvage riders, pointing him instead toward a double door at the end of the chicken house where a woman was hanging two large oil lanterns. Several figures who had been lingering along the waterfront were converging on the doors.

The tavern was already getting noisy by the time the two men entered. Hadrian paused after his first step through the door, unable to suppress a surprised grin. It was hard not to respond to the wood-paneled walls, the fire crackling in the potbellied stove, the motley collection of bottles on the bar reflecting the light of two dozen candles. The impression was one of undeniable cheer.

"Hadrian Boone!" boomed the burly man behind the bar as they approached. He had a broad face and long greying hair tied behind his neck. Wiping his hands, he reached across to grip the newcomer's hand. "Rene Sauger." He offered his name with a wide smile, then pounded the bar with a pewter mug to get the attention of his other patrons. "Hadrian Boone! A founding father of Carthage!" Several customers stared at Hadrian with intense interest as Sauger raised the mug to him, others glanced and quickly looked away.

Sauger poured Hadrian and Sebastian pints of ale and led them to a table by the stove. Hadrian cautiously sipped at his drink, watching the genial publican, trying to fit together the puzzle that was St. Gabriel.

"I'm confused. Am I a prisoner? Or am I a new friend?"

The First Blood sidestepped. "I think that is up to you."

"She's innocent, Sebastian," Hadrian said. "She doesn't know anything. Outside of Carthage she has no authority. She is no threat."

"We know about police. In the old world they were always the enemy of my people." He took a swallow of his ale. "In the old world more than one of my family was thrown into their prisons."

"In the old world."

"We don't need a prison here. You have a prison in Carthage because you have police."

Hadrian didn't know if it was his fatigue or the image of Lieutenant Kenton that flashed in his mind's eye, but he could find no words to argue.

As they drank in silence, Hadrian studied the men at the tables around them, inhabitants of this alien world. Several of them spoke with an uplifting at the end of their sentences, the Canadian accent he had heard at the signal lantern above Carthage. Four patrons sat apart, at a corner table, their clothes dusty, their hard but weary faces lifting as other customers brought them pints and stopped to talk. He realized he'd seen them before, riding into town. Even in Carthage those who regularly made salvage runs were a breed apart, transformed somehow by their repeated visits to the ruined lands.

He gazed with appreciation at the heavy wood beams overhead, the polished wood of the long bar. There were carved flowers and cherubs along its corners. Over it, and scattered on high shelves along the walls, were nearly a dozen stuffed martens, most arranged in attack pose. The long benches along the wall bore the same designs as the bar's carvings. One of the tables was covered with a lace doily.

Hadrian looked back at the bar with sudden discomfort. The chicken house had been a convent, which produced lace. The tavern was in the chapel, the bar an ornate altar, the benches old pews. He glanced back at the martens. Tree jackals. He studied the crowd again. At least half a dozen wore medallions. He shuddered. St. Gabriel was populated with jackals.

"So what shall we serve you for supper?" Sauger asked some time later, stirring Hadrian from something close to slumber. "Our mutton stew is the best for a thousand miles," he offered. It had the sound of an old joke. "Or twenty kinds of soup."

"Twenty?" Hadrian asked incredulously. He hadn't smelled any soup kettles.

Sauger's eyes twinkled. He gestured Hadrian to follow and led him to a door behind the bar. The chamber inside was nearly as large as the tavern itself, though far dimmer. At a candlelit table in the center, wearing a dull expression, sat Dax with a bowl and two tin cans in front of him. Sauger lifted a candlestick and stepped to the nearest wall.

Hadrian stared in wonder. The wall was lined with shelves, every shelf filled with cans of food. Hundreds wore once-familiar labels, artifacts of his childhood, soups and stews often served to him by his mother. The scale of St. Gabriel's salvage was beginning to sink in. "Surely they can't be good after so many years?"

"The cans with leaks and contamination popped open long ago. Most of these are usable. If it's a little stiff we add some broth. We have spices to take the staleness away."

Hadrian picked up one of the cans. It was a most unexpected treasure. He turned it over. With an ache in his heart he read the expiration date. 2024. What marvelous confidence it seemed now, to have printed such a date. In the minds of many survivors there had been no such year, for the end had come first. Civilization had expired, but its soup had endured.

"Chicken noodle," he said, not understanding why he was whispering. "I always liked chicken noodle."

"Two cans," Sauger declared.

"I'll sit in here," Hadrian ventured, gesturing toward Dax, who had not acknowledged him. There was a dark patch on his cheek, a fresh bruise.

Sauger considered the boy with a sober expression, then grinned at Hadrian. "Nonsense. You are ours tonight," he said, then put his hand over Hadrian's shoulder and led him away.

They sat at a table using hallmarked silver. He ate the decades-old soup in a china bowl, the scent of it arousing long-lost memories of sitting in his mother's kitchen after building a snowman. Sebastian, tucking into the mutton stew, watched him with amusement.

In one corner men played darts, throwing at a wooden plank painted with a bear. He realized now there were women scattered among the tables, young ones wearing tight-fitting clothes and makeup. He blinked self-consciously as he became aware he'd been staring at a red-haired woman in her twenties who now met his eyes with an inviting expression.

One of her companions, a tall blond, led a member of the salvage party out a side door. The back of the vest he wore was embroidered with a skeleton holding a shovel. DEATH DIGGER, said the slogan underneath.

Raucous laughter burst from a corner table. Wade and the ape-like engineer from the *Anna* seemed to be holding court with other members of the salvage crew. Clearing their table were the two youths who had arrived with them from New Jerusalem, now wearing the grey clothes of indentured servants.

"What do you think of our paradise?" Sauger asked as he took a seat beside Hadrian.

"You never feel so blind as when you finally learn to see," Hadrian replied.

Sauger seemed to take the words as a compliment. Grinning, he gestured toward the red-haired woman, who brought fresh glasses and an old soda bottle capped with a cork. "You can make vodka from almost anything," he declared, then opened the bottle and sniffed as if it were a fine wine before pouring it out. "Turnips and elderberries, steeped in cedarwood. You'd be surprised."

"I can't help wondering why we in Carthage have been so ignorant of these miracles in the north."

Sauger smiled like a Buddha. He contemplated Hadrian, then lifted his glass in salute before sipping his vodka. "We're just coming into our own, you might say. Before that, it was all about surviving."

Hadrian gripped his glass, struggling with a reflex that demanded he drink, but also hearing the voice that shouted his days as a drunk were over. He stared at the glass and realized he no longer had an appetite for liquor. Somehow it seemed Jonah's doing, as if something inside him had made a pact with his dead friend to stop drinking. "Still, our fishermen have been sailing north for years," he replied.

"Mostly, we discourage them. When they first started appearing on the horizon we'd send canoes out to meet them with furs and woodcarvings and warnings about terrible shoals closer to shore. They kept venturing farther and farther. Once here they found they enjoyed sampling our tattoos and women. They like our tattoo artists. The First Bloods have been inking skin for hundreds of years." Sauger shrugged. "Punic pilgrims, our people started calling them, sailing in for a little quick salvation at the convent before heading back to stuffy old Carthage. No doubt they worry that sharing the secret would spoil their fun. We do like to keep to ourselves."

Sauger raised his glass to Sebastian, who drained his glass with a hesitant nod toward the tavern keeper. Did Hadrian detect distrust in the First Blood's expression?

"But it didn't seem fair for Carthage to keep all her steam trawlers."

"No one stole the *Anna.* She just changed her home port."

"But she's owned by the head of the merchant guild. Funny how he never objected."

Hadrian had landed a blow. Sauger's grin disappeared, and Hadrian continued. "I think that you are telling me that the *Anna* is still part of Fletcher's fleet. Despite the touching monument to her in our cemetery. I remember how the captain wiped away a tear as he laid out the wreath for her dead."

As if on cue a door opened and the man who'd disappeared with the blond woman earlier returned, alone now, carrying his vest in his hand. For the briefest of moments, in the light under one of the bright lanterns hanging from the ceiling, the salvager glanced at Hadrian, then quickly turned his face away. But it was long enough. Hadrian had spent time with him in Carthage, on the docks when they were training men for the first steam ships. The death digger's skin was darker, and now heavily tattooed, his hair longer, but Hadrian knew him. Wheeler. He was one of the *Anna*'s missing crew members. His name was carved on the monument in the Carthage cemetery. The children's choir had sung a song in his memory.

"What I don't quite understand," Hadrian went on, "is why you have gone out of your way to welcome me. Or perhaps you just want to keep the meat tender for your stewpot."

Laughter flashed in Sauger's eyes. He played the role of the publican perfectly, but Hadrian was beginning to glimpse the restless cunning behind his eyes. "We savor your—" he searched for a word, "your uniqueness, Professor Boone."

The two men seemed to be carrying on different conversations. Hadrian forced a sip of his vodka, watching as the blond woman reappeared, now leading away Wade. "I was wondering if I might meet your mayor. Or chairman. The head of your government."

"I like your new friend, Sebastian," Sauger said to the First Blood. "He gets right to the nub of it!"

"I don't understand."

"We have learned our lessons well. We have no government. We live by mutual benefit. Social symbiosis. Everyone embraces their roles. Rethink your world, friend. Ever notice how all the big problems in history were caused by governments?"

"But now St. Gabriel is recruiting for new roles," Hadrian replied. "Putting your agents in the camps. It's a big world, as they say, now more than ever."

"Just trying to make new friends, to find new mutual benefit."

"Or perhaps you are reinventing the world."

Sauger ignored the comment, just gestured around his tavern. "If you need something, just ask."

In a clear voice Hadrian said, "Give me the killer of Jonah Beck."

Sauger's expression grew less genial. "The murder of a prominent citizen. Sounds like an internal problem for Carthage."

"I once thought just that," Hadrian said, then shrugged. "But, as you said, I have to rethink my world. What if our problems started here?" After a moment he added, "How would you even know Beck was a prominent citizen?"

"Old wizards cast long shadows." Sauger signaled to the red-haired woman. She picked up a leather pouch and walked toward them.

The woman dropped the pouch by Sauger, who shoved it toward Hadrian. He opened it. Inside were four cans of chicken soup.

"What price do I put on such treasures?"

His host smiled again. "A gift. Always a pleasure to connect a man to something he will truly appreciate."

"Would that all your prisoners got such treatment."

Sauger shrugged his broad shoulders. "You saw the boy enjoying our bounty. Let's call it two out of three."

The tavern keeper held him with a steady gaze but Hadrian didn't miss Sebastian's glance toward the door behind which the blond woman kept disappearing. Hadrian lifted his glass. "To bigger worlds," Hadrian toasted. Sauger and Sebastian tapped their glasses to his, then the bartender rose with a raucous laugh and left them.

Hadrian forced himself to drink, slowly but steadily, making sure his escort matched him glass for glass. He challenged the big First Blood to darts, then tipsily missed half his throws. As a fiddler began to play he joined the others in a song, then pulled the redhead from her stool. They began to dance. Her skin seemed to shimmer as he held her close, then he saw that it was covered with Angel Polish, the cosmetic from the Carthage fishery.

A brute of a man in sooty denims cut in on a youth dancing with one of the women. When the younger man tried to reclaim his partner a few minutes later, the bigger man lashed out with a fist, knocking the youth to the floor. As he turned to kick him before he could rise, Hadrian recognized the surly engineer from the *Anna*.

"Tull!" Sauger barked, and pointed to the door outside.

The engineer, clearly drunk, halted, glaring at Sauger, then grabbed a bottle and left the tavern.

As the room began to empty, Hadrian clung to the woman with a drunk's ardor until, with Wheeler nursing a mug in a corner and Sebastian asleep at his table, Sauger whispered to her. She led Hadrian to the side door where all the other women had gone. Slurring his words, Hadrian reminded the woman to bring his precious soup, then followed her into the dim corridor.

He had counted six different women who had gone through the door. As his companion led him into the seventh doorway, Hadrian saw three more rooms before the end of the hall.

His companion disrobed in a quick, professional manner. When she wore nothing but her linen smallclothes, she turned and stripped Hadrian to the waist, hesitating a moment over the soiled bandage on his arm. As she touched his belt he tottered backward, twisting so he landed belly down, face to the wall. She laughed, then hearing his exaggerated snores, poked him several times to no avail.

"You old fool," she groused, then sat on the bed and began to dress. His intemperate habits had left him with a remarkable tolerance for alcohol. He waited several minutes after she left, then rose and began doing push-ups to burn off the liquor in his system.

He estimated it was past midnight when he cracked open the door and peered into the corridor. It was empty. He picked up his leather pouch and stepped to the end of the hall. The last door swung open, releasing a musty smell. The room was stacked with crates. As he touched the handle of the next door, a frightened moan came from inside, followed by the sound of furniture toppling over. The door would not move. He stepped back and saw now the padlock holding the door fast.

Retrieving a lantern from the wall, he went back into the storage room. A quick search revealed an iron bar. Moments later he'd wedged it inside the hasp of the lock, then, with a nervous glance down the hall, he gave a violent shove. The screws popped out of the aged dry wood of the doorframe.

As he stepped inside, a figure scrambled away, dragging a table with her. Hadrian leapt to her, clamping a hand over her mouth. When she fought him he slapped her, then covered her mouth again. "It's me, Jori. Do you hear me?"

The sergeant's chest heaved up and down but she stopped resisting as he held her. Hadrian saw that her hands were tightly bound with a rope tied to an iron ring fixed to the table. He quickly cut the bindings, then, with a sinking heart, saw that the room's window was blocked with bars.

"Can you walk?" he asked.

Her voice was tremulous. "At first they just asked questions, gave me food and drink. But when I didn't give them answers, they came back. They caned me, hit me with switches on my legs and arms."

"You have to be able to walk. Now. I know where the horses are kept. We can be twenty miles away by dawn."

Jori bit her lip, scrubbed the tears from her cheeks, and nodded.

They inched down the hall silently, Hadrian fearing what they would encounter when they reached the tavern. He held a finger to his lips as they reached it, then raised the pouch of cans he still carried like a weapon and pushed the door.

Only three candles burnt now, their light so dim that they were halfway across the room before he saw Wheeler still at the corner table, his head cradled in his folded arms. Jori pointed to another dark shape, on the floor by the stove. Sebastian was curled up near the warmth of the fire.

The sky was brilliantly clear, with the light of a half-moon and the aurora enough for them to navigate through the village. They had perhaps six hours until dawn, but before Hadrian went to the stables he had one stop to make.

The paper maker's shop had no lock on its front entrance, only a padlock on the inner door he'd noted that afternoon. He quickly ripped it away with the iron bar, found a candle, and stepped inside.

The secret workroom was well kept, an unusual levering device anchored to its solitary workbench. His first touch of its handle roused memories of visits to a great-uncle's house as a boy. The uncle had been an avid hunter and Hadrian had helped him reload his shotgun shells with just such an instrument.

He pushed the handle down, seeing now the wooden box with the brass bases, a second box with waxed cylinders of the thick grey paper fabricated in the workshop, a third with one of the racks he'd seen in the cache in Carthage, packed with over a dozen loaded shells. He dropped one of the shells into his pocket and quickly examined the rest of the room. There were no pellets, no sign of gunpowder, only one of the small kegs he had seen in the *Anna*, still tightly sealed. He took a step toward it.

"Hadrian, please!" Jori's call was desperate.

He reluctantly stepped away, blowing out the candle as he reached the front entry. Wending their way through the alleys, they soon reached the small paddock adjoining the stable. He paused, watching the stable, seeing no sign of activity.

"We don't need horses," Jori said. Her voice was overlaid with fear.

"And what? Walk for two, maybe three hundred miles? Ten more minutes and we're gone. An hour south of here the heavy forest starts. They won't find us there."

She took a deep breath and nodded.

Jori was surprisingly adept with the animals, calming the two Hadrian led out of their stalls with soft whispers. His heart lifted as he tightened the girth of the last saddle and began tying a blanket behind it. Then suddenly pigeons were startled from their roost at the far end of the building. He tossed Jori a set of reins.

"Go!" he cried. Soft creaks on the floorboards became the pounding of running boots. Standing in the shadows behind the second horse, he swung his pouch of cans. His timing was perfect, hitting the first man squarely in the temple, knocking him to the floor. He jerked the head of the horse around and slapped its hindquarters, sending it toward the other shadowy figures. They would have to make do with one horse.

He began to race out the front doors, leading the horse with Jori already mounted. But half a dozen men leapt in front of them. The horse reared back, throwing Jori off. Strong hands seized his arms. A sack was thrown over his head.

HIS HEAD LAY against the surface of a table, facing a window six feet away. His eyes fluttered open and shut. He smelled eggs and bacon and cigar smoke. The sky was showing a hint of dawn. He did not stir, did not know if he could stir, just watched the stars fade into the greyness. His own light was fading. He was being pulled into a hole in the sky and didn't want to come back.

"No!" he moaned as frigid water suddenly drenched his head. He jerked up, his skull exploding in pain. Slowly he turned, taking in his surroundings. Jori was tied to a chair in the corner just behind him, her mouth gagged. Four men sat at the opposite end of the table, empty breakfast plates in front of them. Sauger, Sebastian, Fletcher, and Wade. Their faces were impatient.

"Last night when I went to sleep, I felt such hope, Boone," Sauger began. "But then I had to start my day with such disappointment."

"Am I to take it you are the leader of this town that needs no government?" Hadrian asked. His head throbbed terribly.

"Like I said, we all must accept the role allotted to us," Sauger said. "You might call me abbot of the order of St. Gabriel."

"Or boss of the criminal enterprise that is St. Gabriel."

Wade glared at Hadrian, then muttered something into Sauger's ear, who held up a restraining hand.

"There you go," he said to Hadrian, "using old world concepts again. Crime is a political construct. When the great khans rolled over Asia, wiping out entire cities, that was not crime to their culture. That was glory, that was destiny being fulfilled. I remember once being hauled in front of a magistrate and fined for not shoveling the snow in front of my house. I said my father had never shoveled that snow for thirty years, and it wasn't a crime then, so why would it be now? He said because the government changed its mind, that's why. That was the disease of the old world. Some crusty bastards sat behind closed doors and decided how I should live my life. Forget the old world. It's gone. Get over it."

"I know a crime when I see one," Hadrian insisted.

"So you declare yourself judge and jury?" Sauger asked in a contemplative tone. "Based on what? Some law no one acknowledges but you? Bullshit. There is only action and reaction. That's the way of nature. When the cougar tries to bring down the stag and gets an antler in his heart, that's not justice, that's the penalty the cougar gambles against for his every meal."

"In other words, if you think you can get away with something, it's worth trying."

"Exactly! If the shifting of the world taught us anything, it was that life is all about the odds, and improving the odds. What were the chances any of us would survive? What were the odds we'd be sitting here today? Where but here could you find such opportunity to improve your life? We offer you fulfillment." Sauger's smile remained but his eyes grew icy cold. "So intimate with the inner workings of Carthage but no reason to be loyal to her. A man interested in reform, much as myself. But last night you jumped the stag and lost. In another month you could have been sitting here, on the most powerful committee in the known world."

"Looks more like a breakfast club that forgot to bathe."

The words brought Wade out of his chair. For the first time, Hadrian saw a gun in front of Sauger. Jori's pistol. The abbot of St. Gabriel touched it. "I'm not going to tell you again, Wade."

"The bastard killed my nephew!"

Hadrian stared at him, confused. "I had nothing to do with the boy brought to the hospital," he said.

Wade fixed him with a venomous gaze.

"I believe," Sauger explained in a level tone, "our friend is referring to the one you killed at my table during your escape last night."

Something icy gripped Hadrian's spine as he recalled the salvager, the one he'd recognized as an original crew member from the *Anna*. "Wheeler was asleep with his head on the table when we passed through," he said hoarsely.

Sauger wiped his mouth with a napkin and gestured Hadrian up. Hadrian rose, steadying himself against his dizziness for a moment, then followed him out the door. They stepped directly into the tavern, where a blanket had been thrown over a figure at the corner table. As

Sauger pulled the blanket away from Wheeler, Hadrian nearly retched. One of the silver forks he'd seen the night before had been driven into the back of Wheeler's neck, up into his brain.

"A careful piece of work," Sauger said in an admiring tone. "But the wrong fellow to kill. Wade is Fletcher's man, and this one was Wade's nephew. We promise his men our protection when they come here. This one was in training, so to speak. Fisherman. Death Digger. Familiar with the streets of Carthage. Proven reliable for special tasks, lots of potential. When Wade first arrived at our little breakfast, I had to restrain him from driving a fork into your head as you lay there."

"Someone didn't want me to speak with him. He was from the *Anna*."

"Fletcher claims you're trying to topple his operation in Carthage."

"His operation is your operation."

Sauger shrugged. "Our alliance is only recent. He has a lot invested in Carthage, over many years. We've just broadened his ambition, so to speak. Merged our business plans. Adjusted expectations."

"I wondered why fishermen would use jackals as their symbol." He gestured to the stuffed martens on the walls. "It was your gang. You just gave Fletcher a franchise."

"You grieve me, Hadrian. You are deep, you are educated. I can speak with you like I can't with the others. We could decide together what to do with your governor. Perhaps make you his successor. You could have had such influence at my side."

"I don't do well at anyone's side."

Sauger ignored him. "I think events may persuade you to reconsider. It will cost me dear to save you. Otherwise, Fletcher will have to kill you, to keep his men in line. If not here, then in Carthage. It won't go easy for you. Wade would like nothing more than to find you some night and have you held down while he hammers a fork into your head. Most likely through an eye, slowly twisting it, to hear you scream. Cruel sons of bitches, those fishermen. Even when I fix things, they won't accept you at our table now."

Sighing, Sauger waved Hadrian away, not bothering to cover the body again. Hadrian bent over Jori before retaking his seat. Her eyes were puffy but her cheeks were dry. She had no more tears left.

Sauger had the air of a judge when he spoke again. Sebastian stood solemnly behind him, like a bailiff. "I think," he said slowly, "perhaps the only real crime is that committed by those who fail to use their given talents to the maximum." He silenced a growl from Fletcher, not with a command but with a glance at Sebastian, who put a restraining hand on the captain's shoulder. Sauger studied first Hadrian, then Jori for a long time, before rising and gesturing Fletcher and Wade to follow him back into the tavern.

When they returned the two fishermen were subdued. Sebastian brought in a tray of bread and hot tea, which he set by Hadrian before untying Jori. Joining Hadrian at the table, she began eating, not daring to look at the men at the other end.

"There is a run across to Carthage tonight," Sauger declared. "You will be deposited near town, free to return to whatever you wish. One last chance, we'll call it. Fletcher and Wade will have little jobs that you will perform. If Fletcher sees one more policeman at the fishery than normal, senses the presence of any detective, he will find you and kill you both. If Buchanan tries to take action against him without advance warning from one of you, I will not be able to save you. As long as you cooperate, you'll have Fletcher's protection. Prove your value, and in a few months we may add to your responsibilities. Great opportunities lie ahead."

Hadrian emptied half his mug, then silently returned the tavern keeper's stare.

Sauger nodded at Jori. "Although you are welcome to stay." He slid a small tin down the table toward her. "Your charms would be most valued."

She stared silently at the container with its familiar label. Angel Polish.

For some reason Hadrian began leaning forward. His head was growing heavy. "Buchanan will throw me in a cell again. I left when Nelly escaped. He will assume I was behind it."

"Excellent. A few days will give you time to contemplate the new world order. But you have always somehow dealt with Buchanan. And," Sauger added pointedly, "prison bars will not stop Fletcher from reaching you if he needs to kill you."

Hadrian's head began to drift down toward the table. He looked over and saw Jori slumped by the plate of bread. The tea had been drugged.

"Sounds too much like the old world order," he said, though he never knew if the words made it out before he lost consciousness.

CHAPTER *Nine*

THEY WERE IN the hold of the *Anna* again, although this time with the cover off and a ship's ladder braced in the opening. Jori was slumped, unconscious, against the opposite bulkhead as Hadrian awoke. He splashed bilge water on his face, then rose and unsteadily climbed the ladder.

The little steamer was building speed, away from the setting sun, into the bite of a cold northeast wind. The St. Gabriel harbor was a mile behind them. He gulped the chill air, shaking the fog from his head, then made his way to the cabin where the helmsman stood. The face of the man at the wheel was in shadow but as Hadrian stepped to the steam pipe that provided heat for the cabin, he leaned over the compass. The hooded lantern over the instrument gave off only a dim light, but it was enough. Fear crept up his spine. It was Wade.

"Slept off your St. Gabe hangover I see."

Hadrian was somehow more disturbed by the bully's level tone than he would have been by a random punch. He retreated and made his way to the small figure huddled in a blanket in the lee of the cabin, watching the smoke etch a purple line across the dusk.

"We're making stars!" Dax exclaimed. The boy pointed to the sparks rising out of the smoke funnel. "Ain't she fast!"

"The *Anna* was always the quickest," Hadrian said as he squatted by the boy. "Faster than she needed to be. The later models had a broader beam, with more power geared to haul nets. She was one of a kind. When I heard she'd gone down in a storm I felt a great sadness." As he spoke he looked to the southeast toward a heavy bank of cloud. In the daytime the *Anna* would be conspicuous in Carthage waters. He did some rough math. It would be well over a hundred miles on a direct course cutting across the inland sea, a harsh, hot run for the steamer to make before dawn. Yet it was possible so long as they did not encounter too strong a headwind and if Wade knew the course, a challenge in the night under cloud cover. Then he recalled the predawn rendezvous routinely arranged by the smugglers. They'd made the surreptitious trip many times before.

He wandered down the short companionway that led to the compartment that functioned as galley and bunkroom to discover Scanlon sitting at the table.

"This ain't your stateroom, Boone," he growled in warning. The hand that clasped a steaming mug had a bandage around it, stained pink. The stump of his finger still oozed blood. Hadrian retreated to the stern deck, stacked now with a fresh load of wood that included six-foot-long logs not yet cut for the boiler's firebox. Climbing the stack, he confirmed that along the stern hung a sturdy little skiff, then collected an armload of wood and descended into the engine room.

The broad-shouldered man at the engine was Tull, the engineer who had been ejected from the tavern the night before. He acknowledged Hadrian with a surprised scowl, then gestured for him to drop his load onto the small pile of wood by the bulkhead. Hadrian did so, then took another step. But as he approached the boiler, the engineer lashed out with the poker he used to stoke the coals, blocking his path, the red-hot tip of the poker embedding in a slab of firewood. Two inches closer, and it would have impaled Hadrian.

He threw his hands up in mock surrender. "I know the man who built this engine," he said in a loud voice over the noise of the machine. "He was always very proud of it." It was all the explanation of his interest in the engine he would offer, and his quick glance was enough to confirm that he still recalled the placement of its regulators and shut-off valves.

"There's logs topside," Tull shouted over the engine noise. "They didn't have time to cut everything before we sailed." There was a strange light in his eyes, a look of amusement that chilled Hadrian. "I was gonna tell the boy to do it, but your back is stronger. There's a saw."

Hadrian gave an exaggerated nod and climbed back up the ladder. He took his time, slowly slicing up the first log as he considered the words of Sauger, the expressions of Fletcher and his men when Sauger had pronounced his verdict, then contemplated the boat and the men running her. The uncut logs meant Sauger had lied. No voyage had been planned for that night.

He had begun a second log when Scanlon emerged to join Wade in the wheelhouse. Hadrian darted into the little kitchen, located the expected kettle of hot water, and poured a mug of tea.

Moments later he was holding the tea in front of Jori, who groggily sipped it, then, reviving, gratefully cupped her hands around the warm mug.

"We're on the way to Carthage," he confirmed.

She greeted the news with a frown and stared into the shadows.

"Kenton won't care about any of this," she said after a long silence. "He won't believe it. All that will matter is that I left the colony without his permission. He'll throw me off the force," she predicted.

He did not reply, did not know how to reply. "I'm sorry," he said at last.

"I'm young. My mother runs a business weaving rugs and blankets. She always wanted me to join her."

"I don't think you understand, Jori. They don't mean to deliver us to Carthage."

"But I heard them. You were there."

"It's their way of keeping us cooperative. Just like they drugged us so we couldn't argue, couldn't resist. The only two people in all the world who seem interested in stopping them are you and me. One of the men entrusted to take us across is Wade, who is certain I killed his nephew. Another is Scanlon, who had a finger shot off by you."

Jori responded with a chiding look. "You always have to be melodramatic about things. They would never go to all this trouble. Sauger promised. He struck a deal with Fletcher. Fletcher wants us as his damned slaves, but we'll be alive."

Hadrian wanted to grab her by the shoulders, to shake her, to shout that Sauger could not be trusted, that he knew in his bones they had at most a few hours to live. But as she returned his gaze he could not find the courage to do so.

He sat down beside her. "Tell me about your mother," he said.

After a long silence, during which she gave him a worried glance, Jori spoke about a loving, always weary woman, a survivor who'd arrived early in the formation of the colony, given birth to five children in the five years thereafter, losing two as infants. Her bedtime stories were always thinly veiled descriptions of the old world, and her hobby of weaving had become their livelihood after Jori's father had died.

"Once when I was ten I found her in the middle of the night by the fireplace writing a letter, back when there was no paper at all, when you had to tear pages out of old books and write in the margins. Her fingers were nearly raw from working the loom all day, and I could see the pain the effort caused her. As I watched she finished and folded the letter, then stood on a stool and hid it up under one of the eaves. It took me days to figure out how to get up there but I finally did. There were a dozen letters, all to my father who had been lost on the lake years ago."

Lost on the lake. In the early years most of those who perished in the deep waters were not fishermen. So many had ended their lives by drowning that the words had become another euphemism for suicide. Emily had told him Jori's father was weak, chronically sick, in constant danger of exile. The suicides would take salvaged railroad spikes and stuff them in their belts before stepping off their borrowed dinghies.

"Whenever anyone spoke about my father in the past tense, she would tell them his body had never been found. She was writing as if he were still alive," Jori continued, "as if he had been building a better place for us somewhere and would send for us any day. She would write about us children and everyday life, what we did in school and the scores in my games. She said once that I would make him very proud. It's funny. I might have understood if she wrote in front of us, to let us think he might still live. But she did it all in secret. I never did tell her I knew about them. I would check sometimes. The letters got fewer and fewer. It's been years since she wrote the last one. But they're still there, up under the eaves."

They sat in silence and listened to the rush of water on the other side of the hull, the churning, mesmerizing flood that took them ever closer to their fate. Hadrian rose and peeked through the knothole he'd opened the day before. The little cargo compartment held half a dozen boxes, smaller versions of the one they'd found hidden in the smugglers' loft.

"I used to wonder about you when you came to our classes and talked with us. No one ever knew about your family. You must have had a family."

Hadrian stared into the darkness. "There was a dog," he offered at last. "It was a few weeks after we began work on the colony. A little grey terrier, not much bigger than a squirrel. But she was tough as nails. Found her in the forest living on mice. There was a little cave where I made her a bed of cedar boughs. Couldn't bring her back or she would've been thrown in the stewpot. I would keep back some of my rations in a scrap of cloth and visit her every couple of days. It would be like a little picnic. We'd play and she would lick my face and curl up beside me for a nap after eating.

"One day I brought her some venison for a special treat. It was starting to get cold. I wanted her to build her strength for the winter. She ate and curled up on my chest and I was singing a lullaby to her. I never should have brought her anything with so much fresh blood in it. I shouldn't have sung the song or I would have heard it creeping up."

"It?"

"A tree jackal. His winter was coming too. There was just a blur of movement and she was gone. He carried her high up a tree. She was screaming for five minutes before she finally died."

Without a word Jori rose and settled at the opposite end of the hold.

Hadrian gazed without focus into the shadows, numb to the cold and the lurching of the boat.

Suddenly his knee exploded in pain. Jori was back, bracing herself on a beam as she kicked him. "To hell with you!" He could see streaks of tears down her cheeks. "To hell with your dead family! I'm sick of all you damned survivors! We're nothing to you! To be real in your world, you have to be dead! We're just shadow people! We never count for any-thing. The only real people to you are in your nightmares. Nothing we do matters! We just playact for you, keep you alive so you can wallow in your grief. Screw you and screw your old world! Your world is gone. It's never coming back! I am not a shadow, Hadrian Boone! And I don't live in a shadow world, you do!" She kicked him again and was gone.

When he returned to cutting logs again, he carried several loads, then crept into the companionway to the galley and opened the small locker there. He quickly studied its contents. Needles and cord for patching nets. A hammer. A coil of rope. He grabbed the hammer and rope, then quickly hid them behind the firewood at the stern.

The increasingly cold wind kept pushing the *Anna* off her course. Wade was fighting the helm when Hadrian ventured inside the wheel-house, basking in its warmth for a moment. "I know this boat," he said. "Let me relieve you."

"Why would I do that, schoolteacher?"

"I want to get to Carthage as fast as you do. You need some food."

"Scanlon's in charge of the galley." As the big man shifted on his feet, Hadrian saw a sawed-off shotgun hanging on pegs near the wheel.

"We're both working for Sauger now," Hadrian tried.

A wave violently hit the bow, breaking over the deck. Wade glanced at the compass, then reached into his pocket for his tobacco plug and bit off a piece.

"You're a horse's ass, Boone. No one works directly for Sauger or Kinzler except Fletcher and Shenker. I work for Fletcher. And you're on my crew now. I think when we get home, you can live behind my shit-house. I'll have you clean my spittoon and chew book pages to soften them before I wipe my arse."

"I guess I underestimated you, Wade. I should have known better, after that magic you worked in prison."

"Magic?"

"The way you were in prison one minute, then suddenly driving the *Anna* away with Nelly and Shenker."

Hadrian had to sidestep as Wade spat tobacco juice in his direction. "You are one dumb fuck. Fletcher said it to Sauger. You're too soft-headed to be useful. No real survival instinct, he said. It's what makes you so unpredictable."

"Maybe it's more like survival isn't my first priority."

Wade gave a snort of laughter. "Exactly," he said, as if his point was proven. He swung the bow into another wave and checked the compass again. "You never understood. You thought I was in prison on account of another knife fight. But I was only there because of you."

"I still don't understand."

"Right. You don't understand shit about the way Carthage works. I was there to keep an eye on you, keep you busy, keep you drunk if need be. Once Buchanan released you, there was no need for me to stay."

"You mean one of the guards in the prison is a jackal."

Wade laughed so hard tobacco juice dripped down his beard. "You never will understand."

Hadrian made his way to the hold and found a corner where he could sit and brace himself against the pitching of the boat. He sat in silence, trying to sleep, but overtaken by new questions and fears. Wade was right. He was too softheaded to understand how Sauger and his league of criminals thought. He stared into the darkness. Snowflakes started tumbling through the open hatch.

She appeared before him again, wrapped in a blanket.

"I'm sorry, Jori," he said before she could speak. "I don't mean you to be a shadow."

"I'm cold," she said, then settled beside him, covering him with part of her blanket.

"Is it true what Emily said?" came Jori's voice after a few minutes.

"What she said?"

"Is it true the ending of the first world was your fault?"

His torrent of emotion broke through. It came out as a groan of pain, but after a moment all he could do was laugh.

He slept and woke to find Jori's head on his shoulder. The hold was filled with moonlight, and the worst of the storm seemed to have passed. He sat very still, feeling the cadence of her breathing against his body, daring to touch a strand of her hair that hung across his chest. He felt his strength returning, his mind clearing. He gently leaned her against a beam and climbed out onto deck. For once survival was going to be his first priority.

When he returned to the engine room he found Tull had made a little nest in the firewood and seemed to be nodding off. He studied the engine once more, and as he returned to the deck a hand reached out of the darkness.

"Dax says we can have soup in the galley," Jori announced. "Scanlon is back in the wheelhouse with the captain."

Hadrian sat in silence at the galley table. The fish chowder was hot and plentiful and he emptied two bowls before looking up to see his companions staring at him. As he pushed the bowl toward Dax for a refill he noticed the boy's pained expression.

"What is it, Dax?"

The boy did not reply but took the bowl and refilled it.

"At St. Gabriel when I saw you in the kitchen," Hadrian said, "they had hit you. Why?"

Dax frowned. "I asked Scanlon if they were his tools at the saw pit. That's all. He didn't take kindly to it, said that's no way to get the secret."

"Secret?"

"You know. I told you about them ghosts."

Hadrian stared at him in confusion. Dax had never explained why he was not interested in crossing over, even while helping others do so. "My God, Dax," he said with a shudder. "You mean the secret of how to die and come back. There isn't any. They don't do it."

Dax frowned again, clearly not convinced. At least he wasn't ready to die. He stared at Hadrian expectantly. When Hadrian did not speak, he glanced nervously at the companionway.

"The skipper came in a while ago," Dax explained. "I said we might have a job of it, watching for that little lantern in this weather. He cuffed me in the ear. But then he calls me to his side and apologizes. Says when we get back he will have me made a full jackal for all my brave work. He says at every ceremony new jackals get a new knife and a silver statue." Dax searched Hadrian's face as if for an answer. "But there ain't no knives and statues. Wade don't know I watch those ceremonies, from the window on the roof of that house by the harbor the jackals use. Why would the scrub lie? And that Scanlon, he has a gun in his belt. The sergeant's gun. Why does he need that?"

The color drained from Jori's face.

Hadrian glanced at the galley hatch, expecting one of the crew to burst in at any moment. Then he spoke in low, urgent tones. "You have to stay awake, both of you, and stay together. Don't drink or eat anything they give you. It's a game they're playing, to keep us from resisting." The real game, Hadrian now realized, was between Sauger and Fletcher. Sauger had exaggerated his interest in keeping Hadrian and his friends alive as a bargaining chip, so Fletcher would be indebted to him when he'd finally consented to Fletcher's demand for revenge. "They don't mean for us to make it to shore. But they can't afford to take the time to stop out in deep water, especially in this weather. When I come to you, you must both be ready and do exactly what I say. No questions. No talking. Do you understand?"

Jori nodded stiffly. Dax, casting confused glances at each of them, finally shrugged. "Okay. Sure."

The swells had begun to subside and the sky had cleared by the time Hadrian finally glimpsed the thin line of darker shadow along the southern horizon. Carthage was visible in the distance, not because of its dim lights but due to the threads of silvery smoke rising into the starlit sky.

He retrieved the rope and hammer, then quickly tied the rope to the bow of the skiff before lowering the boat and tying it to the stern rail.

"In five minutes," he explained to Dax as he descended into the hold, "you must go to the engine room and tell Tull the skipper says it's time to get some breakfast before reaching shore. When I leave, count to three hundred, slowly, then go to him. Scanlon is asleep on a bunk in there. Don't wake him." He turned to Jori. "You need to get past the wheelhouse without Wade seeing you, then after Tull goes into the galley, make your way to the stern."

The engineer was dozing again as Hadrian brought his last load of wood. He quickly slipped into the shadows past the pile of firewood and stretched out in the darkness. Moments later Dax called down as instructed. Tull groggily rubbed his eyes then climbed up to the deck.

Instantly Hadrian was on his feet, loading the boiler to capacity with oak logs, then grabbing a long bolt from the rack of parts on the wall. He fixed the bolt into the holes of the boiler door handle, pulled the hammer from his belt, and pounded the six inches of bolt that extended below the door latch, bending it at a sharp angle. The door would not be opened again. He turned the air intake to maximum, smashed its handle, then, with a silent apology to Jonah, smashed closed each of the stems that served as relief valves.

The grey light of predawn was edging over the horizon as he found Dax and Jori on the stern deck. Carthage was less than three miles away.

"They mean to kill us," he said to Dax, putting a hand on the boy's shoulder. "When the boat stops offshore they are going to shoot us and dump us into the water." His companions stared at him but said nothing. "We are getting into the skiff and rowing to shore. Dax, when we reach land head toward town and find a hiding place."

"We could overpower them," Jori suggested. "Then take the boat to town."

"We can't overpower those three," Hadrian said firmly. "They have guns. And this boat won't exist in another five minutes. The boiler is going to explode."

Jori seemed to sag. "Hadrian, we'll freeze out on that water," she protested.

"We'll die for sure if we stay," he replied, then pulled on the skiff's line. Dax shook his head uncertainly, then leapt into the small boat.

Jori silently pushed past Hadrian and climbed over the side. Hadrian untied the rope then patted the rail and looked back at the fishing boat. "I'm sorry," he whispered to the *Anna*, then eased over the stern.

"We'll head east, a couple miles above town," he explained as he began rowing. They were barely a hundred feet away from the *Anna* when he heard furious voices. He'd prayed the boat would continue on her course, leaving them behind, but Wade now was shouting frantic orders and the *Anna* was coming about, heading straight for them.

Seconds later the pistol began barking. A splinter of wood exploded inches from his leg.

The rising offshore wind was pushing them toward land but the *Anna*'s bulk meant she was being pushed faster in the same direction as she turned in pursuit. Wade's curses grew louder, interrupted by confused shouts from the engineer. Scanlon emptied the pistol then leapt to the bow and lifted a boathook over his head as the *Anna* closed the gap.

Jori frantically put her hands over his, desperately trying to move the oars faster. Dax stood in the bow, lifting the little anchor as if to throw it at Scanlon, who now bellowed in anger.

A moment later the *Anna* was on them, splintering, then crushing the stern of the skiff, and Scanlon was swinging the hook at Hadrian's head with a furious roar.

Then suddenly the *Anna* and her crew were no more. Hadrian did not remember the sound so much as the abrupt rushing of air and debris, the illusion of a brief but powerful deluge as the shards of the boat rained down around them.

The skiff was gone and he was in the water. His clothes quickly filled and the frigid murk pulled him down. Then a hand gripped him and Jori hauled him onto a large slab of wreckage from the *Anna*. There was no sign of the *Anna*'s crew, only pieces of the hull floating in a circle.

"There!" Jori cried, and pointed to a slender form on another, smaller piece of wreckage, fifty feet away.

"Get to shore!" Hadrian called to Dax, and watched as the boy grabbed a plank from the water and began paddling.

"There's a place I know," he said to Jori as she handed him a plank. "Look for a trail that climbs up between two birch trees. Up to the top of the second mountain."

But as he began to paddle something seemed to seize his arm. His shoulder was stiffening. He felt light-headed.

Jori looked up and gasped. "Your shoulder!" she cried. "There's a piece of wood in it!"

Hadrian found himself sinking onto their makeshift raft, the cold water of the lake washing over his legs now. "Take it out."

"Hadrian, it's too big."

"Take it out!" he shouted.

Jori bent over him and pulled.

Only then did the agony fully hit Hadrian. He had a vague sense of her showing him a long splinter as wide as his thumb, then began to taste the salt as his blood mixed with the water washing over their fragile craft.

He tried to rise, to paddle again, ignoring Jori's cries for him to stop, but his strength was gone. He found himself lying on the broken hull as it was tossed by the waves. It began snowing again. A new storm, a freezing storm, was arriving. He closed his eyes, choking every few moments on water and blood, the fire of the pain so severe now it began to banish the terrible cold. He was weak, too weak to move. It had been such a slender hope and in the end all he had done was extend their lives by a few agonizing minutes. The shoreline was still a mile away. He had lost. Wade had been right. He would never understand. He had fought his best and lost. He could never hold on long enough, and when he slipped off the wreckage he would sink forever into the frigid, endless blackness below.

CHAPTER *Ten*

*P*AIN AND FEVER were his world. Hadrian hurt so much, and burnt so hot, he knew nothing beyond nightmarish images and sounds. Dax looked up with him with dead, drowned eyes from the surface of the water. Carthage was being consumed in flames. He was in the fishery being lowered into the maw of one of the chopping machines. Jonah, grey-skinned from the grave, chastised him for wasting his life. Nelly's body swayed in the wind as it dangled from a gibbet. Missiles were dropping on the school of his children.

Cries of anguish roused him from unconsciousness. He fell on a steep, icy trail. Snow packed into his ears. His eyelids were freezing shut. He realized the cries were his own just before he passed out again.

He became distantly aware of blasts of frigid air, of a dark beast nuzzling and sniffing him, of great crackling fires and bitter tastes on his tongue, and always the painful throbs from his shoulder, stabbing like knife blades. Consciousness danced just beyond his reach, never fully touching him but eventually letting him linger in a warm, dark place.

Then suddenly he was awake, gripping the thick beaver pelt blanket that covered him. The walnut-colored face nodding at him was illuminated by a single candle.

"How did you find me?" Hadrian asked in a voice he didn't recognize.

"Not me. She didn't know exactly where she was going when I heard her shouting, pulling you up the trail in the ice storm." His old friend Morgan turned to let him see Jori wrapped in a shawl on the hearth of the big stone fireplace. "Stayed by you all this time, nigh two weeks, breaking down into tears the first days. Helen had to slip hellebore in her tea just to get her to sleep."

A hand reached out from over the black man's shoulder, searching for him. It took all Hadrian's strength to reach up and squeeze it. "You gave us such a fright," the blind woman said. Helen bent and pulled the heavy pelts over Hadrian as his head rolled back in exhaustion.

In the night, Jori was sitting on a stool beside him, watching him.

"Why?" Hadrian asked. "You could have left me to die in the storm and gone back to Carthage."

The question seemed to bring anger to the sergeant's eyes. "I didn't do it for the self-loathing bastard I know, I did it for the man who long ago brought baby raccoons to my classroom and read Longfellow to us." She roughly pushed his hand back into the blankets as he reached out to touch her arm.

The next day he was able to sit up, even reach the table where Helen was ladling out bowls of hot pumpkin soup.

"Sergeant Waller says people are trying to kill you." Morgan shook his head, looking grave.

Hadrian gazed around the snug subterranean home the couple had made more than twenty years earlier. When Helen had started going blind, they had been marked for expulsion from Carthage, but he and Jonah had hidden them, then helped them escape into the steep eastern mountains.

The smell of Helen's bread in the oven almost made him weep.

"Perhaps I could just live here a few years," he said with a melancholy grin. It was the most remarkable habitat he had ever known, two adjoining caves cleverly closed off from the outside with stones and mortar to blend with the cliff face, with access to gardens and stables on the ridge above them through shafts and stairs cleverly utilizing a network of sinkholes. He looked down at Jori's sleeping form by the fireplace. "Has she been farther in?" he asked.

Helen gave a knowing smile. "No one stays unless Aphrodite approves," she reminded him.

Morgan extended one arm to steady Hadrian, then picked up a candle and led him down a tunnel into a musky chamber at the rear. The caves had been empty during the summer Morgan had found them. By the time their proprietor had shown up for hibernation, the two humans had settled in and were not inclined to move.

Hadrian did not approach the ragged old she-bear, who watched him groggily as he knelt several feet away. Aphrodite, on a thick bed of cedar boughs, was preparing for her six-month sleep. The standoff when the bear had first returned to her cave had been stressful, but Helen and Morgan had resolutely claimed the outer cave and eventually Aphrodite had decided there was room to coexist. Since then, the three had become faithful companions.

"She recognized you," Morgan explained, "even came over and licked you when she woke up that first day. Jori almost lost her wits but eventually she let the old girl smell her."

Once Jonah had commented to Hadrian that visiting their old friends Morgan and his sightless wife was like walking into a fairy tale.

"Exactly!" Morgan had exclaimed when Hadrian repeated the words. "Which gives me hope for all else."

"You need to get her back," Hadrian said, still looking at the bear. "Jori could find a way to be safe, once she's with the police again."

"No," came Helen's thin voice. Hadrian turned to see her at the chamber entrance. "She's not ready. She is terribly disconnected."

"Disconnected?" Hadrian asked.

"We speak sometimes. Everything she's been through—in both Carthage and the north—has shattered her view of the world. She's lost her anchor."

"Anchors are luxuries we've learned to live without."

"Don't talk foolishness, Hadrian Boone. And don't speak so harshly of that wonderful girl. She practically died saving your life. She wouldn't take care of herself until she knew you would recover. You damned fool, you are becoming her anchor."

As Morgan turned and left the chamber with his wife, Hadrian lingered. The weary old bear opened an eye and stared in reproof at him.

THE NEXT DAY as Jori slept Hadrian joined Morgan in the chores on top of the ridge. As soon as they left the cavern behind, he asked his friend about the message from Jonah left by Dax at the trailhead.

"I was hoping for some news from one of you," Morgan said, "but that was not so much a message as a shopping list. Plants. Hard-to-find herbs."

"Plants for what?"

"No idea. Jonah was always experimenting. I spent most of the week looking for them but I was glad to do it, after all you and he had done for us." Morgan handed Hadrian a narrow spade and pointed to a row of onions.

Hadrian remembered a lively barnyard, with goats, roosters, and hens in pens along the rough palisade wall that kept predators out. As they pried onions from the frost-heaved ground, Hadrian paused to study the empty pens. "You've reduced your livestock," he observed.

"As a gentleman farmer," Morgan grinned, "Helen always said I was more of a gentleman than a farmer. I can reach the outermost farms in an hour. They are always ready to trade produce for pelts or fresh game."

Now there were no roosters and only two old milk goats. "Helen always loved those cocks," he recalled.

"Too loud," Morgan muttered.

He lowered his bucket of onions. "You mean you're back to hiding your life here?"

"Life moves on. Things change everywhere. You wouldn't be here otherwise."

Hadrian stepped closer and put a foot on the shovel Morgan was using. "What happened?"

"Nothing. We are survivors. The roosters made a grand stew. The other goats are enjoying their freedom in the high peaks."

"What happened?" Hadrian repeated.

Morgan looked out toward distant clouds. "It was over six months ago. I was hunting, tracking a big stag for a couple hours, getting closer to the settlements than I usually like to go, when I heard a terrible screaming. I ran to help but when I saw the men I dropped behind a stump and pulled out my binoculars. Six of them, plus the poor soul they had tied to a log. They were slicing him like he was side of beef, using a huge knife cut down from a sword." Morgan paused, clearly unsettled by the memory.

"The Dutchman? You saw them kill the Dutchman?"

"You forget how many years we've been gone, Hadrian. I don't know many faces, or names, from the colony. It was the one with the big farm off to the south who raised racehorses."

"The Dutchman they called him. Van Wyck."

"Van Wyck," Morgan repeated. "He didn't die well. For a moment I was ready to charge them but there was no saving him by then. And those bastards would have done the same to me if they caught me watching."

"Were there others being tortured? Or just Van Wyck?"

"As I watched they brought up two men, well-dressed townsmen, with their hands tied. They forced those two to watch. I didn't dare move for fear of being seen."

"Did you see the martens come?"

Morgan looked at him in surprise.

"I was there last month when they found the body. I saw the signs of martens."

The memory clearly chilled Morgan. "The piranhas of the forest."

Hadrian looked back around the barnyard. "But that was many miles from here."

"We're only ten miles from his farm. Van Wyck's farm. Even closer to the trail taken by the riders."

"I don't understand."

"They started staging out of his farm after that day. Like salvage patrols. Every week now."

"Salvage parties have been riding out of Carthage for years."

"Not like these. And salvage patrols go out with empty pack-horses. These horses always carry heavy loads. They're tough, heartless-looking bastards, some of the same men who killed that Dutchman. If they caught wind of Helen and me, we wouldn't last five minutes. They'd take everything." One of the rooms in the burrowed labyrinth was Morgan's secret vault, his personal warehouse of salvage, mostly nineteenth-century mechanical devices. They would be nearly priceless in the salvage markets.

"Helen knows?"

"She seldom goes beyond the gardens now. No need for her to know what I saw. She believes the goats escaped and the roosters were taking too much of our hard-won grain."

"You know the land as well as any salvage rider. Where are they going?" Morgan himself had led several salvage expeditions out of Carthage in the early years and still did his own searching for his personal collection.

"The area's stripped bare for a hundred miles to the south. I followed their trail once for a few hours. They circled to the west, far enough south to avoid the exile camps. And they never return this way. They start in Carthage, to get supplies, then they must take a circuit that comes back up to the lake to the west, to minimize their being seen. Like they fear having their secret work discovered."

"I want to see them, Morgan," Hadrian told him.

"Leave them be, Hadrian. You're in no shape to deal with men like that. You need two or three weeks more rest at least. Helen's been smiling like a schoolgirl because she thinks she has the two of you for the winter."

"Just a look."

"You're the one who gave up on saving worlds," Morgan pointed out. His tone was suddenly sharp. "Gave up on everything else as far as I can tell."

His words brought a long, troubled silence.

"There is one thing I never gave up on," Hadrian said at last. "Jonah. In life or death. I intend to find his killer if I have to die doing so."

They gathered the rest of the harvest without speaking. Before they slipped down the ladder that led into the caves, Morgan stopped Hadrian with a hand on his shoulder. "Just don't forget that Jonah never gave up on you."

"What are you saying?"

"The only thing worse than dying in pursuit of his killer would be using his murder as an excuse to die."

As Hadrian gained strength, Jori lost it. His recovery had released something inside her, Helen insisted, had allowed her to surrender to the fatigue that had wracked her body while she kept vigil over him. For reasons he could not fathom, Helen had taken the sergeant into the bedroom, tossing out extra fur blankets for Morgan to sleep by Hadrian at the hearth. She stayed beside Jori for hours, wiping her fevered brow, feeding her thin broth while speaking her healing words.

Hadrian lost himself in Morgan's collection of books, sitting by the fire for hours at a time as winter storms swept over the mountains, soaking up histories of ancient empires. When he wasn't reading, he was playing chess and cribbage with his friend or helping him recondition his old machines. As they set the board for a new chess game one afternoon, Morgan pressed him for further details of Hadrian's discoveries since Jonah's murder.

"It doesn't matter how many shotguns they have," his friend observed as he raised a pawn. "They are so far outnumbered they could never take Carthage by force. It's a sham, a red herring. Like that robbery."

"Robbery?"

"A spice and herb shop was held up by two men with shotguns. They took all the spice, all the money. The owner is in the hospital with a wound on his arm." His friend rose and retrieved a newspaper dated nearly three weeks earlier. "A farmer gave this to me when I was trading for some of his honey."

Hadrian scanned the article. Its tone was alarmist, speaking of firearms being used in crime for the first time ever, calling for the police to be armed now.

"They wrecked the shop with clubs, fired their guns only once, at the front window," Morgan explained. "The owner got hurt because he ran in front of his window trying to save it. The editors want the police turning the city upside down for an armed criminal gang. Hell, those masked men were on the way out of Carthage five minutes after the crime."

"Masked?"

Morgan turned the paper around so he could read it and pointed to it. "A witness's account. They wore masks over the top of their heads, covering everything from the nose up. The witness said at first he thought they were actors going to a rehearsal of some new drama."

Hadrian frowned. "It *is* theater. A well thought-out script penned by a man named Sauger. He understands all the elements of drama. Build from one crisis to the next. Throw in some distracting characters. Keep up the tension so no one has time to anticipate the plot. What Buchanan doesn't realize is that they know what he'll do at every step. He manipulates the newspaper, but Sauger manipulates him." He looked up at his old friend. "They had plenty of ammunition but didn't use it. If the guns are just props in their play, why go to all the trouble of smuggling in so much ammunition?"

"If it's a play, maybe the ammunition is a prop too."

Hadrian's expression changed from uncertainty to worry as he recalled how he had seen no gunpowder in the shop where the shells were produced.

"If I wanted the police to spend their time looking for an arsenal while I was actually up to something else," Morgan observed, "I just might want to make a public display of that arsenal. Hell, half the force would be too scared to look if they think the criminals are the ones who stole all their shotguns. I suspect the people who conceived this drama like surprise endings."

Hadrian rose and stepped to a small pile of clothes, the ones he had been wearing on the *Anna*, now folded on a shelf. Helen had stacked all his belongings along the wall. Pencil stubs. His knife. Pen nibs. Under his bandana, now neatly washed and folded, was the shell he had taken in St. Gabriel, its waxed paper casing worn but still stiff. He handed it to Morgan, who balanced it on his palm, then pressed at its sides before producing a long blade and prying up one of the flaps compressed on the top.

Hadrian's heart skipped a beat as his friend tapped the opened shell over his palm. The powder that poured out was white. It glowed ominously in the firelight. They stared at it in silence.

"If this is as powerful as you say," Morgan said, "it's a whole lot more effective than bullets at subduing a population. Not only does anyone who uses it become your slave, they pay you for the privilege."

Hadrian rubbed some of the powder between his fingers. Jansen's fingers had been coated with such powder. He had assumed the policeman had been investigating the smuggled spices before he died.

"There must be easier ways to transport it," Hadrian said at last. "Why go to the trouble of making the shells?"

Morgan carefully pressed the top flap back into place and set the shell on the table. "You say this Sauger likes to play with people. He needs the fisherman to do his bidding. They're renegades and ruffians, who despise the government. Smuggling weapons to use against the authorities would appeal to them. Smuggling in drugs that paralyze their children, there's nothing of Robin Hood in that. And what better way to keep the police at bay than feeding the rumors that they will face a barrage of shotguns if they try anything."

Hadrian desperately wanted his friend to be wrong. But he knew in his heart that Morgan had stumbled onto the truth about the shotgun shells and Kinzler's mysterious shipments. "Why couldn't I see it?" he asked in a bitter tone.

"Because part of you wants a rebellion against Buchanan to succeed."

The words scorched a place deep inside Hadrian. Not simply because he knew they were true, but because they meant he too had become a pawn in the conspiracy.

THE FIVE RIDERS appeared an hour after dawn, three leading heavy-laden packhorses and two with rifles slung across their backs, looking like guards. Hadrian, terrified he'd be spotted in his hiding place on the ridge above, cautiously raised Morgan's binoculars. The pair with the guns were large, dark-skinned men who had the feral look of St. Gabriel. He studied them, watching the biggest man, the one in the lead, as he turned in the saddle. It was Sebastian, his escort at St. Gabriel.

He stared in the direction of the party long after they'd disappeared into the forest. At every step there wound up being no answers, only more questions. The secret parties were carrying supplies somewhere, had been doing so for months, with men from St. Gabriel freely moving in and out of Carthage. He thought of his conversations with Sauger, who had seemed to know everything about Carthage, even about the circles of government. And when Buchanan had sent a secret scout to the south, he had been murdered before he even left town.

THE EVENING WAS cold, the air thin and clear. In the distance the lake was shimmering with every color of the spectrum. Hadrian watched from his high rock perch, mesmerized as streaks of sunset combined with a budding aurora to reflect off the newly formed ice.

"You're not staying, are you?" The voice came unexpectedly from the shadows of the trail below, from the short path that led to the cave. Jori didn't wait for an answer. "Helen will be so disappointed."

It was the first time she had ventured out since surrendering to Helen's care. It explained why their hostess had decided to prepare what promised to be a veritable banquet.

"She says to be ready to eat in a quarter hour."

"Come see the sunset," he said awkwardly, and gazed into the shadows a long time before realizing she had gone. "I'm leaving before dawn," he declared toward the empty path. "If I tell them they would only argue and ask why, how I will stay alive. It would spoil our dinner."

But the police sergeant was not at dinner. At the table was a woman Hadrian had not met before. She wore a bright blue dress tied with a yellow sash, her long russet hair hanging loose to her shoulders. There was a golden chain around her neck, and she was wearing elegant shoes made in a different world. They sat across from each other, Jori shy about looking at him. For a moment, as she passed a bowl of potatoes, her face in the candlelight had the glow of the shimmering ice. He found himself blushing for staring at her, then remembered the little tin Sauger had given her. She had applied Angel Polish to her face.

As the venison pie was served, Morgan produced a bottle of elder-berry wine, bartered from a farmer, and the atmosphere softened, punctuated by laughter as Morgan spoke of being treed by a bull moose and other misadventures in the forest. When they finished eating, Morgan asked Jori and Hadrian to move the table along the wall. Disappearing for an instant, he returned carrying a large polished wooden box. He carefully set his treasure on the table, then opened the lid, producing a winding handle that he inserted into a hole in the side and turned. A moment later the box burst into music. Jori gave a gasp of joy and ran to the device, round-eyed.

The old gramophone had only half a dozen original records, all big band music, but Morgan had jury-rigged it to accept the smaller 45 records that he now brought from his secret room, most of them nearly a hundred years old. The mainspring was weak, so someone had to sit beside the machine to wind it every three or four minutes. What poured forth from it was real music, music of a kind Jori had never heard. Morgan began to snap his fingers in time and Jori laughed as Helen raised her arms like wings and fluttered around the room.

Hadrian took over when they changed the record and gestured Morgan to the open floor. He gracefully took Helen's arm and they began a slow dance to a tune from the 1920s.

An enchantment settled over the room. The fire crackled, the aging blind woman and her mate floated across the floor without a care, the notes reaching not just across time but across worlds. Once, in the silence between records, they heard the deep hibernating exhalation of Aphrodite, sounding as if the mountain itself were breathing.

Morgan and Helen at last retreated to the chairs. But not before Morgan pushed Hadrian to his feet. Uncertainly, he approached Jori. With a shy smile she accepted his hand and stiffly began to move in time to the melody. They danced through half a dozen songs before she began to relax, dropping her head on his shoulder. Then Morgan inserted another record, gave the handle an extra wind, and pulled Helen back onto the floor.

As the new music filled the chamber, something within Hadrian cracked open. The notes were cutting through long-hardened calluses inside. It was a song not of his youth but of his mother's youth, a tune she'd played again and again, sometimes dancing alone in the kitchen, sometimes dreamingly grabbing her young son for a partner.

Somewhere beyond the sea, the mellow voice sang.

The voice was not just mellow, it had a confident, unshakable joy, of a sort that had been lost to tongues all these years.

Jori seemed to sense the change in him, and the tightness left her as well. It felt as if they had been dancing like this all their lives. When the record was over she asked Morgan to play it again. Hadrian's hand trembled as he put a finger under her chin and lifted her face. With his handkerchief he began wiping away the Angel Polish.

"I know it's silly. For some reason I didn't want to be me tonight . . ." she murmured, not bothering with the tear that rolled down her mottled cheek. He quieted her with a finger on her lips and gently removed the rest of the cream. Then she pressed closer and they danced.

Somewhere beyond the sea, the lost singer crooned, *my lover stands on golden sand and watches the ships that go sailing.*

Outside, another ending of the world was coming. But here, now, in the fairy-tale lair with the blind woman floating serenely over the floor, the dead singer transporting their spirits, the ancient bear snoring in the next room, for the first time in years something real flickered in Hadrian's heart.

CHAPTER *Eleven*

𝓗ADRIAN WATCHED THE farm for half an hour, waiting as a wagon approached the lanky figure with the ax and dropped its load of logs for splitting into rails. He studied the crudely built tower of logs at the edge of the fields as he waited for the wagon to disappear, then took a step forward and paused. He glanced at the trail behind him, half expecting to see Jori.

He had nearly reached Carthage when she had caught up with him, out of breath.

"You aren't ready for this," he had warned her.

"I'm only panting," Jori replied as she lowered a heavy pack to the ground, "because Helen packed half her larder in here for us."

"I thought I left without waking anyone."

"I don't think she slept at all last night. She can see more than most people with eyes."

He looked at the bulging satchel with a pang of guilt. Morgan and Helen needed all their supplies to get through the winter. "You mean she knew I was going."

"She knew we were *both* going. I told her I thought she would try to persuade me to stay."

"What did she say?"

Jori looked away, color rising in her cheeks. "She said if I didn't go, something inside would always wonder if you'd left just to run away from me."

"Jori . . ." he began. "It could never . . ." His words choked away.

"Never what?" she asked.

He looked toward his own feet, toward a patch of snow, anywhere but toward her. "I am never going to be the man you think I can be."

The silence seemed interminable.

"Promise me to be careful," he said finally. Reaching into his pocket, he extracted the round disc of agate. "This was Jonah's," he told her, pressing it into her hand. "When he had problems to solve, he would rub it. For me, it's become something of a good-luck token."

She offered a stiff nod and buried the stone deep in her own pocket. He lifted the pack to his own shoulder. "You will have to tell them you jumped off the boat, that you were hurt in the explosion and found a cave where you were recovering. You don't know where I am, don't know if I am alive."

He had led her to Jonah's cottage and promised he would return there that night before beginning his slow circuit of the town. He paused only at Dax's mill, but found it empty, with no sign of having been inhabited for weeks.

The young man laboring with the ax stared as if paralyzed when he saw Hadrian. He raised the ax as if defend himself.

"You're dead!" Nash yelled. "Drowned in the lake. They said so in the prison."

"In the prison they believe whatever Kenton tells them," Hadrian said, advancing with his hands raised. "I've always been slow to die."

Nash grabbed the head of his ax and extended it handle first, prodding Hadrian's belly. He limped badly as he walked. "It's really you, Mr. Boone?"

"In the flesh. I had to go away. Now I am back."

A grin overtook the young burglar's countenance.

"What's happening to the farms? What are these towers in the fields?"

"Guard towers. There's been raids. Five, six men at a time, always at night, trying to steal corn, cows, pigs."

"Food?" Hadrian asked. "Is it only food they take?"

"So far. Not much really. They usually get scared away, even though they carry shotguns. But the governor says we must be prepared for anything." As he spoke Nash tugged Hadrian into the shadow of the large beech they stood beside. A group of horseman appeared, moving at a fast trot down the road.

"Armed patrols," he explained. "They've been ordered, day and night, through the farms to the south and west of town."

"You mean Buchanan assumes exiles are doing the raiding."

"It has to be, don't it? There is no one else."

"Did the raiders do that to your foot?"

Nash frowned, then looked uneasily back toward the farmhouse. "Men from the fishery. Wade's men." He limped into the open again, retrieving two wedges for splitting the next rail, then glanced at Hadrian with an apologetic expression. "I promised my mother I'd stay away from townsfolk and their troubles."

"Why would Wade's men break your foot?"

"It was nothing. I can walk."

Hadrian picked up a log and brought it to him. "Maybe I'll stay and help. Maybe I'll go to the house and introduce myself."

Nash winced. "Captain Fletcher wanted something I couldn't give him. He thought I was lying, so he had to be sure."

"Wade is dead, Nash. I killed him. What did Fletcher want?"

The youth's jaw dropped. He stared at Hadrian in disbelief. A woman stepped out of the farmhouse. A wolflike dog darted from her side, loping toward Nash. "A painting," he answered, his tone urgent now. "There was a job last spring. He thought I took a painting when I was there. I told them I never laid a hand on it. I only took little things. Jewelry and silver and such." He looked at the dog, nearly on them now. "Jesus. Go!"

"What kind of painting?"

"Birds. Ducks on a lake."

"So you saw it?"

"Never laid a finger on it. They just kept asking about it. They held me down, used a hammer on my foot. After they broke the bone they decided to believe me."

"Who did lay a finger on it? Who was with you?"

"Please, Mr. Boone. My ma will tell the corps if she sees you."

Hadrian backed away.

"It was ducks," Nash yelled as he disappeared into the shadows. "Big ducks taking off at sunrise."

Hadrian turned northward, the threat of patrols keeping him on game paths, watching so intently in the direction of the road that he failed to notice the ruins until he was upon them. Work crews had built the road spur, continuing for perhaps a week before stopping. They'd made good progress on the footer for the bridge, even sunk two heavy posts and laid the ramp that would channel traffic onto the one-lane structure. But now all was ashes.

Jonah's bridge between worlds had been burnt.

He pulled himself away and climbed the next hill, then up a high ridge along a stretch of cliffs. His melancholy grew as he moved through the gnarled oaks and maples that lined the base of the cliffs, studying the overhanging limbs. With a stab of pain he found what he was looking for, the unmistakable collar of scar left where the weight of a hanging rope once chewed the limb down to raw wood. He had been haunted by Dax's secret map since the day he'd seen it. This would have been the first suicide, a girl of eleven, three years before. *One.*

He walked quickly and found another, then another. *Two* and *three.* In the next quarter mile he found the fourth and fifth, futilely trying to fight his memories, to keep the images from his mind's eye. He'd been at many of the trees before, had cut down the limp bodies of children who had been so sure they could find something better than this world. He had faced so many shrieking, sobbing mothers and brooding, broken fathers that there were entire families who shunned him now.

Hadrian had just found the seventh of the death-scarred trees when he heard an odd metallic rattling. He crouched behind a rock for a moment, remembering the police patrols, then realized the sound came from directly in front of him, in the line of trees. In the direction of the eighth tree, the next circle, an empty circle, on Dax's map. He leapt up and ran, ready once again to act as cheater of death.

So wildly, so irrationally hopeful of saving a life was he that when he finally reached the little clearing a wracking sob escaped his throat and he collapsed to his knees. The rope scar was so fresh sap still dripped from it. A length of rope lay on the ground before him, hacked and tattered in several places where someone seemed to have attacked it. On the end closest to Hadrian was a blood-stained noose.

The metallic noise had stopped. On the other side of the clearing Hadrian now saw a square-built figure in a brown homespun robe, holding an old censer by its chain. When William pushed his cowl back, Hadrian recognized the friar, but it did not seem the monk recognized him.

The sturdy friar stared at Hadrian, disbelieving, then quickly crossed himself.

"They say ghosts congregate here," he said in a tentative voice, "that they float over the ridge and watch the town."

"Maybe when the time comes, I will, old friend," Hadrian offered, "but for now I just stumble along like other mortals."

The monk gave a visible sigh of relief and quickly stepped toward Hadrian, arms open to embrace him. "Just yesterday Emily came to me and asked if I might preside over a memorial service for you at sundown one day this week."

Hadrian offered a sorrowful grin, then pointed to the noose. "Was it a child?"

But his companion seemed not to hear. "Captain Fletcher reported three bodies pulled from the lake, said you were on the same boat, and that your body must have sunk. He has offered to speak at your memorial."

Hadrian looked over the long frozen expanse that was now the lake. Near the harbor a course had been laid out for the iceboats that raced in the winter. "I'm like the fish that keeps getting thrown back in the water. Too tough to eat."

"I should say Carthage is better for it," William offered.

"That, Father, remains to be seen." Hadrian gestured to the noose once more. "A child?"

"Two days ago. The only daughter of a carpenter."

Hadrian looked at the censer, from which fragrant smoke still drifted. "I haven't seen this before."

"We have a new member of our congregation. He comes in once or twice a month. He says he was taught that the soul lingers for a year at the site of the death before passing on to paradise. I found him up here, burning chips of cedar. He said the fragrant smoke would summon in the spirits of the forest to keep the girl company. He said he'd lost a younger sister, and that his uncle had done that for her."

Father William's faith may have been shaken but at least he kept trying. He looked at Hadrian with question in his eye, as if asking for approval. Hadrian slowly nodded. "If we can't help them before they cross over, we should do what we can for them afterward."

William sighed. "The girl was up here last week, skipping rehearsal from some play to help me. She asked for you again, asked if it was true you were dead."

"The governor's daughter? Sarah?"

William nodded. "Tears were in her eyes when I said I thought we had lost you. 'How will we remember who we are?' she said to me. Then she started shaking as if she was sick. I asked if I could help her but she suddenly laughed and ran away."

The monk began his circuit around the clearing again, waving the censer. Hadrian placed his hand on the tree. Once, on a similar visit, Jonah had wondered out loud whether the hanging tree felt the pain of the dead.

"Have you seen anything unusual when you come up here?" Hadrian asked after a long silence.

"More unusual than eight suicide trees?"

The question seemed to weaken Hadrian. He wearily sank onto a boulder. "I told you there would be another. I told you about the map. You saw the secret vault," he said.

"And haven't I come up here every day since, trying to stop the next one." William's voice cracked as he spoke. "But I couldn't be everywhere at once."

Hadrian found himself looking at the wisps of smoke floating in the air. "The one who told you about the smoke. Is he always alone?"

"Sometimes he brings one or two others. Not always the same ones. All tall and dark, long hair."

"Where are they from?"

William hesitated. "They must be hunters. They look at everything with great curiosity, as if they are new to Carthage." He shrugged. "Some of my flock just come for the food we provide after the service. Some like our music. Some like my Latin. Some of them, older ones, say they remember priests when they were young. There's an elderly Jewish man from New York. He's teaching us prayers in Hebrew. We are going to take a group to the gallows."

"The gallows is still up?"

"Still up? Buchanan has improved it, made it permanent. Put a little shelter at the top for the hangman, enclosed the stairway. From a distance it looks like a shrine."

"They burn the bridge and turn the gallows into a temple," Hadrian muttered. "Why would he need it?"

"Why the woman, of course. Jonah's murderer."

"But she's gone, father."

William fixed Hadrian with a troubled gaze. "I'm sorry. I know she was a friend. Though it's never been done before, the governor and the judge said it was perfectly legal."

"Never done what?" Hadrian asked with foreboding.

"Hold a trial without the defendant. She's already been convicted, Hadrian. Condemned to hang. Buchanan announced a bounty on her head. A thousand dollars. More than most in the colony make in a year. He gave a speech on the square and vowed that within twenty-four hours of being brought in she will have the noose around her neck."

THE DECREPIT TWO-STORY building had been built as a stable and hay barn many years before, but the town had overtaken it, leaving it lost in a backwater of warehouses that served the shops on the streets beyond.

The wagon-repair business that operated in the former stable offered no indication of the trade plied within, and its gate could be closed for weeks at a time. When it didn't yield to his push, Hadrian climbed a familiar tree and dropped over the wall that enclosed the compound. A tall, shaggy dog with the look of an elkhound trotted over to him, wagging its tail.

He saw that the white-haired man at the workbench seemed to be having difficulty raising the hammer he was using to flatten a strip of metal. Hadrian dropped one of his colorful maps on the workbench, beside a half-eaten bowl of noodles with chopsticks perched on the rim. The man lowered the mallet, then pushed away the bowl and examined the map with obvious excitement.

"You've been away," he said.

"I always come back," Hadrian replied.

As Takeo Hamada slowly turned his face toward his visitor, his eyes softened, the equivalent of a smile for the stoic Japanese man. The cold cigarette he chewed on took on a jaunty angle.

"I have some questions," Hadrian said.

"Of course you do." Hamada's voice was raspy from years of tobacco. He led Hadrian toward the steep stairs to the hayloft, where all the answers lay, past the stall with a cot where Hadrian had often slept the past summer. At the landing at the top of the stairs he paused to light a lantern, which Hadrian held as he unlocked the padlock on the door.

The loft still held traces of hay but its stacks and bales were all of books. Shelves so high ladders were needed to scale them lined the walls. In the light of a high solitary window, dusty, yellowed stacks towered impossibly tall. Hadrian and Jonah had often sent volumes here for safekeeping. Buchanan tolerated the illegal hoard because it was kept so secret and because he himself sometimes had questions only Hamada's books could answer.

"On the northwest shore there was a convent called St. Gabriel," Hadrian began.

Hamada worked the cigarette between his lips as he contemplated the mountains of books, then pointed toward one of the stacks below the window. He approached it warily, as if the books were living things, and pounced on one at the top of the stack.

It was a regional almanac, a commercial publication with maps and listings of businesses and towns. He quickly thumbed through it, then handed it to Hadrian opened to a two-page map of the northwest shore region sixty years before. Hadrian ran his finger northward along the shore, pausing at a beige patch marked as Blue Thunder First Nation Reserve, then moving onward to the edge of the map. No St. Gabriel.

"Search the town listings," Hamada suggested. "They break out business enterprises and important institutions."

Hadrian consulted the book again and picked out half a dozen candidates based on his rough appraisal of the geography. He took only a few minutes to find the entry, chastising himself for failing to recall that the convent had been converted. The enterprise was called the St. Gabriel Egg Farm. "I need to sit with this," Hadrian said, "go through it in more detail."

Hamada gestured him toward a dusty table bearing numerous stubs of burnt-down candles. "We'll leave you here," the Japanese archivist said, turning with his dog toward the entry.

Hadrian worked his fingertip up the coastline again, this time turning back to read the description of each town as he encountered it, not certain what he was looking for until his breath caught. The entry was for a village called Darby, with a single prominent landmark, a favorite with tourists who had liked to snap photographs in front of it. The Darby Correctional Facility had been built decades earlier, after the design of a famous Scottish castle. *Its classical thick granite walls*, read the description, *give little hint of the cells buried inside.* The walls of the prison had probably been destroyed by blast waves but its deep-set cells would have served as the perfect bomb shelter. Moreover, given its remote location and strong lake winds, the site may have escaped biological contaminants. What had Sebastian said? His people had found the convent two weeks before a band of men in grey clothes from the north had, and they had decided to accommodate each other.

He paged through the book, its advertisements giving glimpses of the first world. Car washes, hamburger joints, computer repair shop, radio stations. He gazed back at Hamada, sitting by the entry with his dog. In earlier years, on days of blizzards, Hadrian and Jonah would find their way here, and all three of them would spend hours beside the potbellied stove, enthusiastically digesting the treasures of the barn. But now Hamada had grown distant, even wary.

Hadrian returned the almanac to its stack and moved slowly toward the door, perusing other titles that had surfaced on the tide of books. *Moby-Dick. America's Favorite Folk Songs. Great Battles of the Civil War.* He paused then turned back.

Hamada did not react when Hadrian set the songbook next to him. "I have an old mule and her name is Sal," he recited.

"I'm sorry?" Hamada said.

"She was here," Hadrian said. "Nelly transcribed that song from this book. The corner of the page is folded down. It would have been a day or two before Jonah died. She and Shenker were staying here, weren't they?"

Hadrian expected a denial. "I don't keep a guest log," Hamada said instead. "You know well enough that anyone interested in my books is welcome to take sanctuary in the stables downstairs."

"And you know very well the owner of that house where they were taken was lying when he said they were there, keeping him against his will."

Hamada stroked his dog's head. "They'd burn us down and not blink an eye," he said.

Hadrian put a hand on the old man's shoulder. "Who is it, Takeo, who is scaring you?" If civilization were a religion, the old man would be a saint. He had suffered much on account of his books.

Hamada's voice was hollow when he finally replied. "We should have taken the books into the mountains years ago, Hadrian. It's too late now."

Hadrian considered his companion's mournful air, then looked about the compound. A member of Hamada's family was missing. "Your other dog. Is she all right?" The two oversized shaggy creatures had been fixtures in their master's life for more than a decade.

The reply was long in coming. "She was gentle as a kitten," Takeo sighed sorrowfully. "Never harmed a soul." He stroked the head of the dog at his feet. "This one will bark at strangers, he's the sentinel. But she would just run and greet them as if everyone was an old friend."

A knot began tying itself in Hadrian's stomach. "What happened?"

"It was nearly three weeks ago. I heard the first cry in the middle of the night. That must have been when they put the first nail through her. By the time I got there they were gone." Hamada whispered now, as if he didn't want the surviving animal to hear. "They nailed her to the gate, then cut her throat."

There was nothing to say. Hadrian offered a match to light Hamada's cigarette. "Takeo," Hadrian said at last, "when I asked for that almanac, you went right to it. It was on top of the pile, yet had little dust on it."

"I went to his funeral, I had to. Wouldn't have missed it."

"Jonah? Jonah used the almanac?"

"He came a few times this past year, usually leaning on a boy like a weary pilgrim. He began to take a special interest in the almanacs."

"You mean he used other almanacs?"

"Last winter he spent a whole day here, looking at maps, cross-checking the almanacs and old business directories." Hamada inhaled deeply on his cigarette and cast a sidelong glance at Hadrian. "You are his executor?"

The question gave Hadrian pause. "I am the closest thing, I guess."

"If you find the one, it goes back here." Hamada's words came out like an order.

Hadrian cocked his head, confused. "Do you mean a book was taken?"

"By mistake, no doubt. Jonah knew the importance of keeping the books together. But he was the only one ever to show an interest in the directories."

"When?" Suddenly Hadrian had the sense of touching something important. "When did it go missing?"

Hamada grimaced. "Last winter, before the Year-End Festival."

"What did it cover? What geography?"

"South and west. The old industrial towns."

"Think, Takeo, old friend. Jonah must have given some hint of why these books were suddenly so important."

"He said his wife once worked at one of those complexes to the southwest. A medical researcher. I thought looking at them somehow made him feel closer to her. I keep my wife's book of favorite poems close to my bed."

"What complex? Surely Jonah wasn't planning to go there?"

But Hamada was done talking. He just shook his head from side to side, then rose and locked the door to the loft before settling back to pet the old dog. He had the expression of a captain who knew he would soon go down with his ship.

The Globe Theater was an over-painted actress, dressed in Victorian style, its ornate woodwork offering a pretense of culture that was well suited to its many productions of Shakespeare and Shaw. Hadrian lingered in the shadows beside the stage as students streamed in for an after-school rehearsal.

A bulletin board beside him held bills for the season's offerings and lists of cast members. Near the top was a faded broadside announcing a lecture Jonah had offered six months earlier. *How Shakespeare Invented the Citizens of Carthage.*

He watched as young actors emerged in costume. Two girls in doublets picked up wooden swords and practiced a duel. A boy passed by wearing the bottom half of a donkey.

Suddenly he was aware of a presence at his side.

"Art thou some god, some angel, or some devil, that mak'st my blood cold?" came the whisper. Sarah Buchanan wore an uncertain grin but fright was in her eyes.

"Not thy evil spirit, Brutus," Hadrian replied without thinking.

"I have heard but not believed the spirits of the dead may walk again," the girl recited.

"You're mixing your scripts, Sarah," he said.

The girl threw her arms so tightly around him he struggled for breath. He pushed her back, holding her at arm's length.

"You were gone," she said in a rush. "People told me you were dead but I didn't believe them. I heard my father speaking to you one night, yelling at you, and ran down to see you. But he was alone, just drunk."

"I've been worried about you, Sarah. Father William is worried about you. I looked for you at the old mill."

"An unlessoned girl," she replied, "unschooled, unpracticed, yet not so old but she may learn."

Her peculiar theatrical ramblings disquieted him. There was something new about the girl. Her energetic joy had been replaced with a nervous fatigue. Her eyes seemed to move in and out of focus. He shook her. "Sarah, that day you saw the body in the sewage pit. Who did you tell about it?"

"For murder, though it have no tongue, will speak with most miraculous organ."

Other actors were beginning to stare at them.

"Sarah, speak straight. Did you tell someone?"

Pain flashed in the girl's eyes. "We didn't see a body. We saw a funny black stick that happened to look like a hand. The governor said so, it must be true."

Hadrian's heart sank. The girl, once his prize pupil, was oddly adrift.

Sarah looked down and giggled. "Silly me, I put my shoes on the wrong feet."

A boy in a harlequin suit paced through the crowd, ringing a bell. "Places," he declared.

When her eyes found him again they seemed almost playful. "What does the director do when he realizes he is in fact just another actor? He drinks, drinks alone, drinks all night. It's hard getting the script one page at a time." Suddenly she became grave and seemed about to weep.

The harlequin passed again, ringing the bell. A girl pulled Sarah away. As she disappeared behind a curtain she turned and mouthed two words. A chill rose up his back. He could have sworn they were *Save me.*

CHAPTER *Twelve*

*I*T WAS NEARLY sunset before he reached Jonah's darkened cottage. Hadrian ventured inside only long enough to retrieve the hidden vault key before lifting a lantern from the porch. The chamber behind the vines was as he had left it more than a month earlier. As he closed the door behind him he felt an unexpected calmness. Even now the faint scent of Jonah's tobacco still hung in the air, and for a moment he had the sense of having just missed the old scholar.

He quickly lit the candles, then settled at the little desk, moving to one side the sword-knife he had left there and retrieving Jonah's chronicle from its stand. He slowly leafed through the colorful manuscript, conscious more than ever that its pages must somehow unlock the secrets that had been plaguing Carthage and the camps. Sarah's words hung like a cloud over him. The colony was indeed being played like a puppet, and the closest thing he had to a script were the pages in front of him.

He paused over an entry from nearly a year before, reading its description of how the lacrosse championship was played during a snowstorm, then another, weeks later, describing the long graceful ice-boats launched on the lake every winter. The artwork decorating these corners was of migratory birds and, as with most of the others, connected by intricate flourishes in rich, varying colors. He went back to earlier entries from two and three years before. In the margins they all had short verses, Latin phrases or just words that read like mottos. He turned back to the later page about the iceboats. The margin art had changed, the margin words had disappeared. What was before him now seemed exaggerated somehow, almost garish. He drew the lantern closer, examining the long right-hand margin, lifting the magnifying lens. A long, curving, undulating line of black ink had been laid first, with red, green, and brown lines woven over it. He forced himself to look at only the black ink, then grabbed a pencil and traced the black line on a separate sheet of paper.

Excitement surged within as he completed the line. They were letters, grossly squat and widened. It was a visual game he'd seen Jonah play with children. When the paper was slanted away from the reader, they assumed normal proportion. *The eagle suffers little birds to sing.* It was Shakespeare. Standing alone, the words read like a warning. He transcribed the black shapes in the remaining margins. *For a single healthy birth*, the top of the page said. *A banquet of corncob and frog stew*, read the next. The phrases appeared both unconnected and strangely disturbing.

He returned to the page from eighteen months earlier, describing the loss of the *Anna.* On the next page, for the next week, he read the Latin sentence *mundus vult decipi ergo decipiatur* in the margin. The world wants to be deceived, so let it be deceived. He stared at it, puzzled and unnerved. Surely Jonah had not learned so quickly that the loss of the *Anna* had been fabricated.

He pushed pages back and forth, confirming his suspicion. All the early pages had borders with plain text, but, starting a year earlier, the border text was concealed.

Hadrian tried one more, reading first the main text describing the opening of the new public bathhouse and expressions of pleasure over the running water heated by steam, using designs of old Roman baths. Again, he traced the black lines of the margin text. *Not so much the famous journalist who is mourned but the delicate painter matched so perfectly with his poet mate. A song broken amid its lyrical chorus.*

Hadrian lowered the pen. Nelly had spoken of how her television anchorman husband had died the week before the baths had opened. Jonah was not in fact offering random musings about life outside Carthage in the margins, he'd been recording events in the camps as they happened.

He quickly pulled fresh paper from the shelf and began paging through the journal, transcribing as he read, pausing over another margin entry disguised in a vine. *Malesuada fames,* he read in Latin. The hunger that encourages people to crime.

His gaze drifted back to the little stand where the journal had been kept. It was of recent vintage, he realized, not salvaged. Holding the light close to it, he began to examine its joints, then tilted it, feeling a shifting of weight beneath the top.

It took him five minutes to find Jonah's hidden drawer. The leather packet inside held dozens of papers of various sizes and shapes, all bearing the same handwriting. The bottommost pages were written on the backs of title pages torn from old novels. The first few were nothing but poems. His gut tightened as he read.

Reading crumbling books by bullrush lights
It's not the way we expected to grow old

In the land of the free and the home of the brave

He could only bear to read the opening of a haiku-like verse:

How cold are the freshly washed
faces of our dead

The later messages were all reports on life in the camps. An attempt to organize a school had failed because too many families were preoccupied with sickness and foraging for food. A new push by the Tribunal to organize midwives was described, driven by the appalling number of exiled women who died in childbirth. The list of diseases Nelly had spoken about. Others were only short questions on roughly torn slips. *How long to soak the bark?* asked one. *Antibiotics lie at the end of our rainbow*, said another. Still another gave a list of pots and pans and their capacity, asking if they would suffice. They were the other end of Jonah's correspondence with the camps.

He continued to stare, rubbing at his chin as realization edged into his consciousness. He had misunderstood the sequence, which meant he had misconnected the pieces. Jonah had not been randomly reporting on events in the camps, he had been participating in them. Jonah had started teaching the camps about making drugs, then, months later, hallucinogens had begun to appear in Carthage. Slowly Hadrian leafed back to the page where the margin notes had been first hidden, then replayed in his mind his conversation that afternoon. Jonah had begun disguising his margin notes after the directory was stolen from Hamada's archives.

At last, exhausted and famished, he lowered the pencil and closed the book, pressing it to his forehead for a moment. He had not simply missed the sequence, he had missed all the important links. Nelly had told him Jonah corresponded with her about medicine. He himself had seen letters surreptitiously being delivered to the camps. But this changed everything.

He'd assumed there had been occasional contact during the past few months but the journal confirmed that the correspondence had been constant, growing in frequency. And as the correspondence grew more active so too had the criminals. Jonah had not been engaging in casual letter writing, he had been launching his own conspiracy to counter them. But the trusting old scholar had unknowingly chosen as his messenger a fledgling member of the jackals.

Jori was asleep at the dining table in the cottage, her head cradled in her folded arms. Arranged on an oily cloth in front of her were a small revolver, its magazine open, and four bullets. She had been cleaning a new weapon.

Hadrian rekindled the smoldering fire and sat smoking one of Jonah's pipes, staring into the flames. A log had crumbled to ash before he heard movement behind him, the soft metallic click of bullets being loaded into the revolver, followed by the spinning of the cylinder. Moments later Jori appeared beside him, extending a mug. "I bought fresh milk in town," she offered, then pulled up a chair beside him.

"I did like you said," she explained, "but waited until lunch when the offices were mostly empty. When I stepped inside Buchanan's office Bjorn was about to leap on me, said I had to be taken to Kenton right away. Buchanan called him off, saying that I no doubt had an amusing story to tell. He waved Bjorn outside and shut the door. By the time I finished speaking about the *Anna* and St. Gabriel I think he had stopped listening. He laughed, said I should see a doctor about the effect of my injuries on my brain."

"But you came back with a gun."

"He said that, in any event, I'd been brave, that I deserved a second chance for trying to penetrate the camps. So I am temporarily assigned to his flying squad."

Hadrian lowered the pipe and leaned forward. "You understand what happened?"

"I never understand the governor."

"Trust his actions, not his words. He has to dismiss your story officially, but appointing you to his flying squad means he is worried you might speak the truth. Easier for him to keep an eye on you. A lot harder for Fletcher to reach out to you."

"There's talk all over town. The Council is in some kind of dead-lock. The others won't ratify the man Buchanan appointed to fill Van Wyck's seat on the Council. They say they don't know him, that he's a stranger."

"You mean the head of the millers' guild."

Jori nodded. "He made a speech praising the governor for his bold action in recapturing the assassin. This miller no one knows even suggested canceling the next election as a distraction in this time of public disorder."

"They're calling Nelly an assassin now?"

"Everyone is waiting for her to be brought back and executed. With the size of the bounty, it will be any day now." Jori bit her lip. "He won't stop until she is dead, Hadrian."

IT TOOK HIM nearly half a day to find Dax, and he succeeded only because he gave up searching for the boy and followed the bait. It was midafternoon when the boy entered the back of Mette's cafe. Dax had been hiding in plain sight, trimming his hair, wearing the dark clothes prescribed for students. But he could not hide his craving for Mette's maple sugar pastries. Hadrian waited by her backyard stable until he reappeared several minutes later, watching as Dax stopped to pet a cat.

Off-balance already, he had no time to react as Hadrian darted out of the shadows and grabbed him by the belt. But as Hadrian pulled him toward a bench the boy slammed a knee into his groin.

"Hello to you too," he gasped, staggering backward.

The boy's expression changed from fear to shame as he recognized his assailant. "Stone the crows!" he exclaimed. "I didn't know you was . . . you could have just . . ." His words trailed away as he helped Hadrian to the bench. "I'm cheered you ain't dead."

"I have to stay in the shadows," Hadrian explained. "Which means I had to find you in the shadows. You've gone back to school after all."

The boy brushed off his pastry, which had fallen in the dirt, then broke it in half. He shrugged as he gave one piece to Hadrian. "Three squares and a warm bed."

Hadrian nodded thanks. "You didn't tell me about your present for Jonah," he said.

Dax studied Hadrian warily.

"Ducks taking off at dawn. He would have liked it."

His listener's eyes gave nothing away.

"Some of the jackals broke your friend Nash's foot trying to find out where that painting is. Why?"

"Ain't seen Nash, not for weeks."

"He's on their farm with his mother. Staying out of the way. You were his budge, the one who climbs inside and waits until it's safe to unlock doors. Why would the jackals be interested in that painting? Was it stolen from Fletcher?"

"Never in life!" Dax exclaimed. "He'd drop me in the fish chopper if he caught me. It was just some house. White clapboard, white fence, big stone chimney. Sometimes the owner works nights."

"Where's the painting, Dax? You never gave it to Jonah."

"He told me his birthday was next month. I was waiting for that. It's at the mill. Mergansers. He liked mergansers, the ones with the big green crests. Once we watched some take off, running like clowns on the water, and he laughed and laughed. Second floor," Dax added. "An old feed bin filled with empty burlap sacks. Except the bottom sack ain't empty." He bit into his sugary cake.

He watched the boy eat. "What was it like the first time you went to the camps?" Hadrian asked.

"I was scared. Jonah had given me a note to explain I was helping him. But we always heard about the monsters and mutants who lived there. You know, two heads, with skin like snakes."

"But you went anyway."

"Mr. Jonah gave me a note," he repeated. Dax looked up as if remembering something. "Kenton asked for you. When he first found me last month he put me in jail for a night to help me remember where you were, no food or water for twenty-four hours. I said I thought you were dead."

"Good idea."

"I mean I really thought you were dead. I saw that piece of wood in your back, then saw the waves crashing over you."

"It was a close thing." Hadrian finished his piece of pastry and licked his fingers. "What I don't understand, Dax, is how you had the time to travel so often to the camps."

"Weren't just me. We split it. Jonah let me pick two others, from the orphans."

"Who? Where are they now?"

"Told you. They got taken to iron salvage."

Hadrian gazed at the boy, trying to unlock the mystery of his words. "The two Kenton took for salvage runners? He couldn't have known."

"Bad luck is all. They were with me when he came that night. He knew they were my friends. Worse for them."

"Who has the words for the camps now, Dax?"

"There's always families trying to get notes out. But nothing for that Nelly and her friends."

"But what about messages from the jackals to Kinzler?"

The boy looked with worry into the stable's deeper shadows as if suddenly frightened of something. "We should go," he said.

"When did the jackals start sending messages to the camps?" Hadrian pressed.

"Last fall. Nelly had given me one of those carved ironwood knives they use in the camps, with a turtle shell handle. I was outside the fish plant, opening clamshells with it when one of the jackals grabbed me. He asked who I stole it from. I said no one around here. Two days later they found me, took me to the jackals' place, that white house by the docks. One-eyed Fletcher was waiting for me. He asked me questions to see if I knew my way around the camps."

"They thought you went there to steal things."

Dax nodded. "Captain Fletcher took off his eye patch and looked at me with his dead eye, the zombie eye, and told me if I ever told anyone about our talk that eye would see me."

"That's when they said you could become a jackal."

Hadrian watched him cast another nervous glance into the shadows. "We should go," he said again.

"Is that when?" Hadrian pressed.

The boy grimaced. "No, not then." He stood, made a gesture toward the alley.

Hadrian silently studied him. "Not then," he ventured, "because the promise to make you a jackal came when you stole the book from Hamada for them."

Dax went very still. "You don't know that."

"You were in and out of Takeo's barn for Jonah. But he'd never ask you to steal a book. Listen to me. I need to know what it was," he said more urgently. "What book was so important to the jackals?"

"A di-rect-ory." The boy pronounced the unfamiliar word slowly.

"A directory of what?"

Dax took a step toward the light. The pain on his face was unmistakable. "Businesses. Later, I saw it on Kinzler's table in that compound of his. I'll get it back. I said that into the phone the day they put Jonah in the ground. I kept seeing Jonah's face when I was going to die in the icy water that night the boat blew up. When the waves starting breaking over me and my hands were too cold to hold the paddle, he kept calling to me, like he was on the shore waiting. That's why I didn't pass out, why I stayed alive. He kept me alive for a reason. I went to his grave as soon as I got back to town—before I even found dry clothes. I promised him again I'd get it back." Suddenly they were interrupted by a low groan from the back of the stable, growing in volume to a howl. Dax ran.

Hadrian, too, began moving quickly away. But then he paused as the howl became a long sob. Mette seemed not to see him as she darted out of the cafe carrying a small tin bucket. He ran into the shadows behind her, halted six feet away as she unlocked a door and slipped inside what appeared to be a workshop, leaving the door ajar.

Peering inside, Hadrian could see chairs in various stages of repair, all of which hung on the wall to make room for a low cot. Mette bent over a limp figure on the bed, murmuring words of comfort in Norwegian, sounding like a mother soothing a sick child. Her patient was a blond man in his late twenties, and he wasn't confined to bed by a sickness, he was bound to it by ropes across his elbows and knees.

The man quieted under Mette's touch and she poured milk from her bucket into a mug for him, then retrieved a vial of powder from inside her apron and emptied it into the milk. As he drank the man's eyes seemed to regain their focus, gazing gratefully at Mette before widening with fear as he glimpsed Hadrian behind her.

The Norger woman spun around with surprising speed and seemed about to launch herself at him before she froze. "Hadrian!" she gasped. Then she collected herself and extended her arms for an embrace. "Hadrian, thank God!" she murmured warmly, folding her arms around him with a sigh of relief.

She quickly explained that the man on the cot, now sinking into unconsciousness, was her nephew Arne, a shipwright who lived with his parents near the waterfront. A quiet, steady worker, he had recently begun acting peculiarly, borrowing money from his parents, shouting out in the middle of the night, acting tipsy though he never touched a bottle of spirits.

When he sliced himself in the leg with a shipyard adze, his parents had kept him at home under orders from the hospital. But he had soon grown violent, repeatedly hobbling outside at night and reopening the wound, then returning much calmer despite the blood running down his leg. Next they discovered he'd been stealing his mother's jewelry. But only when he had started howling like a wolf at all hours did they ask Mette for help. Living in the commercial district, she had few neighbors to complain of the disturbance.

"He asked me to tie him like this," Mette explained as her patient drifted off to sleep. "He has to face this sickness alone, he says. His medicine helps," she added, dabbing at the sweat beading her nephew's forehead.

"Mette, I need to know where you get his medicine."

She shook her head. "I don't really know. After the first couple days a friend from the fishery showed up, saying he could get a powerful medication that would help Arne. I don't mind paying."

A chill crept down Hadrian's spine. "Do you know the name of his friend?"

"He won't say. He comes every evening. Says they miss my nephew at the shipyard."

"Does he wear dark glasses?"

"What a strange question," she said distractedly as she lifted the mug to Arne's lips again. "Yes, yes, he wears shaded glasses. It's becoming quite a fad. Wears glasses and has a snake tattooed around his wrist."

They sat in silence, Hadrian wringing out the cloth as Mette washed her nephew. "Jonah used to come almost every day, you said," he observed as she finished. "Did he ever leave you anything to hold for him, something secret?"

"Never. I think he believed sharing too many secrets would endanger his friends. Sometimes he borrowed things from my kitchen. Measures and pots."

Hadrian nodded, then pulled out his transcription of the code from the last journal page, the one Jonah had tried to destroy. He spread it out on the side of the bed. "Does this mean anything to you? It's important. I think it's some sort of code."

She lifted the paper for only a moment before reaching into her pinned-up hair and extracting a pencil. "Not a code, Hadrian," she said in a patient voice. She laid the paper on her knee and began making marks between the clusters of letters and numbers. H2G, then MAN4MG, SS3G, BC2CC. "Like this. You might want to ask Emily at the hospital what the letters stand for—their lab has some system for abbreviating ingredients they use."

"I don't understand."

"It's not a code, Hadrian, it's a recipe. I use the same shorthand in my bakery. H two grams, MAN four milligrams, SS three grams, BC two cc's."

Hadrian looked at her in wonder. He had tortured himself trying to understand it, trying to make something more complicated of it. Startled and grateful, he stuffed the paper back into his shirt. The recipe would be useless without the missing pieces, but an important part of the puzzle had fallen into place.

As he stepped toward the stable door Mette gestured him to stop. She rose, removed the bright woolen scarf from around her neck. "I just knitted it," she said, draping it over his neck. "You need it more than me. Winter's come early."

Hadrian retreated into the shadows of the alley. It was nearly an hour before a tall man entered the stable, five minutes before he left the building. Hadrian followed him down the hill, grateful for the snow that had begun to blow in from the lake. The drug dealer hurried to get out of the elements, straight back to the smugglers' apartment where Jansen had died.

THE OLD MILL had a haunted air under the moonlight. Small dark shapes scurried across the floor as he opened the door. He reached along the wall until he found the hanging lantern, lit it, and moved up the narrow stairs. Well-worn hemp sacks did indeed fill the feed bin, empty except for the rectangular object in the last one.

In the dim light he admired the framed painting, an expert rendering of mergansers on a slow running takeoff toward the rising sun, then looked out the window at the moon, bright enough for him to use the forest paths. He returned the painting to the sack. It was time for Jonah's present to be delivered.

An hour later he laid the painting on the trestle table of Jonah's dining room. Jori listened silently while he described its mysterious connection to Fletcher's men, then she turned it over and pulled a knife from her pocket. She pulled back the cover to reveal two sheets of paper inside. Hadrian carefully laid them on the table and arranged several candles around them before pointing to the upper right corner of each. "Page thirty-three," he read, "and page eighty seven." They were cut from a ledger, both sides crowded with handwriting.

Jori lifted the first page and began reading. "Franklin Bishop," she said. "Age fifty-six. Cause of death cardiac arrest."

"Jonathan Hampden," Hadrian read from the second. "Age forty-nine. Cause of death cardiac arrest."

The first sheet was dated over a year earlier, the other three months after that.

"Why?" Jori wanted to know. "Why would someone steal death reports for men who died of natural causes?"

"More importantly," Hadrian asked, "why would Fletcher care if they did? Who was he protecting?" Was he at last beginning to glimpse the unknown players inside Carthage?

They sat and read the full reports out loud. Both men had died of heart attacks after consuming large dinners, and heavy quantities of alcohol, at the same waterfront restaurant. One had been a shipwright, the other a miller. They had no obvious family connection. Their death examinations had been conducted by two different doctors.

Hadrian stared at the names again. "I knew them," he said with sudden realization. "Or at least knew *of* them. Each was the head of his guild."

THE LITTLE COTTAGE a block away from the hospital was surrounded by gardens, many planted just with herbs but others just for the pleasure of their flowers. Late-blooming asters and coneflowers swayed in the breeze. The last golden leaves of elderberries drooped from the cold. Hadrian waited in the darkness, watching the house, then circling it at a distance, following the tracks in the shallow snow that led from the street to a clump of evergreens at the side of the house. Squatting, he studied the packed snow where someone had stood and stomped their feet from the cold, not missing the half-dozen fresh cigarette butts by the tracks of heavy-treaded shoes. He rolled one of the butts in his fingers, knowing from the touch of the parchment it was a Bookstick.

He rounded the house once more, making sure there were no other tracks, pausing to study the well-lit kitchen, then climbed up onto the front porch. Testing the front door, and finding it locked, he retrieved the key from the lintel of the front window.

Two of those at the kitchen table leapt up in alarm as he entered. Emily stayed seated. "I don't recall leaving my door open," she said, but made no effort to conceal her weary smile. She did not seem surprised to see him. Jori had visited the hospital.

"There is a community of criminals on the north shore," he said abruptly. "They mean to take over Carthage."

No one spoke. The two men, both tall lean figures with muscular hands and leathery faces, dropped back into their chairs. Hadrian recognized them now. Melville and Wilmot, the farmers who served on the Council with Emily.

It was the doctor who stirred first. She rose and gestured Hadrian closer. "First let me see how your arm and shoulder are healing," she said, motioning for him to pull his jacket and shirt off. Only after she had leaned close to the wounds, uttering low syllables of approval as she pushed and stretched the skin around the scars, did she pull out a chair for Hadrian. "Only you could find a way to sink a ship a second time," she said, then confirmed that Hadrian was acquainted with the two Council members. They were stalwart, trustworthy men who Buchanan had originally nominated for service on the Council because they would be quiet, backbench members who would always support his government. Yet here they were, meeting with the independent-minded Emily, far from Buchanan's scrutiny.

"From the beginning," Emily instructed him as she passed a mug of tea. "First you took my mare to the camps. Fortunately she found her way back without being eaten. That's all I know."

"New Jerusalem," Hadrian began. "That's what they call the camps now. The promised land." He choose not to offer every detail of his past month but spoke of the smugglers, the *Anna*, Kinzler's mysterious walled compound, and his discovery of St. Gabriel. He spoke for nearly an hour, accepting more tea, then thick-sliced brown bread and butter. He hesitated about proceeding when he recognized the pain and anger on the faces of his audience. But there was no real surprise. They had harbored suspicions of the truth.

At last he rose to stand at the window and survey the grounds outside. "How often have you been meeting like this?"

"Three or four times," Emily said. "Why?"

Hadrian tossed onto the table the Bookstick butt he'd retrieved from the snow. "Someone has been watching. He wore police shoes. There may be several on the force who smoke these but only one I know for certain."

The farmers cast worried glances at Emily. "Bjorn!" she exclaimed. Then she rose and pulled shut the curtains. "Buchanan is furious at us. He selected Van Wyck's replacement but we have withheld our approval."

"The head of the millers' guild," Hadrian confirmed with a nod "On what grounds do you protest?"

"Officially, we need none. The vote has to be unanimous, or we go to a full election."

Why, he asked himself, was it suddenly so important for the millers to be represented on the Council? "Unofficially?"

Emily grimaced. "The drugs are spreading. I have half a dozen patients with hallucinations or in comas. Buchanan has started proceedings to exile anyone whose eyes bleach out. They're mutants, he says, technically covered by the expulsion laws." She glanced uncomfortably at the tall farmer to her right. "Wilmot's daughter is one of them. And no one knows anything about this man from the miller's guild. He came in from some distant farm, was raised to guild master overnight when the last one died unexpectedly. There was talk of bribery."

"The last one," Hadrian said. "A man named Hampden."

Emily nodded. "He died more than a year ago."

"A few months later the head of the shipwrights' guild also died. Both of heart attacks. And both their replacements have been raised to the Council." He reached into his coat and pulled out the two death reports.

The doctor, recognizing the format of the pages, slowly reached for them. "What have you done?" she demanded, heat rising in her voice. "You can't just—"

"I didn't cut these from the death lists. Someone else did. And the jackals have been trying to find them ever since." Hadrian quickly explained what he knew about the reports. "They were hidden at a house behind the square. White clapboard with a stone chimney and a white fence."

Hadrian watched as Emily's face tightened. "I know who lives in that house," she grimly declared. "He's on duty at the hospital tonight."

Thirty minutes later Hadrian sat with Emily in her office at the hospital, a large leather-bound book opened in front of them on her desk.

They had quickly located the official death reports. The pages were not missing from the book although the two pages in the ledger were in a different handwriting. Both had been signed by Dr. Jonathan Salens, owner of the house off the square.

"It makes no sense," Emily said after reading through the notices in the book. "Salens signed the original reports in the book and someone made duplicates over the names of two other doctors."

Hadrian pushed down on the ledger book, pressing the pages flat to the binding. "No," he said after a quick inspection. "These pages from his house were the originals. They were cut out and the new ones replaced them." He pointed out how new sheets had been inserted and secured with expert stitches. "No one would notice. No one would care. Routine reports. Routine deaths signed by one of your doctors."

"Except Salens was not the examining doctor," Emily growled. She consulted a pocket watch. "He should be out of surgery now," she said, and pushed back her chair to leave the office. Hadrian bent and reread every word of the reports, then took a seat in the shadows behind the door.

Emily returned moments later, engaged in pleasantries with the thin, black-haired doctor he'd seen tending Jamie Reese weeks earlier. Salens, he recalled now, had quickly moved away when Hadrian had asked about the fisherman, had been the one who had reported Reese's death as an industrial accident. The atmosphere abruptly changed as she closed the door and pointed to the ledger on her desk, opened to the first of the reports. "Fabricating official records is a crime."

"So the police found the painting," Salens said in a tight voice. "I told them not to trouble themselves when they asked about it."

"If there is any hope of you not becoming a hospital janitor by this time tomorrow, you'd better start explaining right now."

Salens sank into a chair. His good looks seemed to fade as Emily dropped the two stolen pages beside the ledger. "Two men died of natural causes," he said cautiously. "The reports in the ledger are accurate."

"You did not conduct the examinations. Why then is your name on them?"

When Salens did not reply Hadrian stepped from the shadows. "Because the changed reports are in his handwriting."

Salens stared at Hadrian with resentment. "I wouldn't sign another doctor's name," he said stiffly. "That would be wrong."

A bitter laugh escaped Emily's lips.

"They are the same reports," protested Salens.

"No," Hadrian said. "There are several differences. In your reports you left out the fact that each ate at the same restaurant before his death. The Blue Gander. And you made sure a symptom was left out of the official record. Blue-black discoloration of the skin along the forearms."

Salens stared into his folded hands. "They both died of cardiac arrest. None of what is written is a lie."

"It became a lie by its omissions," Hadrian corrected.

"Who told you to do this?" Emily demanded.

"No one."

"Very well," Emily said. "I will send for the police. Lieutenant Kenton would find such a case of great interest. The governor will probably know by morning."

"No!" Salens exclaimed. "You can't!"

"Then who told you to do this?" Emily pressed. "What else have you done?"

"It isn't like that," Salens said. "I never . . ." He glanced up at Emily with a desolate expression. "There was a girl at the tavern behind the Blue Gander. A working girl. I'd lost a lot of money to the owner at the poker games there, more than I could afford. I was going to lose my house. The owner said he had a way for me to pay it off, said he had a girl, his best girl, who would be out of work for months if something wasn't done."

Emily threw up her hands. "If she were sick she could have come to the hospital."

Salens looked down.

"I don't think she was a waitress, Emily," Hadrian inserted. "She worked in the rooms upstairs."

Emily went very still. "Surely you wouldn't . . ." her voice cracked. "God no, Jonathan," she moaned. New births were vital to the survival of the colony. Performing an abortion, or having an abortion, was not simply a felony, it was tantamount to treason to many minds.

Salens's voice was filled with pleading now. "You don't understand. These girls would be taken to herbalists or black-market midwives. God knows what damage would be done. One of her friends died of hemorrhaging last year."

"You did this and then the owner used it against you to get the death reports changed," Hadrian stated. "Who was it?"

He knew the answer before it left Salens's lips. "He has grown rich from the fishery these past years. He fancies becoming the richest man in the colony. Talks about building a mansion that will rival that of the governor."

"Fletcher!" Emily spoke the name like a curse.

A knot was forming in Hadrian's gut. "Was it he who hosted the dinners before Hampden and Bishop died?"

"I don't know," Salens murmured. "I suspect so. He just said he would turn me in for what I did to the girl if I didn't fix the ledger."

"He told you what to write?"

"He told me what to delete."

The silence was like thin ice.

"What were you thinking?" Emily asked at last. "Why keep the original pages?"

When Salens did not speak, Hadrian offered the answer. "Insurance. If Fletcher sought his help again, he'd have the leverage to say no."

Salens sighed.

"Did he?" Hadrian demanded. "What else did he ask for?"

"He told me to check certain records in the laboratory, to change the inventory sheets so nothing would be missed. I told him no one had time to keep accurate records and he dropped it."

"But you checked anyway," Hadrian suggested. "Out of curiosity."

"Records are kept, but only of current inventories to see when stock has to be replenished. There were some levels of an antiseptic that were lower than normal."

Emily approached Salens, hovering over the young doctor like a vengeful fury. "Of what exactly?" she demanded.

"Silver nitrate."

She struck him on the cheek with her open hand, hard, then pointed to the door. Salens's face lost its color. He did not speak as he left the chamber.

"I don't understand," Hadrian said.

"He did," Emily spat. "The heart symptoms could have been induced by any number of agents that are freely available in the colony. A concentration of yew, rhubarb, bloodroot, or half a dozen other herbs could have done it. But they can vary widely in their effectiveness, and most could be reversed by a good doctor. The discoloration along the arms means silver nitrate, which isn't available anywhere but in our lab. We make our own. The effects of ingestion would be irreversible. It would have guaranteed death."

CHAPTER *Thirteen*

*T*HE ZEUS WAS the largest of the skipjacks left to winter in the ice, tied at the end of its solitary wharf. The thin crust of snow on her deck crunched as Hadrian stepped on it. He looked back at the clapboard house by the shipyard that had become the refuge of the jackals, then at the distant dock where ice freighters were launched, the only wharf where men seemed to be working. No one seemed to have noticed him, no one had followed. Perhaps no one had even seen the dim cabin light he had sighted when scanning the harbor through the telescope in Jonah's workshop.

His heart leapt as a cat jumped out of a shadow and disappeared down a companionway. He noticed movement on the lake, an iceboat speeding toward the docks, and quickly followed the cat into the darkness. The hinges of the cabin door gave a low groan as he stepped inside the chamber. The solitary candle lantern on a large table revealed an oddly disjointed chamber. On one wall drawings were tacked, artful charcoal renderings of cats and fish and sailing ships, some of them fanciful images of huge square-rigged men-of-war. On the opposite wall, between portholes, were nailed the leathery skins of several sturgeon.

The far end of the table held a small arsenal. A long-handled ship's hook leaned beside a pole with a spearhead. On the table lay two clubs, a knife, and one of the heavy cleavers used for chopping off fish heads. Beyond the weapons, a small brazier smoldered beside a pile of blankets.

As he inched along the table, another cat emerged from under it, hissing a warning. The pile of blankets began to stir. One of them suddenly rose and extended a knife at him.

"If you came to steal, I'll slice you belly to brisket!" the figure warned.

Hadrian wasn't sure whether to laugh or run away. The sturdy stranger who threw off the blanket was fully a foot shorter than himself but had the most muscular build, and most leathery skin, of any woman he had ever met. He held up his hands, palms outward. "I only seek a word, Captain Reese."

"Tell him to go fuck himself. And his tree dogs too."

Hadrian ventured a step closer. "I don't know who you mean. My name is Hadrian Boone. It's about Jamie. I just wanted to—" Her fist slammed into his jaw before he could finish the sentence. She was suddenly all arms and legs, pounding him, then kicking him as he dropped to his knees.

"Goddamned scrub!" she snarled. "How dare you show your face!"

As Hadrian tried to raise his head a cat leapt onto his neck. When it began to sink its claws into his skin he rolled into the pile of blankets, knocking it off and burying his head. Captain Reese jumped on him and pummeled him through the blankets.

He fought for breath, finding a gap in the blankets. "I never hurt your son!" he shouted. "I tried to help him! I am trying to find his killers!"

The pounding did not stop immediately, but slowly it diminished. When it finally stopped he ventured a look and saw his attacker on a stool, wearing a stunned expression. "Killers?" she murmured. "My Jamie died because of the hospital. You and that bitch doctor are why he died. Everyone says so."

He silently rose to his feet and straightened his clothes. Three cats were on the table now, staring at him. "Then everyone is lying."

"My name is Hadrian Boone," he began again. "I am . . ." he had no idea how to describe himself anymore. "I am trying to help. I am fighting the same people your son was fighting." Blood trickled from his lip.

"Jamie weren't any fighter," his mother said. "He was the hero from the *Anna*." She leaned back, opening a porthole. Her hand extended outside and returned with a ball of snow. Hadrian accepted it and pressed it to his bleeding lip.

"There was a police investigation into Fletcher's smuggling. I think Jamie had begun to realize, like I have, that the smuggling was a cover for much worse things. He was going to help with the investigation. But Fletcher found out."

"No. He had an accident. The hospital should have cured him but it didn't."

"Captain, how did Jamie wind up on the *Anna*? Did he ever speak to you about the sinking?"

"Fletcher said my boy had no future on a sailing ship. It near broke my heart but when Fletcher needed an extra hand I let him go off to see what those steamers are like. All soot and noise. It was just his second trip out when she went down."

"But surely he told you about it."

"Sailors don't talk of such things. Bad luck. Two died, two survived. I went to church for the first time in years when he came back alive."

"The *Anna* never went down that day. I saw her, I sailed on her last month. Fletcher staged the sinking. He didn't want your son as a sailor, he wanted him as a jackal. But Jamie had second thoughts. Because he had a good upbringing," Hadrian suggested. "Because you taught him right from wrong. So Fletcher saw to it that Jamie went out on another of his boats, then they forced drugs into him. The drugs put him into a coma. The only thing the doctors did to hurt him was to tell two of Fletcher's men that he would probably recover. They came back in the night, from the jackals' house, and suffocated him with his own pillow."

Captain Reese stared into her rough, callused hands. A big grey cat moved to her side as if to comfort her.

"Fletcher and the men in St. Gabriel killed your son."

In the long uneasy silence Hadrian lowered himself into one of the chairs.

"St. Gabe is a wicked place," she said at last.

"You've been there?"

"Only to take on cargo. Ordered by Fletcher. I told him I already had a full hold and he said that wouldn't be a problem."

Hadrian studied the woman, sensing invitation in her words. "Fletcher's steamers take the smuggled salvage."

The captain went to a cabinet and pulled out a bottle of whiskey and two glasses. When Hadrian declined his glass she poured her own, then turned his upside down and dribbled some of the spirits onto the upturned bottom. The grey cat eagerly licked it up.

"Fletcher hates the sailboats. Keeps trying to use the guild to shut us down. All the 'jacks are owned by independent captains, no one who kisses his arse. But he knows what I think of the government, so he asked me to haul something special. I'd walk ten miles barefoot on the ice to rile that son of a bitch Buchanan. I think the police were sniffing around his smuggling operations. No one ever pays attention to the skipjacks. We come and go without any hoopla. No wood to take on, no smoke to show our path. Last month when he asked me to start carrying some of those men from St. Gabe, I asked for payment. He nearly hit me. Said the payment I get is not having jackals burn my hull to the waterline."

As she spoke raucous cries rose outside. They both bent to a porthole to see a small crowd on the main wharf, cheering a procession coming from the iceboat that had just docked. Four men with ice poles were herding someone in a cloak toward town.

"Pay me shit and they rake in a thousand for a little afternoon cruise," the captain muttered.

The figure fell as a pole prodded a shoulder. When the prisoner rose, the cowl slipped away. With a shudder Hadrian saw her bald head.

"Buchanan will have to schedule the execution between ice bullet races if he wants it done this week," Captain Reese said.

"How did they get her so easily?" Hadrian wondered out loud.

The captain shrugged. "Word is there was some kind of trap out on the lake. No one is going to outrun an iceboat."

Hadrian fought his emotions as he turned back to the table. "Wooden boxes," he said. "That's what you hauled first. Boxes full of shotgun shells. They would fit easily under this table."

Reese drained her glass and poured another. "I never said I looked inside them."

"Jamie did. Inside the boxes, and inside the shells. It was why he suddenly was interested in talking with the police."

"No. You don't compass it. The government goes too far. People have to defend themselves. It's only right the fishermen have shotguns."

"Jamie discovered that most of the shells contained drugs. Lying about the *Anna*'s sinking, helping with the smuggling, that was just part of getting ahead in the fishery. But shipping illegal drugs into Carthage was different."

The captain's glass stopped in midair. "No," she said in an uncertain tone. "That's old world. We don't have such things now. It was ammunition. Everyone has the right to bear arms, I don't care what the damned governor says."

"Do yourself a favor. Find one of those shells and cut it open. It was the powder inside that got your son killed. It's killing others in the colony. You've been helping the jackal drug runners."

Captain Reese spoke no more, just stared into her whiskey. She seemed not to notice as Hadrian rose and left the cabin. The grey cat escorted him off the ship, then ran back inside.

Hadrian made his way carefully up the darkened back stairs of the theater building. He had confirmed that Buchanan's carriage was parked at the front and knew he would have to be subdued if Hadrian confronted him in the Governor's Box in the middle of an act. But as he peered around the corner of the back hallway he froze. Bjorn hovered in front of the door. Buchanan was taking his bodyguard everywhere now. Hadrian retreated down the stairs.

Minutes later he slipped over the fence into the governor's compound and found a hiding place inside the little smokehouse at the rear of the property. As he closed the door something glinted in the moonlight that leaked through a gap in the planks. Atop an upright log lay a small hammer and a piece of shiny metal. As he stepped toward it a piece of porcelain broke under his foot. He picked up the porcelain, then found three more pieces nearby. They were from the face of a doll, a blond doll that had been beaten with the hammer. He lifted the metal. It had been a badge, one of the replica police badges the governor gave away as tokens of appreciation. It had been pounded flat, its embossing destroyed. He looked back at the doll, realizing he had seen it before, at the mill. Someone had taken a hammer to the angel.

He lowered himself to the ground, leaning against the wall. In a little pool of moonlight the angel's eyes stared unblinking at him.

Hadrian did not realize he had dozed off until he was awakened by the furious barking of a dog. The door was flung open. He was still groggy as Bjorn seized him by the collar, dragged him outside, and heaved him toward the kitchen of the governor's house.

"I knew the rumors of your death were too good to be true," Buchanan said as Bjorn shoved him into his downstairs office. "You were seen at the theater. Bjorn doesn't work alone when I am out in public."

"I should have known you would need protection round the clock now." Hadrian stepped to the fireplace to warm himself. "The citizens are restless."

Buchanan stared at him without expression, then gestured Bjorn out of the room. "Where have you been?"

"Discovering a whole new world. Meeting the people who have turned you into a puppet."

A glint of amusement appeared on the governor's face. "We went ahead in your absence and updated your official record. Just in case. Permanent exile will just take a quick vote of the Council now."

"The new face of justice in Carthage. Condemn the accused without a hearing."

"She will hang," Buchanan said coldly. "I will make you watch."

"And when I find the real killers your political career will be finished."

"You have no notion of what is happening in this colony. Don't evade your responsibilities for weeks then show up just to criticize me."

"It is not me you need worry about. It's your Council. They've begun to wonder about the guild heads taking over the government. Fisheries, merchants, shipwrights. The ones crucial for smuggling. Have they actually begun paying you cash, or is it still just extravagant gifts?"

Buchanan said nothing, but glanced out the open door as if deciding whether to let Bjorn take over.

"And now the millers. Have you wondered at all about that, Lucas? Have you done an inventory of the grain?"

"Don't be so naive. The guilds pay the taxes that support the government. And having the guilds provide administrative support saves government expense. The millers are now responsible for security at the silos and administering the retail distribution. A waste of time for government."

"It doesn't hurt that they bring you so many things you treasure. Brandy. Fine furniture from God knows where." Hadrian ran his hand along the back of an elegant settee and gestured toward the grandfather clock and a sideboard with a dozen bottles of salvaged liquor. "Have you ever seen a duty certificate for any of this?"

Buchanan took a step toward the door.

"The last head of the millers' guild was murdered," Hadrian said to his back, "and the new one was probably living in the north until a few months ago. If he's confirmed on the Council, the guilds won't have to listen to you ever again. They will control you, and control the Council. The colony will be theirs. No need for messy revolutions. They will probably even let you stay in the mansion. So far you're doing fine as their figurehead."

Buchanan seemed distracted. Defiance was certainly on his face, but as he looked back out the door so was pain. Hadrian edged across the room to follow his gaze. Bjorn was not outside the door as he expected, but sitting at the end of the hallway, at the base of the stairs to the second floor.

"You have no proof of anything," Buchanan said flatly. "You flee the colony on a lark and leave me to clean up. That bitch had a fair trial. A jury convicted her. Kenton provided testimony that she invaded a citizen's house, held the owner prisoner. Witnesses saw her running back there from the library after Jonah was found dead."

"Lies. Who was there to defend her?"

"Emily made a statement. More like a plea for mercy."

Hadrian lowered himself into a wingback chair by the fireplace, within sight of the stairway. "The town in the north is called St. Gabriel. They are sitting on treasures you cannot imagine. They stole the *Anna* and had Fletcher lie about its being sunk. They killed your scouts to keep their operations secret. Then a policeman. Surely you haven't been able to sweep Jansen's murder under the rug too?"

The sound of crashing dishes suddenly erupted from the kitchen next door. A woman called frantically from somewhere. Buchanan cursed then strode out of the room, snapping at a maid who appeared in the corridor.

An instant later Hadrian was at the sideboard. He grabbed one of Buchanan's precious bottles and hurried to the cellar door. With a glance toward the kitchen to make certain no one watched, he opened the door, rolled the bottle over the first step, and ran back into the study as the bottle noisily bounced down the darkened stairs.

Seconds later he heard Buchanan's furious curse. "Bjorn!" the governor shouted. "He's in the cellars again!"

As soon as the two men disappeared into the cellar Hadrian darted down the hall and up the stairs. A stout woman in an apron lay sprawled, asleep, in a chair by the first door. He slipped past her and pushed open the door to find himself in a bedroom lined with shelves full of books and dolls. Dora, the governor's youngest daughter, sat in a chair by the bed, her cheeks red and swollen. She had been crying. The girl held the hand of her older sister, who lay under a heavy quilt.

At first Sarah appeared to be sleeping. But then Hadrian saw her pallid cheeks and the tremors in her fingertips. He knelt at the bedside and gently took the hand held by Dora. Sarah's pulse was slow, dangerously slow.

He did not move as footsteps pounded on the stairs. Bjorn seized Hadrian by the shoulder and seemed ready to pummel him when he was restrained by the voice of the governor. "Wait. Hadrian is an old friend of the girl's."

The bodyguard scowled but retreated into the hall. Buchanan moved to Hadrian's side. "Speak to her. Maybe she will react to your voice."

Hadrian uttered the girl's name, twice, three times, then very carefully lifted an eyelid. Her iris was fading. "She should be in the hospital," he said.

"They have more than they can handle already," Buchanan said. "The first one died in their care, as you know."

Hadrian glanced up. Was the governor acknowledging that he now knew the truth about Jamie Reese? "I just saw her two days ago at her rehearsal. How long has it been, how long since the coma?"

"That night."

"Before that?"

"School. Homework. Her usual routine. But she was acting restless. And distracted. Went out in the backyard at all hours, looking at the sky, sitting in the smokehouse."

"They're bringing it in from the ruined lands."

"It?"

"Drugs, Lucas. My God don't you see? St. Gabriel is eating away Carthage from the inside while it erodes our resolve with treasure from the outside. You don't control the colony anymore. You don't even control what comes into your own house."

"Impossible. My Sarah doesn't do drugs. I've had guards here these past weeks. No one could get drugs to her without being noticed."

"Unless she wanted them," Hadrian shot back. "You've got to close down the smuggling depot in the cave beyond the icehouse. Pull back your patrols from the farms and put them in the fisheries where they belong."

"The outsiders are nothing but peasants," Buchanan said stubbornly. "Powerless shadows. We have nothing to fear from them."

But as he spoke Bjorn reappeared in the doorway. The big Norger's face was a storm of emotion. He said nothing, only pointed down the hall, out the window at the end. Hadrian rose and followed Buchanan, seeing with panic the flames that flickered over the town, then running, reaching the window as a long, agonized groan left Buchanan. The shadows had power after all.

The flaming structures at the south end of town were like five giant fingers about to close over Carthage. Bells began ringing. Fire brigades were already galloping. But Hadrian knew they would be too late. The silos containing the colony's winter grain were engulfed in flame.

THE END OF the world had come again. More than a few of the older men and women who had labored to build Carthage sat against trees and openly wept. Mothers held young children tight against their aprons so their tears would not be seen. People walked about with blank expressions, not wanting to believe the catastrophe before them.

The entire winter's supply of grain was gone. The dry kernels and the seasoned oak walls of the structures had provided the perfect fuel, burning so hot that the silos had been impossible to approach. The fire companies could do little more than spray water on the nearby buildings, and even then two stables and a dozen horses had been lost. There would be no bread, no porridge, no pastries, no pasta, no more of the grain coffee drunk by many. The supply of wild game would quickly be exhausted. Milk cows would be confiscated for meat. The colony would be left with salted fish and pickled vegetables. By midwinter even those supplies would be short.

Lucas Buchanan walked among the ruins with an impassive expression.

"How will you feed us now?" a woman with a child angrily yelled at him.

"What's the point of your damned police if they can't stop this?" a man shouted.

Buchanan ignored them. His police were out in force now, surrounding him, guarding the rope barrier Kenton was erecting to keep the onlookers from the ruined silos. Only one of them showed any interest in examining the site.

Jori knelt, studying a large crockery pot that had been shattered by the heat. As Hadrian approached he spotted more of the ceramic shards, from demijohns and larger containers. Jori held one of the pieces up to him.

"Smell it," she instructed.

The acrid odor was faint but unmistakable. Turpentine had been in the crock. Hadrian picked up another shard and discovered the same scent.

"They wanted them to burn all at once, fast, so there would no chance of saving even one. They got away fast. One of the ice freighters is missing," she added. Her face twisted with emotion as she watched a woman, pale as a ghost, walk by with an infant pressed to her breast. "The children," Jori said in an agonized tone. "My God, Hadrian, the children."

He walked among the ashes, considering the night's work. It had taken several men, with a wagon full of the solvent used to accelerate the flames. History was indeed repeating itself. The agony of their first winter would be theirs again. He did not respond at first when he realized Buchanan was standing next to him.

"There are small inventories scattered about at bakers and the mills," the governor said in a hollow voice. "The farmers always keep a little extra. We will establish a rationing board."

"It's taken months, probably more, to put this together. Wheels within wheels. Crimes within crimes. I never suspected the scope of their ambition."

"Speak plainly," the governor snapped.

"The pieces were all there. The guilds always cut corners. The merchants had secret salvage trips. The fishermen had their smuggling. The millers had found a way to divert some grain to eventually sell to the exiles. It took the genius of those in St. Gabriel to combine it all. When they found they could make drugs they were unstoppable. The sum of the parts became far greater than the whole. The smuggling made them rich. Now destroying the grain brings Carthage to its knees. The drugs provide the deathblow."

"Nonsense," Buchanan said, but his voice lacked conviction.

"With our granaries gone, they'll expect you to beg for food," Hadrian said.

"They can't possibly have enough."

"They were running the *Anna* back and forth for months hauling salvage one way and grain on the return. And what's enough? Their point isn't really made until people start dying. But they won't offer us the means to stay alive, not yet. St. Gabriel first wants the people here desperate, so they won't question what their new government does so long as it feeds them. Then the drugs will destroy any resolve to resist. You'll end up begging."

"Like hell," Buchanan growled.

"And when you refuse they'll make it clear to the people that you have turned down the means to avoid starvation. They won't have to get rid of you then, because they know the people will. How long will your flying squad last when five hundred citizens storm your mansion?"

"To hell with them!" Buchanan remained defiant. "I will not beg!" As he spoke a wagon drove by, laden with a family and their household furnishings, no doubt bound for relatives on some distant farm. A man struggling with belongings jammed into a blanket on his shoulder walked by. The disintegration of Carthage was beginning before their eyes.

"You *will* beg for it," Hadrian said, "you'll pay double, triple what it is worth, transfer the entire government coffers to St. Gabriel if that's what it takes."

"You forever misjudge me. I will destroy them."

"No. You misjudge them. I am not speaking of the governor. I am speaking of the father. They will keep Sarah addicted for a while, then withhold the drugs. She will start to scream, scream until her throat is bloody. She will weep with pain, she will shout hideous things at you and her sister. She will suffer things no child should ever suffer. You have already shown those in St. Gabriel that there is no boundary between what you do for the state and what you do for your family. As part of the negotiations they will secretly offer you what Sarah craves. You will not refuse."

Buchanan's expression turned desolate. "My little Sarah," was all he said.

Jori approached, with cool determination in her eyes. She held his gaze a moment before he turned back to the governor. Hadrian sighed and gazed toward the western horizon as he spoke.

"Their power rests with the drugs and the grain, but also with their secret allies in Carthage. Unless we find those working inside Carthage, the ones who always seem to know our every step, we can trust no one. And the truth is not here. It is out there," he said, gesturing toward the wilderness. "So we will go find it, the three of us, and follow the trail of evidence back here."

Buchanan watched a family of older colonists go by with their belongings piled on an oxcart. The veterans were the first to leave, because they knew what lay ahead. Hadrian knew the governor was glimpsing the same nightmarish memories of their first two winters, when dogs and cats, sparrows and mice had gone into stewpots, when bodies had gone into mass graves, when women had offered their bodies for half a loaf to keep a child alive.

Hadrian did not believe Buchanan had heard until he slowly turned to him. "Three?"

"Nelly's coming. She can get us inside closed doors. She possesses secrets that will help. But she will never reveal them in your prison."

"The people have to see we are still in charge," Buchanan said. "They need a distraction," he said after a moment. "I should move up her hanging."

"Nelly is a thorn in St. Gabriel's side. They made sure she was here when Jonah died. They've made her a pawn in this, just like you. They *want* her hung, to eliminate any dissidence on their side. Her death will mark the point of no return. She must go with me. Say she is still in official custody."

"Never."

Hadrian closed his eyes a moment, then opened them to the sound of an animal-like whimpering. A young man was traveling with his fleeing parents, who had been obliged to tie him down in their cart. He was laughing hysterically one moment, muttering gibberish the next. Their voices were despairing, stoic pain on their faces as they tried to soothe him.

Buchanan watched them, saying nothing.

Hadrian fingered the shell of powder in his pocket. He hated himself for saying the words even before they left his mouth. "I will leave you enough of the drug to last Sarah a week."

Buchanan stared at the family disappearing over the hill before speaking. "Bjorn will go," he suddenly declared. "He will have orders to kill her if she tries to escape."

CHAPTER *Fourteen*

The FISHERY HAD a haunted air about it in the winter night. The larger boats lay trapped by ice against their wharves. Smaller ones, hauled by teams of oxen onto log racks, resembled stranded whales. The moonlight, filtered dim and blue through a bank of fog, rendered the solitary sentry an otherworldly scarecrow.

The iceboat freighters lay beyond the guard, tethered to the dock as if they might float away. Hadrian and his three companions crouched for a quarter hour in the shadow under one of the boat racks, assuming the sentry would soon move away from the shed where he lingered to patrol the rest of the docks. When the moon finally rose out of the fog and lit the man's face, Bjorn rose.

"I know that Norger," was all he said before marching deliberately toward him.

He spoke only briefly with the guard, pointing down the docks. Even from the distance it was clear the big policeman was berating the man for staying out of the cold wind instead of making his rounds along the waterfront. No one ever argued with Bjorn. The sentry offered a gesture like a salute and trotted away.

They chose for themselves a sleek midsized craft with a small cockpit that opened through a hatch into the oval-shaped hold. As Nelly settled into the hold beside their packs, Hadrian and Jori collected blankets from the other boats, quickly cutting the rigging on each as they did so. Jori lit the onboard lamps then began to explain how Hadrian and Bjorn must push the outrigger struts to position the boat out on the open ice where it would catch the wind as she unfurled the mainsail.

Bjorn bent to untether the boat, then paused and suddenly sprang to the shadows behind a piling and heaved out a small figure. The boy's legs flailed the air as Bjorn held him at arm's length. Dax ignored Bjorn, calling to Boone.

"I know you'd have to go!" the boy said. "As soon as I saw those jackals steal the ice freighter after the fire last night I knew you'd be following."

Bjorn slowly lowered the boy to the ice and Dax scrambled to the strut, where he began pushing. When the boat did not move, he quieted and fixed Hadrian with a solemn expression. "I told you. I have to get that book back so Mr. Jonah can rest on the other side."

Bjorn snapped a curse and was about to pull the boy away when Hadrian held up a restraining hand. The Norger glared at the two a moment then shrugged and motioned Hadrian to join him on the struts.

In past winters Hadrian had crewed on the ice bullets, as the small racing craft were called, and had suffered so many rough landings on the lake ice when the unstable boats had veered or toppled that the bruising and discomfort had begun to outweigh the thrills of the winning runs. This larger boat was a different creature. The bullets might behave like erratic hares, but as the craft they were on now picked up speed, she was a long graceful snow leopard, loping toward the silver horizon.

As Bjorn, Nelly, and Dax settled into the compartment under the heavy blankets, Hadrian leaned on the rail beside Jori. Her eyes darted from the rattling sail to the rigging, the outriggers, the compass, the ice ahead. He had never seen her so confident, so at ease with herself. She was in control, at a task at which she obviously excelled. Everyone remembered her as a lacrosse star, she had told him when they had argued about who should pilot the boat, but her passion had always been ice sailing.

"Following the coast, it's nearly a hundred miles to the camps," he said, raising his voice over the wind. "Can we make it by dawn?"

Jori's face seemed to shine as she watched the shoreline speed by. "Much sooner. Funny thing about these ice luggers. With their shape and displacement, they'd sink like a stone in the water. But on the ice, riding on the outriggers, they are speed demons. We're doing thirty knots at least." She paused and gave him an inquiring glance. "But the camps aren't our destination," she ventured.

"There must be a salvage trail leading from them to the southwest. From the harbor we'll have to slip through New Jerusalem to find it."

She asked no more, only nodded, then lifted his hand and rested it on the tiller. She spoke no more of the dangers ahead, but only of the rigging and headings, pointing out how the compass had been cleverly mounted in a case embedded with mirrors and crystals that concentrated the light so the needle was illuminated by the small oil lamp built into its base. With her gloved hand resting on his, she showed him how only the subtlest movement was needed to shift direction, then moved to the side, letting him steer. "A good skipper watches the needle and embraces the music," she told him. For a quarter hour she stood silently, the wind whipping her hair, the stars filling her eyes. At last she yawned and lowered herself to the deck, wrapping herself in a blanket before leaning against his legs.

Hadrian had seldom known a feeling of such exhilaration, of such freedom. He was on a strange icebound planet, between known worlds—the catastrophe that was Carthage behind him, the ruined land of killers and thieves ahead. But for the moment, in between, as the aurora danced overhead and the ship ghosted across the empty lake, he was free. Gradually he understood Jori's words, gradually the music reached his consciousness. When they were in perfect trim, the tight rigging ropes emitted a low humming noise as the wind stroked them, the brass pulleys offered a baritone drone, the runners sang on the ice.

He was not sure when Nelly awoke, simply became aware of her kneeling at the hatch below him, her head cocked, listening to the song of their passage. After several minutes she rose and faced forward, loosening her blanket, letting the cold wind whip into her. She had seemed hesitant about leaving the prison with Hadrian, and he realized that of all the mysteries that plagued him, one of the most painful was why Nelly had seemed so ready to die on Buchanan's scaffold. It had not been for Kinzler, and certainly not for the criminals of St. Gabriel. He almost had convinced himself that she was just worn out, too weary of the world and the mess that humans had again made of it to care about living. But there was no resignation in the woman who stood before him, scoured by the wind.

"I didn't know the grain was to be burnt," she declared when she finally turned to him.

"I never thought you did," Hadrian replied.

"That grain was part of Jonah's dream of unification. He wrote me about it. There was finally enough to share with us. Wouldn't it be a world shifter, he wrote me, if New Jerusalem brought the medicines to cure the sick of Carthage and Carthage opened her silos in gratitude?" She raised her chin toward the stars.

"Jori saw log buildings on the island offshore from Kinzler's compound. Two stories, with only a single door and a small hatch opening near the top. Did you ever ask what they were for?"

"They were hidden from shore by the trees. Men from St. Gabriel did the construction. Storage, Kinzler told us. Warehouses for all the trade we expected."

"They've been stealing grain, Nelly. Stealing for months. Many, many tons of it. That must be where it is. Now that they've crippled Carthage they will use it to get what they want."

"Impossible. Kinzler knows how our crops failed. Some of our families have been close to starvation already. He would never hide the means to keep us alive."

"Kinzler hates Carthage as much as Buchanan hates the camps. And Kinzler is only one of the officers. Sauger is his general. He controlled the *Anna*, he controlled Fletcher. This is their final play, Nelly. The camps would mean nothing to Sauger without Kinzler's help in making drugs. Destroying grain and selling drugs. That's how Sauger and Kinzler gain power."

"You're mistaken. Kinzler would never support such crime. He wants only the best for the camps."

"I've seen his little compound. He brings in the drugs from out in the ruined lands and refines them there for shipment to St. Gabriel."

Nelly turned long enough to cast a frown at Hadrian. "You've spent so many years fighting Buchanan you see conspiracy in everything. Kinzler uses that compound to repair the machines brought in from salvage. He makes drugs there, yes, he processes the willow bark according to Jonah's recipe so we can make our own aspirin pills. He's made belladonna from nightshade. That's a poison if not handled correctly, so security precautions have to be taken. He explained it all to the Tribunal. We were going to learn how to make more medicines.

Jonah was experimenting on simplified ways to produce them. Even Carthage has the same serious diseases, just not as widespread. We want to cure everyone."

"The drugs Kinzler makes cure people of their very lives," Hadrian said in a distant tone, wishing for a moment he could just lose himself in the music of the ice again. He turned back to Nelly. "Corresponding about aspirin was innocent enough. Then you started asking Jonah questions about the other medicines and the equipment needed to make them. Eventually Jonah remembered a place that would have everything necessary, a place he thought could have survived. The pharmaceutical facility where his wife once worked."

Nelly sighed. "He told you?"

"No," Hadrian admitted. "He went to old Hamada and found a book, a directory with maps showing exactly where it was. He wrote you asking if you'd be able to go and check there. He asked if he should send the directions out of that directory."

"Kinzler told me he knew the area, said everything there was destroyed, no need to bother."

"Because they wanted it to be their secret, not yours. They told you not to bother, then they had Hamada's book stolen for them." He watched her face to see if she understood what he was saying. "They found the place and are using it to make the drug that is killing people. They are sending supply parties to it every week." He recalled his dinner with Nelly and Kinzler. "You said Shenker was often away. Where does he go?"

"You make it sound like Jonah and I made all this possible, like we opened the door for these hoodlums from St. Gabriel."

When Hadrian did not answer, she turned her face into the shadows. She had nightmares, she had told him, about Jonah saying he forgave her for his death. She had begun to realize it was her letters, her questions, that had been the beginning of the end for Jonah. "Those men in St. Gabriel wanted to combine with us, to have a joint government, a united front against Carthage. The Tribunal declined their offer."

"When? When did the Tribunal reject this merger?"

"Early last summer."

In his mind's eye Hadrian revisited the pages he'd deciphered from Jonah's chronicle. "It was you who stopped it, Nelly. Because Jonah had sent you a letter explaining that St. Gabriel was controlled by escaped criminals."

She didn't reply, just pulled her woolen cap lower over her head as if she finally felt the cold.

"My God, Nelly, it's why they made it so easy for Fletcher to capture you out on the ice. Why were you out there? It had to be because Kinzler or Shenker told you to go."

Nelly stared toward the horizon. He realized she had not spoken about the bruises on her face and arms. "They said one of the First Bloods had been hurt by wolves," she explained, "that his dog team had been attacked and he needed help. But a band of fishermen ambushed me."

"Did you ever see an injured First Blood that day?"

"That iceboat came before I got to him."

"Exactly. Thousands of square miles of ice and Fletcher's crew happens to pick the spot where you are. Your hanging would have guaranteed the camps and St. Gabriel would unite against Carthage. And Kinzler and Sauger would be rid of you. You had become an impediment to them. There never was an injured man out on the ice."

She still would not look at him. "You're wrong."

"Where was your Shenker when Fletcher came for you? He was with you before the library fire, to make sure you performed your role, make sure you became the villain Buchanan wanted and the martyr they wanted. You said Shenker and you were separated the night Jonah died, that he was watching the rear of the library. What if he went inside the library? Jonah understood what was happening, he knew about the drugs. He had been working on a cure, a way to break the addiction, a way to end Sauger's plans. He was going to explain the conspiracy, tell you about his breakthrough, how it would turn every-thing around. Having you introduce the antidote would be the per-fect way to unite the camps and Carthage at last. Where was Shenker? Where was Kinzler? Your first escape was a tactic to fan the flames. It was part of the script, just like your recapture was. They didn't free you this time, I did. They wanted you to hang as much as Buchanan wanted it. Jonah had to die . . . and so did you."

Nelly once again did not reply. She tightened her scarf and moved forward to the front of the boat, staring out over the ice, a lonely fig-urehead in the shimmering night.

"SHE'S TOO BEAUTIFUL, Hadrian," Jori protested when Hadrian explained what they would do with the iceboat when they arrived at New Jerusalem. It was an hour before dawn.

"She won't be lost, she'll just stray a bit," Hadrian reassured her. "Just ease toward shore and tack about. We'll roll off with the packs. Then you aim her toward the center of the lake, tie the tiller down, and join us. The jackals will be no more than two hours behind us. This mast is over thirty feet high. It will glow like a beacon as the sun rises. They'll follow her, recover her. It buys us another few hours."

Jori reluctantly agreed. They hit the ice hard as she expertly swung the boat about.

They had begun stealing across the ice to the compound when Bjorn suddenly turned in alarm. His prisoner was missing. His hand went to the gun at his waist, then Hadrian pointed to a shadow running toward the nearby island. They caught up with Nelly as she approached the first of the squat two-story buildings. The heavy door was locked but Nelly spotted the rough timber ladder lying on the snow nearby. Hadrian silently helped her ease it in place under the hatch by the eaves. She was at the hatch moments later, flinging open its small door then leaning into the opening. Even from below they could make out the rich, sweet scent of the grain. She seemed to go limp for a moment, then closed the hatch and slowly descended.

"He is saving it, for when we need it most," she offered unconvincingly, then let Jori lead her away toward the shoreline.

They watched the compound for five minutes, waiting for its sentry to appear. Then Hadrian conferred briefly with Bjorn and began walking straight toward the main gate. He had nearly reached it when a man appeared with a shotgun in one hand, a lantern in the other.

"I'm looking for Kinzler," Hadrian announced, his breath fogging the air. His hand touched the sword knife he had retrieved from Jonah's vault, his only weapon. "A message from St. Gabriel."

"In the outlands, getting the big shipment," the guard said as he raised the lantern toward Hadrian's face. "Hell, Sauger knows that—" He collapsed to the ground before finishing his sentence. Bjorn had silenced him with a blow to the back of his head, then grabbed his shotgun as he fell.

They stayed along the inside wall, in the darkest shadows, confirming there were no more sentries, then entered the building closest to the gate.

"Just as I said," Nelly declared, as Hadrian held the lantern over a workbench strewn with small hand tools, gears, and springs. At least three mechanical clocks lay in pieces.

"Your chairman doesn't need a walled compound and an armed sentry to fix timepieces," Hadrian pointed out. "Are you saying you've never been inside here? You were never curious?"

"I told you about the dangers of the belladonna he was working on. And trade with St. Gabriel has become the key to our survival. The salvage they bring to us for repair has to be protected. You know people here are desperate. If they could steal a clock and get it to the black market in Carthage, they could earn enough to keep them alive for months. And Kinzler did show us, the Tribunal, showed us this shop and the little lab where he makes the medicine."

"Take us there," Hadrian said, "to his little lab."

She lit a second lantern and led them to a door at the end of the central building. They found themselves in a small, warm chamber with two wooden racks that held large metal trays where a white brine was slowly evaporating. Under each tray was a small brazier with glowing coals to accelerate the drying.

"And the rest of the building?" Hadrian and Jori exchanged a glance. They had been in the main chamber of the building before, when Hadrian had tried, and failed, to rescue Jori. He hadn't had time to study the contents of the room.

"Storage. Vats for soaking the willow bark, to make the extract that gets evaporated. It's a simple process, but unwieldy on this scale."

Hadrian led the way now, into the main entrance. There were indeed wooden containers along the back wall, the vats Nelly had just described. The adjoining wall had a large stove built into it, bearing several heavy cooking pots. As he began lifting the lids off the vats, Nelly's eyes narrowed with worry. There was no aspirin being prepared in the room. The vats contained a brown pasty substance that, judging from the residue in the pots on the stove, had been poured into them after being heated. Along the wall opposite the

stove were more trays, where the same paste had been spread in lay-
ers. On the ones nearest the door the paste had dried into a familiar
white powder. Under the table lay several empty kegs, waiting to be
filled.

Hadrian opened the door of the cabinets that lined a wall. Clay
crocks jammed the shelves. Several held only turpentine, but most also
contained an orange scum on the surface. He found a spatula and ran
it over the bottom of one of the crocks, scooping up a brown sludge.
"They bring the main ingredient from the factory in the ruined lands,"
he said, "then precipitate this by treating it with the solvent, cook it,
and dry it in the trays."

Nelly stood very still, saying nothing, then marched to the shelves
and began tipping over each of the crocks, letting the pungent turpentine spill out over the wooden floor. Hadrian slowly retreated, pulling
Dax with him out the door just as Nelly threw the lantern onto the
volatile solvent. It burst into flame.

Outside, Jori showed Nelly the kegs of turpentine stored along the
palisade wall. Bjorn did not object when Nelly gestured for him to carry
them to the doors of the other buildings, where she kicked out the
bungs that plugged them. He began pouring out the contents of another
keg onto the frozen ground, making rivulets of the liquid leading to the
buildings from where he stood. Nelly tossed a burning stave into the
solvent. They were already across the little isthmus and into the forest
when the explosions broke the silence of the night.

WHEN NELLY HAD brought them to the well-worn trail that would
take them to the southwest, she stopped, turning to Bjorn with her
arms extended. The big Norwegian was unable to hide the admiration
with which he regarded the bald woman. She had managed to destroy

Kinzler's compound without a word, still shackled. The policeman hesitated, glancing at Jori, who technically outranked him.

"If we encountered a salvage party," Jori suggested, "a leading member of their Tribunal may be able to talk our way through." Hadrian reached for his knife.

Bjorn seemed relieved as he cut through the cords. "But I am still responsible for you," he reminded Nelly, who replied with a weary grin.

After the first hour, Dax and Jori took the lead over the steep, icy terrain. Most of the trail followed old roads, apparent not so much from the concrete shards sometimes visible through the snow as from the trees. They followed swaths of trees that were no more than fifteen or twenty years old, twenty-foot-wide ribbons between much taller trees of fifty, even a hundred years' growth.

They pushed hard, not certain of their destination, staying always on the most heavily used tracks, crossing over crude log bridges erected where highway overpasses had once existed, passing snow-packed campsites showing frequent use by men and horses. As they traveled, the cold bite of the air lessened and the snow began to thin, until finally it was present only in scattered patches.

Twice they leapt to cover as Dax whistled warnings, watching salvage parties ride by, their pack animals piled high with treasure. Once, in the night, they heard the blood-curdling roar of a great beast. Hadrian remembered the tales of zoo predators liberated a generation earlier. At dawn one morning he caught a glimpse of what he would have sworn was a monkey, watching them from a tree.

On the third day, as Dax and Jori paused at a ledge that overlooked a long, low valley, Hadrian realized their journey was over. His companions were puzzling over a row of regularly spaced hills, covered with plant growth but strangely angular in shape, vine-covered mesas that rose fifty, even a hundred feet above the low valley floor.

"Buildings," he said. "At least once they were buildings," he amended as he saw the uncertainty on the faces of Jori, Bjorn, and Dax. Now the structures were just part of the landscape, no different from the Mayan temples long ago lost in the jungle. It was as if nature had decided she was finished with the experiment that was mankind.

"But it makes no sense," Jori said. "Why would buildings need to be so tall?"

"It was just something people did," Nelly said in a voice that was almost a whisper, glancing at Hadrian. From long experience they knew it was not possible to fully convey to the new generation the mass of population, the mazes of highways, the acres of asphalt and concrete, the transmission lines and millions of automobiles that had defined the old world.

"It would have been a perfect bio sink," Nelly said at his shoulder. The steep, tall ridges on either side of the valley may have protected the buildings from blast waves, but the deep bowl would have trapped the biological agents that had spread across the landscape.

"For years," he agreed, remembering how Standish and his party had died there two years after the settlement of Carthage. Even now he was wary of sending any of their party into the valley. But then he saw a thin plume of smoke rising from the opposite hillside. Although the smoke seemed to rise up directly from the ground, with no sign of a fire, fifty yards below it he now spied a clearing whose shadows held several men and horses. He scanned the surrounding terrain, then watched as several of the distant figures disappeared into a wall of vegetation.

"Jonah described it as one of those low-impact buildings," he explained, referring to the environmentally self-contained buildings that were used for new industrial operations in the years just before the shifting. "It must be built into the hill, underground, with a small entrance from the outside."

"It's what Jonah meant when he wrote to me that it might have survived," Nelly told them. "It would not have been under attack by the elements because it was built into the earth itself."

As Bjorn led the others down the slope, Hadrian lingered, a vague recollection trying to break through to his consciousness. He scanned the valley floor once more, all the way to the low river bottom where the structures ended, and then the memory burst through. He had been to this town. He had taken his son to a baseball game here, sat in the community park at the river bottom, eating a hot dog and cheering as boys sprinted between bases. Studying the end of the valley, he saw it as it had been then, then as it would have been when Standish had led his salvage party there. It was the deepest point in the valley. The little park had been the biosink where Standish had died.

Staying off the cleared path now meant traversing the thickets that crowded the slopes. It was late afternoon by the time they reached Hadrian's objective, the square mountain of brush and vine directly opposite the old pharmaceutical factory. It had been a four- or five-story office building. Most of its windows had been blown in so that impenetrable mats of roots and tendrils crowded inside, extending deep into the interior space. The first-floor lobby area had been stripped by salvagers, its walls now covered with vines. Hadrian paced along the walls, finding a patch of new growth where vines were reclaiming a section that had been torn away by salvagers. He probed the vegetation, discovering a door handle, which he pulled open to reveal a stairwell. He lit a candle and began climbing the stairs.

The door on the third-floor landing gave way when Bjorn and Hadrian put their combined weight against it. He quickly located an office window in which the glass had shattered and pushed the vines aside. They were overlooking the buried factory, only a hundred yards away.

As the others set up a camp in a conference room, he studied the pharmaceutical plant. He saw how the slope over the buried building had been cleared, revealing box-shaped structures that must be sky-lights and vents. Before the light faded, a large party departed, pack-horses full. Only five mounts were left.

Nelly arrived at his side in time to watch as a big man with a rifle appeared and took up a sentry position on the slope above the entry.

"Nelly," he said. "Tell me why Jonah thought this plant would provide the answer to your problems."

"He knew it well because it was where his wife worked as a senior researcher, making pharmaceuticals. Cancer drugs mostly."

"He wasn't sending you for cancer drugs."

"No. The plant was a prototype, using simpler technologies based on natural processes and heavy use of water. Fermentation with molds and bacteria. It required lots of water for the vats, for washings, for precipitation tanks. He said it would have the simple lab equipment we needed to refine our aspirin and make permanent supplies of it. If we were lucky, he said, we might find enough vats and other equipment to begin making penicillin. Do you know how many in the camps and Carthage die every year of pneumonia? Penicillin could save most of them. His letters had more and more enthusiasm about the possibilities. He was doing research on his own and reminded us that in the years before the ending there had been many discoveries made for producing medicines from fermentation. The bacteria in the vats replaced entire factories.

"But he warned us that a salvage team had died there long ago. And Kinzler said there was nothing left." She paused. He saw the pain in her eyes as she gazed out over the dead town. "We don't need sal-vage. If I had my way, we'd wait another hundred years before letting anyone into these places."

"They would have manuals in there," Hadrian said. "Chemistry books. A library on chemical molecules and how to make them in those vats."

When Nelly didn't reply he pointed to the water tower nearly obscured by trees near the top of the ridge, still catching the light of the setting sun. "Is that part of the operations?"

"I have never been here," she reminded him. "But yes, I would think so. Manufacturing plants had to be self-sufficient by the time this one was built. It would have had its own water source to run turbines and for all the water used in the process. The tank, and probably a lake to feed it."

Nelly fell silent as she stared at the entry to the plant with its armed guard. "When he produced the first batches of aspirin, Kinzler was elected to the Tribunal," she told him. "When he negotiated an alliance with St. Gabriel, he was made chairman." Then she walked away.

Hadrian watched the stars rise over the ridge and the invisible factory below, recalling how the weapons that had ended another world had also been launched from subterranean bunkers.

When he finally returned to their makeshift camp, Nelly was at the table by Dax, explaining objects the boy had scavenged and piled before him. He gripped a stapler like a treasure, testing it again and again with scrap papers, then gleefully demonstrated a handheld hole punch to Hadrian.

As they shared a paltry meal, their supplies nearly gone, Hadrian explained his plan. The few horses left meant there would only be a handful of men inside. They should try to distract the sentry at dawn, he proposed, then steal into the factory and take the others by surprise.

"You said they have guns," Nelly observed. When Hadrian nodded she offered a sly smile. "Then I think we just go in conspicuously, parading our prisoners," she declared, and explained her own proposal.

Jori, Bjorn, and Hadrian took two-hour shifts as sentries. Toward the end of his shift Hadrian found a window on the opposite side where the vines were thinner, allowing a wide view down the moonlit valley. The landscape had been settled for centuries, with the original natives displaced by farmers, then by industrial works as the canal to the ocean had pierced it. For perhaps two hundred years out of millions, it had teemed with human activity, had been a place of mule-drawn barges and bulldozers, steam locomotives and computer-chip factories, marching bands and shopping malls. Then in one sudden storm the humans had been scoured from the landscape.

When he turned at a low whistle from Bjorn, coming to relieve him, Dax was standing at his elbow, silently staring out the window. The boy followed Hadrian down the hall as he handed over the shotgun to the Norger. He was about to find a place to sleep when he saw the unsettled expression on the boy's face, and he recalled how withdrawn the boy had seemed since entering the town. Picking up two of the lit candles, he handed one to Dax, and gestured for the boy to follow him down the hallway. The salvagers who had visited the building had not been thorough. Offices seldom held much of value for the colony. They had not touched some of the inner doors. Hadrian pulled a fire extinguisher from its wall cabinet and smashed a rusty door handle. The door led into another stairway.

Dax said nothing as they walked down, then paused with wide eyes as they entered the garage under the building. Hadrian raised his candle over a red convertible, its tires flat, its top in mildewed tatters. Dax approached hesitantly as Hadrian reached through the top, popped up the lock, and opened the driver's door. After a moment Dax reached out and touched the steering wheel, then looked up in disbelief.

Hadrian pressed the latch for the trunk and to his surprise it popped open. He pulled Dax, still in his silent paralysis, to the rear of the car, then recited the names of the incongruous items arrayed before them. A tennis racket. A chainsaw. A baseball bat. A hair dryer. He retrieved the lug wrench and began walking along the other cars, forcing open the trunks with the wrench as he did so. As the boy walked from one to another, gazing at the objects they contained, emotions swirled on his face. Confusion, anger, bitterness, and melancholy.

"This is the world that is behind us, Dax," he declared, "not the one on the other side."

HE KNEW HE would not find slumber, so he took the guard shift after Bjorn, letting Jori sleep through her watch. Strange waking dreams came to him as he surveyed the ruined landscape. In his mind's eye the vegetation retreated and the buildings and streets emerged. He saw cars and trucks, pedestrians entering cafes and shops, policemen directing traffic, the neon lights of fast-food restaurants, a school bus loaded with a high school team, an old woman walking a terrier. He began hearing people making small talk in the corridor behind him, the whirl of office printers, and elevator chimes. He shook his head violently, muttering a curse. He was done with shadow people, he wanted them to leave him alone.

Then suddenly came a scent of licorice, and he wanted more than anything to be with one of the shadows. He stopped breathing, fearful of breaking the spell, as he inched around. His son was wearing the uniform of his junior baseball team, smiling expectantly, his shaggy blond hair jutting out from his cap, a piece of red licorice from his pocket. As the boy raised his glove for Hadrian to toss him a ball, tears welled in his eyes. He did not move for fear of losing the boy, but his son pushed back his wayward hair and patted his glove, as if expecting Hadrian to throw. He took a step forward, seizing on a ridiculous hope that he could touch the boy. But the closer he came, the more tenuous the specter became, until there was only an arm extending from a shadow, still holding the glove.

Bjorn found him at one of the open windows, looking through the vines.

"She's not in her blankets," he announced. "She didn't eat tonight."

Hadrian puzzled at the tone in the policeman's voice. It was not anger, but a mix of worry and disappointment. "Nelly needs time to herself," he said. "As much as she needs food."

Bjorn stepped to his side and gazed out the window. "She reminds me of my grandmother."

Hadrian paused, not certain he had heard right. "You remember your grandmother?"

"My mother had a photograph she had brought with her, from before. A strong face like Nelly's, with eyes like burning wicks. My mother would speak of her so often she was like another member of our household when I was young. My grandmother was a bold woman. Lived alone and had a dory she rowed out in the sea to catch codfish. Always made sure people did the right thing. They said she was the conscience of the village."

It was an extraordinary speech for the big Norger, the most words Hadrian had ever heard him string together at one time. Nelly was no longer his prisoner. "You're right, Bjorn. She is the conscience of the village."

"Sometimes I watch her when she sleeps. It makes me . . ." Bjorn struggled for words. "It makes me feel peaceful. But when she is awake I think sometimes she is afraid of me." There was chagrin in his voice now.

"She just doesn't know you well enough," Hadrian ventured, realizing that perhaps he too did not know the Norger well enough.

"She would listen to you. This is a place of death. Not safe."

At last Hadrian grasped the plea in Bjorn's words. "Of course. I will find her," he replied. His companion gave a relieved nod. He refused to take the shotgun from him, as if Hadrian would have greater need of it.

Hadrian grew more concerned as he searched the open rooms of the floor. He found a gap in the vines over one of the shattered windows and leaned out over the town. The moon was bright now, bright enough to show a narrow track through the thickets that once had been streets, bright enough to cast a silvery pall on the statue that sat atop an outcropping in the middle of town.

He heard, but did not see, the creatures that stalked him as he moved along the trail, cursing himself for not bringing a lantern. When he reached the broad clearing, he saw it was strewn with outcroppings of various sizes, none more than a dozen feet tall. As he climbed onto the one he had seen, it gave a strangely hollow sound. He pushed his foot through the loose snow and matted vegetation to a metal surface. A truck. The mounds were all vehicles abandoned in the town square, covered with two decades of plant life.

Nelly did not seem to notice him. She was staring down the ruined street, the moonlight washing her face. She had been weeping.

He froze as he bent to sit beside her, then quickly swung the shotgun up. A few feet below her sat a black wolf, gazing intently at her. She pushed the gun barrel down. "He's been here for an hour," she said. "He likes my singing."

Hadrian knelt beside her, keeping the gun ready. The animal was huge, larger than any wolf he had ever seen. He opened his mouth to warn Nelly that the rest of the pack must be close by when she suddenly began to sing.

There was no stopping her once she had started one of her chants. Indeed, after a few moments, he had no interest in doing so. Her deep, lilting song-prayer seemed to wind out into the world like one of the vines, wrapping its tendrils around the heart of any creature that listened. Hadrian stared at her. The wolf stared at her. More tears began streaming down her cheeks but still she sang. Her breath hung about her in the cold air, like a halo in the moonlight.

Hadrian thought he heard segments of old folk ballads, of rock songs, of earlier dance tunes and hymns, all woven into one rich tapestry of sound. She seemed to sing impossibly long between breaths. An owl landed on a nearby tree, turning its horned ears toward her.

When she finally stopped, the silence was like a sacred thing, the time between priests in a cathedral. Hadrian wanted to throw his gun away.

"How often have you come out into the lands?" he asked after a long time.

"Never. I knew I couldn't bear it." Hadrian recalled her brooding silences on the iceboat, on their trek along the trail. She had been harboring her fear, not of the jackals, not of the wild animals, but of the ruins she knew she would finally have to encounter. "I still can't bear it, Hadrian. Ever since we arrived there's been a terrible weight pushing down on me."

The wolf below gave a low utterance that hinted of impatience.

Melancholy overtook her face. "It's his world now," she said peacefully. "I won't come back again."

Suddenly Hadrian understood her song. It had been a eulogy for the lost world, a farewell that had taken all these years to give.

"We should go back," he suggested. "Bjorn was worried."

"A sweet boy. I can see it in his eyes. I can see his pain. When you grow into an ox everyone expects you to be an ox, even if you are something else inside."

Restless, hungry cries came from the brush. The wolf uttered a low growl of rebuke and the sounds stopped.

"We should go back," Hadrian repeated.

"I can't. Go. You need your sleep. I am not done."

"Then I am not done."

Nelly smiled again and studied him as if for the first time. "Put down your gun, Hadrian," she said softly, then gestured him to rise so she could reposition him. They sat back to back, legs folded under them, and she began a new litany. After the first few minutes he found himself making humming sounds, as if something inside him anticipated the rhythm, had somehow recognized the song. He lost all track of time. He realized other sounds were coming out of his throat, sounds that came out as if of their own volition and somehow harmonized with those of Nelly, sounds that sometimes continued during the long minutes when her song choked away and she sobbed in pain. When he looked down, two smaller wolves were watching from his side of the old truck.

There was a blush of dawn in the east when Hadrian finally turned and, with a hand on her knee, quieted her. The wolves were gone.

"We had a whole world once, didn't we," she said, her voice quite hoarse. "Now everything goes dark."

"Not everything, not for us," he said as he reached out and helped her stand. "Surely you don't forget."

"Forget?"

"You and me and Jonah. We are the ones who rage against the dying of the light."

CHAPTER *Fifteen*

THEY WERE THIRTY yards from the entrance to the factory when an arrow hit a boulder beside them and exploded. A tall muscular figure emerged from the shadows, nocking another arrow in his bow. Sebastian said nothing as he circled the group, studying them with more amusement than alarm. Jori and Hadrian were in the front, hands tied with their shoelaces, Nelly behind them holding Jori's gun, Dax in the rear holding the baseball bat they had found in the garage.

"I was sad when I heard you had died," the First Blood said to Hadrian.

"Me too. I wanted to stay alive to get even with you for drugging my drink."

Sebastian grinned. "You needed the sleep."

Somehow Hadrian found it hard to resent the man. "I didn't think we'd be greeted with artillery," he said, pointing to the blackened rock.

Sebastian extracted one of the strange arrows from his quiver. "Something Kinzler devised. Good for scaring away wolves. They're thick as flies around here." The arrow ended not with a point but with a shotgun shell mounted in a sleeve. "The shell slides back when it strikes, slams into a pin that fires it. Shenker calls it a toy. You can't go in there," he added, as Nelly pushed Hadrian toward the entrance.

Nelly straightened up and spoke with an unusual tone of authority. "Of course I can. You know damned well I'm a member of the Tribunal of New Jerusalem, Sebastian. One of your many brothers cuts my firewood. I have important messages for Kinzler. These two followed me after I escaped from Carthage, so the boy and I got the jump on them. They need to be interrogated." She put her hand on the door handle.

Sebastian put his foot against the door and fixed her with a solemn gaze. "I heard you last night," he said to Nelly. "I didn't believe my brother Nathaniel when he told me about your singing. He said the dead from the old world spoke through you." There was an odd tone of invitation in his voice.

"Who I speak for today is the Tribunal. Where is Kinzler?"

"You missed him. They're taking a shipment back for Sauger. The biggest one yet, the one they've been waiting for. Kinzler left yesterday, to rendezvous with Fletcher at the harbor."

"Then you will take my prisoners and let me rest before I set out to catch up with him."

Sebastian's skeptical gaze shifted back and forth from Hadrian to Nelly, then rested on Jori. "You still a policeman?"

"I am sworn to the service of Carthage," she replied defiantly.

Sebastian grinned. "I like her," he said to Hadrian, then pointed to the sword-knife in Hadrian's belt. He silently handed it to him.

Nelly did not resist when he reached out and took the gun from her hand. Sebastian handed his bow and quiver to Dax, trading for the bat. "Guard the door, boy," he said, and pulled the door open. As he stepped inside, Hadrian resisted the temptation to look about for Bjorn, waiting in the rocks.

Lifting a lantern from a table by the wall, Sebastian directed them down a long, descending corridor whose aged carpet was caked with mud and mildew. They walked past several dimly lit chambers packed with large stainless steel tanks connected to a web of pipes, in the last of which a man in a tattered lab coat was leaning over a vat. Hadrian heard the low hiss of steam running through pipes overhead. He remembered the smoke he had seen the day before.

Some elements of the factory were frozen in time. Safety stations with fire extinguishers and fire axes were built in the walls, covered with the grime of many years. A bulletin board displayed notes for a church social, a bake sale, a company picnic. A faded banner boasted WE ARE PROUDLY SAVING LIVES ALL OVER THE WORLD.

At last they reached a brightly lit conference room, one of the chambers under a skylight.

"Idiot!" a man shouted from the shadows at Sebastian as they entered. "No one is ever allowed to—" Shenker's words died away as he stepped forward and recognized the intruders.

"You'll be pleased to know I escaped again," Nelly declared.

Shenker's face showed no pleasure at all. "Of course."

"An impressive facility," Hadrian observed. "We never would have imagined one of the old factories could be rehabilitated."

The scar on Shenker's cheek moved up and down as he clenched his jaw, looking from Nelly to Hadrian. He gave a grunt of satisfaction as he spotted the sword-knife at Sebastian's waist and pulled it away. "I thought I'd never see this again. A gift from my one-eyed friend." He looked back at Hadrian and replied. "Adapted. Only a small part of the equipment was still usable. But it was enough."

"The miracle," Hadrian suggested, "is that you manage to make chemicals that don't kill a person outright."

Shenker offered a lightless grin. "There were startup difficulties. We don't have the ability to run lab simulations. There had to be experimentation."

"Human trials, you mean."

"Salvage crews are accustomed to high attrition in their ranks."

Hadrian considered Shenker's cold announcement. "St. Gabriel salvagers being sacrificed by exile scientists. Interesting way to build an alliance."

"Not Sauger's people," Shenker shot back.

Sebastian went very still. The only thing that moved were his eyes, slowly shifting from Hadrian to Shenker. The salvage teams had been largely composed of First Bloods.

"Still," Hadrian prodded, "hard to believe you could accomplish so much."

"When Jonah Beck starting speaking of penicillin, Kinzler saw the opportunity for something even bigger. We could never synthesize the complex drugs they used to make here. But they had a whole library about chemical production from colonies of mold and bacteria. Some of those colonies in the vats had been dormant all these years, just needed heat and water to come back to life. It took weeks to find the right ones, but once we did, all we needed were the vats, heat, water, and drying tables."

"You must be very proud of yourself," Hadrian said.

Shenker sensed the sarcasm in his voice. "Be proud of your dead professor. He made it all possible. When we saw those letters we realized the possibilities."

"I don't actually recall showing you those letters," Nelly inserted.

Shenker circled them, then peevishly grabbed the bat from Sebastian and with it tapped Jori and Hadrian on the shoulder, pushing them down into the chairs. He studied Nelly again, then pushed her into the chair beside Hadrian and shook his head at Sebastian. "Good thing we don't rely on you for your brains. Kinzler's going to be furious with you. She knows too much now to be useful." He circled the table, eyeing Hadrian as he stroked the heavy end of the bat, then sighed and tossed it behind him.

"You're slowly poisoning people," Nelly declared.

"You made sure we read our history," Shenker reminded her. "There's always been drugs. Opium eaters. Hashish smokers. Cocaine snorters."

"They were on the fringe of society. We have no fringe to spare."

"You are thinking about it all wrong. The new world will have a new currency. Before we're done we'll have carpenters and masons and shipwrights ready to work for us all day for a spoonful of powder. Carthage will pay for what it did to us."

"You'll have carpenters and masons crawling up the walls."

Shenker glanced at Sebastian. "We'll always have strong horses to carry our loads. It's the way of the world."

The First Blood pointed at Hadrian. "Sauger will want him in St. Gabe."

Shenker gave a weary sigh. "This is politics. I don't debate politics with salvage horses. You fail to understand the art of making martyrs." He pointed to Nelly. "Her body will have to go back to Carthage. You can claim the reward and spend it on Sauger's whores."

"I understand why I have to die, but why did Jonah have to die?" Hadrian asked.

"Because he was so fucking clairvoyant." Shenker stepped to a desk by the wall and returned with a book, a well-worn directory of businesses and their products, then sat down. "As soon as he discovered this was missing, he was on to us. Put the pieces together immediately. Nelly told him about the history of St. Gabriel and the way men in grey came to it. He was the one who guessed that meant prison uniforms. Somehow he figured out what we were doing here, knew the effects of what we were making. Always a step ahead."

"So you killed him, like you killed the early salvage crews."

"They were different. They were experiments. I watched one of them take a swallow of that first batch. His eyes went into the back of his head. He was dead before he hit the floor. Trial and error." He shrugged. "The old drug companies kept warehouses of monkeys to use. We went through the first crew in a week."

Nelly's face twisted with anger. "You as good as murdered them," she hissed.

"The will of the people will not be denied."

Hadrian could actually hear the wind of the baseball bat as Sebastian swung it, then the sharp crack of breaking bone. The back of Shenker's head collapsed so abruptly from the blow that Hadrian doubted he felt a thing.

"Deny that, prick," Sebastian spat. "My brother was in that first crew."

Shenker didn't move. He just looked down at the floor as if he had lost his thought. Blood began dripping out of his nose.

Nelly seemed to stop breathing. Jori stepped to her side as if to defend her.

"They treat us like this," Sebastian said with a sigh. "Their pack-horses and lab monkeys." He poked Shenker. "You always talk too much." Threat was still in his voice, as if he were daring Shenker to respond. One of the dead man's eyes began filling with blood.

"My mother is building a cabin in the forest," the First Blood said conversationally, looking at Hadrian now. "She says we can make a better life there."

Hadrian nodded, then spoke in a whisper. "Give thanks for such a mother."

Sebastian looked at the bat in his hand, then glanced self-consciously at Nelly. "I'm sorry," he said, and threw the bat into the shadows.

"I'm sorry," Nelly said back, not bothering to wipe away her tears.

"We're going to destroy this place, Sebastian," Hadrian said. "The others need to leave. Alive."

Sebastian nodded. "We're under a lake. Everyone worries about the old pipes breaking and flooding the place." He gestured down the corridor. "The main water intakes are in a room at the end of the hall. Up a ladder to a wall of valves. I'll show you." He handed the pistol to Jori. "The others are just exiles paid to work here. They won't argue with you."

Hadrian handed the book Shenker had been holding to Jori. "For Dax," he said, then followed the First Blood into the corridor.

Sebastian grabbed an ax from a hall fire station and led Hadrian to the mechanical room. Quickly they climbed the ladder up a steel scaffold to the intakes. Hadrian began opening valves as his companion pounded the ax into the big cast-iron pipes. A split appeared in the brittle metal of a main and the pipe began to groan, then burst. As Hadrian frantically climbed down through the cold torrent, Sebastian smashed open another pipe, disappearing behind a cascade of water. Hadrian lingered, waiting for Sebastian as the deluge rapidly rose around his calves, then suddenly the big man appeared, laughing as he slid down the ladder rails.

The water rose with frightening speed, surging at their knees now, forming an angry wave as it reached the narrow hallway, then poured into the production rooms. Sebastian could not stop laughing as he slammed the ax into one vat, then another, on down the row, splitting them at their seams, oblivious to the flood swirling at his waist. By the time Hadrian was able to pull him away, several other tanks were floating away.

Outside, the three operators were sitting on the ground with their hands on their heads, staring in confusion at Bjorn, who pointed his shotgun at them, and Dax, who aimed one of the explosive arrows.

Sebastian, who'd darted into a small room by the entrance, emerged holding two packs. "Food for our journey back," he announced.

Bjorn frowned as he hung the packs on saddles. "There's only enough horses for us," he said.

"Dax will ride with me," Hadrian explained, and gestured his companions to their mounts. Water began spraying out of the seams between the closed entry doors. Dax paused long enough to stuff the book Jori had given him into a saddlebag.

As the rest of the party rode away, Hadrian helped Dax mount behind him, then turned his horse to look at the chagrined exiles who had been forced out of the factory. Lifting the pack from his saddle horn, he dumped out half its contents, then pressed his heels to his mount and was gone.

THEY SAT AT their campfire that night long after the logs had burnt to embers, with Nelly offering a low, sad humming song toward the sky and Dax staying closer than usual, not objecting when Jori held his hand. The boy had been unusually quiet. The ruined lands had deeply affected him.

Something had been troubling Hadrian all day. "Last spring," he asked Dax at last, "did you take Jonah to one of the ghosts?"

"There was one from St. Gabe who was a ghost. He brought us toys and told us about the other side. For half a day he lay in the grass by the mill after taking his medicine. I forgot Mr. Jonah was coming to read to us. I was shaking him, calling in his ear, when Mr. Jonah appeared. He spent a long time studying him, holding his wrist, looking into his eyes, smelling his breath, wanting to know what kind of medicine he had taken. Then he just stops breathing. His white eyes were open, and we watched as they went all dull, like dirty marbles."

Dax paused and pushed back his wayward hair. "Mr. Jonah knew he wasn't from Carthage. He asked about others like him, and I told him about all the ghosts and their travels. He said this one would travel no more, for we had just seen the dying of his light.

"Then Mr. Jonah gets out a paper and starts taking notes and finds the sturgeon-skin pouch that had the last of his medicine. He said there'd be no reading that day, that I was to go to the fishery and tell them to take the body home."

Jonah had watched the dying of a ghost's light. The words echoed in Hadrian's head long after the others had fallen asleep.

THE LAST NIGHT before New Jerusalem, Hadrian's restless sleep was disturbed by a faint rattling. At first he thought the noise was the scolding sound of a little night animal on the nearby ledge, a wood mouse or vole chattering its teeth at an intruder in its nest. But it did not cease as he approached the moonlit ledge. Sebastian was just one more grey mound on the boulder-strewn landscape, but then he moved, and Hadrian saw the glint of his gun barrel. The sound was coming from the First Blood, from his hands. As Hadrian inched forward he heard the words. *Hail Mary, full of grace.* The First Blood was counting prayer beads.

Sebastian continued for a few moments after Hadrian sat beside him, finishing his rosary prayer. "I'm sorry," Hadrian said. "I couldn't sleep. I didn't know anyone else was here." The ledge overlooked a river and a broad expanse of forest. Miles away could be seen the silver plain of the frozen lake.

Sebastian raised the beads in his hand. "My mother was raised in one of those old Christian schools. She prays every day, gave beads to each of us when we began salvage trips. She's not going to like it when I tell her I killed that Shenker."

"Shenker killed your younger brother."

"I won't tell her that part. It would ruin her."

"Then tell her he was a murderer who was trying to kill many others."

The First Blood nodded. "And you know what she will do? She will pray for Shenker's soul. She will ask me to join her. I don't think I'll be able to do that."

They watched the sky in silence. A meteor, or a dying satellite, burnt out high overhead.

"Do you ever think how it might have been at St. Gabriel," Hadrian asked, "if you'd sent Sauger and his men away when they first showed up?"

"There were three dozen of us but most were children and women. I was only five or six. Our men had been away at jobs in the cities when the sky fell in. Sauger had a dozen strong men. They helped build our first house. That place where Sauger has his tavern used to be our church. The chicken farmer had preserved that chapel all those years, because he had religion too. At first they would come and sing like everyone else, listen when my mother read from her Bible."

"But today it is a place of slaves and thieves and killers."

Sebastian was silent a long time. "I guess what a place is like depends on its founders," he said. "Sauger said you were a founder, at Carthage."

The words hurt more than Sebastian intended. "I guess it depends on which founders prevail," Hadrian replied.

They grew silent again, watching the sky.

"Did Shenker ever speak about killing Jonah Beck?" Hadrian finally asked.

"He got drunk once and bragged about cutting the heart out of Carthage." Sebastian looked at him questioningly.

"Shenker worshiped Sauger," Sebastian continued when Hadrian did not reply, "said he was a genius."

"A genius at using people, and disposing of them when he finishes with them," Hadrian said. "You and the First Bloods do Sauger's heaviest lifting. He convinced the merchants, the fishermen, the millers to continue what they were doing, just let him manage it for still greater returns. Only a handful at the top know the truth."

"Most of the salvage teams," Sebastian added, "get paid in credit at Sauger's tavern. Liquor, food, and women." He quieted a moment, seeming to consider Hadrian's words. "I don't know who helped Shenker kill your friend Jonah, if that's what you mean to ask. Sometimes there'd be meetings with people from Carthage, but usually they were far out on the lake. Two or three of the steamers would meet and then new orders would be issued. Men would be needed to help unload grain. We would be sent to Carthage to pick up supplies to take by horseback to the factory."

"Where in Carthage?"

"A horse farm south of town. A wagon would meet us at the docks and drive us there. A big place, with racehorses. Sometimes the owner would be there, but we weren't ever in his company."

"You mean the Dutchman?"

"Not him. He's dead. Some of the fishermen still laugh about how he died. The new owner. From Carthage."

Hadrian leaned toward the First Blood. Sebastian was speaking about the last piece of the puzzle, the keystone, the invisible link to the government. "You've never seen him?"

"Never. Comes at night, in a black carriage, stays at the big house and has some of those jackals for guards. In Carthage they always do the security. On this side Sauger likes us to do it. A group from my tribe is waiting at New Jerusalem, to escort Kinzler's big shipment."

"Sauger relies on your people. Your mother, you say, is building a new place in the forest."

Sebastian stared at him. "I don't understand."

"You could be a founder, Sebastian. You and your mother and your surviving brothers. Tell your people what Sauger is doing. Destroying children in Carthage. Driving us to starvation. You could cut him off from his salvage. If he sends others, you would know how to stop them. We don't need more salvage in this world. We need to be our own people. You could have good friends in Carthage. There's an old priest I would like to introduce to your mother."

An owl called from the forest behind them. They listened to another answer, far below.

"When I was young," Sebastian said, a strange ache in his voice now, "my grandfather used to sit at a campfire and burn fragrant wood. Cedar, apple when he could get it. He said the smoke attracted the spirits of our ancestors and their old gods. Once I asked if I could stay with him, to speak with them, and he said I was too young to learn all the words that must be spoken, that he would teach them to me when I was older. I left but hid in the trees. He sat there for hours, waving his hands in the smoke, calling out old words, sacred words. We have had ancestors in these lands for thousands of years he told me once, and their spirits were close by when we needed them. But all those who knew the words for summoning died in the shifting. Now after so many years those spirits think we have forgotten them. All I can do is borrow my mother's spirits now," he said, raising the rosary.

"I think the words are waiting in your heart," Hadrian replied. "I think when you find them the spirits will hear."

In the morning Sebastian was gone.

THE ICE FREIGHTER bound for St. Gabriel still sat in the New Jerusalem harbor when they arrived, small kegs that appeared to be the last of her cargo being loaded from sleds. With the compound burnt down, the drugs inside the kegs would have to be refined in St. Gabriel, but once they were, there would be enough for hundreds of doses. As the pilot knocked ice from the rigging, Hadrian counted at least eight men on or around the boat and not for the first time that day wished he could have persuaded Sebastian to stay with them after reaching the shoreline. At least two of the crewmen had rifles slung on their shoulders. He paused and surveyed the shore, recalling that there were supposed to be even more guards. Sebastian had said his tribesmen were to escort the shipment to St. Gabriel, but they were nowhere to be seen. He looked back at the warriors in his own party. Jori had her pistol, Bjorn the shotgun, and Dax the bow and quiver given to him by Sebastian.

Hadrian surveyed the harbor from the edge of the woods, desperately seeking some means for blocking the boat. A team of horses with an empty sledge stood by the lake. A small, sleek ice bullet was tethered to the dock. A large brazier burnt at the foot of the dock, with half a dozen children gathered around it, watching the activity at the large vessel.

As he turned to tell his companions to dismount so they could approach more stealthily, a buckskin mare charged past him.

"Nelly!" Hadrian's cry was futile. She had no intention of stopping, or of being inconspicuous. When her horse balked at stepping onto the ice, she flung herself off and began running to the freighter.

"They'll kill her!" Hadrian shouted, and kicked his horse forward as Nelly slipped, falling, and two of the crewmen intercepted her.

It was Bjorn who reached the ice first, leaping off his horse and unslinging his shotgun as he ran. As her captors dragged Nelly onto the boat and other men began leaning on the struts, sliding the vessel into the wind, Bjorn began shooting. His shots went wild. He emptied the gun and tossed it aside, then charged, resembling nothing so much as a Viking berserker. Hadrian watched with sudden hope as Nelly struggled free. But she did not jump off the boat, she leapt onto a diminutive figure sitting in the cockpit, draped in furs. As she knocked the man's hat away Hadrian recognized his gold-rimmed glasses and narrow pockmarked face. Instead of fighting back Kinzler began gesturing frantically for the crewmen to drag her away. Hadrian could not hear the questions she fired at the chairman, but her enraged tone was unmistakable. Kinzler had no interest in her words. He had his precious cargo on board and was destined to conquer Carthage with it. He slapped Nelly and shook his head as a sailor roughly pulled her away.

The sail began to swell as the freighter caught the wind and turned north. Bjorn continued yelling, pulling down a crewmember who was scrambling on board. With a mighty leap from the back of the downed man he caught the railing and pulled himself onto the deck, where two sailors began hammering him with the poles used to steady the ship. One of the men flew through the air, landing unconscious on the ice as Bjorn made his way toward Nelly. But suddenly two more men appeared, one slamming a heavy club into the Norger's arm. Bjorn collapsed and an instant later was tossed overboard.

For a moment the man at the tiller turned toward Hadrian and Jori, now at his side, showing a scarred, sneering face partly covered with an eye patch.

"Give her up, Fletcher!" Hadrian demanded.

The captain offered a mock salute. "Another thousand in bounty!" he retorted, and seemed about to turn over the tiller to a crew member when he was abruptly thrown off balance, stumbling onto one knee.

Jori gasped in surprise. Hadrian followed her gaze to Bjorn, standing now, with one arm limp at his side but the other arm wrapped around the trailing tether line. He had pulled the rope so hard he'd jerked the bow of the boat off course, swiveling it on the glassy surface. As they stood watching in disbelief, the Norger twisted, winding the rope around his body and pulling once more, jerking the bow toward him again.

"Give her up!" Bjorn roared, then, incredibly, began stepping backward, pulling the ship with him.

It had been a long time since Hadrian had heard a rifle, and at first he didn't recognize the flat crack as it echoed off the ice. But then he saw Bjorn's leg jerk, saw the blood spurt from it. He tried to run to the Norger but his sudden movement caused him to slip and fall. As he struggled to get to his feet everything seemed to move in slow motion, in the freeze-stop movement of old film. The rifle spoke again and Bjorn's body jerked as a bullet struck his belly. The boat began to turn back with the wind. The rifle cracked once more and his second leg erupted with blood. As Bjorn collapsed the boat began pulling him forward.

Hadrian ran, slipping and sliding, but reached the bleeding man too late. Bjorn held out a bloody hand and Hadrian leapt for it, grabbing it, then just as suddenly lost his grip. Bjorn fixed him with a desolate grin. "Don't let them take her," he said. Then he was gone. The freighter found her wind and slipped away with a burst of speed, dragging the Norger behind.

No one spoke. He stared at the speeding boat and then looked down at his bloodstained hand.

It was Jori who finally stirred. "So close," she said as she steadied Hadrian. "I thought Bjorn was shooting at the men at first."

"What do you mean?"

"I thought he was aiming for the crew and missing. But he hit what he was aiming at, every time."

"I don't understand."

"The strut. He was shooting at the center of the rear strut, trying to collapse it. I think he almost succeeded. I saw splinters flying."

Hadrian looked up with a dazed expression.

"They're fast," she said, then pointed at the little bullet boat. "But we can go faster. They're staying close to shore, worried about the fog interfering with navigation. They won't catch the full wind. Farther out we can go much faster. We can sail out and then back at them. If we can ram the weakened strut they'll lose the outrigger."

Hadrian and Dax began running toward the ice bullet.

HADRIAN KNEW ENOUGH to stay out of Jori's way as she piloted the sleek little vessel. He kept his arm around Dax and leaned as far back in the single passenger seat as he could. Ice crystals thrown from the runners stung his face. The wind tore at the rigging until it seemed certain it would rip away, and still the boat increased speed. He recalled a lecture years earlier, when the first ice bullets had been built, in which one of his math teachers had used diagrams and formulas to demonstrate why the bullets could travel at least five times the speed of the wind. The canvas on such small iceboats did not function so much as a sail as a vertical wing.

He lost all sense of time as they hurtled out onto the lake, watching the clouds soar overhead, keeping an uneasy eye on the fog banks that crept along the shore. Surely it would be impossible to calculate the navigation and speed precisely enough, surely they were more likely to get lost in fog or hit one of the patches of thin black ice that appeared unexpectedly on the lake and sink. But then he saw the savage determination in Jori's eyes. He pulled the blanket tighter around the boy and listened to the song of their passage.

Then abruptly Jori swung the rudder and the vessel veered toward shore.

"We've got her!" she exclaimed, and Hadrian bent upward to see the big mast, perhaps two miles away, no more than half a mile from the shoreline. "Fletcher's staying even closer to the shore than I expected, which means he's risking even more patches of thin ice." As she adjusted the sail for still greater speed a new grimness appeared on her features. "Behind the boat," she said. "The bastards are still dragging Bjorn. What's left of him. Like a trophy."

Moments later Jori began to explain how Hadrian and Dax would have to roll off at her signal, how she would stay with the boat until the last second to be certain the bullet collided with the strut.

Hadrian wanted to protest, to point out the terrible odds against their survival, to remind her that their enemy had rifles, that with his near-frozen limbs he could not move as fast as she wanted. But he saw the glint in her eyes and said nothing.

It happened in an instant. He heard someone shout from the freighter as the bullet boat was finally spotted. He felt Jori's shove as she cried for him to roll off, saw the bullet career wildly as it lost the weight of its two passengers, saw her fight to stabilize it, then in an explosion of wood splinters the two vessels collided.

The freighter spun violently about, losing its wind, throwing two startled crew members onto the ice. A shrill voice rose from the deck of the ship. Kinzler, rising from a small mound of furs, flung curses at Jori, at Fletcher, at Nelly and the crew. Fletcher began barking orders for his men to pull away the remains of the bullet. The freighter still stood upright. The bullet had slammed into its target and cracked the strut, but it was still holding.

No one seemed to notice as Nelly lowered herself to the ice and ran back to the end of the tether rope. She froze as the bloody mess came into focus. Hadrian prayed Bjorn had died quickly. Most of his clothing had been peeled away by the ice. Much of his skin had been shredded as well.

Hadrian stepped to Nelly's side and led her away, toward Jori, who sat on the ice, stunned from the collision.

Fletcher lowered himself from the hull and walked along the tether line, pulling out his belt knife to cut it. As he did so, a howl rose from the now fog-shrouded shore. He turned to Hadrian with a heartless smile. "Wolves. They smell the blood. They'll be here soon. Ten, twelve, maybe more. They can run a lot faster on the ice than you can." He paused to study the damage to his boat, muttering a curse. "You're not worth the bullets it would take to finish you. I told Sauger to let me kill the two of you that night at St. Gabriel but he wouldn't have it. Doesn't like to foul the nest where he lives."

As he spoke Kinzler stumbled out onto the ice, throwing splinters of lacquered wood at them, missing widely. "I'm glad you're hurt, you damned bitch!" he screamed. Hadrian looked back at Jori, who still sat on the ice, brushing the frost from her hair with a dazed expression.

No, not dazed. She was staring at the surface of the lake. The freighter had come to rest on a patch of black ice.

The cries of the wolves increased as the pack spread the news of the imminent meal. Hadrian saw shadows in the murk now, moving with the fog out onto the ice.

"You can't be allowed to do this!" Nelly shouted from his side. He grabbed Jori's shoulder and pulled both of them back.

Kinzler seemed amused as he climbed back onto the boat and sank into his furs. "We'll be feasting by a fire tonight while your cold bones rattle across the ice," he taunted.

The sound was like that of a firecracker. One of the exploding arrows had struck the ice near the bow of the ship.

Fletcher spun about to see Dax nocking another arrow. "Fool! You can play with your toys as you die!" he snapped as the boy sent another arrow in a high arc to land near the stern. Fletcher's men mocked the boy, mouthing small popping noises as they laughed. The fog was moving quickly toward the boat now. Wolves howled again. Oddly, crows began calling from the mist.

"You had a chance at greatness, Nelly," Kinzler told her as he tucked on his elegant fur cap. "Now look at you. You won't run half a mile before they're at your throat."

A third arrow from Dax's bow landed, then a fourth, all in a radius five feet from the boat. Hadrian pulled his companions still farther away from the corpse as Fletcher directed his crew back on board.

The crows called as loud as the wolves now. Even Hadrian could smell the blood. The fog was nearly upon the boat when suddenly there were four of the small explosions, in rapid succession, along the pattern started by Dax. Fletcher, busy with getting his vessel underway, did not seem to realize the arrows had not come from the boy. A strange grin lit the boy's face as he saw four ghostly shapes at the edge of the fog. The lead phantom made another crow call and three more appeared. Dax raised his own bow. Eight arrows were aimed at the damaged struts.

"Peculiar thing about your boat, captain," Hadrian called to Fletcher. "It doesn't float."

The snarl on Fletcher's face was replaced by confusion as he saw the men at the edge of the fog. The strangers fired an instant after Dax released his arrow. The struts shuddered as the shells exploded against them, then broke away. As the hull slammed down, the weakened ice groaned and broke along the line started by Dax. The largest of the intruders skied to Hadrian's side. Sebastian offered a grim, silent nod.

Fletcher yelled at his jackals to get their weapons and was climbing down when the slab under the boat upended.

The heavy vessel sank like a boulder. Hadrian glimpsed Fletcher trapped between the ice and the hull as he went under, saw Kinzler futilely struggle to get out of his heavy furs. A crewman trapped in a rope uttered a frantic cry, then there was only the mast, sinking into the black water.

CHAPTER *Sixteen*

HE LINE OF figures bent with heavy loads moved out of
the fog toward the docks like a frost-covered snake. A dog
barked in fear. A woman gasped and ran into the building
as if to hide. A girl cried out and darted away, warning of spirits rising
out of the ice.

"God be praised," Father William, at Hadrian's side, exclaimed as
he hurried to a ladder and climbed down to the ice.

"Bring it now," Hadrian called to Wilton. The farmer turned
toward the shadows between the buildings and whistled. A heavy farm
wagon pulled by a team of horses appeared, filled with burly workers.

The figure at Hadrian's side threw off the hood of her cloak to
better see the column of strangers, most bent under a heavy bag of
grain, some hauling at tow ropes in front of sleds stacked with bags.
"I think," Emily said to Hadrian, a rare note of joy in her voice, "that
is the most beautiful thing I have seen in years." Buchanan's rationing
system had already taken effect, and most of the city's population was
going to bed hungry.

Hadrian had puzzled over how Nelly would organize her first caravan, but she had insisted she would find a way when she had hurried him off to arrange its reception in Carthage. Now he saw a familiar face and understood. Sebastian kept the bag of grain on his shoulder until he dropped it onto the wagon, followed by his brother Nathaniel and half a dozen more of the First Bloods, who then hurried to help the others. He stepped to the edge of the dock. At least half the party were Sebastian's tribesmen.

When Nelly finally appeared she looked close to collapse, the fingertips sticking out from her tattered gloves frostbitten. Emily quickly guided her into the fish plant, where hot tea and soup were waiting, followed closely by Jori, who'd brought a carriage to take Nelly to Mette's house once she had eaten. Hadrian glanced with worry toward town. Those in the caravan who were not tribesmen were clearly on their last ounce of strength.

But they were far from out of danger. With a sinking heart he now saw a man with a boathook appear from behind a stack of barrels, then two more with fishing spears. Sebastian stepped to his side, picking up a fish club.

"Stand tall, you scrubs!" came a sudden shout.

The fishermen stiffened and looked back at the compact woman who began calling out orders as she arrived with a dozen more men. Captain Reese of the *Zeus* had brought the crews of the skipjacks and was quickly positioning them as guards. Hadrian pushed down Sebastian's club and looked back at the big house that had been the jackals' headquarters. Its windows were blackened, its doors smashed in. While he was gone the jackals had been attacked in a running street fight, the smugglers' apartment stripped and its door nailed shut. The next day the paper had referred to an accidental fire gutting the house on the waterfront. Hadrian no longer had any doubt who had caused it.

They'd nearly finished loading the grain into the wagon when a buggy appeared, from which a plump man in spectacles emerged. Hadrian stood in the shadows as Emily walked up to the man, the editor of the colony's newspaper. Gazing in wonder at the precious cargo and the strangers who had brought it, he took from Emily a folded paper, which she read before handing it to him.

"The people of New Jerusalem," she recited, "freely donate this grain to the schoolchildren of Carthage."

DR. SALENS'S FACE had grown gaunt since Hadrian had last seen him. When he saw that Hadrian had followed him into his house as he carried wood to his stove, Salens did not speak. His eyes drifted toward a carton on the table, containing a stethoscope and a framed certificate. He lifted a bottle marked with a medicinal label and took a long swallow.

"I just have one question, Doctor," Hadrian said, "one thing that's been troubling me. You said the police couldn't find your painting after it was stolen. But surely you wouldn't have asked for their help, not with those death ledger sheets in the back."

Salens cast a sullen glance at Hadrian. "I didn't say that. I just said they couldn't find it."

"I don't understand."

The thin, dark man gazed at the bottle in his hand. "You're the one who caused all my problems."

"Fletcher's dead," Hadrian replied. "I saw him drown."

"She won't even speak to me."

"The camps are getting a new clinic. It's going to be hard on whoever goes as the new doctor. They won't trust him. A lot of his early patients are going to be too sick to save. They'll hate the doctor for giving them false hope."

Salens was slow to react to the invitation behind Hadrian's words. He put the bottle down. "They came to me," he said at last. "I didn't report the lost painting. They came to me and asked what it looked like."

The meeting room at the rear of the newly restored library was lit only by a solitary oil lamp when Lucas Buchanan angrily shoved the door open. He paused, trying to make out all the faces at the long table.

He decided to address Emily. "You didn't say there was a Council meeting," he growled, gesturing to the two farmers who flanked her. "The others should be notified."

"The others are gone," Emily replied in a level voice.

"Then you must wait until they return," the governor snapped.

"If you refer to the heads of the millers, merchants, and fishing guilds, they have all disappeared. We have it on good authority Captain Fletcher is dead. It seems that when they received word about that particular accident, the other guild masters fled. One of the ice sloops was seen going north, toward a place called St. Gabriel. Perhaps you have heard of it?"

"Don't be ridiculous. You can't just—"

"Sit down, Lucas. Now."

"That grain came directly from the camps. An obvious admission of their crimes."

Emily pointed to the chair across from her. "Sit down."

The governor stared at her a moment, then gestured his new bodyguard out of the room and sullenly pulled out the chair. As he did so, two more lamps were lit. His eyes flared as he saw Hadrian sitting in the corner.

"It is a long and convoluted story," Emily continued, "that apparently begins with the Dutchman and arrangements you made with the smugglers."

"Hadrian will tell you anything to turn you against me," Buchanan protested.

"Actually the evidence has been presented to us by your own trusted Sergeant Waller. And you must stop interrupting or we will rule you out of order and remove you."

For a moment Buchanan leaned forward, seeming to consider leaving the chamber, but then he studied the stern expressions of the other Council members and sank back in his chair.

It took Emily nearly half an hour to recite the facts that had been presented to the Council, reviewing the smuggling, the drug network, the subversion of the guilds, the destruction of the drug factory, the deaths of Bjorn, Kinzler, and Fletcher, even the assistance provided by Sebastian and the First Bloods.

"Hadrian Boone is just trying to get a seat on the Council," Buchanan charged. "He wants to pretend nothing has changed."

"I think he would be the first to admit much has changed. And yes, the Council *is* changing."

"I don't understand."

"The three of us"—she gestured to the two farmers who flanked her at the table—"with you make all that is left of the Council. An emissary from New Jerusalem has presented a formal proposal. Their Tribunal has unanimously voted to merge with us. One Council, one colony, with two settlements. For us to accept such an extraordinary change we need a unanimous vote as well. Before you leave this room the four of us will vote to accept the proposal."

"Impossible! You cannot ignore the other Council members."

"We have police out looking for them, interviewing those present at the docks when that ice sloop mysteriously departed. An interesting question, Lucas, is whether you really want us to find them. Before they could participate again on the Council they would have to answer some very inconvenient questions. About what happened to their predecessors in the guilds. About how Captain Fletcher and a committee in St. Gabriel directed their votes. About how you and they were always voting together. About the murders of Jonah Beck, Micah Hastings, Officer Jansen, and two former guild masters. By the time we finished we would need a new wing on the prison.

"Alternatively our first order of business can be a vote to expel them, thereby formally ending their roles in the Council. We will then vote to accept the proposal of unification with New Jerusalem. We are prepared to recommend your continuation for a term as governor of the combined colony, with much-reduced powers of course. The police will report to the Council. The schools and hospital will report to the Council. No more censorship. You will be an administrator."

Hadrian saw now that Buchanan held something in his hand. His marble rook, clenched now with white knuckles. Hatred flared in his eyes as he gazed at Hadrian. For a moment Hadrian thought he was going to throw the rook at him.

"There will be much work for you. A clinic, a new dining hall, houses to be built in New Jerusalem. That bridge across the ravine and a new road to connect the towns."

Buchanan stared only at his chess piece now. Hadrian almost felt sorry for him. He well knew the feeling of worlds collapsing around him.

"The emissary from New Jerusalem believes they have an antidote to the drugs, Lucas, a cure for the addicts," Emily said in a softer tone. "The recipe was developed by Jonah, just before he died. We will dedicate a floor of the hospital to their recovery. Your Sarah will have a bed there."

Hadrian had whispered an apology to Jonah when he had pulled the plaque from the wall in the vault and uncovered the complete formula for the antidote. He had noticed the newness of the plaque when he'd first sat in the vault with Jonah's journal. It had been placed there, he was now certain, after Jonah had witnessed the dying of the light in the addict at the mill. The antidote had been his weapon to defeat the criminals, and in the end it had worked. Emily had immediately made sense of the recipe when Hadrian had explained how to read it. H had been for hellebore, MAN for mandrake, SS for solomon seal, BC for black cohosh.

Emily's words quieted Buchanan.

"Emissary?" Buchanan looked toward the shadows at the other end of the room.

"The new chairman of their Tribunal." Emily made a gesture toward the side door. Nelly stepped forward, Jori at her side.

Buchanan shot up from the table. "She is a convicted murderer!"

"She has the right of appeal. You know the law because you wrote it, when you controlled the Council. The appeal is to the Council. We have heard the evidence. She killed no one. Sergeant Waller heard the confession of Jonah's true murderer before he died. Perhaps you would like us to call the witnesses you put forward at Nelly's trial to see if they wish to stand by their testimony?"

Buchanan again sank back into his chair. Hadrian rose and stood at the end of the table. "There is still a final piece of the puzzle," he stated. "The one who made everything in Carthage possible, the one who was able to keep everything so secret, the reason the drug dealers could operate openly. I'm talking about the one who arranged Jonah's murder and then Nelly's escape from the prison. Those who plotted from outside Carthage were powerless without the involvement of someone in the government."

Buchanan spoke in a flat voice. "You said Fletcher is dead. We were watching him. We knew what was going on. Kenton stayed on top of it. He told me about everything. That secret journal. Signals on trees, secret boats at dawn. Black market smuggling, that's all Fletcher was interested in. Fletcher is dead," the governor repeated.

Hadrian looked past the table to Jori. Her eyes were filled with warning as their gazes met, as if she somehow anticipated his lie. He broke away, and took a deep breath before addressing Buchanan. "I have one of the drug dealers finally, ready to talk. Let the corps know. He's meeting me tonight at sundown, at the cavern warehouse used by the smugglers."

THE TRAIL THAT curved around the edge of the steep ravine had not been used since the last snow. Hadrian's boots crunched loudly in the still air. He paused at the outside of the sharp turn, surveying the landscape. Tatters of red cloth still hung in the old signal tree. The crews working on the new ice road to New Jerusalem, laying sand and straw to ease the passage of wagons, were streaming back to town. The cemetery lay in quiet repose, with a single solitary figure in a red coat kneeling at Jonah's grave.

Dax had waited for Hadrian before going to Hamada's barn that afternoon. The old man had welcomed them with a new energy, then introduced them to one of the exiles who had carried grain, a grey-bearded professor sent by Nelly to discuss a new library in New Jerusalem. Dax had asked Hamada to be seated at his desk, then solemnly presented the missing book. Hamada couldn't stop grinning. He seemed to have lost ten years in age.

"I guess you think I'm a fool for putting that old phone in his grave," the boy had said as they left the compound. "I know now it is just one of those old things. As good as a rusty nail."

"Jonah would have understood."

"Maybe it was better," Dax had said after a long silence, "when I thought I could speak to those on the other side."

Hadrian gestured him to a bench overlooking the lake. Children were skating along the shoreline. Dax watched them with a distant expression. Not for the first time Hadrian considered the torment the boy had endured, the many ways in which his world had been shattered, how he'd been forced to deal with truths most adults would flee from. In the time Hadrian had known him, Dax had outgrown his childhood.

"I once knew an old man from China who would write letters to his mother," Hadrian said at last. "She had died years earlier, on the far side of the world. He would take each letter to a quiet spot and light a match to it, then watch the ashes rise up to heaven. He said he knew his mother always received his messages.

"I'll tell you a secret, Dax, that no one in all the world knows. I write a letter to each of my dead children on their birthdays. I take it out on a ledge by the lake and burn it at sunset."

The boy considered the words a long time in silence, then finally nodded. "There are things I have to say to Mr. Jonah. I don't have any paper."

"I know where we can find some."

The library was almost empty in the middle of the afternoon. No one seemed to notice when Hadrian took Dax into the now restored workshop on the second floor. Hadrian helped the boy settle at the desk, pulling paper, pen, and ink from the drawer, then told the boy he would cross the street to visit Mette.

"I am a baker without flour," the Norger woman had said in greeting, then insisted he stay for a plate of apples sautéed in maple syrup. Her nephew, one of the first to receive the new medication, had been awake and asking about his family when she visited him that morning.

Half an hour later he returned to find Dax folding his letter. As he handed the boy a bag of sweets sent by Mette, Dax pushed the letter toward him. "I don't know. I never learned how to pray or anything like that."

Hadrian hesitated, then saw the boy's anxious expression and lifted the letter.

Dear Mr. Jonah,

I am very sorry you had to die. Sometimes when I walk in the woods I feel you by my side. I was the one that stole that book and never told you. I wanted to be a jackal. But Mr. Hadrian showed me the true things about jackals. We stopped them good, and they are in a big black boat at the bottom of the lake. I know about your old world now and I am sorry it got broken. I think I understand about keeping the spark alive.

Out in the ruined lands I heard a wolf and smiled cause I thought it might be you. Mr. Hadrian and me have nobody else now. I will ask him to help me learn the constellations like you wanted me to. And maybe we can read books together sometime. He and I have to protect the spark now. I want to be the boy you thought I was.

Amen,
Dax

Hadrian refolded the letter and returned it to the boy. "No one could do better," he whispered to Dax.

As he watched now, he saw a small flame flicker at the head of the grave. He did not move until all the ashes of Dax's message had spiraled up to Jonah.

Minutes later he shoved the long bar on the cavern entry with his shoulder, let it fall to the ground, and dragged it away before swinging open the doors. The tattered wingback chair was still in the entry, across from the mounted moose head. He sat down and waited.

A deer appeared and began browsing on the shrubs that jutted out from the bank before disappearing behind the door against the steep bank. A crow cawed from the far side of the ravine.

The sky was deep purple when a cloaked figure appeared around the bend, carrying a lantern. Lieutenant Kenton offered no greeting as he set his light down on a barrel. "The governor explained things, said the bastard might try to get away, that we'll want to hold him. I can hide," he suggested with a gesture toward the shadows of the tunnel, "take him from behind." He tossed his cloak behind the barrel.

Hadrian gestured toward a bench on the opposite side of the entry. "Take a seat. It's a fine evening. The stars will be out soon."

"You never listen, Boone. I have to hide."

"The bastard's already here."

Kenton's head snapped toward the tunnel. His hand went to the pistol on his belt.

"Sometimes the best place for a pig to hide is right in the barnyard. I always underestimated you, Kenton. You were the perfect instrument for Sauger."

The lieutenant lowered himself onto the bench. "I hear long spells out on the ice can damage your brain, Boone. You need a good long sleep in a small warm cell. I can arrange that."

"It's hard to put together a puzzle when you don't know if you have all the pieces, don't even know its final shape. Lots of misleading pieces. I was impressed when I heard you were looking for that map of the suicides. But you weren't trying to help the children, you wanted to make sure it didn't reach the wrong hands. Once I had all the pieces, though, it was remarkable how quickly they fit together. It's been months since the Dutchman died, but he was sending messages through you until a few weeks ago. You told Buchanan you got them through someone in the guild. You spent a lot of time in the horse barns at the fair. It's where you went after we found Hastings's body, to arrange for Jonah to be killed that night. You probably checked on your racehorses. How are your stables in the south? The Dutchman spared no expense in building them. Were you there when the martens were feeding on him?" He should have known, Hadrian chided himself, that night he had waited in the governor's smokehouse. Sarah had attacked a police badge with a hammer.

Kenton drew out his revolver and slowly rotated its cylinder, checking that they were all loaded. "He wasn't cooperating. Too rich already, no motivation. The other two guild heads were resisting. We made sure they were there when we cut into his gut. My mistake was not tying you down beside him. Still, it kept the other guild heads on good behavior for a while."

"Until their replacements were lined up. Then Fletcher poisoned them."

"We could have turned it into a war. St. Gabe would have been outnumbered but those fighting for Carthage would have reported to me. Do you know how many would have died then?"

"We should no doubt be grateful. But there is the matter of the dozens you would have starved to death this winter."

"Name a revolution where people haven't died." Kenton sighted his pistol against the light of the lantern. "I had so many chances to kill you, so many times Buchanan was on the verge of asking me to. But he was weak. He always held back, as if he owed you something. And after a while you were so powerless you hardly seemed worth a bullet." Kenton aimed the pistol at Hadrian's knee. "Today, however, I am willing to use half a dozen."

"I've come up in the world. Jansen only justified two of your bullets."

Kenton shrugged. "Jansen was uninspired. No ambition. The stupid bastard didn't know what a shotgun shell was. He had actually had cut one open trying to understand what it was. I told him I could make him rich. The fool said he had orders from his sergeant, said he had taken an oath. He didn't even understand when I had put the first round in him. I'm not sure he'd ever seen a pistol fired before." A ragged laugh escaped Kenton's throat. "He saw the blood on the front of his shirt and was confused, asked if I had done that, the idiot. I said here, let me show you, then put the barrel close to his heart and shot him again. He had no more questions after that."

"Killing Jonah was your big mistake."

"You know damned well I was with you when he died."

"You arranged it when you went to the fair that day. As soon as he knew Hastings had been murdered Jonah might have started connecting the evidence. Buchanan hadn't forgotten about that little valley where Hastings's father had died. He was going to secretly send him there. Except he shared the secret with you and told you Hastings had probably told Jonah. You couldn't risk Jonah's knowing that Micah Hastings had been murdered before he even left. It would raise too many questions about that little valley he was going to. You ordered an earlier schedule for the patrols by the library that night. Then Shenker went in through the rear door. But the second man, I never understood who the second man was."

Kenton knew Hadrian presented no threat to him. He was happy to gloat. "Sauger needed someone who came from Carthage, knew his way around the streets, knew what I meant when I explained I was sending the police patrol early, and to wait until they passed that Norger cafe. They say he wound up with a fork in his brain."

Hadrian sighed. "Wheeler. I was afraid he died because of me."

"He did. The sap told Scanlon he knew you, that you had been his schoolteacher. He was homesick. They thought he would talk to you."

The lieutenant stretched his arms and rose, stepping closer, aiming his pistol at various parts of Hadrian's anatomy and counting. "One, two." Hadrian's knees. "Three four." His elbows. "Five, six." His shoulders. Then over the edge you go. There's a nest of tree jackals near here. They'll find you sometime in the night."

"I don't think so. You're not quite that stupid."

Kenton's eyes lit with amusement. "You're going to stop me?"

"Sergeant Waller knows about you. If I don't come back she will come for you."

"That bitch? Nothing but a schoolgirl with an attitude."

"But such an attitude. Before she comes she will tell Buchanan and the Council. You'll be in prison the rest of your life if they don't hang you. No. You'll leave me and run to St. Gabriel. That's your only chance. Regroup with Sauger."

"She hasn't told anyone or I would know it."

"She's waiting to see if I get back. Leave now, Kenton. We'll give you until daybreak."

Kenton spat a curse at Hadrian. He absently scratched his temple with the barrel of his gun and seemed about to concede when the door against the embankment creaked.

The lieutenant moved surprisingly fast, lowering the pistol to cover Hadrian as he leapt toward the door. As he slammed the door with his shoulder someone on the other side groaned in pain. He reached into the darkness and dragged out Jori Waller. He swung her out by the front of her coat, and when she struggled he slammed her violently against the heavy oak door. She collapsed. Kenton pulled away her pistol and dragged her to Hadrian's feet.

"I forgot about that deer trail," he said. "Imagine. The only two people in the world who can do me harm. Bad news, Boone, you only get three of my bullets now. A knee, an elbow, and an eye."

Jori stirred. Kenton kicked her. She held her belly and gasped. He considered his two prisoners before extracting one of the brown shotgun shells. "A week's worth of fairy dust. With half of this in each of you I can tell you to fly like a bird and you'll leap into the ravine. No need to explain messy bullet wounds. I'll write the report myself. Another tragic accident by overdose. You will pour it into her, Boone, then I—" Kenton paused, cocking his head toward the road.

The figure coming through the shadows made no effort to conceal his approach. The snow crunched loudly under his feet. He paused at the entrance to clean it from inside his shoes. Buchanan wore a suit and black overcoat as if arriving from a state function.

"Good job, Lieutenant," the governor announced. He seemed unaware that the trail behind him clearly showed he had come from behind the door, where he must have been listening with Jori.

Kenton shot him.

Buchanan dropped to the ground as blood began seeping through his shirt and up over his collar.

"Idiot!" Kenton snapped, then looked back at Hadrian. "He's the damned fool who caused all the problems. Bringing you in to investigate the dead scout, then Jonah's murder. He couldn't stay bought. He thought the money that came to him from Fletcher was just to keep quiet about the smugglers."

Buchanan stirred, rolled onto his side, one hand in his coat, the other gesturing Kenton closer.

"Lieutenant," the governor gasped, "Come closer, where I can see you. Everything is so dark." He spoke with a wheeze, seeming to struggle for breath.

Kenton, strangely obedient, crouched over the bleeding figure.

Hadrian should have known the governor would have kept the best of the pistols for himself. It was a small, powerful semiautomatic he fired through his coat, four quick shots aimed at Kenton's heart. Buchanan was suddenly up, flinging off his coat, leaning over the dying policeman. His wound, though bloody, was in his shoulder. The governor grabbed the drug shell in Kenton's hand.

"You dared to put this in my Sarah!" he screeched as he straddled Kenton. He broke the shell open and began pouring its contents into Kenton's gaping mouth. The lieutenant tried to roll, tried to pound Buchanan with his fists but he had no strength left. Buchanan emptied the shell and pummeled Kenton's face until Hadrian finally rose and pulled him away.

Kenton was dying quickly of the gunshots but it was the drug that choked away his last breath. He gave a deep cough that sent out a spray of blood, then he moved no more. His eyes were fixed on Hadrian as they lost their light. His face was ghostly white with powder.

Epilogue

*T*HE FIRST CARAVAN from Carthage to New Jerusalem took several days to organize. Not only did wagons to carry grain back have to be located but Nelly and Emily made sure they were loaded with blankets, barrels of pickled fish, and building supplies. They had stopped taking volunteers for the construction crews when the rolls swelled to two hundred.

At the big table in the hospital's kitchen Hadrian stirred at the sound of grates being opened on the big cast iron stove. He had fallen asleep over a glass of milk.

"You look like a wreck," Emily muttered as she dropped a log into the firebox. "When's the last time you slept in a bed?"

Hadrian rose and extended his arms over the stove. "I spent the afternoon upstairs. A quarter of your nurses have left for New Jerusalem and there are three dozen addicts in residence."

"Some will be ready for home in another week. Lucas had Sarah out on the veranda today." Jonah's antidote worked slowly, taking several days to reverse symptoms, but it was working nonetheless.

When Hadrian looked up, Jori was at the door, dressed for travel on the ice. Emily retreated from the room as the sergeant laid a heavy backpack on the table.

"They're going to open a new police station in New Jerusalem," Jori declared. "They've asked me to head it. An iceboat is being held for me."

"Rather sudden."

"I'm supposed to start recruiting in the camps tomorrow."

Hadrian slowly turned, finding it strangely difficult to find words. "There is a lot of work to be done."

She took a hesitant step toward him, then another. "They're starting regular mail service in a week or two. I can write you if I know where you'll be."

Hadrian shrugged. "I'm going to try to decipher some of Jonah's project plans. The library workshop. Try me there."

Suddenly her arms were around him, her head buried in his shoulder.

"Jori . . . I can't . . . I'm too . . ."

When she looked up at him a tear was rolling down her cheek. She brought up a hand and covered his mouth. "Shut up."

"I don't know how it would have been without you," she offered after a moment. "I mean I never would have . . ."

"Shut up," he said, and put his arms around her.

There were no more words spoken. From the chair where he had been sitting he lifted the woolen scarf Mette had given him and wrapped it around Jori's neck. He remembered a pack of tea he'd bought that day and darted into the adjoining room to bring it to her. When he returned she was gone.

Hadrian ran into the frigid night without bothering to find his coat. He was panting for breath by the time he reached the knoll overlooking the moonlit harbor. The iceboat was being hauled out onto the lake. He watched as the big sail filled and the boat leaned, gathering speed. He stood in the chill air, not moving until she was out of sight.

HE WAS AT the library by dawn, working on the detailed drawings for the new bridge, then sorting through Jonah's stack of plans. After several hours he stepped out onto the balcony to watch the town below. When he returned to the desk he pushed the files aside and pulled out several sheets of paper, setting Jonah's inkpots and pens in front of him.

He did not know when he drifted off to sleep, was just suddenly aware of someone draping a blanket over his shoulders. As he straightened in his chair Dax pointed to the pages he had been working on.

"Chronicle of the Unified Colony, Year One," the boy read from the top page, then straightened the blanket. "It's cold in here. You need to take better care of yourself."

"What I need," Hadrian replied, "is a walk to clear my head."

Outside they bought some roasted walnuts from a street vendor and strolled to one of the little parks overlooking the waterfront. Wagons were on the ice road now, their horses and oxen newly shod with cleats, beginning their long trip to New Jerusalem. Children were skating along the nearest dock. A cloud plump with snow was settling over the town.

"You should be in school," Hadrian said to the boy as they sat on a bench.

"I tried school," Dax said. "I get confused about what we're not supposed to know and what we really have to know."

"I think that will change," Hadrian offered.

"I'm just tired of it," Dax said in his old-man voice. "I wish there was a place I could go that has no time, not of this world, not of the last one, where I could just lie by a fire with books for the winter."

Snow began falling on the cobbled streets below. Hadrian absently scratched his cheek as he watched the skaters. "You know, Dax, I might know such a place. I could take you there, stay with you for a day or two. You'd be welcome to spend the whole winter reading books in front of a fireplace." He realized that for the first time in months a contented smile was spreading across his face. "But tell me something first. Are you frightened of bears?"

Author's Note

NDINGS OF WORLDS have occurred throughout human history. Some have been abrupt, like the annihilation of the original, ancient Carthage by the Romans. Some have been gradual, like the destruction of the Tibetan world over the past fifty years by the Chinese. But none have encompassed all of humankind. Only in recent years have we developed the capability for annihilation on a planetary scale. While there may be many reasons to believe that such a nightmare will never occur, the moment that capability became real, global apocalypse entered the realm of the possible.

This novel is certainly not meant to be a prophecy, but implicit in its backdrop are predictions about the state of technology and science after such universal destruction. Even with highly trained scientists among its inhabitants, it seems likely that a society of survivors with no electricity and no internal combustion engines would turn to early industrial age technologies. Locating the Carthage colony on the Great Lakes endowed its inhabitants with an environment rich in minerals, timber, water, and wildlife, meaning that simple technologies like those for making matches, paper, cloth, glass, and lumber would be readily available. Once foundries and forges were developed, steam engines and other simple machines would not be far behind. The setting on the inland sea also means the colonists are able to travel long distances by water—and in a region of long winters with few roads, incentives would be great to advance the iceboat technology of an earlier century.

The effects of global destruction on the external trappings of a community of survivors strike me as far easier to anticipate than the effects on the human psyche. Certainly baser human cravings and prejudices would not become extinct, yet nor would dignity, honor, and spirituality. With survivors comprising a random cross-section of modern society, there would be ample opportunity for the glory, and the shame, of humankind to be exhibited. It was this unique mix of worlds and peoples that drove my curiosity in writing this book. A stage on which a twenty-first-century cast relying on nineteenth-century technology struggles with murder, starvation, tyranny, and even the meaning of civilization itself provides fertile ground for imagination.

As my characters became more like companions on this journey, I began to sense an inevitable tension between the survivors, who must shoulder the nearly unbearable weight of memories of the past world and collective guilt over its fate, and the new generation, who would have to cope with inexplicable physical and emotional remnants of the old world. After being severed from their world would survivors lose all confidence in their past, would they shy away from history? Would the lost world seem more a myth than a nightmare to the new generation? How would it feel to glimpse the possible dying of humankind's light? What would define the people who were the most successful survivors—and how far must humanity be sacrificed for the survival of humans? Of all the mysteries explored on these pages, perhaps the greatest is the nature of the spark that must be kept alive.

—ELIOT PATTISON

Printed in the United States
by Baker & Taylor Publisher Services